# The Substance of Things Hoped For

# The Substance of Things Hoped For

## A Novel

TOM NOYES

THE SUBSTANCE OF THINGS HOPED FOR
A Novel

Slant
An Imprint of Wipf and Stock Publishers
199 W. 8th Ave., Suite 3
Eugene, OR 97401

www.wipfandstock.com

HARDCOVER ISBN: 978-1-7252-7722-9
PAPERBACK ISBN: 978-1-7252-7721-2
EBOOK ISBN: 978-1-7252-7723-6

*Cataloguing-in-Publication data:*

Names: Noyes, Tom.

Title: The substance of things hoped for: a novel / Tom Noyes

Description: Eugene, OR: Slant, 2021

Identifiers: ISBN 978-1-7252-7722-9 (hardcover) |ISBN 978-1-7252-7721-2 (paperback) | ISBN 978-1-7252-7723-6 (ebook)

Subjects: LCSH: Noyes, John Humphrey, — 1811–1886. | Guiteau, Charles J. — (Charles Julius), — 1841–1882. | Collective settlements — New York (State) — Oneida.

Classification: PS 3614.O98 S83 2021 (paperback) | PS 3614.O98 (ebook)

03/17/21

# Contents

# *Prologue*

MOSQUITOES AND SWEAT BEES SWARMED their beards, and cottonwood seed drifted down around them like snow.

The older man sat on a damp log, his hand on his throat, and regarded the younger man hovering over him. "You startled me, Son," he said. "What do you need?"

"Not sure," the younger man answered. "Not sure I'm the one in need."

The older man watched a cloud-colored moth rise from the log and disappear over the younger man's shoulder. "Most folks understand I come out here alone in the morning," he said. "Alone on purpose. This time is precious to me. I try to guard it."

"And yet this morning you beckoned me," the younger man said.

"I did not beckon you," the older man said. "It would seem there's been a misunderstanding."

"And yet we are of one mind," the younger man said.

"I'm not sure that's the case," the older man said.

"As I am unsure," the younger man said.

The older man rose slowly from the log, cracking his knees. "I'm headed to the turtle pond. You may walk with me, I suppose. If there's nothing pressing to address, though, let's make it a contemplative walk. Let's not speak. We'll be walking together in one sense, but in another sense we'll each be alone. Can we agree to that?"

"Your words at breakfast this morning I heard as a beckoning."

"My homily," the older man said. "You could have said so straightaway. You have a question?"

"Bear ye one another's burdens," the younger man said.

"That was my theme, yes. From Paul's Letter to the Galatians. Chapter six, verse two. Neither you nor I nor the rest of the family would be here in Oneida if not for these words. As I said at breakfast. We are all here to fulfill these words."

The younger man rubbed his beard roughly with both hands and smashed a mosquito above his eyebrow, leaving a spot of blood. "Verse five says, 'For every man shall bear his own burden,'" the younger man said. "You skirted that verse."

"I see," the older man said. "Paul saying on the one hand that we should share our burdens and on the other hand saying that each is responsible for his own burden. You're concerned by the apparent contradiction."

"The contradiction as well as the skirting," the younger man said. "You presented as clear and straightforward that which is not clear and straightforward. Not in context. You offered it out of context to make it sound clear and straightforward, but it is not. Not in context it's not."

"You followed me into the woods to correct me," the older man said. He tilted his head back and studied the bright canopy. The branches shimmered silently, bird-less. "You're here to set me straight."

"I heard your words as a beckoning," the younger man said.

"I regard these two verses as more complementary than contradictory," the older man said. He turned and proceeded down the path a few steps, but the younger man remained anchored in place. "Come," the older man said, gesturing to the younger man to follow. "The turtle pond."

"I thought you might be walking away to leave me behind as opposed to walking away with the intention that I should make to accompany you, so I did not make to accompany you," the younger man said.

"Another misunderstanding," the older man said, and he gestured once again to the younger man, who with his first step stumbled and sunk his foot ankle-deep in a mud puddle. The older man had not previously noticed the puddle. It were as if the puddle had sprung into being precisely so the younger man, who now winced and yelped and limped in a tight circle, would stumble into it.

"Are you hurt?" the older man said.

The younger man bent over to squeeze his wet ankle with both hands, and then straightened slowly and breathed deeply. "I thought at first I'd twisted it badly, but now I don't believe I twisted it badly," he said. He hopped on one foot and then the other as if to compare. "No. It would appear I didn't twist it badly despite thinking at first I'd twisted it badly," the younger man said. "It would appear I merely dampened it."

"Good," the older man said, and the two men started together down the path. "So, once again, about your concerns with this morning's homily...."

"The contradiction as well as the skirting," the younger man said.

"Yes. As I was saying, I think both concepts are part of the same truth," the older man said. "As a family rooted in the spirit of love, we become one body, and as one body we bear our collective burden. In that sense we bear each other's burdens. But as each family member is unto himself a part of that body, a component of that body, the collective burden necessarily becomes each member's own individual burden. In that sense, then, each of us bears his own burden, but the burden each of us bears individually is the collective burden of the united body. Do you understand now how both verses are true even though they might seem incompatible upon first hearing?"

The older man paused to allow a reply, but he heard only the squeak of the younger man's wet shoe.

"There are other possibilities, of course. Other interpretations of this passage," the older man continued. "Paul is not a simplistic writer. Perhaps he was trying to communicate to the Galatians how some burdens lend themselves to sharing while other burdens are more individual in nature. I can say I myself have borne both kinds. I imagine many folks have. Another consideration is that there might be those among us who are required to bear more than their fair share. Perhaps the sharing of burdens is not always perfectly equal."

The younger man wiped his nose on his sleeve, regarded his sleeve, and then wiped his sleeve on a tree. "Why didn't you speak to all this at breakfast?" he said.

"Most folks think slowly early in the day," the older man said. "Best to keep things simple."

When the pond came into sight, the younger man quickened his pace. The older man watched him forge ahead, pry loose a small stone from the muddy bank, and hurl it into the water. The younger man's exaggerated effort and loud grunt did not match the result. The older man had seen children throw farther.

"Why do you suppose we're led to do this?" the older man said. He bent to pry loose his own stone and lob it underhand into the pond. "Not just you and I. Everyone. It seems well-nigh instinctual. What is it about rocks and water that leads us to want to throw the former into the latter?"

"The sight and sound of the splash," the younger man said. "Then, if there are geese on the water, the scattering of the geese. Then the rippling out. Then the pronounced quiet, which is quieter than the quiet before the splash and the scattering of the geese if there are geese. Then the thinking about the rock settling newly on the bottom. The thinking about the cloud of sediment rising and the rock settling newly on the bottom forever."

The older man nodded. "I won't forget that answer," he said.

"It shall come to pass," the younger man said.

"What shall come to pass?" the older man said. When he leaned back on his heels and put his hands in his pockets, he felt the pencil and two letters he had forgotten about. One letter to read and one to finish writing. The letter to be read was the most recent in a series from the younger man's anxious father. The older man already knew what it would say, what it would ask and what it would offer. As for the letter to be written, the older man knew from experience that no matter what he wrote, she would not reply. He did not know if she would even read it. This knowing and not knowing made writing the letter simple in one sense and arduous in another.

"Did you hear me?" the older man said. "What shall come to pass? Finish your thought, Son."

"It is finished," the younger man said, and he flung another stone.

# PART I
## 1823–59

## John Humphrey Noyes Encounters a Fox

BY THE TIME WE WERE AWARE of its presence, the fox was already heading for us, splashing through the reeds and mud of the swamp in full trot. My younger brother George shouted at it and shouted at me to shout at it, but the animal was not intimidated. It lowered its shoulders and head, flattened its ears, and picked up speed, putting me in mind of an arrow. The sounds emanating from its grinning, panting mouth, though, could have been human. The loud, insistent squawking of a discontented baby.

George picked up the large, muddy stick lying at his feet and held it out to me. When I accepted it, he turned and ran. His sudden bolting enticed the fox, who tried to dart around me to pursue George. As the animal rushed by, I surprised myself by swinging the stick down like an axe across its back. It yelped and spun, gnashing wetly at the air between us. When I swung again, this time landing the stick on the fox's neck, its front legs collapsed, and its head slammed, muzzle-first, into the mud. On the third blow, the stick broke across the top of the fox's head. Black blood seeped out of a gash on its crown, and its foamy gagging turned to strained wheezing.

At a distance I had thought the fox to be large, but now, as it lay still at my feet, I was struck by its taut scrawniness and grew afraid that if I stared long enough one of its blade-like ribs would poke through its skin.

When I looked up in George's direction, he was still running across the swamp towards home. "George! Come back here!" I called, but he gave no heed. I watched him trip over the roots of a black gum tree, pull himself back to his feet, and continue running without so much as a backward glance.

When I caught up with my brother at home, I first made sure to shame him for his cowardice, and then I proudly rendered him the tale of how I had extinguished the fox. On the first point, he did not seem at all chagrined. In fact, he told me I had demonstrated stupidity for not running away like he had, and he asserted that even though he was the younger and I the older, it was now proven fact that he possessed more common sense. How had I, he wondered, nearly reached the age of twelve without knowing enough to run from rabid animals? Of what other basics of survival was I unaware?

On the second point, George did not believe me about killing the fox. He even denied remembering arming me with the stick—this especially confounded and infuriated me—and he told me that, even if he had equipped me with such a weapon, he doubted I possessed the physical strength necessary to swing it hard enough to slay a squirrel or field mouse, let alone a fox.

We argued bitterly for a while before I suggested it was an easy enough matter to settle. I would hit George with a stick on the top of his head, and then he could tell me whether or not I had swung it hard enough to kill a fox. When he balked at this suggestion, I offered another. We would simply go back to the swamp. Either we would find a dead fox, or we would not find a dead fox. George was initially reluctant to accept this course of action. He said he was worried to return to the spot because he imagined the fox would likely be there waiting for us, still very much alive and game for bloodshed. When I told George that I suspected the real reason he did not want to go was because he did not want to be proven wrong, he had little choice but to solemnly acquiesce.

There was no dead fox at the swamp. There was a swatch of matted fur and a mess of tracks where the animal and I had tangled, but there was no carcass. The stick, now two sticks, was there, but George told me that proved nothing. "There are sticks everywhere," he said. "Wherever there are trees." When I dropped to my hands and knees in the muck to scour the area for blood, George snickered above me, shaking his head. "You are putting on quite a show, John," he said. "This is a farce. Would it not be simpler for you to own up to your fib? We could then be done with this foolishness, and you would have a clear conscience."

I stood to face him, told him to recant, and when he would not, I shoved him in the chest, sending him stumbling back onto his hind end. "There is your farce and your fib," I said.

8

"Beating me will not make your lie true," he said as he pulled himself up and wiped his hands on his trousers, "nor will it make me believe you."

"Your belief or unbelief does not determine what is true, George," I answered. "Nor does what you think in your muddled brain matter a whit to me. Now go do what you always do and tattle to Mother like the petulant brat you are."

George studied me silently for a moment before his eyebrows rose and his finger pierced the air between us. "I know what happened to the fox!" he said.

"I told you what happened," I said.

"I mean I think I may know, if it indeed were killed by you like you say, why and how its body has disappeared."

"Go on," I said.

"I believe the varmint must have been resurrected from the dead!" George said, and then he folded his soiled hands at the top of his chest, and his voice quieted to a reverent tone as he bowed his head. "To save us from our sins."

Before I could grab him to give him a pummeling, he was off running across the swamp towards home again, this time cursing me bitterly over his shoulder. I considered giving chase, but I knew he was a fast runner—I was rarely able to catch him even though my legs were longer—and when I watched him stumble over the same set of tree roots he had met with earlier, I thought it sufficient comeuppance, at least for the time being. I took care to cackle loudly enough at his clumsiness to ensure his hearing.

A few months later, just after his tenth birthday, George was dead, cut down by a vicious fever. He was bed-ridden the last few weeks of his life, and on several occasions, against my mother's orders, I entered his room to attempt to persuade him to believe me about the fox before it was too late. With each passing day, my obsession grew more fervent. I could not help but suspect that George's affliction had something to do with his rejection of the truth of my story, and I was persuaded that if I could convince him to believe, he might be healed or, at least, be better prepared to face final judgment.

As George's death appeared to grow more inevitable and loom more closely, desperate measures were taken. During the final stages of his illness, my mother gave birth to her fourth son, her ninth and final child, and she named the new baby after George. She and my father thought this might make the dying George happy, give him a glimpse of his family's affection for him before his departure, but their well-meant gesture did not have its desired effect. George did not say much about the situation, at least nothing I heard, but I sensed that there being a new George in the household—a fresh, innocent version, who demanded more than his fair share of our mother's diligent and tender care—greatly injured him and made his last days even more miserable than they would have been. In some sense, the birth of his namesake seemed to depress George more thoroughly than his own imminent death. Or perhaps the birth of his brother made his own impending death more concrete and immediate. If he had been harboring hopes of a recovery, he now understood those hopes were empty. He knew there was not enough room in one family for two boys named George. He would have to go.

Is there anything more tragic and mysterious than an action born out of grace and selflessness that instead functions to harm and destroy the soul meant to benefit from it?

Infant George could not have been more than a week old when I sneaked into my dying brother's room early one morning and gently awakened him by cupping his hot, damp head in my hands and pressing my lips against his ear. I told him I would always miss him greatly—even in my old age I would never forget his brief life—and I assured him he had nearly always been, for the most part, a good and capable brother. Moreover, I confided in him that he was my favorite brother, what with little Horatio and the new baby George being entirely useless as companions, and I told him I had decided to forgive him for wrongfully accusing me of lying about the fox, whether he would repent of his disbelief or not. My final gift to him.

As I spoke to George, I remember liking the way he smelled, pungent like cold coffee, and being cognizant of how deeply and desperately sad this scent made me. I had not at that time in my life felt such sadness.

My gift of forgiveness enraged George. When I drew back from him, I saw his dim eyes had widened, and his teeth had clenched. He was able somehow to summon the strength to lift his head and tell me clearly and slowly that he rejected my grace. He said so twice to ensure my understanding, and as he spoke, tiny drops of hot spittle landed on my face. He then eased his head back onto his pillow, reached over to his nightstand, and rang his bell.

Since my mother was still asleep with infant George, it was my father who answered my dying brother's beckoning. He did not even hear

George's complaint before grabbing my elbow and ushering me out of the room and then out of the house and into the rain. He looked up at the dark sky and seemed to doubt himself for a moment, but when he looked back at me, he regained his resolve and informed me matter-of-factly that I would not be welcome back inside until supper. If I protested or tried to sneak home any earlier, I would not be welcome back until tomorrow morning's breakfast. When he asked if all was clear, I did not answer, and I tried to look as hurt and as pitiful as possible, but he shut the door anyway.

As I tramped through the soggy woods that morning, I spent the first couple of hours pouting, wallowing in self-pity and indulging in self-righteousness. I staged an imaginary exchange with my father at the end of which he saw the error of his ways and, as part of his apology, confided in me that of all the wonderful things he had done and experienced in his life, nothing had brought him more pleasure and pride than to be able to claim me as his son. If it sometimes seemed the opposite, he told me, if sometimes his temper seemed to flame most quickly with me compared to his other children, whom he also loved, albeit with a more traditional paternal fondness, this was only because he strove to not let on to them how he truly felt about me. To spare their feelings.

This fantasy satisfied me enough to allow me to turn my thoughts to my brother, and after much deliberation, I decided the best course would be to reverse strategy. Instead of forgiving George, I would ask George's forgiveness for lying about killing the fox even though I had not lied. I thought affording him the opportunity to exercise the grace of forgiveness, even unnecessary, misdirected forgiveness, might be something that could bring him some final moments of peace. It struck me then that dying might not be so bad if one were blessed to enter into it free and clear of concern, if one were not distracted by the loose ends and nagging troubles that informed the life being left behind.

Having settled on this new tack, I directed myself out of the woods to our neighbor's farm and into his horse barn to escape the rain. I nested in a clean, dark corner behind some empty bushel baskets and scraps of lumber and wrapped myself in a horse blanket I found draped over one of the stalls.

I napped in fits and starts until dusk. On several occasions I was awakened by Mr. Sharpe wandering into the barn. He talked sweetly to his horses, asking one named Archer when the weather was going to clear, and assuring another named Patty that when it came time for her colt to be born, he would take good care of the both of them. I wondered what I would say to Sharpe if confronted—I hoped he would be as kind to me as he was to his animals—but that situation never came to pass. If he did catch sight of me that day, he graciously decided that the best thing to be done was leave me be.

By the time I returned home that evening, I was thoroughly convinced that my plan for George was a perfect one, and I was eager to enact it. But I was too late. He was gone. I knew this before anyone told me. I knew the moment I opened the door to find my mother shivering in grief at the kitchen table, weeping over the sweetly sighing infant nursing at her breast.

# John Humphrey Noyes Heeds God's Calling

AN HOUR INTO HIS SERMON, FINNEY paused to mop his forehead with his handkerchief, folded his hands under his bearded chin, and walked a slow, silent lap around the altar. I considered the possibility that he did so simply because he needed to gather his thoughts, but a lesser part of my nineteen-year-old self, the unjustifiably self-assured part of me, the part informed by unearned cynicism, suspected him of showmanship and interpreted his gesture as pretense.

Of course, the self I grew up to be, the self who went on to deliver thousands of lectures and homilies over the next few decades, would have chided my younger self for questioning Finney's sincerity. Throughout his lifelong ministry, the man was nothing if not faithful and uncompromising in his fervor for God and justice, and on this night, his lengthy pause was surely legitimate and honest in its aim, designed to afford his words opportunity to germinate in the hearts and minds of the congregants. A rhetorical device, to be sure, but not a duplicitous one. One might compare this technique to a master poet's use of caesura, or to King David's employment of the Hebrew word "Selah" to denote moments of holy silence in his psalms.

At the moment Finney looked up after his silent stroll around the makeshift stage, appearing as if he were about to recommence preaching, a stout, bosomy woman in one of the first few rows tipped out of her chair and into the aisle. Her flailing limbs and choking cries suggested a drowning victim. While a man who appeared to be the woman's husband attended to her, a young girl, most likely the couple's daughter, looked on with fear. While I imagine most eyes were on the collapsed woman, I studied the girl and her confused grief. Too frightened to weep. Her fragile features and expressive clarity commanded my attention more urgently and resonated with me more powerfully than did her mother's gyrations. The way in which the girl's body leaned forward then back, forward then back, rocking itself as if for comfort, and the way in which her mouth repeatedly opened and closed, as if over and over again trying and failing to come up with words, enamored me. She was perfect in her brokenness. What occurred in my life that night had as much to do with the image of this girl as it did with Finney's message.

It did not take long for another body to drop. This one belonged to a young man around my age who had been sitting a few rows behind the woman. He flopped himself violently up and out of his seat like a slippery trout and then rolled onto his back and writhed madly like a flea-bit hound. When one of his companions reached down to him, the young man snapped his jaws, yipped and hissed, and this is when I remembered the rabid fox that had chased George and me through the swamp outside Putney, just a few miles from where I now sat. So George was present for my rebirth that night in Reverend Finney's meeting—present in the perfectly complete way in which only the dead can be present—and eventually I would see my way clear to claim this presence as a promise that we would one day be together again, reborn jointly into new life.

The congregation's responses to the growing commotion in the tent varied. Some of the young man's companions smirked and appeared to stifle guffaws. Other folk though, responded with fear and trembling. A few parents near me put their children on their shoulders or allowed them to stand on their seats so they could see the spectacle, while others quickly and sternly rounded up their charges and herded them out of the tent as if saving them from a fire. I remember empathizing with both responses and wondering what I would have done had I a child with me. Perhaps, I thought, the best course of action would be to let the child's response be my guide. If she seemed intrigued and desired a clearer look, I would oblige her, but if she were upset by the spectacle, like the sweet-faced daughter of the afflicted woman at the front of the tent, I would respond by holding and shielding her, and once out of the tent and in the fresh air, I would smooth her hair away from her face, hold her chin in my hand, and meet her eyes to reassure her the danger had passed.

Somehow through all the commotion, despite the weeping, laughter, and pained, joyous yelps of the now numerous bodies that had leapt and fallen and continued to leap and fall, Finney's voice persisted. He did not sound as if he were shouting or straining; rather, his voice reached my ears on a different plane than the other noise, cutting through the cacophony without competing with it. This was an amplified, insistent, yet carefully controlled eloquence I had never before heard nor would ever hear again, certainly not from the pulpit, although perhaps on a few occasions in the coming years I would have the privilege of hearing musical instruments, most especially Frank Wayland-Smith's violin, come close.

"The wages of sin?" Finney inquired, raising a tight fist over his head. "Death!" he answered. "The gift of God?" Finney continued, raising his second fist. "Eternal life!" he bellowed. At this moment my knees buckled, and the air left my lungs. I had to close my eyes to stop my head from spinning, and when I re-opened them, they were no longer my eyes, they were two warm stones in my skull, and my skull was a warm stone, and my ears were warm stones, and in my mouth my tongue was a warm stone, and my teeth warm stones, and it was all I could do not to swallow and choke on them as I staggered outside into the newly descended night, the blackness overhead pocked by the pinpoint light of thousands of warm stones.

My memories of the rest of that evening are hazy. I remember shuffling along the road and then through a field and then woods and more than once losing my balance and tumbling to the ground. I remember lying on my back in a bed of pine needles and mud, my head throbbing on a flat rock, watching clouds drift across the face of the nearly full moon. I remember being awakened three times: once by the sound of rustling in a nearby thicket, once by a mosquito's sting on my neck, and once by the musk of a skunk. Each of these instances felt like a beckoning, a warning, a blessing.

I remember upon arriving home my mother's arm around my shoulders and her look of concern as she helped me out of my soiled clothes and into bed, and I remember her calling to wake Harriet and Charlotte and her instructions to them to fetch a cup, a washcloth, a pitcher, and a bowl. When my sisters brought these items but no water, I remember my mother asking them if it were possible their brains might have leaked out of their ears while they were sleeping. This does not sound like something my mother would say, but it is what I remember her saying.

I spent the next three days in bed with my father's Bible. I read the Gospels and the Acts of the Apostles straight through numerous times, and when not reading them, I drifted off and dreamt of them. The last verse of John's Gospel afforded my imagination opportunity to create visions of new renditions of Christ's power and grace. "And there are also many other things which Jesus did, the which, if they should be written every one, I suppose even the world itself could not contain the books that should be written. Amen."

So I dreamt the miracle of Christ's healing the Samaritan twins' crippled mule and the miracle of His turning the overbearing Pharisee into a camel. The miracle of His turning the coins in Judas's money purse to scorpions, only to later heal with tearful kisses the knave apostle's swollen, wounded fingers. The miracle of His raising from the dead all the rotting, stinking fish that had washed up on a Galilean beach after a storm, only to do nothing with them other than to leave them there to flap themselves to death again. The miracle of His opening a beautiful young woman's prideful heart so she was able to overcome her selfishness and reciprocate the love of the homely but godly man who wanted to make her his wife, only to have the homely, godly man change his mind after discovering, much to his sorrow and shame, that the very thing he had found most beautiful and desirable about the woman was her former arrogance and unattainability. The miracle of His swapping a rich man's sound hand with a poor man's withered foot, leaving both men worse off than they had been. The miracle of His transformation of an old, dying woman into a fat, healthy infant, who, despite her astonishing origins, was left alone much of her life and grew up an orphan. The miracle of His cleaving a ferocious fox in two with His staff only to resurrect it, only to have it bite him, only to cleave it again.

I had requested the Bible immediately upon arriving home in my disheveled state the night of Finney's revival, but my mother had paid no heed. Each time I had asked, she shushed me gently and continued to dab my face with the cool washcloth and urge me to sip water. Covered as I was in dirt and perspiration, smelling of skunk and burning with fever, she had good reason to think me delirious, and her worry clogged her ears. She did not respond to my request until I pushed her hands away roughly and raised my voice. This display immediately earned her ire. "In the morning," she said before dropping the damp washcloth on my chest and exiting the room brusquely. I did not see her again until the next afternoon when she delivered fresh water and bedding, and even then she did not speak to me. She was coldly quiet with me for a week, even after I was up and around, even after I explained to her what had been behind my furious insistence, even after she said she understood and, despite my pleading, refused to forgive me because forgiveness, she said, was wholly unnecessary.

It was my second brother George who, under instructions from my mother, delivered the Bible to me. I know this not from my own recollection but from what George later told me. He said I stared at him as he stood at my bedside, but I would not extend my hands to receive the book. After a few moments, he cautiously rested the Bible on the bed next to me, and it was only then I spoke. "Which George are you, George?" I asked. "Are you the first or the second George? The original or the replacement George? The living or the dead George? Do you believe now, George, that I broke the fox's back and crushed his skull? I am sorry I killed the fox, and I am sorry I claimed killing the fox when I did not kill the fox. I ask your forgiveness and extend you forgiveness, George."

My brother said these words frightened him so that he could not breathe. When he ran out of the room and back to his bed where he wept into his pillow, my father and mother heard him and inquired of him what was wrong, but he would not tell them. He refused to go to school that day, and in order to get him to come to supper that evening, my father had to threaten him with a lashing.

George recalled this for me forty years after the fact. We were in Oneida, the two of us picking strawberries into one basket on a warm June afternoon.

# Charles Grandison Finney Loses His Voice

I READ MR. NOYES'S LETTER once with my own eyes and then had Lydia read it to me aloud. This is something I would ask of her occasionally, and she was always amenable. Anything that, for better or worse, I wanted to absorb fully: a challenging passage from one of Paul's epistles, an article critical of my ministry, an entangled mass of sentences from Emerson. Somehow her voice enhanced my perception and sharpened my discernment. This is one of the ways in which the loss of Lydia has often made me feel lost, even after I married Elizabeth, whom I also lost, and then even after I married Rebecca.

For a time I was ashamed of the way I missed Lydia. I accused myself of idolatry, of being unfaithful to my subsequent wives, and went so far as to confess the persistence of my grief as sin. I realized later I was wrong to do this, to repent of undying love, to confuse a gift from God with iniquity.

After Lydia finished reading Mr. Noyes's letter, she removed her spectacles and held the pages on her lap. Rather than look at me, she turned to the hearth where I had just started a fire. The spring night was warm but damp, and I had wanted to dry the air.

"You have something to say," I said.

"Oh, I don't know," Lydia answered, re-creasing the folds of the letter between her fingers. "This Mr. Noyes, he's the Perfectionist from Vermont?"

"Putney," I said.

"Well, his use of commas is, to put it kindly, innovative." She re-opened the letter and slid her spectacles back on. "Men write to you for a variety of reasons, but Mr. Noyes's motivation is especially peculiar, isn't it?"

"It strikes me he has more than one motivation," I said. "He wants to discuss abolition, resurrection of the saints, Perfectionism, and at least a half-dozen other subjects."

"Primarily, though, he wants to enter into correspondence with you so you can vouch for his sanity," Lydia said. "He wants to answer his critics by referencing connection with you. He wants to be able to say to his detractors, 'Reverend Finney thinks me to be of sound mind. In fact, he and I are in agreeable correspondence.' He wants you to legitimize him."

"I didn't deduce that," I said.

"He all but states it," Lydia said, and she rose and walked to my desk to hand me the letter.

"If you're right, I think Mr. Noyes might have chosen more wisely. Being associated with me is just as likely to bring him trouble as approval. Of course, you of all people should know this."

She tried to hide her smile by turning to walk away, but I snatched her hand and held it so I could see her grin.

In replying the next day to Mr. Noyes's letter, I strove to be both polite and honest. I told him I recognized we had much in common, especially in our passion for the abolitionist cause, and I took a moment to implore him to keep in mind the slave owners in his ministry, reminding him that we should work for the salvation and repentance of the captors even as we worked for the freedom of the captives. I went on to tell him I had heard of him, and what I had heard had both compelled and concerned me. In any case, my schedule was such that I had already taken on more writing commitments than was responsible, so I could not promise an ongoing correspondence. I closed with the suggestion that if he ever found himself in New York City, he should feel free to call. I wrote this to be polite, not imagining it would come to anything. At any rate, it did not take Mr. Noyes long to accept my invitation.

It was true that, in one sense, I felt a bond with Mr. Noyes. When one has been deemed a heretic, it is natural for one to feel a certain affinity with other heretics. My own complicated relationship with Calvinism—what it means to have free will, what it means to be among the elect, what to make of the relationship between sanctification and sin, what to make of the notion of eternal security—has, over the years, stirred ill will against me. There have also been accusations of the more personal variety.

My language is too coarse; I do not possess the necessary sophistication to be a legitimate representative of the gospel; I rely on histrionics to frighten people into salvation; my pulpit prayers are not sufficiently deferential. Of course, the most popular critique focuses on the boisterous nature of my meetings. I remember early on in my ministry, in a town where Presbyterians held sway—I believe this was Mayville, possibly Rensselaer—I thought I was in trouble when seven men fainted within the first twenty minutes of my sermon. As the fallen were attended to and I soldiered on, I admit my mind was not on my sermon. I was sure I would be invited to leave town that night, and such invitations were not always polite. The Lord was good, though. All the fainters turned out to be well-respected Presbyterians.

Of course, there were many other memorable meetings. The young man in Watervliet who frothed at the mouth and gnawed on the back of his chair like a misbehaving puppy, the old woman in Cohoes who took to the aisle to belt out misremembered hymns as she disrobed, the Montpelier man who snapped his spectacles in two and ate a hank of his own hair. In Victor a few years back, three entire rows of congregants lost the use of their arms. In Stephentown, a mass sneezing attack descended like a plague. In Hamburg, vomiting. In Sherman, a group of men sitting together in the rear of the tent commenced punching themselves in the face, each his own, when I referenced Christ's pardon of the good thief. I have seen more than a few pistols drawn. One on me. The bullet whizzed by my ear, passed through the tent, and killed a horse. That the horse was discovered to have belonged to the shooter some took as a sign, and upwards of a hundred lost souls were found that night.

Even my most fervent detractors cannot argue with the results. Over the years, the Lord has seen fit to win thousands of souls at my meetings. Mr. Noyes claimed to be one of them.

Most decisions made at a revival meeting are fairly similar. Once the candidate has made it to the anxious seat at the front of the room, it takes more courage to turn tail in front of family and neighbors and decide against salvation than it does to go through with it. I freely admit this inclination influences the measures I've used. Of course, the anxious seat has the potential to attract the individual who longs to be the center of attention, who, for reasons apart from redemption and sanctification, aspires to be at the front of a room. Indeed, I have seen folks come forward to make a decision for Christ in one town on Tuesday and then do a repeat performance a few miles down the road on Thursday. If not for the attention, then perhaps the thrill? So be it. Better to find salvation twice than never to find it. That said, I admit to finding satisfaction in reflecting on another kind of conversion that I like to imagine often occurs after my meetings, the kind where, rather than rising from his seat and coming forward in public view, the embattled soul trudges home, retires to bed, tosses and turns until morning, wrestling with God like Jacob with the angel, and then, in the new dawn, perhaps silently, perhaps alone, surrenders himself. Incidentally, this is the kind of conversion Mr. Noyes claimed and described to Lydia and me during his visit. He began recounting the experience before we had even invited him to remove his coat. He still had snowflakes in his beard.

When I preached, I would often hold my Bible to my chest for the duration of the sermon, opening it not even once. I would recite from memory the scriptures I needed. Mr. Noyes said he had heard me preach several more times after his conversion and suggested my recitation sounded like composition. "As if you were the author of the words you spoke," he said. He told me that in my voice even the most familiar verses sounded fresh. "I heard them from you as if for the first time," he said. "'For God so loved the world He gave His only begotten son.' Your voice had the power to make me forget everything I had ever heard so I could hear these precious words anew."

I understand he meant this as a compliment. Perhaps he was even being sincere. Nevertheless, I find his notion misguided. I am not the author of the message I carry, nor is the message new. Of course, neither is the message old—it, like its beginning-less, endless source, is, was, and ever shall be—but I think people of this age have come to regard the message as old. Used up and stale. So they search for a newer message, one that goes beyond what is already complete and fully perfect. Of course, there is no such message, no true one, so such a search is folly. Worse than folly when one claims to have found such a message. Worse still when this false message is shared with others and represented as having been born of God.

Given the misdeeds that I later heard were being perpetrated by Mr. Noyes and his followers, I regretted not being able to share these impressions with him during his visit. Perhaps he might have changed course. Unfortunately, I had little choice in the matter. On the afternoon of his unannounced visit to my home, I was suffering from a harsh cold, and whenever I tried to speak I was overcome by coughing. The tea Lydia prepared seemed to agitate my throat rather than soothe it. Given my condition, Mr. Noyes had free rein. Lydia tried unsuccessfully to interject on a couple of occasions, but she did not persist for fear of coming off as rude. Mr. Noyes did not pause except to sip his tea or catch his breath, and even in these instances he would interrupt himself mid-sentence so as to provide no real opening for another speaker.

After an hour of filling our home with words, Mr. Noyes abruptly took his leave. Just before he left, though, as the three of us were gathered at the door, he insisted on praying over Lydia and our unborn child. Lydia acquiesced, figuring agreement would hasten his exit. The resulting supplication was thankfully straightforward and brief, but it was also disconcerting given Mr. Noyes's placement of his right hand on Lydia's stomach and his left hand on my cheek.

When our door closed behind Mr. Noyes, the resulting silence was deep, resonant, and relieving. After a few moments, Lydia announced she was exhausted, and when I answered her by recommending a nap, I was bemused to find my throat had recovered and my cough had disappeared. When I suggested that I might chase down Mr. Noyes and invite him back so I could have my say, Lydia informed me if I did so I would never see her again nor meet our unborn child.

Julia was born a few months later. Over the next few years, as our daughter grew along with Mr. Noyes's notoriety, Lydia increasingly regretted allowing the man to pray over Julia. She was a fussy, demanding child compared to her older sister and brothers, and when she would show impertinence or otherwise try her mother's patience, Lydia would wonder whether it was somehow Mr. Noyes's influence. I found this amusing and assured her Mr. Noyes had no such power. "You and I prayed for Julia on a daily basis prior to her birth," I reminded her. "Our prayers would've cancelled out Noyes's. Julia's occasional troublesomeness isn't supernaturally inspired. We've just been spoiled by her siblings' uncommon contentment. Helen, Charles, Jr., and Frederic obviously take after the Finneys, whereas Julia seems to be growing into the spitting image of your mother." Lydia and I disagreed about the merits of this joke. It was unique in this way. For the most part over the years, our respective senses of humor were in perfect harmony.

Julia was ten when her mother died. Lydia would be proud and relieved to see the wonderful woman she has grown up to be.

The only pleasure I derive from recalling Mr. Noyes's visit to my home stems from the fact that Lydia was there, and any opportunity I have to recollect her warm presence I count as a blessing. As for Mr. Noyes, my predominant feeling towards him is pity. Had he ever been afforded the opportunity to love a woman in the way I loved Lydia, I believe that love would have steered him away from the nonsense he convinced himself and his disciples to believe and the travesties he and they committed. Such love might have saved him from himself more effectively than even God's love. I realize this notion is outlandish—perhaps even foolish, perhaps even blasphemous—but I suspect this is true of many of the truest truths I know. As I grow older, this suspicion deepens.

# *Jane Howe Guiteau Endures Her Pregnancy*

WHEN I LAUGH AND WEEP and will not rise from the bed even in the afternoon, Luther does not understand why I laugh and weep and will not rise from the bed even in the afternoon. He does not understand that I laugh and weep and will not rise from the bed even in the afternoon because he who abides in me laughs and weeps and would not have me rise from the bed even in the afternoon, and Luther's lack of understanding weighs on him like a curse as I weigh on him like a curse and as he who abides in me will weigh on him like a curse, and the weight stirs Luther to anguish and anger, and the anguish forces him from the bed, and the anger drives him from the room.

When Luther slams the door, I stop laughing and weeping, and I roll over onto my side and shiver because he who abides in me stops laughing and weeping and rolls over onto his side and shivers.

There is a kind of man whose anger clamps down on him like a trap clamps down and imprisons him in a room, but Luther is not the kind of man whose anger clamps down on him like a trap clamps down and imprisons him in a room. Luther is the kind of man whose anger drives him from a room.

FRANKIE SAYS SHE REMEMBERS inside of me.

Her breath smells like sour milk, and her cheeks are sunburned, and she is sticky with sweat so that her hair clings to her forehead and mouth and back of her neck. She climbs into bed to lie next to me and to rest her hand on me where he who abides in me abides in me, but I brush away her hand.

Was it like being in the root cellar?

*No. Not like the root cellar. There was not the cold smell of potatoes. What else was it not like, Mother?*

I don't know what it was not like. I can't know. I am on the outside of myself, so how could I know what it was not like on the inside of myself? Was it like nighttime in the woods?

*No. Not like nighttime in the woods. There were no trees and no critter sounds in and under the trees and no yellow eyes staring out from behind the trees and no paths winding among the trees. What else was it not like? Do more, Mother.*

Frankie tries again to rest her hand on me where he who abides in me abides in me, but again I brush away her hand, and I roll away from her onto my side so I cannot smell her breath and she cannot reach me where he who abides in me abides in me.

Was it like swimming in the pond? Was it like when you hold your breath and dunk your head and blow bubbles like a frog and stay under as long as you can before you have to come up so that you don't drown?

*No. Not like under the pond. It did not taste like fish smells, and it did not sound like nothing, and it did not feel unpleasant under my feet and especially between my toes like pond mud and pond weeds feel, and I was not frightened that a turtle might gobble my foot.*

Was it like sleeping? Like a dream?

*I want to feel the baby move, Mother. Please? Please don't say I mustn't. Why mustn't I? Please may I? Just for a moment? I said 'please.' If you let me please feel the baby for a moment, I won't ask again to please feel the baby for a long time. I promise I won't ask for a long time.*

Was it a place in which you would have wanted to stay if you had been allowed to stay? Like a cool, clean bed or a warm kitchen where pies are baking? Or was it a place you wished to leave? Like a sweltering barn or an outhouse with spiders? Was it a lonely place? Was it a hiding place?

*No. It was not lonely. I was only a baby. Not even a born baby. Not even born babies can't feel lonely because they don't know what lonely is because they don't even know there are people. And it was not a hiding place. I was not even a born baby, and not even born babies don't even know what hiding is because they don't even know anyone to hide from. And it was not like a bed because there were no pillows. And it was not like a barn because there were no cats. And there were no pies and there were no spiders. What else was it not like? Do more.*

When Frankie sits up and reaches over me to try again to rest her hand on where he who abides in me abides in me, I surprise myself by smacking her cheek, and she cries out in confusion and despair, and her confusion drives her from the bed, and her despair drives her from the room.

When Frankie slams the door, I cannot laugh or weep because he who abides in me cannot laugh or weep, so I press the heels of my hands into my eyes too firmly so that my face will cave in and loosen and cool and not feel so tight and hot, but I cannot press the heels of my hands into my eyes firmly enough for my face to cave in and loosen and cool and not feel so tight and hot.

THE REVEREND SUMMONED BY Luther to curtail my laughing and weeping and occasional fits of temper holds my hand securely in his hand like my hand is something that might be lost or pilfered if it is not held securely in his hand.

*You have no cause to be agitated with your husband, Mrs. Guiteau. No cause to be cruel to your daughter. No cause to be harried and distraught to the point of harshness. No cause to lash out. To bring a child into the world might seem on its surface a trial to endure, but it is not a trial to endure. Not on balance. On balance it is a blessing in which to rejoice. You've previously been blessed in the same manner, so you know that bringing a child into the world is on balance a blessing in which to rejoice rather than a trial to endure. This is something in which you can take solace. Your previous experience of having been blessed in the same manner. You are someone who has already become a mother becoming a mother again. Let the mother you already are comfort and counsel the mother you are becoming.*

He who abides in me would not have the reverend summoned by Luther to curtail my laughing and weeping and fits of temper pray over me.

*May I pray over you now, Mrs. Guiteau? The both of you? You and your baby? Christ would have us cast our cares upon Him, for He careth for us. Would you be willing to allow me to help you do that now? To cast your cares upon Him?*

He who abides in me would not have the reverend summoned by Luther to curtail my laughing and weeping and fits of temper bring Luther into the room so he may also pray.

*And may I bring your husband into the room so he may also pray? Luther has cares to cast, too. He has his own cares, and he has your cares, which he counts as his cares. This is what it means to be a husband. I am going to call Luther into the room so he may also pray.*

When the reverend summoned by Luther to curtail my laughing and weeping and fits of temper releases my hand, he does so gently, like my hand is something featherless, furless, freshly hatched, slick and blind. Something fragile and new that's just come into the light.

## John Humphrey Noyes Goes Swimming

WITHIN DAYS OF MY experience at Finney's tent meeting, I penned a letter to Larkin, my brother-in-law and supervisor at the law practice in Chesterfield, to inform him I had decided to give up my legal studies and would not be returning to clerk for him. I explained I was no longer his apprentice, but Christ's.

Larkin was prompt and direct with his reply. He assured me his words were rooted in love and endorsed by my sister Mary Jane. "When one is nineteen, one's emotions are loud and overblown," he wrote. "We implore you to think around this temporary fervor and reconsider your rash plans. We do not want to pity you in the years ahead. We do not want you to live a life diminished by regret."

I addressed my reply to Mary Jane only. I told her she should make no plans to pity me. Rather, it was I who pitied her and her husband, two lost souls who evidently held worldly comfort so dear they dared discourage another's commitment to Christ. "Of course, you can be assured the pity I feel for you is rooted in love," I wrote, and I closed by informing her that if she cared to pursue future correspondence, she should address subsequent letters to Andover Seminary, where I would be matriculating as soon as possible.

Unlike Mary Jane and Larkin, my mother was pleased to learn of my seminary plans. My father, though, had never been more satisfied with me than when I was working with Larkin and, conversely, had never been more disappointed in me than when learning of my new intentions. His reluctance to stake my tuition was finally assuaged by my mother, who, despite my father's ambivalence towards religion, helped him recognize the futility of keeping from God what is God's. Even in their advanced years, my mother had significant influence over my father by way of his passion for her. He would often retire to their bedroom in the evening thinking one way about a matter only to emerge the next morning with a fresh point of view. I do not think this reflects weakness on my father's part, nor do I believe my mother to have been unwholesomely cunning. Rather, I think it speaks to the restorative and healing power of amativity. Bodily love can cleanse; it can correct; it can work like prayer to enhance and clarify. I can recall many amorous interviews over the course of my own life that refined my thinking and sharpened my judgment.

My father was a man worthy of admiration, but his mind worked differently than mine, and in our differences we frustrated each other. The evening before I left for Andover, as he smoked his after-supper pipe in the parlor, he quizzed me about my aspirations. "My aim is no longer to dissuade you, John," he said. "I ask only that you help me envision the life you have in mind for yourself."

"I do not have a life in mind for myself," I said. "It's Christ Who has in mind a life for me."

"I beg your pardon," he said, raising his eyebrows. "In that case, please tell me about the life Christ has in mind for you."

"You are patronizing me," I said. "At best that's what you're doing. At worst you're patronizing Christ."

"That's a bold thing to say to me," my father said, removing the pipe-stem from his mouth and pointing it at me. "Surely it's not Christ inspiring such disrespect and arrogance."

"I hope we do not spend our last evening together in cross conversation," my mother called from the kitchen. She did not show herself, but the knowledge she was within earshot was enough to temper both my father and me.

"Of course not," my father answered. He nodded to me. "No one wants cross conversation. That's not what this is, is it, John?"

"No, sir," I said.

"Although it is cross conversation in a sense, isn't it? You're off to make a minister of yourself, to bear witness to folks about the power of the cross. And here we are talking about it, so we are having a cross conversation."

"Yes. I see, Father. Very good."

"Now who is being patronizing, John?"

"I am, Father."

"Yes. Well. Your life as a preacher. Unpatronizingly, I would ask that you paint me a picture."

"I'm not sure what I can say about my future, Father, other than it is in God's hands," I said. "In seminary I will enter into fellowship with and learn alongside like-minded men. I'll seek to use this learning to discern what and how to preach. Then, according to God's will, I will do what I've been trained to do. I cannot tell you anything about my finances. I know you are highly concerned about that aspect of my future, but I wish you wouldn't be. It isn't your responsibility."

"You don't need financial assistance from me? This is news."

"Beyond seminary, I mean. After that, I will not be a burden to you. The Lord is my shepherd."

"Listen to yourself, John! You are already preaching! Perhaps you do not need seminary!" My father smirked but then shook his head and waved his hand in the sweet smelling smoke above his head as if to shoo away his own words. "How about a wife, John? How about a family?"

"John wants those things," my mother called into the room. "Of course he does."

"With God's grace I will have them," I said.

"I am sure of it," my father said, and he reached in his pocket to pull out his watch although we had already had supper, had no obligations, and were expecting no company. This habit of my father's irritated me, and I told myself I must never acquire it. My father was successful in business, had served with distinction as a congressman, and was admired and respected by all who knew him. A wise young man would have considered him a good candidate for emulation. At the time, though, I was not a wise young man. I had already assembled a long list of my father's traits that I swore I would resist inheriting.

"You are always welcome back here in Putney, John, and I know Larkin and Mary Jane feel the same about your returning to Chesterfield," my father said. "Please remember this."

"Be assured I will never return to Chesterfield," I said. "Mary Jane erred in marrying Larkin. She should've been dissuaded."

My father stood to crack his knees, another habit of his that I detested, and then sat down again. "Yes, Mary Jane erred in marrying Larkin, the kind, generous, diligent, responsible, successful lawyer."

"All the things I am not," I said. "Understood."

My mother came into the room, wiping her hands on her apron, and stood in the space between my father and me. "Your father is not saying that, John," she said, her voice thick and quiet. She nodded to my father. "Please tell your son you are not saying that."

My father motioned for my mother to sit and then pensively emptied his pipe. I knew whatever he was about to say would be intended for her ears as much as mine.

"Despite what you may believe, John, I respect what you're doing," he said. "You're acting with passion and conviction, and most worthwhile things a man accomplishes are rooted in these inspirations. There's no shame, though, in a young man doubling back once or twice as he finds his way. I believe I have told you the story of how I almost became a lumber man, and you know the first time I was approached to run for office I declined."

"You will see, Father," I said. "God does not double back."

"Well, I am no theologian," my father said, and he smiled reassuringly at my mother. "Along these lines, though, I have wondered about God creating the world, declaring it good, and then destroying it. Perhaps not even God is above doubling back, John. Perhaps they'll speak to this in seminary."

"You must write home regularly, John," my mother said, and with these words my father and I both recognized our conversation was over. "More regularly than when you were at Dartmouth."

"I will be very busy with my studies, Mother," I answered, "but never too busy to write to you."

WHEN I RETURNED HOME six months later, disgraced and discouraged after withdrawing from classes, my father was not smug. I sensed skepticism when I recalled for him how, during my last days in Andover, when desperate for an answer from God regarding whether it was His will that I stay or leave, I fortuitously opened my bible to Matthew 28, where the angel at the empty tomb tells Mary and her companions, "I know that ye seek Jesus, which was crucified. He is not here."

When I complained to him, though, about the professors and other students, specifically their penchant for theoretical debates about doctrinal minutiae rather than genuine revival and transformation, I detected some sympathy. Although I doubted he completely understood my dilemma, he told me it was a sign of good character not to compromise one's most closely held convictions. Larkin and Mary Jane were gracious, too. There was not a hint of condescension in their words when they wrote to tell me how delighted they would be to welcome me back to Chesterfield.

Instead of being appreciative, though, I found these kindnesses mortifying. I felt abandoned and duped. I wondered if I had misinterpreted God's mission for me, or worse, mistaken fever-induced visions as divinely-inspired ones, allowing Finney and a tent full of simpletons to persuade me I had found something real when in fact I had been fooled by false fervor. Whereas in Putney I thought I had felt God's clear presence in those weeks after Finney's meeting, in Andover He'd seemed silent and removed. I searched for Him in my peers and professors, but He was not there. He would not even reveal Himself in the scriptures, which I studied each night until my eyes grew bleary.

I was working up the will to swallow my pride and accept Mary Jane and Larkin's invitation when Christ once again revealed Himself to me. Where I finally re-found Him, or, I should say, where He re-found me, was in the lovingkindness and wisdom of my mother.

She invited me on a walk one spring afternoon, and I relented, allowing her to take the lead as we meandered silently through the woods before reaching Sacketts Brook. We then walked upstream a while on the trail to the swimming hole I had frequented as a boy. As I followed my mother, I discovered she was no longer young. At least she was not as agile as I remembered, skillfully negotiating slippery rocks and leaping from bank to bank with three or four offspring in tow and another cradled in her arms.

When she found a spot that suited her on the bank, she sat and patted the grass next to her. As soon as I was settled beside her, she pulled my hand onto her lap and squeezed it. This was no tender caress. Using both of her hands, she clamped down as firmly as she could until her fingers turned white. Underneath the strained grimace she wore, I detected a smile.

"What are you doing, Mother?" I asked, snatching my hand away.

"Do you remember?" she asked. "You and George? You'd compete to find out who could squeeze the hardest and who could persevere the longest without surrendering."

"We did this with you?"

"No," she said, laughing as she took off her bonnet and tilted her face to the sun. "With each other. I feared the two of you would end up maimed, but I couldn't dissuade you. When I scolded, you'd apologize, but then you'd get in the creek and have at each other underwater or go behind some trees where you thought I couldn't see."

"We were very competitive," I said, plucking a few pebbles from the mud and flicking them into the gentle current. "What was wrong with us?"

"One afternoon neither of you would surrender, and after hours of defying my instructions to stop, both of you were hurt. By evening I was dealing with two sobbing boys. Four little hands purple with bruises."

"I suppose I do remember that," I said.

"There was another version of the game that involved trading blows to the shoulder, and another featuring kicks to the shins."

"We were awful boys!" I smiled. "You must have thought us demon-possessed."

"Your father called you spirited. Despite my frustration, he liked when the two of you battled. When I'd make you and your brother quit each other for a while, he was almost as disappointed as the two of you. That was the worst punishment I could assign you and your brother, by the way. If I told George he had to play east of the house and told you to head west, you both would wail like grieving widows. You were addicted to tangling with each other. I realize now it was how you loved each other."

"It is good to sit here with you and remember George, Mother. I did love him dearly, you are right. But what has you thinking about our boyhood nonsense?"

"I think you are surrendering, John," she said. "I suspect you are considering retreating to Chesterfield to accept a lesser life for yourself, and it pains me to see you abandon your conviction."

I rose and stepped towards the creek. "I can't return to Andover," I said. "I don't expect you to understand, but the spirit there. . . . Instead of completing in me the work Christ had started, the place sapped my resolve. What Christ had ignited was extinguished a little with every lecture, every exam. And my fellow students? When not arrogant and cynical, they were low-minded and crass."

"So you will reject God's call then," Mother said. She stayed seated as she spoke, her hands in her lap and her eyes on the water. "You were disenchanted by a human institution and disappointed by a handful of young men, so you've decided God was wrong."

"I cannot go back," I said.

"You had a brother who did not have the opportunity to live past the age of ten, and you've been afforded the privilege not only to grow into a man, but to grow into a man whom God has chosen." She stood and put her bonnet back on. "Are there other seminaries in America? As you know, your brother Horatio is headed to Yale in the fall. Is there a seminary there?"

"You know there is," I said.

"I need to head back to prepare supper," my mother said, and she put her hands on my shoulders and kissed my cheek. "It wasn't my intention to sadden you, John. I do think, though, that if George were here, he wouldn't allow you to give up without offering you an earful, and I didn't want the fact that he's no longer with us to prevent him from having his say."

After watching her disappear down the trail and into the trees, I stripped off my clothes, descended the bank, and swam in the cold, dark water until dusk. I kept waiting for my body to become accustomed to the frigid temperature, but it never happened. I never stopped being cold. Even after I had redressed and was back at home, eating supper, I could not completely rid myself of the chill. Even months later, studying in my room at New Haven, I would now and then be surprised by a shiver. Even decades later, I still had not warmed the whole way through. For this I was always thankful.

# John Humphrey Noyes Furthers His Education

IN HEADING TO YALE, I believed God was affording me the opportunity to start anew. I eventually realized, though, that in His wisdom my slate would not be wiped completely clean. It would not be a new work Christ would start in me; rather, the work He had already commenced would continue. Andover had not been a misstep. It had been a first step.

The only Andover students with whom I forged any meaningful connection were those committed to foreign missions. Only they seemed dedicated to authentic spiritual work. Those already committed to mission boards spoke passionately of their respective destinations—Burma, Africa, China—and I was envious of the security they had in knowing how and where God would use them. I would not go so far as to call these men friends—the dark, perpetual agitation that defined me during this time left me ill-equipped to cultivate relationships—but we occasionally prayed together, and they introduced me to the practice of mutual criticism, which offered me moments of comfort during those trying days. As I listened to my peers enumerate my shortcomings, I felt reassured. In the shame and pain I found warmth and light. On more than one occasion, when told my time was up and the group intended to move on to critique someone else, I tearfully begged for a few more moments of reproach. If my companions thought me a glutton for punishment, they did not fully understand my state of mind. That said, neither were they fully wrong.

In my courses at Andover, I had been introduced to two passages that I could not stop puzzling over even after arriving in New Haven. When each turned out to be the subject of a lecture during my first few weeks at Yale, I decided God was sanctioning my attentiveness to them, so I continued to pore over Matthew 24, where Christ speaks of the Last

Days, and Romans 7, where Paul simultaneously affirms and declares himself emancipated from Mosaic Law.

I was not cautious about sharing the controversial truths God eventually revealed to me through these passages. The revelation I gleaned from Matthew regarding the fact that Christ's Second Coming had already occurred was exciting, although at the time I was unsure of its practical relevance. As for the doctrine clarified for me in Romans, though, confirming the joyous truth that anyone abiding in Christ was no longer a sinner, I was energized by its life-changing implications. It meant I was perfect. The barrier separating my humanity from my divinity had been destroyed. It also meant, however, that all around me were deluded individuals who considered themselves to be in good standing with God despite their acceptance of their sin. They believed in Christ's transforming power and humbled themselves daily in begging forgiveness, but this continuous cycle of sin followed by repentance was itself indicative of their damnation. It was not enough to repent. They needed to recognize and claim the promise of perfection in order to be truly restored and made whole. It was clear to me now my mission field would not consist of heathens, unaware of Christ and the redemptive story of His death and resurrection. On the contrary, many of the souls living outside God's grace knew the Bible front to back better than I. Truth be told, I believe I would have had an easier time bearing witness to the lost in Borneo or Singapore or Hawaii rather than here in our so-called Christian nation.

My professors at Yale were accustomed to passionate young men espousing "new" interpretations of scripture and so were initially patient, if somewhat patronizing, in listening to my ideas. They allowed that the timing of Christ's return and the issue of Perfectionism had been and would continue to be legitimate, debatable topics—they took some satisfaction in informing me that my assertions were not entirely original— but they cautioned me about the difference between healthy intellectual inquiry and unconstructive doctrinal meandering.

One faculty member with whom I spoke frequently was Professor Gibbs, a kind, boyish-looking man who suggested I might be better suited to follow in his footsteps and teach at a seminary rather than shepherd a flock. "For scholars, belief is a continuum, at least it is Monday through Saturday," he said. "To be open to newness and nuance is what defines the dynamic mind. There is a difference, though, between discussing alternative viewpoints and opinions in the classroom and preaching these notions as God's truth from the pulpit, where one has the responsibility to privilege tradition over personal conviction."

"Even when tradition is false?" I asked. On this occasion, Professor Gibbs and I were standing outside the lecture hall in a soft rain. Passersby had their chins tucked into their chests and their shoulders hunched as they hurried by us, but Gibbs and I, absorbed as we were in our conversation, could not bother to be bothered by the rain. "Even when tradition is stale and built on the foundation of misinterpretation?" I said. "Even when personal conviction is God-breathed?"

Before Gibbs replied he smiled uneasily, like he could not decide whether to be proud of or embarrassed for me. "Yes, Mr. Noyes. Even then," he said, and before I could offer a rebuttal, he clapped my damp shoulder to let me know our conversation had come to an end.

As I matured I came to understand the nature of Professor Gibbs's advice. I even eventually saw the wisdom in it. All wisdom is not wise, though. While I would go on to create difficulties for myself and my followers on occasion by sharing ideas too quickly, and while I even would be forced periodically to revise my message, I could never condone a kind of preaching that would seek to hide truth from the hearer. It would be better to stay silent. Silence would at least be a lesser kind of cowardice.

Word spread quickly among my classmates about my ideas, especially my notion of Perfectionism. For weeks a steady stream of my peers visited my room to engage me. Some came out of simple curiosity, a few came out of concern for my soul, but most came simply looking for a fight. At the time, my brother Horatio was a classics student and, unfortunately for him, my roommate. Our small room was located off the chapel, and whenever I received an interrogator, Horatio would be forced to relocate to the dim, empty sanctuary to squint over his books or stretch out on a pew to try to sleep.

For the most part, I was as foolish as my opponents in these rhetorical duels. Like them, I equated rightness with the ability to win a debate, and these back-and-forths functioned primarily as proving grounds for overly earnest young men who wanted to sound intelligent. That said, while I did not change many minds in these discussions, the exercise helped me clarify for myself the finer points of my convictions. Sometimes during these debates it was not until I heard myself say something that I knew it was something I believed. While it might be going too far to suggest God was always speaking through me in these discussions, I hold that He was always present with me. While my counterparts would often become flabbergasted and tongue-tied, I was able to keep my bearings.

One young man who visited my room was rendered unconscious as a result of our exchange. In the moment, I wondered if I had killed him. He was the last such visitor I had—given his fate, I suppose this is unsurprising—and he came alone. Most of the young men who knocked on my door arrived in small groups. There was usually a leader who did most of the talking, and the others were there to watch. When I opened my door to welcome Todd, I respected him right away for his independence.

I believe his name was Todd. I recognized him as a fellow student, but he was not someone with whom I had previously spoken. Even before confirming his name, he announced his intention to inquire about a rumor he had heard, that I believed myself to be equal with Christ. Despite my visitor's fragile makeup—his arms wire-thin, his neck long and stringy like an old rooster's—I gave him credit for possessing genuine purpose. If not polite, he was at least straightforward.

Todd's announcement chased Horatio from the room. His arms overflowing with books, he nodded to our guest and hurried out the door as if the room were afire. As much as my brother loved poring over Homeric poetry and Ciceronian oratory, he had no patience for long-winded exchanges between living people. This would never change. Although he would eventually join me in Oneida and serve there faithfully, he always preferred the company of books to the company of people. On occasion this would frustrate me, and I would feel personally insulted, but eventually I grew to understand and appreciate his inclinations. While I always believed Horatio could have better managed his love for literature to allow for more meaningful human interaction, it is probably just as true that most people have the opposite problem; that is, they spend too much time together in idle banter and not enough time in conversation with books. It is a balance with which I myself would struggle over the years.

In making his escape on this particular evening, Horatio abandoned a fresh cup of tea. When I moved over to his desk to adopt it as my own, I invited Todd to sit in the chair I had just vacated, but he remained standing for a few seconds before cautiously taking a seat as if I were out to trick him.

"What exactly do you want to know?" I said, "and why exactly do you want to know what you want to know?"

"I want to know if it is true that you count yourself equal with Christ," Todd said. "I do not usually entertain gossip, but given the nature of what I have heard, I thought it my duty, first, to let you know that such a rumor is being spread about you and, second, to dissuade you of this false notion if it indeed turns out to be an accurate representation of your opinion."

I took a sip of Horatio's tea and studied Todd's face. He tried for a few seconds to return my gaze before leaning forward to prop his elbows on his knees and stare at the floor.

"I do not count myself to be equal with Christ," I said. "None of us is equal with Christ. To make such a statement would be both evil and insane."

"Of course not," Todd answered. "I mean, of course." He rose from his chair. "Please understand it was not I who was saying this or ascribing these words to you, but. . . ."

"You came to confront me about something I supposedly said. You were ascribing words to me."

"I beg your pardon?"

"While I am not equal with Christ, I am akin to Him as is anyone who has been saved by his perfect sacrifice. Do you not agree?"

Todd sat down again. "Akin? Well, I can see how. . . ."

"In Christ I have been remade. In Him I am sanctified and holy. Sin has no part in the new creation I am."

Todd straightened and folded his arms on his chest. "Christ has provided propitiation for your sin through His perfect sacrifice. Through grace God counts your faith as righteousness. Your sinful nature, though, remains. You are not a perfected work. You will not be until. . . ."

"Until when? What is God waiting for? His grace and mercy are perfect now. If I accept them with genuine faith, then I am made perfect. God's power over sin is complete. Do you think it incomplete?"

"What I don't believe," Todd said, "is that you are without blemish or fault." He tried to say more, but he could not get the words out. He began to wheeze, and his eyes grew wide as he struggled for air. When he brought his hands up to his slender neck, it appeared as if he were making to strangle himself.

"I do not pretend to perfection in externals," I said, raising my voice to be heard over his hacking. "A book may be perfectly true in sentiment and yet be deficient in grace of style. God's eye is on the root, not the branches, of my character. I am not saying I am perfectly intelligent or perfectly mannered. I am saying I am without sin." I regarded Todd's reddening face. "Are you sure you might not want some tea?"

Todd's eyes rolled back, his body went limp, and he slumped forward, falling slowly and softly out of his chair. I was surprised at this development. Almost immediately, though, my surprise was replaced with a wholly perfect peace. Even as I regarded Todd expiring on my floor—I believed at the time he was expiring—I felt calm and assured. It was akin to how I had felt during the mutual criticism sessions at Andover, but while the warmth and light I had gained from those exercises was generated from an outside source, this all-encompassing peace filled me from within. To say that I was imbued by the Holy Spirit begins to explain what I felt, but it might be more accurate to say the Holy Spirit possessed me so that I was in that moment more than myself and also somehow less than myself. As Todd eventually coughed and sputtered himself back to consciousness, I was devoid of fear and guilt. I was devoid of sympathy. The peace I felt was a jealous peace and could not afford space to these other temperaments. As I knelt over Todd, splashing tea onto his face, I was put in mind of baptism.

Upon coming back to himself, Todd's reaction to the sight of me suggested he did not feel what I was feeling. He was equal parts angry, embarrassed, and frightened, and he lashed out with accusations and threats as he wiped tea off his face and stumbled out the door. A few days later I heard he had withdrawn from classes and left New Haven due to ill health.

I was not far behind Todd in leaving Yale. Ignoring the counsel of Gibbs and my other professors, I became bolder in communicating my truth to anyone who would listen, not only inside the walls of the seminary but also outside. As my notoriety and infamy grew, Horatio pleaded with me to exercise restraint, to consider the consequences my recklessness would have not only on my life but on the lives of those linked to me, but I did not heed his advice either. What finally doomed me was my public criticism of the lengthy, ostentatious pulpit prayers of Dr. Taylor, Yale's most celebrated and esteemed theologian. Word of my invective eventually got back to the man himself, and I was summarily expelled.

I continued to stay with Horatio for a short time as I contemplated my next steps, and my presence distressed him. I would later come to sympathize with his predicament better than I did at the time. He was doubly afflicted, concerned for his brother, who, in his eyes, was foolishly ruining his future, but also concerned for himself and the threat posed to his own good standing.

On one of the final nights I spent as Horatio's roommate, I made one last attempt to persuade him I was not a fool. "To whom are men like Taylor praying when they hold forth in such dramatic fashion?" I asked. "You are a student of oratory, Horatio. Do you think he is intending to honor God with his overblown vocabulary and long-windedness, or is he seeking to reinforce his own supposed brilliance and piety with the young men in the pews who are attending his seminary? Is he communing with Christ or cultivating admirers?"

"I don't care," Horatio answered. He lay on his back, his hands folded behind his head on his pillow. As he spoke, his eyes remained closed. "Taylor is an important professor. I am a student. The third party is God, who, I assume, can take care of Himself."

"Long, tortured, formal prayers are unnecessary for those who have achieved perfection," I said. "There are no needs for which to ask, not even forgiveness."

"So then make your own prayers short, John, but why critique the prayers of others?" Horatio opened his eyes and propped himself up on his elbows. "Does your supposed perfection require you to point out everyone else's imperfection?"

I moved to his cot and sat at his feet. "That is an excellent question, Brother. I recognize the wisdom in it. I don't think there is an easy answer to it. I will have to ponder on and pray over it."

"Yes. Well. Just be sure to make your prayers terse, direct, and unartful." Horatio sat up and pulled a book from the nightstand onto his lap.

"You are quick, Horatio. You are like Father in this way."

"Considering how you feel about Father, I'll take that as an insult," Horatio said.

"Please don't," I said. "I didn't mean it as such." As I rose from his cot, I had already begun to miss my brother, and I regretted that I had not appreciated more fully the time we had spent together in that cramped room.

"Either way," Horatio said, "you're more like Father than I am."

"All Father and I do is quarrel," I said.

"'They do not comprehend how each thing quarreling with itself agrees; it is a connection turning back on itself.'" My brother smiled, satisfied. "Heraclitus said that."

I returned his smile and tapped the book he held. "When you're done reading the books others tell you to read, Horatio, you should write one of your own."

# Charles Guiteau Mourns His Mother

IN FREEPORT THERE WERE trains; in Ulao there are ships. That a ship doesn't sink, that it isn't swallowed up. There is a secret to a ship. Buoyancy. There is no secret to a train. The train moves over the track that was made for the train to move over. No track, no train. No water, no ship, but water is God-given. So a ship is preferable to a train twice-over, first due to buoyancy and second due to God-givenness. And third due to the wake a ship leaves behind. Thrice-over. The wake feathers up and then spreads out and then falls back into what was there before there was a wake, which was just water. There is water, and then the ship, and then white feathers, and then water again. And fourth due to the factor of how the white feathers attract the gulls that dive down at the ship, thus incorporating the sky. A train does not leave a wake. A train does not attract gulls to dive down and thus does not incorporate the sky save for the steam that rises and then dissipates formlessly. Train tracks are never white feathers.

My father does not like me to go into my mother Jane's room, the room that would have been my mother Jane's room had she moved with us to Ulao, had we not left her behind in Freeport, left her behind buried there, because he does not like me to talk to her, because he does not believe she can be talked to, because he does not like to be reminded, so I only go into the room that would have been my mother Jane's room when my father is not home. My mother Jane is not yet dead in the room that would have been her room. She is still dying in the room that would have been her room. I think if only I could help her out of the room, but she tells me it is not the room. She tells me there is nowhere I could help her to where she would not be dying. She tells me she does not want to talk

43

about dying. She does not want me to talk about ways to make her not die. She wants to talk about things other than dying, but it is impossible for someone dying not to talk about dying. She tells me what she would love to eat if she had an appetite, and that is about dying; she tells me stories of when she was a girl in New York, about how she loved apples and ate too many apples so that when she grew up she no longer loved apples, and that is about dying; she tells me how my brothers and sisters and I are similar to and different from one another, and that is about dying; she tells me about giving birth to me and about how after I exited her body the brain fever entered to fill the void, and that is about dying; she tells me about how she felt when her head was shaved by the doctor, how her bald head felt to her hands, how her hands felt to her bald head, how she felt when regarding her bald head in the mirror, how she couldn't stop regarding herself in the mirror until her hair grew back, how even after her hair grew back her head was still bald sometimes in the mirror, and that is about dying; she tells me how my father used to hold me, coo at me, bounce me on his knee, kiss my chin, tickle my feet, watch me sleep with his face close to my face, and that is about dying. When my mother Jane asks me what I am learning in school as a way to get me to confess to her what she already knows, that I am not going to school, that I am spending my days on the bluffs watching the ships turn the water to white feathers, that is about dying; and when my mother Jane thanks me for coming into the room that would've been her room, and closes her eyes, and tells me that she's tired now and that she'd have me leave her so she can rest, that is about dying; and when my mother Jane asks me to promise to come back tomorrow, that is about dying.

When my sister is waiting for me on the other side of the door of the room that would have been my mother Jane's room, and I can tell she has been listening because I can tell she has been crying, that is about dying, too.

*You know you should be at school, Charles. You know Father doesn't want you in that room. You know he doesn't want you talking to Mother. You know these things. I've told you before that if you have to talk to Mother, it would be better for you to talk to her quietly, inside your head, rather than out loud in the room. Or, better yet, you could talk to me about Mother rather than talk to her. That would be better for you because it would be less lonely, and it would be better for me because it would be less unsettling, and it would be better for Father because he wouldn't have to know. We could talk elsewhere. Away from the house. We could take a walk and talk about her. You could show me where you go to watch the ships when you should be at school. We could talk about her there. I would like that. I miss her, too. But she is at rest now in the bosom of her heavenly father. She was not at rest when she was alive, Charles, but she's at rest now, so we can be at rest. You can be at rest. That's what Father wants for you. That's what I want. And that's what Mother would want. Mother would want for you to be at rest.*

I cannot be at rest. Miss Blood will soon be my new mother, and the room that would have been my mother Jane's room will be my new mother Blood's sewing room. When my new mother Blood becomes my new mother, her name will no longer be Blood. Frankie says this is why my new mother Blood wants to marry my father. To replace her awful name.

*I was making a bad joke, Charles. Miss Blood could marry anyone to change her name. That is not why she is marrying Father. Women don't get married just to change their names. The truth is I don't know why Miss Blood wants to marry Father. Perhaps she doesn't know why. Perhaps when our mother agreed to marry Father, she didn't know why. If I agree to marry Mr. Scoville, I hope I'll know why, but I might not. If you can convince a woman to marry you one day, Charles, it's likely she won't know why.*

Frankie pulls on her shawl and hands me my jacket. She wants me to take her to the bluffs. To where I go to watch the ships rather than go to school. On the way, she tells me that if I continue not going to school, then she will have no choice but to tell Father. I tell her that our cousin Candace saw me on the road this morning and told me that she will not tell anyone I have not been attending school. Candace told me the teacher does not ask where I am or if I am coming back, and the other students do not ask where I am or if I am coming back. Candace told me the teacher is relieved by my absence, and the other students are relieved by my absence, and Candace herself is relieved by my absence. I am also relieved by my absence. If Father finds out I have not been going to school, he will make me go back to school, and everyone will be unrelieved.

*You are still a boy, Charles. Your truancy does not depend on your preferences, nor Candace's preferences, nor your classmates' preferences, nor even your teacher's preferences. It's up to Father.*

I take Frankie to a spot on the bluffs where we can watch ships, but I do not take her to the spot where I usually go to watch ships instead of going to school. The spot where I usually go to watch ships instead of going to school is closer to the log chute. Father says it takes ten acres of trees to send a steamer from Ulao to Buffalo. At the top of the chute are the cursing, spitting woodsmen who cut the acres, and at the bottom of the chute are the cursing, spitting lakemen who burn the acres. The spot closer to the log chute is the spot where I usually go to watch ships instead of going to school because if there are no ships on the water to watch, there might be wood sliding down the chute to watch, and if there is no wood sliding down the chute to watch, there might be cursing, spitting woodsmen and cursing, spitting lakemen to watch, and if there are no cursing, spitting woodsmen and cursing, spitting lakemen to watch, there might be circling gulls to watch, and if there are no circling gulls to watch, I can watch the ascending and descending stairway next to the chute and remember the morning I spent ascending and descending the stairway until the cursing, spitting woodsmen and the cursing, spitting lakemen told me to stop ascending and descending the stairway and go to school.

*This is a nice spot, Charles. I can see why you come here. You should not come here during school, but I can see why you do. A nice spot like this is worthy of a picnic. We should have brought sandwiches. I should have thought to bring some. I don't always think of the things I should think of, do I? I don't think of things a mother should think of. The reason I don't is because I am your sister. If I marry Mr. Scoville and he and I have children, then I will think of things a mother should. For my children I will. I'm sorry I don't always think like a mother for you. Before our mother passed, she told me that I would be your mother now, but she should not have said that. And Father acts as if I am your mother, but he should not do that. I know you don't want me to be your mother, and you shouldn't want that. I know that you don't want Miss Blood to be your mother, but I am glad she will be your mother so that I can be your sister again. Do you understand this? I am not saying this well.*

As Frankie talks, she braids three long blades of grass, and then bends the braid into a wreath, and then crowns herself with it, and then braids three long blades of grass, and then bends the braid into a wreath, and then crowns me with it, and then says that she and I are the princess and prince of The Bluffs. Of Ulao Bluffs. Of Ulao. Of Wisconsin. Of Lake Michigan. Of the Great Lakes. Of the United States of America.

To trace the screeching gull overhead I tilt my head back, and the three long blades of grass that Frankie braided and bent into a wreath slide off my head.

*Father loved Mother, Charles, but Mother worried him. Even before she started to die she worried him because she sometimes seemed to be elsewhere. She would sometimes do things that might have made sense elsewhere but didn't make sense where she was, in the place where her husband and children were. She would sometimes say things to people who might have been present elsewhere but who were not present where she was, among her family. When you love someone, you want them to be in one place at a time. You want them to be wholly in the place where you are. Mother was not wholly here.*

*You are like Mother in this way, Charles. You are often elsewhere. That this elsewhere is a place where you talk to Mother, who is at rest in the bosom of her heavenly father, is worrisome and unsettling to Father and me, who love you and want you to be wholly here with us. You and I need to be wholly with each other as brother and sister, and both of us need to be wholly with Miss Blood as mother. If we are wholly with Miss Blood as mother, we will be wholly with Father. Mother is wholly at rest in the bosom of her heavenly father, and you cannot be there with her.*

*I am not saying this well, Charles. What I want you to understand is that you need to choose to be here with Father and me, and you need to choose not to be elsewhere. You need to make a choice. Just like every morning you choose to come to the bluffs rather than go to school. I am not saying you are making the right choice in coming to the bluffs—in fact, you are making the wrong choice—but you are making a choice, and the nature of the choice acknowledges that you can't be in two places at once.*

*I am not saying this well, Charles. Am I asking you to forget Mother? I am not asking you to forget her, but I am suggesting she takes up too much room in you. She is at rest in the bosom of her heavenly father, so she shouldn't take up the room of a living person in you. She should take up the room of an at-rest person. An at-rest person should take up less room than a living person. If she took up less room in you, there would be more room for living people, and then you wouldn't be lonely.*

*I am not saying this well, Charles. In any case, I had better talk to Father this evening about your school. Unless you promise me that you'll start back tomorrow, I had better talk to him this evening.*

Frankie stands and walks to the edge of the bluff. With one hand she holds down her skirts against the up-breeze, and with the other she secures to her head the three long blades of grass that she braided and bent into a wreath. She cranes her neck over the precipice to glimpse the shoreline. She straightens and turns to me and tells me that it makes her dizzy to look, and then she takes one step closer to the edge to crane her neck over the precipice to glimpse the shoreline.

This spot on the bluff is empty. Empty of ships and logs and gulls and cursing, spitting woodsmen and cursing, spitting lakemen and descending and ascending stairs. This spot on the bluff is empty, but this spot on the bluff would be emptier. If Frankie took two more steps to rise into the sky and dissipate formlessly like steam, this spot on the bluff would be emptier.

When Frankie again straightens and turns to me, this time to tell me to join her at the edge of the bluff, she is startled, and she stumbles, and she clutches her throat. She is startled, and she stumbles, and she clutches her throat because I am already there.

# Abigail Merwin Recalls
# and Reconsiders Petrarch's Sonnets

MR. NOYES WROTE TO ME regularly. Letters spanning six decades. Their frequency would ebb and flow, and they would vary in terms of length and tone, but they were always there. Always on the way.

I do not blame Mr. Noyes for being perplexed by my decision to stop seeing him. In addition to being young, we were fervent, and youthful fervor is especially conducive to confusion. We spent much time together in prayer and felt a kinship in what we believed was being revealed to each of us through the other. This spiritual excitement was easy to mistake for romantic love. I realized the mistake first and thought Mr. Noyes would eventually see it, too, but he never did. He seemed determined to interpret our parting as not only tragic but cosmically so. He wanted to equate my rejection of him as a lover with my rejection of God, and later, after I married Merit, he went so far as to suggest that Satan had commandeered my life, asserting there had been hints of evil in me from the beginning. At the same time, he admitted to me that when we prayed together, he sometimes lengthened his petitions so he could stay huddled with me a few minutes longer, and he confessed that on more than one occasion his eyes remained open, his head unbowed, so he could study my face.

As the years passed, Mr. Noyes became more insistent in his conviction that our time together had been immensely significant. I noted, though, that as his missives became more strident, they also became less personal. In these letters I was less a person and more a symbol. Furthermore, he was forever revising my meaning. In one paragraph I would be cast as a gracious, divine promise whose time had not yet come, and in the next I was the personification of a curse. Within the span of a couple years

I would be everywoman, a messenger angel, a wily demon, the matron of a new generation, a cruel witch, and a divine pen used by God to inscribe His sacred will onto the pages of Mr. Noyes's heart.

In addition to his ongoing project of reconfiguring and re-interpreting me, Mr. Noyes would occasionally reminisce in his letters about the first time he saw me, but these recollections were more myth than fact. I wore a gray dress that day. I remember this not because I am vain but because Mr. Noyes wrongly states in some of his letters that the dress was blue, and in others letters he colors it black. This is not one of the more stunning inaccuracies of which he convinced himself, but it always especially vexed me, even more than his comparisons of me to a dragon or a pox. The absurdity of the fact that this man, precisely and maniacally obsessed with me as he was, could commit and repeat such a careless oversight makes me, even now as an old woman, want to weep and laugh at the same time. Run off into the woods and howl. Beat something with a stick. I have become convinced through Mr. Noyes's unrequited correspondence with me that madness can be contagious. A few years back, when some of my fellow Americans were surprised to learn of the link between Mr. Noyes and the deranged murderer of our president, I was not among them.

Mr. Noyes and I met in New Haven. He attended my family's church one Sunday, arrived late, and slipped into the pew behind us. I was perched between my mother and father, both of whom Mr. Noyes has labeled as "homely." In one letter he uses the word "repellant." He seems to want to insist on their ugliness—my "lump-faced" father, my "painfully plain" mother—in order to make a case for what he characterizes as "the miraculous nature" of my beauty.

According to Mr. Noyes, he did not listen that Sunday to the sermon or the prayers, nor did he join in the singing of hymns. Rather, he writes, "I meditated on and sang silent praises to your set of perfectly formed shoulders and worshiped the exquisitely shaped back of your bonneted head." He says he was in love with me even before he saw me in profile when I turned to comfort my mother, who, according to his recollection, was suffering from "a sneezing fit worthy of a diseased hog." By this time he had already decided he and I were to be married, somehow coming to the conclusion that, from birth, I had been "claimed and set apart" for him by God.

The first letter I received from Mr. Noyes after leaving New Haven and moving to Ithaca with Merit is the only one I ever answered, and answering it was a mistake. I should not have responded, not even to put into writing what first I and then my brother and then my father had already attempted to make clear to Mr. Noyes in person. He evidently considered my written reply, curt as it was, an open-ended invitation to converse, and he used my words as fodder for more than fifty years' worth of delusion.

"If you are being genuine in your representation of what God has revealed to you about your future with me," I wrote, "then why has He not delivered to me a similar revelation? Why do I feel oppositely, that to acquiesce to you would be to deny God's will? Please do not waste any more time waiting for my heart to turn in your direction. It will not happen."

These brief sentences afforded Mr. Noyes occasion to hold forth in future letters on the subjects of celestial time versus earthly time, Satan's methodologies, the hypostatic union, divine economics, and phrenology. It also led to multiple comparisons to biblical figures. Over the years, perhaps unsurprisingly, he composed portraits of me as Eve, Delilah, and Jezebel, but he also linked me to Sarah, who "haughtily and foolishly laughed at a God-breathed promise"; Miriam, who "was afflicted with a horrific skin rash as comeuppance for her superciliousness"; Vashti, who, "out of vanity, was banished and replaced for not fulfilling her role, for not heeding her calling"; and Sapphira, who "was slain where she stood for withholding what was owed."

It did not take long for me to realize that Mr. Noyes was not only stubborn and selfish but also ill, and there were moments when I feared my rejection of him had triggered his madness. This guilt is partly what kept me from answering any more of his letters. If I were somehow a muse for his insanity, then it seemed the best course of action would be silence.

I foolishly shared some of my thoughts about Mr. Noyes with Merit one evening, and he saw fit to respond by slapping my face, hard enough that I saw spots. This was the only time my husband ever struck me, and within the hour he was apologizing as he wept and stroked my mouth—I ended up with his head on my chest and my hands in his hair, comforting him—but before we slept that night, he offered a second apology, which served as a clarification of the first. He said he was sorry not for his anger nor even necessarily for the strike he had delivered but rather for the fact that his anger and his hand had landed on me rather than Mr. Noyes. This explanation seemed to imply I was somehow at fault for getting in the way of Merit's righteous wrath. The twisted logic of my husband's apology was reminiscent of Mr. Noyes's numerous apologies for his angry, vindictive letters, which tended to be brief statements of contrition buried in the middle of other angry, vindictive letters.

My daughter was conceived that night in the lull between Merit's first apology and his second. Days afterward, I left Ithaca to visit my parents and informed Merit I did not know when I would return. I wonder if I would have returned at all had I not discovered while in Connecticut that I was with child. Prior to this development, my father had been encouraging me to consider divorce, and I was beginning to wonder if a husbandless life might not just suit me. In any case, after I returned to Ithaca, Merit and I never spoke of Mr. Noyes again, although the letters kept coming, and I know they must have tortured Merit. Perhaps he never spoke of them because he came to think of the letters as his penance for striking me. Perhaps he thought if we conversed about them he might reach that level of anger again, and that frightened him.

Still, if I put myself in Merit's place, I cannot say I could have kept quiet. I do not imagine most people could have. If Mr. Noyes was unique for his prolific loquaciousness and self-assured oratory, Merit was unique in his capacity for silence. This is not to say he was simple or banal. Quietness can have as many moods and tones as speech. There is bereft quietness, satisfied quietness, mournful quietness, busy quietness, pensive quietness, mindless quietness, and even joyful quietness. It is possible, of course, that quietness is what first drew me to Merit, especially considering how I had just disentangled myself from Mr. Noyes, who not only loved words but lusted after them, especially if they were pouring forth out of his own mouth. It might also be true, though, that Merit's quietness explains why a small part of me always anticipated Mr. Noyes's next letter even as the larger part of me prayed it would never arrive.

For a stretch of a few years after the birth of my daughter, I determined that any new letters would go unread as reading them would make me something of an accomplice to Mr. Noyes's madness. If he were just writing letters into the air, composing words that never found purchase, they would be nothing but harmless noise. The babbling of an infant. The squawks and grunts of a barn animal. So I would burn the letters in the fireplace when Merit was out, or I would walk into the woods, wade into the creek, and tear the pages into pieces over the sluggish water.

I soon found, though, that I was mistaken. Unread words do hold sway, perhaps even more than read words. An unread letter with your name on it, even after it has been burned or drowned, is a difficult thing to put out of your mind. You miss it despite never having had it. You think it might have told you something you do not yet know about who you are.

So I stopped destroying the letters. I would read each one dutifully, allow myself to puzzle over it for a few hours, and then place it with the others and hide them, but lazily, so as not to make it too difficult for Merit to find them if he wanted. I felt I needed to hide them because I suspected Merit might prefer I hide them, but I also felt I needed to make them available to him in case he changed his mind. So I would keep them in a hat box in a closet for a few months and then stash them under canvas in the barn and then stow them among the squash and potatoes in the root cellar. There were times in our life together when I wanted Merit to be reading the letters, and there were times when I hoped he was not reading them. Even now that he is gone, I do not know in which direction I should have hoped.

At one point in his correspondence, Mr. Noyes made the claim that he had heard my marriage to Merit had grown "fragile and troubled," and this seemed to energize him. "When I am thinking of you, which is always," Mr. Noyes wrote in one letter, "I am a god with a bursting heart. You are my entirety. I owe both my sweetest dreams and most horrific, blood-curdling nightmares to you. Even if you are of the devil, it makes no difference to my heart. Even if you die, even if you make up your bed in hell. My desire for you is eternal." What good could have possibly come from Merit reading these deranged words? Conversely, how could I in good conscience have kept from Merit this sort of unhinged bombast?

Surely Mr. Noyes's brand of madness was peculiar, but I found some of the themes in his letters quite familiar. Man's love of woman is burdensome for man. My father seemed to love my mother with this precept in mind. Reluctantly, as if she were a bothersome task. When I came of age, he loved me in this dutiful way, too. And my suitors, even the sane ones, some whom I loved back and some whom I did not, seemed, at least on occasion, simultaneously consumed by and disgusted by me. They wanted me, wanted me to yield to them, but whether I relented or not mattered little in the sense that desire would eventually become tinged with resentment. Even Merit. I suspect that, in addition to whatever else I was to him, I was also a problem. If you are loved often enough in ways like these—if love is as often as not tinged with coldness, with anger—it makes you wonder whether you want to be loved. You might begin to think of ways you can be unloved, unlovable, of words you can say, actions you can take, expressions you can wear on your face to discourage love. And when you catch yourself living so as to discourage love, you might begin to wonder what good love is, and what good living is, and what God intended for you, and if this is what He intended, then what good God is.

In some of his final letters to me, Mr. Noyes compared himself to Petrarch. He explained the poet had fallen in love with a woman named Laura after seeing her in church and then spent the rest of his life writing sonnets about his unrequited love for her. Mr. Noyes copied many of these poems for me. Some praised Laura's beauty; some bemoaned her rejection of the poet's love; and some expressed the poet's shame over his misplaced worship of Laura rather than Christ.

Although the poems struck me as melodramatic and overwrought here and there, I found many lovely moments. In comparing himself to Petrarch, Mr. Noyes said that while he empathized with many aspects of the poet's predicament, he was not ashamed of his pining for me like Petrarch was of his pining for Laura. In Mr. Noyes's mind, his pining was not sinning but rather "instructional suffering," and he believed he had learned much from this suffering over the years. "A Christ-like suffering, from which springs eternal hope and love," he writes. "If you are my Gethsemane and my betrayal and my denial and my cross and my tomb, you are also my resurrection."

I think Mr. Noyes believed there was nobility in Petrarch's and his own literary insistence that they connect with their respective beloveds via pen and page in lieu of the flesh and blood connection they were denied. He believed he and Petrarch were heroes of love for basking in rejection's light. How does he account, though, for my silence in the face of such heroic love? How does Petrarch account for Laura's silence? Perhaps now that the two scribes are together, they can work in tandem to formulate an answer.

I have thought recently, now that it is too late, about how I might have done well to reply to each of Mr. Noyes's letters with a blank page. Perhaps this emptiness would have communicated what I needed him to understand. Of course, it is possible that these wordless letters would have had no effect on him. I can imagine him opening one, settling in at his desk with the clean page in front of him, and proceeding to write at the top of it, "Dearest Abigail."

In his final letter, sent just prior to his death, Mr. Noyes writes, "That you and I never abided with one another means less than the fact that we have always and will always abide in one another. This is grace. God's will is fulfilled," and he closes by telling me he loved dearly and missed bitterly the children he and I never had together. He describes them to me in detail. Three perfect sons, three perfect daughters. Heirs to an eternal kingdom.

## Harriet Holten Noyes Picks Raspberries

FROM THE BEGINNING, their marriage was the way it was. Harriet appreciated this, appreciated knowing where she stood, and she eventually came to realize there was no other place she would have liked to stand. No better available place.

She and Mr. Noyes had worked out the logistics via a series of frank letters. In her first letter, she had tried too hard to be agreeable. She had read his statement on marriage in the *Battle-Axe* and was intrigued but also confused. "When the will of God is done on earth as it is in heaven, there will be no marriage," Mr. Noyes had written for all the world to see, and now he was asking her to be his wife. She decided she would answer in the affirmative but assure him she had no expectations in terms of traditional marital relations. She would be satisfied with a brother-sister relationship if that is what he deemed best. She thought this was what he would want to hear, not only because of what he had written but because this is what other men had told her, that they preferred to consider her a sister. So she had read between the words of his proposal. This was his accusation. He was frustrated by her assumption that what he was asking for and offering was less than ideal. His anger stung her, but she was ultimately glad for it, glad she had been wrong.

He eventually explained to her how the woman God had initially intended for him had proven to be ill-fitted for his ministry and how her rejection of her calling had ultimately clarified and broadened his understanding of his own. "So I turn to you, Miss Holton." The wounds of his disappointment and abandonment were still fresh. She could tell. "So I turn to you." It was not romantic. She was glad it wasn't. She had read everything he had written, not only on the topic of marriage but also his pamphlets on holiness, abolition, and the Second Coming, and she had been convinced by his straightforwardness and conviction. She would've been disappointed if his proposal and its accompanying explanation were flowery and clichéd. She wouldn't have believed them. She liked that she could believe him. So she turned to him.

*To follow God in all things is to be holy. Yes. The notion that mankind must wait for Christ's return in order to be holy is an ill-conceived argument advanced by the Deceiver. Yes. Christ's return occurred in 70 AD, so waiting for Him is a fool's game. Yes. God's redemption and sanctification is, was, and ever shall be perfect, so waiting for perfection is also a fool's game. Yes. Now is the time to gather. Now is the time to set ourselves free. Yes. Now is the time to set the Negro free, but not only the Negro. Now is the time to set free all men and women. Yes. Not only from slavery but from all institutions and conventions rooted in ignorance. Yes. From the limitations of earthly marriage. Yes. From the ruinous sham that earthly marriage has become. Yes. Now is the time to bring about paradise by inhabiting paradise. Yes.*

Her faith in him would never wane. Not in Putney and not in Oneida and not in Wallingford and not in Brooklyn and not in Niagara Falls. Even when others wavered, she did not. Even when his siblings wavered. Even when his mother wavered. He told Harriet this was because only she knew him truly. Those who thought him less than he was eventually grew to resent him, and those who thought him more than he was eventually were underwhelmed and disappointed. Harriet, though, knew him with a clear-eyed exactness, so her faith was sustained.

When their respective fathers died, there was some money, enough to set up the community in Putney. At the center of the community with Harriet and John were the Skinners, the Millers, the Smiths, and the Cragins. On the periphery there were others, off and on, here and there. Some single, some married. Some would come and then leave and then sometimes return and then sometimes leave again. Staying was what was hard. To come and to leave were easy in comparison. Even before the community's neighbors were angry and vengeful, they were suspicious and confused and disapproving, and many who came to the community could not abide being misunderstood or disapproved of or suspected of anything. They would begin to misunderstand and disapprove of and suspect themselves, and then the misunderstanding and disapproval and suspicion would fill them up, and the only way they could think to empty themselves was to leave. The center of the community was unmoved, though. Harriet and John, the Skinners, the Millers, the Smiths, and the Cragins. This was how it was.

Of course, it occurred to Harriet that since her husband was the man at the center of the center of the community, she, his wife, should be the woman at the center of the center. It made a certain kind of sense. This was not how it was, though. It made sense to Harriet that she should be the woman at the center of the center of the community until she watched Mary Cragin pin up her hair or heard her speak or watched her sip a cup of tea or watched her smile. Then it would make no kind of sense. There was no room for jealousy. There should never be room for jealousy—Harriet agreed with her husband that jealousy was the greatest threat to the community—but in this case, jealousy wouldn't have only been wrong, it would've been absurd. It would've made no kind of sense for Harriet or any of the other women to be at the center of the center instead of Mary.

Harriet liked Mary. She was smart and quick, and when she talked, which was often, she held the men's attention. Harriet liked to watch the men listen to Mary. They listened as if something were at stake. Some of the other women, most notably Mrs. Smith, did not like Mary. During a meeting held at the Smiths', Harriet watched Mrs. Smith accidentally dump a cup of milk in Mary's lap, and then, afterwards, as Mary continued to chat with the men as the rest of the women were cleaning up, she witnessed Mrs. Smith accidentally jab the handle of a broom into Mary's ribs. The broom handle left a bruise, which Mary showed to Harriet the next day. They agreed the colors were lovely.

It was a few months later that John finally articulated to the Cragins the proposal he'd been mulling. Harriet and he had spent the afternoon with the Cragins fishing at the brook. The four of them had shared two poles. John and Harriet shared a pole and caught two fish while George and Mary caught none, and then to change the luck, Harriet and George shared a pole while Mary and John shared the other. No one caught any fish during this stretch. At one point, John and Mary moved around the bend past the meadow to try a different hole, but when they returned after the better part of an hour, they reported no luck. Finally, the men shared one pole while the women shared the other. This arrangement yielded three fish for the men and only one for the women, but Harriet and Mary's fish was by far the biggest of the day. The four of them cheerfully argued over the meaning of this, and then when it began to rain they hurried back to John and Harriet's cabin, and there they took turns reading aloud until they were hungry for supper, and then Harriet and Mary prepared the fish along with some turnips and biscuits. "Sacketts Brook trout is the best trout," they told each other. "Isn't it the best trout? Where is it better? The more beautiful the brook, the tastier the trout. It's a fact!" And then they were quiet, waiting for John to say what he needed to say.

He said "we." Sometimes "we" seemed to refer to himself and Harriet, and sometimes "we" seemed to mean the four of them, and sometimes "we" seemed to include the entire community, and sometimes "we" seemed to mean himself and God. "We believe the time has come to put faith into action, to broaden and deepen our marriage bond by inviting you, friends, to join with us in sharing and perfecting our love. We already share so much. We already love and edify each other and see each other as partners in Christ. There is but little that separates us. We are separated only by earthly boundaries. To overcome these, we will need courage and resolve, but if we aspire to experience our love in its fulness, if we aspire to complete it and honor it, we need to move forward."

As John spoke, Mary nodded with her eyes steadily on him, and Harriet nodded at her folded hands on the table, and George did not nod, but rather closed his eyes and aimed them at the ceiling.

When John finished speaking, Mary appeared ready to answer, but George broke in first. When he spoke, he faced Mary but directed his words to John. "Are you asking permission prior to embarking on a voyage, or have you already set sail?"

"George," Mary said, "John is not Abram."

"But you, Mary, are Mary," he answered.

"George," John began, "it is in part because of the indiscretions that occurred between Abram and Mary that Harriet and I believe the time is ideal to enter into this communion with you and your wife. As a sort of corrective. What occurred between Mr. Smith and Mary was impure because it was unsanctioned and unblessed. The four of us can demonstrate to our beloved brothers and sisters how shared marriage, complex marriage, should work. I think we have the duty to do so."

George turned to Harriet. "This is what you believe, is it, Harriet? That Mary and John and you and I are dutybound on this matter?"

"Among the four of us, you, of course, are the one who needs to summon the most courage," Harriet said. "You were harmed and deceived, and now you're being asked to trust."

Mary patted Harriet's wrist and broke in. "When Mr. Smith took liberties with me, George, he did so without consulting you. He did so without consulting his own wife. And I made the mistake of not confiding in you right away. Due to my confusion and shame, it took me too long to confess and beg your forgiveness. This is different. Here are John and Harriet in tandem coming to us in tandem. Here am I, imploring you to demonstrate that your trust in me has been restored."

"My question has not yet been answered," George said. "I need to hear from you, John. I need to know if this is a proposal or a confession."

"I have walked with Mary, and I have been tempted to take her into my arms," John said, "and I have told her of my temptation, and she has confirmed to me her desire for me to take her into my arms, but I have not taken her into my arms."

George shook his head and waved his hand in front of his face as if he were scattering gnats. "If I say no, what happens? You hold that this is God's intention, right, John? You have been exhorting us for the last few months about the role sexual love should play in celebrating and abiding in His kingdom. So why am I even being asked? Your suggestion that I have a choice in the matter is deceptive, and I resent it."

Mary leaned across the table to snatch both of her husband's hands and hold them to her cheek. "I will not participate in this without your blessing," she said. "It is not my marriage that I seek to bring into line with God's perfect plan. It is our marriage. I will not commune with John if you do not commune with Harriet. If you allow this to happen, though, I promise you our love for one another will not decrease; rather, it will increase."

"You are done with Abram, right?" George said, his voice breaking. "He will have no part of you? No part of this?"

"Abram and Mary have both repented, George," John said. He pushed back from the table and crossed his arms. "I don't think any good can come from further reference to their indiscretion."

"Not indiscretion. Indiscretions," George said. "More than one."

"What's important is that they have put that wickedness behind them," John said. "Mr. and Mrs. Smith do not have permission to share their marriage at this time. They are not ready. Only we are ready. You and Mary and Harriet and I. We are the only ones at present mature enough in our faith to enter into this practice."

"With Abram I was unfaithful to you because my heart was not right," Mary said to George. "With John I will be faithful to you because my heart is right. Do you understand? Do you believe me? Please say you believe me."

The four of them sat at the table in silence for a few moments before George rose and walked around the table to where Harriet was sitting. "Harriet, would you like to walk with me? It sounds like the rain has stopped."

"Thank you. Yes," Harriet answered after she looked to John, who nodded in approval.

They walked for a few minutes in silence through the damp meadow before George spoke. "Harriet, I hope you won't be offended or disappointed if we share only conversation tonight."

"Of course, George," Harriet said. "We don't even have to share that if you'd prefer. We can simply walk and enjoy the evening together."

"Thank you, Harriet. Thank you for being kind," George said, and then his face changed, and he placed his hand on Harriet's back, turning her in the direction of his and Mary's cabin.

After a few weeks the Skinners, too, were invited to commune with the Cragins and the Noyeses, and then the Millers, and then a few other couples from the periphery whom John had deemed fit, and it struck Harriet that as different from one another as Mr. Noyes and Mr. Cragin and Mr. Skinner and Mr. Miller and the other men were in terms of their minds, mannerisms, and personalities, their similarities as lovers were just as pronounced. If this realization surprised and disappointed her, it also relieved her. She wondered if the men felt the same way about her and Mary and the other women. She somehow doubted it.

Harriet considered these things one afternoon as she walked Sacketts Brook alone. Since the community had taken the step it had, it seemed solitude was more difficult to come by. When she and John weren't interviewing with other couples, there were meetings. Everyone was on edge due to the rumors about John's impending arrest, and in the meetings folks discussed different scenarios and courses of action, but Harriet believed John was right to insist that they take no action for the time being. "Whatever happens, the Lord will work it together for good," he told his followers on more than one occasion. "Perhaps our neighbors' ill-conceived fervor will be quelled, perhaps it won't. Worse comes to worst, we will have won the opportunity to explain our love for one another in a court of law. I'd relish such a forum to spread our message and purpose."

Harriet had brought along on her walk a basket that she intended to fill with raspberries. Near the footbridge were several bushes that she'd spotted on a recent excursion with Mr. Miller, and Mary had promised she would make pies if Harriet picked the berries.

Just as Harriet approached the footbridge, she heard grunting. Her immediate thought was a bear, but the sound had a human quality that unnerved her even more than the thought of a bear, so she dropped to all fours and stationed herself behind a large walnut tree. Peeking around the side of the trunk, she saw a man's hat floating above the tall grass and then a hand reach up and knock the hat off the head that had been wearing it. From this vantage point Harriet couldn't see anything else. Before she considered the wisdom of the idea, she hoisted herself into the 'V' of the walnut tree's split trunk, affording herself a better view of the spectacle.

Peering through the leaves, Harriet couldn't make out either of the couple's faces right away, but she was able to follow the choreography of their bodies. Harriet was put in mind of kneading dough and bobbing for apples. When the man grunted—there was the bear—the woman would stop sighing and panting, and when the woman commenced sighing and panting, the man would stop grunting. It sounded to Harriet like the two were having a conversation. The man made it sound like a spirited debate, and the woman made it sound as if she were trying to change the subject.

Harriet was initially nervous she'd be noticed by the couple, but the longer she watched, the more secure she felt, not only because of the leaves and branches she hid behind, but because she realized the lovers' senses were wholly invested in each other. She imagined she might jump down from the tree, do a jig, and recite the Declaration of Independence at the top of her lungs and still not be noticed.

After a while the man stood, his back to Harriet, and produced a handkerchief from his jacket pocket. His trousers were nowhere to be seen, but from the waist up he was fully clothed. As he wiped his face and neck, the woman rose from the grass and turned to him. Mary. She smiled brightly at the man, laughed loudly at something he said, and then took a few steps over to a young sapling, which she gripped with both hands as if it were a throat. She leaned her hips into the tree, and the man, hurrying behind her, lifted her skirt, and the two commenced to have another conversation.

Eventually, of course, the couple's lovemaking came to an end. The man and Mary helped each other dress—Mary knelt to draw up the man's trousers, and his hands worked quickly to re-button Mary's blouse—but they kissed and nuzzled one another throughout the process, and once fully dressed, they rubbed their bodies on one another and mashed their faces into each other's in such a way as to suggest they were set on re-igniting the ritual rather than getting on with their lives. Harriet had grown exhausted just watching and was equal parts impressed and put off by their persistence.

The startling call of a low-flying crow is what finally broke the spell. They each took a step away from the other, looked to the sky, and laughed. "I beg your pardon!" the man called out to the bird, and Harriet identified the voice. Abram Smith.

It was a few evenings later that Harriet and John took a ride in one of the community's carriages. Abram claimed the wheels had seemed off-kilter when he took it to Montpelier earlier in the week, but George had taken it to the mercantile since then and said it was riding fine. John had been called on to settle the matter. Harriet had asked to accompany him. She thought it would be a good opportunity to have John alone so she could report what she'd seen.

The sunset was stunning. The hazy, humid weather had given way to thunderstorms around suppertime, and now the air was cool and still, the sky backlit with colors so bright they seemed to shimmer.

"I like the orange streak at the top," John said, pointing. "Have you ever seen that color?"

"Beautiful," Harriet said. "John, I need to tell you something."

"Is it something that is going to ruin my evening?" John said, continuing to study the horizon. "If so, can it wait until morning?"

"If you'd rather," Harriet said.

"Look at that shade of purple hovering below the orange just above the tree line," John said. "I have seen that color before. Do you recall when Mrs. Smith poked Mary in the ribs with her broom?"

"Mary's bruise," Harriet said. "I didn't know you had occasion to see it."

"How's that?" John said. He shrugged one shoulder and rubbed his beard against it. "Did you know I was of the mind to remove the Smiths from the community after that incident, but Mary argued for them to stay? Convinced me they would come around? She was right, I think."

"Yes, no one's been accosted with a broom for months," Harriet said.

"What is it you wanted to tell me?" John said. "You'd best tell me now. Otherwise I won't be able to sleep."

"Oh, it was nothing," Harriet said. "It is nothing. Let's not bother with it."

"No?"

"The wagon seems to be riding fine, don't you agree?" Harriet said.

"You're right," John said. "It's anyone's guess what's on Abram's mind half the time." He patted Harriet's hand. "Are you absolutely positive you have nothing you need to tell me?"

"I am," Harriet said. "I am also a bit chilly. Let's get back, please."

"All right then, Wife," John said. "Let's get you back."

# Etta Hall Makes a Recovery

I SAY I AM THANKFUL to God and to Mr. Noyes and Mrs. Cragin for rescuing me from my illness, and I am. I am thankful. But thankful is not the only thing I am.

I'm ashamed to admit it, but I often miss being sick. I found comfort in my illness. Most days my pain was subtle, bearable. I could rest in it. It held me. Even when my vision faltered, the effects were not altogether unpleasant. Objects and faces haloed in blurs of soft color, like watercolor flowers.

I do not want to be misunderstood. I did not want to die, and I suppose if one stays ill long enough, dying is what one does. It is also true, though, that if one stays well long enough, dying is what one does. Perhaps in being healed I was rescued from an early death, or perhaps I was rescued from a long, restful life of quiet if sometimes doleful contentment. In any case, I was rescued.

It is difficult to express my thoughts about my illness and subsequent healing without sounding capricious and ungrateful, so I do not express them, not even to Daniel. This is one reason why the blessing of my healing has created distance between us.

There is this: when you are ill, you know you are on the minds of those around you, those attending to you, and since folks are always lifting you up in prayer, you know you are on God's mind, too. So there is a warmth to be found in illness, a hospitableness, and there is a relief. From responsibility. You aren't held accountable for the needs of others. It is acceptable to be concerned first and foremost with yourself. I believed it to be acceptable in any case. I allowed myself to believe it. I feel some guilt about having allowed myself to believe it, and I feel some guilt about my occasional desire, even now, to fall ill again so I could go back to believing it.

What good would I serve in sharing such a reflection with my husband? If there is a distance created between Daniel and me by my not sharing it, would not there also be a distance created by my sharing? Perhaps even a greater distance?

It was Daniel who called in Mr. Noyes to minister to me. He tortures himself with this fact. On the one hand, it worked. I was healed. But on the other hand. . . .

The doctors we had seen had not been able to help. There were two. Each took a different tack to tell Daniel and me the same thing. The first did not know what was wrong with me and communicated this by presenting us with a long list of possible diagnoses. The second did not know what was wrong me and communicated this by presenting us with no list. Of the two, Daniel preferred the first, and I preferred the second. Daniel appreciated the list because it made him feel like we had something tangible with which to work. When the doctor handed it to him, he could fold it two times and place it in his pocket. I did not appreciate the list. To read it was to feel sicker.

So Daniel called Mr. Noyes whom he heard had led some sick folks back to health, or at least he had heard Mr. Noyes's claims that he believed himself capable of leading sick folks back to health. Daniel admitted to me that he felt foolish and irresponsible calling Mr. Noyes, but he would have felt just as foolish and irresponsible not calling him.

Each time Mr. Noyes came to our home to minister to me, Mrs. Cragin accompanied him. All of the visits save for the final one were the same. Mr. Noyes would pace the room as he held forth, while Mrs. Cragin would stand still at the foot of my bed. She would regard me with a tight smile on her narrow face, or she would stare at the quilt folded over my feet, or she would study a spot on the wall as if there were a painting hanging there, but there was no painting hanging there. Daniel had wanted and expected to be in the room during these visits, but Mr. Noyes worried his presence might dilute or distract me from the full attentiveness of God's healing power and would not allow it. It hurt Daniel to hear that he was ill-equipped and unfit to take part in his own wife's restoration. If this is not precisely what Mr. Noyes said, it is precisely what Daniel heard, and this preliminary resentment that Daniel did not act on prepared the way for the final resentment that he did act on.

As Mr. Noyes paced the room, his hands would often flutter about his face like agitated birds. Other times his fingers wrestled with one another, plucked the buttons of his jacket, or wormed their way into his eyebrows and ears and occasionally his nose. When he would commence speaking, I always found myself trying to listen intently, and when he finished, I always found that I had drifted off. It was often difficult to discern if Mr. Noyes was directing his words to me or to Mrs. Cragin or to the both of us or to himself. Or praying. Sometimes I suspected him of praying. If the intended audience for his ramblings was difficult to discern, so was the content. Sometimes the point seemed to be that my faith needed to increase, that God was waiting on me so my healing could be enacted. Other times Mr. Noyes seemed to be making the case that we were the ones waiting on God. If there were a consistent theme in these litanies, it seemed related to how Christ-likeness was not only a spiritual state but also a physical state. Christ was the Great Physician and His love and grace the perfect medicine.

During the era of my illness, almost two full years, everything in my life blurred together. My days and my nights, my sleep and my wakefulness, my dreams and my reality. Mr. Noyes's and Mrs. Cragin's visits were no different. Mr. Noyes's meanderings did not lead one to the other like cobblestones on a path. Rather, his words accumulated, like snow does, into a heavy blanket, and as happens during some stretches in winter, in Vermont, the storm persisted as if forever, and the line between the heavy blanket and everything else on the landscape eventually disappeared.

As it turned out, the storm of Mr. Noyes's words was merely preamble. It was not even that. It was less than preamble. Mr. Noyes could have been reciting nursery rhymes. He could have been speaking a lost language. His words did not matter. What mattered was Mrs. Cragin's swooning. The afternoon visit during which she swooned was the only visit that mattered.

I was the sole witness to her swooning. This matters somehow. Mr. Noyes was characteristically engrossed in his own words, his eyes closed in reverence or concentration, so Mrs. Cragin's swooning was only for me. She swooned onto my bed. It was soft and gradual, like the melting of ice or the closing of a flower. When I was a young girl, my brother found a squirrel's tail in the woods, and after he chased me around with it for a while, we took turns brushing each other's cheeks with it. Mrs. Cragin's swooning was that soft. When she landed on my bed, the quilt barely wrinkled under her. I did not alert Mr. Noyes to what had happened because I did not want him to know. I wanted to keep the swooning to myself. The swooning had me feeling in a certain soft and light way in which I wanted to keep feeling, and I sensed if I alerted Mr. Noyes to the swooning, then my feeling in this way would end.

In addition to feeling soft and light, I felt strong. Seeing and feeling the weightlessness of Mrs. Cragin's body across my legs made me feel strong. It was as if through her swooning something in her had been emptied so I could be filled. Her body, the way it slumped half in and half out of the bed, like she was both climbing into and sliding out of it, awakened mine. When Mr. Noyes finally noticed what had happened, he looked at me accusingly, but I had not engineered Mrs. Cragin's swooning. Rather, her swooning engineered me. From that point on, I was well. I knew I could be well. Perhaps I could have been well all along if I had wanted badly enough to be well. This notion has crossed my mind. The question of whether Mrs. Cragin's swooning planted something new in me or activated something that was already there. Either way, her swooning invited me to be well. It changed me in that way. Through invitation.

Mrs. Cragin's swooning changed Mr. Noyes, too. He was eventually able to revive her by gently squeezing her shoulders and smoothing her hair and repeating her name softly and sweetly. I did not know his voice could sound tender and quiet like that. It was Mrs. Cragin's swooning that invited him to sound like that. Whether that tenderness and quietness was already in him or was newly introduced to him through Mrs. Cragin's swooning is a question. Either way, it changed him, too.

The steps I took with Mr. Noyes and Mrs. Cragin from my bed to the front porch were the strongest, surest steps I had taken in months. Mr. Noyes supported one side of Mrs. Cragin, and I supported the other. I was able to keep my eyes open the whole time because even when we threw open the door, surprising Daniel, who was whittling a stick into a stick with a pointy end, the sunlight did not feel like a blade cleaving my head. Even glinting off Daniel's knife the sun did not feel like that. When Mr. Noyes yelled to Daniel to help him lift Mrs. Cragin into the wagon, Daniel did not respond right away because he could not take his eyes off me, could not believe what he was seeing, could not believe that I was able to stand and walk and keep my eyes open in the sun. When Mr. Noyes yelled to Daniel a second time, I reached out my hand to touch Daniel's face. I did this to assure him that I was all right and that he could help someone else now.

When Mr. Noyes and Mrs. Cragin returned to our home a week later, one might imagine that the visit would have been celebratory, but it was not. Despite our initial relief and joy, Daniel and I had shared some tense days since my healing. He asked me continuously how I felt, and that quickly grew tiresome, and he sensed I found it tiresome, and he had trouble understanding how I could grow impatient with him asking me how I felt, considering the context of the sudden end to my two-year illness, considering how this question reflected nothing but his love and concern for me.

I felt Daniel's love and concern like a heaviness, though. I wanted to be out from under the weight of his love and concern, and that was a self-ish thing to want. I felt some guilt about wanting it. I was not ill anymore, so I did not have any right to be selfish. And if a part of me missed being ill so that I could feel selfish, I felt some guilt about that, too. And this guilt felt like a second heaviness. And so neither of us was looking forward to Mr. Noyes's and Mrs. Cragin's visit. We knew we should be grateful, but we felt like we owed them too much, and we did not know how to make restitution, and that not knowing made us somewhat resentful towards them. And since we did not know what they wanted—I think we both suspected that they would want too much—we were also suspicious of them.

It turns out Daniel and I were right to suspect them of wanting too much. When Mr. Noyes finally expressed his desire to Daniel that we share our marriage with him and his followers in exchange for my wellness, as propitiation for it, the tension between Daniel and me broke somewhat, the distance between us closed for a moment, because we were of one mind in denying Mr. Noyes his request.

Mrs. Cragin seemed relieved by our refusal. She tried not to let on she was relieved, but I sensed she suspected we would say no, and I imag-ined she had tried to warn Mr. Noyes. So she was relieved we had said no not necessarily because she thought no was the right answer but because our saying no made her right. I could tell this by the way she kept smooth-ing her skirt with her hands under the table and the way she arched her eyebrows and the way she looked at Daniel and me but not at Mr. Noyes. I sensed she was saving for later her looks for him.

When Daniel raised himself up to usher Mr. Noyes and Mrs. Cragin out of our home, Mr. Noyes stayed in his seat and advised Daniel and me that before we gave our final answer, he wanted us to do two things. First, he implored us to speak with the Leonards, Stephen and Fanny, who had recently enlisted in his group. He assured us that this couple would tell us that not only had their marriage survived its opening, but that it had been deepened and strengthened. The second thing he asked us to do was pray with him, then and there. In making this request, he slid his hand across the table to cover mine. This is when Daniel took hold of Mr. Noyes's coat collar and helped him to his feet in the direction of the door.

Early the next morning, Daniel rode into Brattleboro to the sheriff's office to tell what he knew. Out of obligation to the greater good, he told me later. He took care not to wake me when he left, but I had not slept at all that night. I was having difficulty getting used to sharing a bed again. I had only been pretending to sleep.

## John Humphrey Noyes Does Time

WHEN THE SHERIFF arrested me, I asked if he would be putting me in shackles. He in turn asked me if shackles would be necessary. He sounded tired in his asking.

"None of this is necessary," I said, but I could have just as easily said, "All of this is necessary."

I was arrested in Brattleboro in mid-morning on the street just a few steps from the sheriff's office. "I wonder how you might have made it more convenient for them," Larkin would say to me later. He did not understand at first. He and Mary Jane were in Putney to visit Mother—since Father's passing, they visited her often—so I knew I would have his services at the ready, and I did not want the spectacle of the sheriff coming out to the community, which had been the rumor. The children did not need to see me being led away like that, and although I trusted that most of the adults would act peacefully and responsibly, I worried about some of the more impetuous personalities. I did not want a reenactment of Peter and Malchus.

I had the cell to myself, but even if it had been filled with murderers, drunken brawlers, and train robbers, I suspect I would not have paid any heed to them. My mind was as crowded as my cell was empty. Larkin and Mary Jane. Todd. Professors Gibbs and Taylor. Abigail. Father. George. Daniel and Etta. With me sitting in jail, they might consider their concerns confirmed, their complaints validated. Even as they haunted me, though, I was encouraged by them in the same way the Apostle Paul was simultaneously haunted and encouraged by the Sanhedrin. I anticipated my opportunity to speak in my defense and in defense of the other faithful even as I dreaded it, in the same way, I imagined, that Christ and Stephen and Peter and Paul must have both anticipated and dreaded their respective testimonies.

After a couple of hours in the cell, I rose from the stool, the only available piece of furniture in the wretched place, and moved to the door. I cleared my throat to rouse the sheriff, who was napping at his desk, his large head nestled heavily in his stout arms. "Excuse me, sir?" When he didn't answer, I tried the door to my cell, which, of course, remained locked. Still, I was right to try. One can never be sure how the hand of God might work, by what design of His the faithful might reap and realize the substance of things hoped for. "Sir?" I raised my voice. "Sheriff? Excuse me?"

When the sheriff finally lifted his head, his eyes remained closed, and they remained closed as he walked over to my cell where he leaned against the bars and rubbed his face with his hairy hands. A bear summoned from hibernation.

"What is it?" he said, and then he continued without allowing me to answer. "Word has been sent to your lawyer in Putney as you instructed. Your brother-in-law, Mead Larson. As soon as your bail posts, you'll be free to go."

"Larkin Mead," I said. "All right then. As long as word has been sent to my mother's home. As I said previously, that's where he's staying. So, yes, that was my concern. Sorry to bother you. I simply wanted to confirm that the wheels of justice were turning," I said. "Also, I need to use the privy, please."

"Your counsel has been notified, Mr. Noyes. As I just finished saying." The sheriff stood straight, tucked his chin and coughed wetly, and then finally opened his eyes to study his prisoner. "So it's not me you're waiting on. It's Mr. Larson."

"Mr. Mead," I said. "Larkin Mead."

The sheriff smiled faintly. "As for the wheels of justice, they started turning when you were arrested this morning. Going forward, if I were you, I'd hold out hope for something other than justice."

"How's that?" I asked.

"Justice probably wouldn't serve you too well, Mr. Noyes. Not if it's true that you and your followers take turns stealing each other's wives." The sheriff leveled his finger at me. He seemed to be aiming for a spot in the middle of my forehead. "I knew your father a bit. I don't imagine this would be a proud moment for him."

"We do not steal, but we do take turns. I suppose that's one way of putting it. To not take turns would be depraved. As for my father, I knew him a bit, too." I held up a finger. "As pleasant as this is conversing with you, I really do need to use the privy please."

"Not me," the sheriff said. "Not my wife."

"Understood. Which is why I'm here on this side of the locked door, and you're there on the other side."

"Look at that," the sheriff said. "We agree."

"It shouldn't go unnoticed, though, that both of us are imprisoned, albeit in different ways," I said. "In fact, I'd argue that, by the grace of God, I'm a good bit more free than you."

"Not interested in debating you, Mr. Noyes."

"Have any innocent men ever ended up here where I am, sir?"

"No," the sheriff said. "Not in my jail. My jail is for the guilty only. I'm not set up here to deal with the innocent. They get sent elsewhere." He smiled disdainfully. "Rutland, I think."

"Good," I said. "I'm in the right place then."

"You're guilty?"

"Of living my life and encouraging others to live theirs according to God's good and perfect will. Yes. As charged," I said. "The privy now. Please. Or a chamber pot. Whichever is customary here. Please."

"As I already mentioned, Mr. Noyes," the sheriff said, "you won't find the debate you want here. I'll tell you this, though. Another man touches my wife, he doesn't make it to jail." The sheriff pushed himself off the bars of the cell and rubbed his nose. "That man doesn't see jail."

"Is that what defines your love for your wife? Selfish ownership protected by threat of violence?"

"That's part of it," the sheriff said. "I believe the Lord would want me angry if another man lay with my wife. The jealous love I have for her isn't an empty feeling. It has purpose behind it. It helps preserve the vows we took."

"I wonder how your wife feels about your jealous love for her."

"You don't think she wants me to love her jealously? You think she'd prefer I abandon her to other men?"

"There are options other than jealousy and abandonment," I said.

The sheriff folded his hands behind his head. "I have a question for you, Mr. Noyes."

"Ask it, and I will do my best to answer," I said, "as soon as I return from the privy. Or make use of a chamber pot."

"When your wife becomes pregnant, what is it like not to know whether it was your seed or another man's that found purchase in her?"

"We do not indiscriminately impregnate our women, sir," I said. "This is but one of the false rumors that's besmirched our community."

"With all due respect, Mr. Noyes, you seem to misunderstand some fairly elementary facts regarding men and women's bodies and how they work together."

"You think of the love act between a man and a woman as primarily propagative, but that's not necessarily or ideally so." I tried to smile, but my growing discomfort made doing so difficult. "The privy, sir? A chamber pot?"

"What do I think?"

"You think of sexual love as a means to an end. The end being offspring."

"That's how it works, Mr. Noyes. How do you believe you sprung into being?"

"Children are a blessing but not the only blessing bestowed by the love act. In paradise there will be no more pregnancy, no more births, but there will still be sex. The amative properties of sexual union are just as holy as the propagative properties. Now, sir, I must insist. The privy. A chamber pot. Whichever. Please."

"Who knows what heaven will be like?" the sheriff said. "Down here on earth, though, love produces babies."

"It needn't. Like all gifts from God, we have a responsibility to be good stewards of sex. We men particularly. With training and commitment, we can celebrate the divine act without sharing our seed, and we can help our women preserve their bodies and lives for activities other than child-bearing."

"Onan's sin," the sheriff said. He raised his chin, proud of this tidbit of knowledge. "This is how you propose men be good stewards of God's gift? Through waste?"

"No," I said. "Rather through continence. God has bestowed upon mankind complimentary gifts. Passion and self-control are not mutually exclusive." I put my hand on the door. "Now please," I said. "The privy. A chamber pot."

"You need to remove your hand from the door, Mr. Noyes."

"I apologize," I said, showing him my palms and raising them to my shoulders. "I am simply eager to use the privy. Or a chamber pot. Either would suffice."

"You are a crass and vile man, Mr. Noyes. All the more so because you link these sexually depraved ideas to notions of holiness."

"I am crass and vile and my ideas are depraved because I believe men should learn to practice self-control and because I hold the opinion that all mankind should think through the best, healthiest, and most responsible ways to cherish one of God's greatest gifts to us? You are not the first person to insult me in this way, but I have yet to see the fairness in it."

"You are also a snake. Of the same ilk as the one that tempted Eve in the Garden."

"I have heard that, too."

"You just heard it again," the sheriff said, and he turned towards his desk.

"I understand that our conversation has come to an end, sir," I said. "So now, the privy. Please. Or a chamber pot."

"What's that now?"

"I need to use the privy, please. Or a chamber pot, please. Whichever."

He turned to face me fully again. "The privy?" he said, raising his eyebrows. "You need to use the privy? Why didn't you simply say so?"

"Please," I said.

"You need to piss then?"

"I do."

The sheriff tapped his moustache. "I'm confused," he said. "I was under the impression you'd trained your body to practice continence."

"Your assertion makes no sense," I said.

"Then you and I have something in common," he said. "Nothing you've said to me has made sense."

"The privy please, sir?" I said. "Or a chamber pot?"

"When things get desperate, most of the incarcerated duck into the far corner of the cell," he said, nodding at the wall over my shoulder.

"No chamber pot? I should just relieve myself against the wall? That's the arrangement here?"

"Absolutely not," he said. "That's disgusting. It will get you into even more trouble than the trouble you're already in."

"Please," I said.

"I'm sorry," he said. "My mind is a bit spotty today. What is your question again?"

When I didn't answer, the sheriff retreated to his desk, and I returned to the stool. I alternated between sitting and standing for the next hour. Both positions seemed to worsen my condition.

When Larkin finally came through the door, he looked at me and nodded before presenting to the sheriff the receipt for my bond. I was surprised by the flash of embarrassment and shame I felt when Larkin saw me behind bars. I immediately recognized this as being indicative of a weakness on my part, and I became ashamed of the shame, embarrassed of the embarrassment.

"I need to speak with you outside, Mr. Larkson," the sheriff said.

"Mr. Mead," Larkin said. "Larkin Mead."

"Please," I said. "Larkin, I need to use the privy or a chamber pot right away. The sheriff here has not been responsive to this request."

"The privy?" the sheriff said to Larkin. "This is the first I'm hearing of it. In any case, I'm afraid I can't release the prisoner until I have a word with you. It will take but a minute."

"All right," Larkin said. "Quickly please." He turned to me. "Just a minute, John."

The two of them were gone for more than a half-hour. By the time they returned, I was no longer in need of a privy or chamber pot. When the sheriff unlocked the door to let me out, he smiled broadly.

It was a mostly silent ride to my mother's house. When I asked Larkin why he and the sheriff had been gone so long, he told me the sheriff himself announced his need to use the privy and then had disappeared for twenty minutes. Other than that, we didn't speak. I know Larkin could smell me because I could smell myself.

At my mother's house, I waited in the barn while Larkin fetched a pair of his trousers for me. After I changed, we stayed in the barn to discuss my legal situation so as not to upset my mother. I told Larkin that I would like Mary Jane to be present for our conversation, but he told me she wasn't interested in seeing me just then, and then he surprised me with a burst of anger and frustration. He told me he had half-a-mind to cuff me in the ear and launched into a lecture about my foolhardiness and arrogance. He seemed to be incensed by two things. First, that I had "commandeered" my followers to practice complex marriage. Second, that

I hadn't conferred with him about the legal ramifications before doing so. As he grew more heated, so did I.

"Larkin!" I said. "If you do not want to represent me at trial, simply say so! Scratch that! Do not say anything! You are fired!" I spun away from him, kicked a milking stool, and in the process split the seat of my borrowed trousers. This humiliation didn't quiet me, though; rather, it increased my fury. "I will reimburse you for any expenses, and then we will be finished with each other. I would be better off representing myself in this matter I believe. If I need any counsel, I will seek it elsewhere."

"And now I'm down a pair of pants, too," Larkin said. "I packed only two pairs for this trip, not taking into account the possibility that I might have to bail you out of jail and you might piss yourself in the process. My own fault, I suppose."

"I expect you can add the cost of the trousers to my bill," I answered.

After a few moments of silence, Larkin spoke first. "John, listen to me." He'd lowered the volume of his voice, but it was still informed by exasperation. "You and your followers are guilty of these charges, correct? You are transgressing the bonds of marriage?"

"Yes," I said. I righted the stool and perched myself upon it. "In breaking man's law, we are following God's."

"Man's law is what I'm concerned with here. You will without question be convicted. Do you understand?"

"I am persuaded the Lord will not allow that to come to pass," I said.

"John," Larkin said, "there is no question."

"God will provide me the words to make my defense," I said.

"You need to leave, John," Larkin said. He walked to where I sat and crouched in front of me. "You need to leave Vermont."

"That would violate the bail you just posted," I said. "I'd be a fugitive."

Larkin shook his head. "I highly doubt the courts will invest the resources necessary to pursue you. The likelihood is you are regarded as an embarrassment more than a threat. If you disappear, I imagine those citizens making the complaints against you will be relieved and reasonably satisfied."

"Have you ever before advised a client to violate his bail, Larkin?" I said.

"I have not," he said. He stood and shrugged. "At this point, though, I see it as your only good option."

"I recognize the wisdom in your advice," I said, remembering how I had tried to open the locked door to my cell just hours earlier. "Moreover, I understand what God is saying through you. The substance of things hoped for."

Larkin looked at me quizzically before continuing. "There's one very important thing I need to communicate to you, John. One thing I'd have you keep in mind as you make your plans for where to go from here. You need to realize your actions reflect on and affect the lives of others. Not only your community members, who seem to put great faith in your judgments and inclinations, but others, too. Mary Jane and myself. Your other siblings. Your mother."

"You will see, Larkin," I said. "All things will work together for good."

"You must remember it is not only God who loves you, John," Larkin said, and then he looked up into the rafters where two sparrows chased each other up and down the length of the barn.

"They're forever building their nests in here," I said. "Father hated the mess."

Larkin nodded. "If your father were still with us, he'd agree with what I'm telling you, John. You must remember it is not only God whom you love."

# John Humphrey Noyes Stakes His Claim

I WAS INITIALLY PUT in mind of the prophet Elijah, who, in fleeing a drought and an angry king, was hidden by God at the Brook Cherith. There ravens sustained him, brought him flesh to eat, until God raised him up to defeat the prophets of Baal. I thought my banishment to Oneida was destined to be temporary like his. I anticipated an eventual triumphant return to Putney. It did not take me long to realize, though, that I was not Elijah but rather Joshua. I would not be returning to my family in Putney; rather, they would be following me to Oneida. Our Promised Land.

The property belonged to Jonathan Burt, a New York Perfectionist, who seemed motivated to help me out of equal parts sympathy and admiration. He and his wife Lorinda knew of my community in Putney and were intrigued by the project, and upon hearing of my legal troubles, he sent word by way of Larkin. If I needed refuge, he would count it as a privilege to see to my needs in Oneida.

I had difficulty deciding whom to take with me as a companion. Harriet and Mary each said they were willing to go when I asked, but I detected reluctance in each. The illegality of my flight concerned them, I am sure, but perhaps foremost in their minds was what they would be leaving behind—friends, lovers, children—and the fact that the duration of my trip was unknown. On a sort of whim, then, I asked Fanny Leonard if she might consider making the journey with me. My arrest and its connection to her had not diminished the vivacious spirit of our interactions, and I imagined her energy would keep me encouraged and stave off loneliness. Fanny initially seemed eager to accompany me, but when Harriet and Mary caught wind of the possibility, they both opined strongly that taking Fanny with me would be unwise as she, in their mutual opinion, remained spiritually immature. As for Fanny's husband, Stephen, word reached me that he was quite put out and was even talking of leaving our community if that is what it would take to keep his wife in proximity to him. Somewhat reluctantly, then, I decided to turn towards the men in search for a traveling companion. To my surprise and disappointment, however, no one volunteered themselves. While the Apostle Paul had Barnabas, Timothy, and Silas, I evidently had no one. At first I was hurt by this. At best it struck me as a sore lack of comradery; at worst it felt like betrayal. Eventually, though, I came to realize that God was at work, that my family's reticence was likely indication that He wanted me to Himself for a time, so I made the difficult decision to proceed alone.

The Burts' land, located about a half-day's stagecoach ride from Syracuse, sprawled over the grounds of an old Indian reservation. The sawmill was still operable, and some simple log homes remained. Their haphazard arrangement amongst the trees as if they had been carelessly dropped there put me in mind of giant nuts or pinecones and made me feel small in a strange sort of way, as if I were one of the Israelite spies who, upon glimpsing the Promised Land for the first time, had reported it to be a land of giants.

Upon my arrival, Mr. Burt invited me to stay with him and his wife in their roomy farmhouse, but I felt led to spend my nights in one of the cabins. So the first order of business was to choose one. My host led me on a tour of all of them, and when I selected as my abode the homeliest, most dilapidated structure on the lot, I could tell my choice made Mr. Burt curious. He did not speak up to question me, but if he had, I would have told him that I had chosen the cabin that most resembled the state of my soul. Weathered, exhausted, beaten down.

On my first evening in Oneida, after dinner with the Burts, I apologized for my reserve and blamed it, rightfully so, on my physical and spiritual exhaustion. I told them I was thankful for their hospitality and assured them that I was typically an enthusiastic conversant. "I hope you'll have me back tomorrow so I can redeem myself," I said, and they were graceful in reassuring me that they were not offended and fully expected to see me in their home for every meal during my stay. Before I set out for my cabin, Mrs. Burt provided me a jug of water, a lantern, and two blankets, which smelled faintly of the cabbage and potatoes we had just consumed.

I was not accustomed to retiring to bed so early in the evening, but my diminished condition was not conducive to reading or writing. Even if it had been, the weak light cast by the ancient lantern was not sufficient for any activity other than to set up my bed and crawl under the blankets. Once sleep descended upon me, I saw with striking clarity much that my waking eyes had been unable to see. I have never, neither before nor since, dreamt so much and so vividly as I did that night in the old Indian cabin. My dreams were legion, and they stretched widely and plumbed deeply.

Ever since I was a boy, women had populated my dreams more frequently than men. I had my share of amative reveries, of course, especially as a young man, but even my non-sexual dreams almost always predominantly involved women. This night in Oneida was no different. Harriet, Mary, and Fanny all made visitations, as did my mother, Mary Jane, and Lorinda Burt. Each of these presences stunned and moved me.

In one dream, Fanny and I solaced one another in the Brattleboro jail cell under the watchful eyes of the sheriff as he begged our forgiveness for his sins. In another, my mother and Mary Jane argued with one another behind my back as I sat in a chair in the kitchen of my childhood home. Every now and then I would catch a flash of silver out of the corner of my eye, and I realized eventually that the two were taking turns cutting my hair with shears. Then, in the same room, I was suddenly out of the chair and kneeling on the floor, and my mother and sister had been replaced by Harriet and Mary, who were sitting in chairs above me, weeping bitterly, as I washed their feet. I was puzzled by their histrionics until I realized my brother George's body was stretched out on the floor next to me, and my hands along with Harriet's and Mary's feet were stained with blood. When the outside door swung open, a fox, more orange than red, slunk into the room. It curled its flame of a body in a tight circle as it lay next to George, draped its bushy tail over its paws, and opened its mouth to speak. "A perfect sacrifice," it said. "Holy and acceptable unto you."

There were many other dreams, some of which I remember the details and some of which I do not. Of all my visions that night, the one I remember most vividly involved Mrs. Burt. She and I lay together in my Indian cabin, our bodies tangled together under the pungent blankets. I clung to her not only out of passion but also for warmth and to calm my fear. Through the cabin's cracks a cold wind blew, and I could see the orange light of a tremendous fire and hear the whoops and cries of Indian warriors circling us, closing in. Just as it seemed they were upon us,

Lorinda rose naked from the bed, walked to the door, and flung it open. A parade of warriors then entered the cabin, bowing to Lorinda as they passed, and presented to me bundles of furs and baskets of food. The meat they gave us to eat was delicious. When I asked what it was, one brave laughed and shook his head as if he intended to keep secret from me the answer to my inquiry. This agitated Lorinda, who admonished the Indian in a strange and severe language I had never heard before. She turned to me then and said, "We are eating fox." She said this to me in the same mysterious language in which she had addressed the warrior, but I now understood her perfectly.

I was sleeping soundly the next morning in the aftermath of these dreams when Jonathan knocked on the door of my cabin. This is what he told me later. He entered when there was no answer and spoke my name several times to try to rouse me, but I would not stir. When he was satisfied I was still among the living—he said my vigorous snoring reassured him—he allowed me to continue sleeping. Hours later, when I finally awoke on my own and saw the sun high in the sky, I sheepishly found my way to the Burts' cabin where they were just sitting down for the midday meal. I apologized for my rudeness, but I also expressed how I had never enjoyed a more invigorating and refreshing night of slumber. I briefly considered sharing with them some of what I had dreamed but ultimately decided against it. Lorinda seemed cross—I suspected she was irritated by my sleeping late and missing breakfast—so my words during the meal focused mainly on repeating my thankfulness for my hosts' hospitality and my admiration of their beautiful property.

Save for meals, I spent the next few days largely on my own, exploring the grounds. The pond, the brook, the woods—the entire landscape was charged with awe-inspiring wildness and affected me similarly to the dreams visited upon me during my first night in the place. Even though I did not know what the future held for me, I felt simultaneously energized and at peace. I passionately missed my Putney family and knew that I would eventually need to lead them with conviction in one direction or another, but I did not feel despair. Rather, I looked forward to discovering how I would ultimately respond. At bottom I knew all would be well, that whatever actions I would take had already been ordained to lead my family and me in the direction of goodness, hope, and holiness. In the direction of paradise.

On my third day in Oneida, there was another guest at dinner, Dr. William Gould, a neighbor of the Burts and a fellow Perfectionist, who already knew much about my Putney family and me and was keenly interested in hearing my impressions of Oneida. When I told him it seemed to me that only a mad man would ever leave the place, he and Jonathan smiled at one another, and I felt Lorinda watching me as I watched them. "We are glad you feel that way, Mr. Noyes," Dr. Gould said. "We were confident you would."

Dr. Gould had read some of my writings and was intent on quizzing me about them. He seemed most enthusiastic about my letter on marriage that Theophilus Gates had published. When I wrote the letter, I had no intention of seeing it in circulation. I had written it to a friend nearly a decade before to outline my critique of traditional marriage, and although this friend accused me of allowing my personal strife regarding the news of Abigail Merwin's impending marriage to influence my thinking on the subject, he was struck by the cogency of my arguments and asked if he could share it. He proceeded to pass the letter to one friend, who passed it to someone else, who passed it onto Gates in Ithaca, who published the letter in his broadsheet. When I read the letter in print, I was surprised to see that it was attributed to that prolific genius Anonymous. When I asked my friend about this, he was surprised by my surprise. He had left my name off the letter when he had shared it out of caution and concern for my well-being, and he held that the uproar it was causing proved he had done the right thing. Of course, I came forward as the writer of the letter as soon and as frequently as possible from that day forward. The words were mine, and I had a responsibility to lay claim to their consequences. If one of those consequences would be for Abigail Merwin to hear about and read the letter, so be it.

Although his plate was still half-full, Dr. Gould crossed his knife and fork on the table beside it and leaned his shoulders forward. "Mr. Noyes, you write in your *Battle-Axe* letter, 'Exclusiveness, jealousy, and quarreling have no place at the marriage supper of the Lamb.' You also write, 'I call a certain woman my wife. She is yours, she is Christ's, and in Him she is the bride of all saints. She is now in the hands of a stranger, and according to my promise to her, I rejoice. My claim upon her cuts directly across the marriage covenant of this world, and God knows the end.' That is outstanding, Mr. Noyes. Such clarity and authority. I could imagine it nestled into Paul's letters somewhere. Perhaps 1 Corinthians where he speaks to the subject of marriage."

"You memorized this letter?" Jonathan pointed his fork at Dr. Gould. "Of course, Lorinda and I have read the letter, too, and we were also intrigued by it, but we didn't commit it to memory! That's outstanding, Dr. Gould! And to suggest that it could be scripture! If I'm understanding you correctly? What a compliment!"

"You are not a writer, Jonathan," Lorinda said. "How do you know if it's a compliment? If it is a compliment, it's a dangerous one, isn't it?"

"I'm sure I couldn't recite the letter myself, Dr. Gould," I said. "I am impressed and honored. To be honest, I have had this letter recited back to me on other occasions, but not out of admiration."

"Do you believe as Dr. Gould that your letter belongs in the New Testament, Mr. Noyes?" Lorinda said. She passed the gravy to her husband, who was busily eating and hadn't asked for it, but upon receiving it, he paused to pour it heavily over his plate.

"I didn't mean that literally, Lorinda," Dr. Gould said. "No one, of course, could add one jot or one tittle to scripture. And as for memorizing parts of the letter, don't be too impressed with that. It is something that comes to me quite easily." He tapped his temple before picking up his utensils again. "If it's a talent, it's not an extremely useful one, but as I grow older, I'm glad I don't appear to be losing it. I only wish my body was as nimble."

"Still quite a feat," Jonathan said.

"Well, thank you, Jonathan," Dr. Gould said. "In any case, I just wanted to tell you, Mr. Noyes, that you could not have written more articulately, and I hope you'll consider it a compliment if I tell you that I detect an enthusiastic pride behind the words. Reminiscent of Emerson, I think. An author in awe of his own ideas. As a prophet writes. It's a risky sentiment to convey on the page—readers might interpret such a tone as self-important and as a result grow weary of it, correct?—but I'd opine that Emerson pulls it off for the most part, and you do, too."

"The Apostle Paul, Ralph Waldo Emerson, and the prophets," Lorinda said. "I apologize, Mr. Noyes. I should've done better than chipped beef and biscuits."

"Nonsense," I said. "Since I've been here, I've eaten more like a king than a prophet. Prophets didn't always fare so well. Elijah, if you'll remember, ate like a bird. Literally! Beak to mouth at the Brook Cherith. In all seriousness, you are a skilled cook, Lorinda."

"Yes, everything is delicious," Dr. Gould said. "As always, Lorinda." He smiled quickly at her and then turned again to me. "May I ask one more question about your writing, Mr. Noyes? I don't want to be a pest."

"Please," I said.

"Well," he began, "my admiration aside, here we are a decade later, and most of your readership remains unconvinced by your vision." Dr. Gould paused, perhaps anticipating interjection, but when none came, he continued. "There's your group in Putney, a group now in crisis, and that's about it. You have free love contingents here and there in Ohio and elsewhere rejecting marriage altogether—I'm sure you cringe at their perversion as do I—but in terms of the view of marriage you endorse in the *Battle-Axe* letter, I wonder how you don't find it completely frustrating that you were not and are not being heeded. If I may, I find it frustrating for you."

"Perhaps you are being a bit pessimistic, Dr. Gould," Jonathan said. "Besides, does the quality and veracity of an idea or a conviction depend upon its popularity? I should hope not."

"If no one here at the table liked the chipped beef I prepared for this evening's meal—if no one were convinced by it—we would deem it bad chipped beef, wouldn't we, husband?" Lorinda said.

"Unconvincing chipped beef," I said and chuckled. "When I was a boy and my mother fell ill for a time, I remember my father preparing some unconvincing biscuits that my brother George and I fed to the dogs when our father wasn't looking." Everyone at the table, even Lorinda, smiled. "I understand your critique, Dr. Gould," I said.

"Is it a critique per se?" Dr. Gould answered. "I did not mean it as one."

"It is a critique. Sure it is. And it's a fair one as far as it goes," I said. "I suppose if I use Christ as my measuring stick, though, I'm not doing too poorly. At the beginning of His ministry He had twelve apostles, and at the time of his crucifixion, he had eleven."

After a brief moment of surprise at my words, Dr. Gould erupted in laughter, and Jonathan smiled unsurely. Lorinda shook her head, either at my answer or at Dr. Gould's response to it, and then rose from her seat to fetch an apple pie out of the oven.

"Very good, Mr. Noyes," Dr. Gould said. "Do you think God has a sense of humor? I do. I think He's probably much more mirthful than most folks believe. In any case, speaking again to the question of your writing's negligible impact, I think you're in good company with Emerson," Dr. Gould said. "His letter about the Indian crisis to President Van Buren was penned around the same time as your *Battle-Axe* letter, and although he was as rightminded as you in terms of his subject, and although he expressed his sound ideas as eloquently, his writing didn't affect change either. 'However feeble the sufferer and however great the oppressor, it is in the nature of things that the blow should recoil upon the aggressor.' An exquisite sentence among many other exquisite sentences! Emerson crisscrosses them one upon the other as if to create a lattice for the ascension of his sentiments. A poet as well as a seer. And yet here we are."

"I've been thinking a lot about Indians during my stay here in Oneida," I said.

"It's difficult not to think about their former presence here," Jonathan agreed, seemingly relieved by the direction in which the conversation had turned. "And you sleeping in that cabin every night."

I nodded. "Despite all the beauty, there's a certain melancholy in the air that informs everything. Not only the cabins and the sawmill, the things they made with their hands during the time they spent here, but also the trees, the sky, the water."

"It's a gravely unfortunate aspect of the American story," Dr. Gould said. "As is the enslavement of the Negro, of course."

"All of these issues are connected," I said. "Slavery and the Indian problem, sure, but marriage is a crisis, too. They are all issues of freedom and love. The lack thereof. A violence-tinged sense of entitlement is the poison at the center of each of these wounds, and greed and self-love cause them to fester."

"Perfectly expressed," Dr. Gould said. "The question is, will writing more letters and essays and treatises facilitate healing? I'd venture to say no."

"Writing is but part of the antidote," I answered. "For me, my efforts at building the community in Putney is the other part. There my family and I aim to practice what I preach."

"Is it possible that as noble an effort as Putney was, its time has come to an end?" Jonathan asked.

"I don't think so. I hope not," I answered. "Due to my circumstances with the law, you mean?"

"Yes, in part," Dr. Gould answered. "It would seem you and your followers have worn out your welcome in Vermont."

"It is true we might need to relocate," I said. "These considerations weigh on me, I can assure you."

"Perhaps you might consider the possibility of reorganization to complement any future plans of relocation," Dr. Gould said.

"Reorganization?"

"Shared leadership," Dr. Gould said. "Jonathan and I would be humbled to help you on both scores. We have discussed this in detail and believe we're being led to join you in your ministry if you would have us."

"Move my family here?"

"Here you are," Jonathan said, glancing at Dr. Gould. "You said yourself only a madman would leave."

"He was paying attention!" Dr. Gould exclaimed. "For a time there, Mr. Noyes, Jonathan seemed in such deep fellowship with his vittles that I thought we'd lost him."

"I admit to finding Lorinda's chipped beef wholly convincing," Jonathan said, and I detected in his voice some annoyance at Dr. Gould's teasing and some self-pride in his decision to rise above it.

"Perhaps my husband was on the quiet side, Dr. Gould, because as you were holding forth, there wasn't much room for him or anyone else to make themselves heard," Lorinda said as she entered the room, pie held aloft.

"Have you been talking to Mrs. Gould, Lorinda?" Dr. Gould answered her. "In any case, be assured that I now feel sufficiently chastened for my verbosity. That said, I must press on."

For the rest of the evening, Dr. Gould and Jonathan laid out for me their vision. Under their plan, I would summon the entirety of my Putney family to relocate to Oneida, and we three men would together preside over and grow the sanctified remnant that would soon usher in God's promised kingdom on earth as it is in heaven. That their vision so closely matched mine I took as a sign that this land had been ordained for my Putney family and me, that in Oneida, God's kingdom would be rooted and realized, and the faithful would abide in His glory forever.

There were important aspects of Dr. Gould's and Jonathan's vision, though, to which I objected, but I was not prepared that evening to articulate my arguments. Rather, I told them I was encouraged and honored by their proposition and asked if we could reconvene in the morning to converse further after I took the night to contemplate their generous offer. They agreed to my request, but I could tell they were surprised and disappointed by my measured response. Still, they smiled and shook my hand enthusiastically when I made my departure for my cabin. Lorinda, who had stayed quiet during our conversation, asked if I would need to be roused in the morning for breakfast. She said she did not wish to prepare food that would not be eaten. I noted Jonathan's embarrassment at his wife's question, but I simply smiled and assured her I would be present at her table with time to spare.

I did not sleep that night. No dreams to inspire, frighten, or puzzle me. Rather, I thought through Dr. Gould's and Jonathan's words and tried to discern the best way to proceed. I did not pray according to how most people think of prayer. People often imagined me to be a tireless, habitual pray-er, but I was not and never had been. God was present in me and I in Him. What purpose did it serve to formally address my own God-inhabited soul and to waste energy trying to find words to ask my own God-inhabited self for guidance and comfort? It struck me that traditional prayer, like those recited in churches and by folks on their knees at bedtime, often had the potential to do more harm than good. Folks used prayer to shift and shirk responsibility to a far removed, invisible spirit and away from themselves. One eventually had to rise from one's pew, from one's knees. What then? Better to think of prayer not as words to be waited on but rather as sacredly guided perpetual action, akin to breath and heartbeat insofar as how it is compelled not by one's own conscious will but by something deeper, more intrinsic.

One concern of mine was Jonathan's use of the word "gifting." He had said he would be gifting the land to my Putney family and me. He had seemed proud of this—he obviously considered his gesture a grand one—and I suspected that he, and perhaps even more so Lorinda, had been underwhelmed by my expression of appreciation.

As for Dr. Gould, the first aspect of his person to give me pause was his profession. Many doctors I had known placed too much trust in their own judgments and, despite their claims of allegiance to science and objectivity, too often dealt in conjecture and assumption. I noted, too, that they often thought their supposed expertise in medicine somehow lent them expertise in all things. Over the course of the evening's conversation,

I gathered that Dr. Gould fancied himself a man of letters, a political authority, a historian, a horticulturalist, a chef, and a woodsman. It was no surprise, then, that he had offered to situate himself, along with Jonathan the land-gifter and myself, as a co-leader of the new Oneida Community. This, of course, would be unacceptable.

By the time dawn broke, I had formulated my response. I waited outside the Burts' door until I heard the first sounds of stirring and then entered with an armload full of firewood and a jacket pocket full of eggs that I had taken the liberty to gather from the Burts' hens. My other jacket pocket was also full, but not with eggs.

After bestowing my gifts on Lorinda in the kitchen, I sat myself at the table where Jonathan and Dr. Gould, who had evidently spent the night as the Burts' houseguest, were yawning themselves awake, and I dropped the bag of gold pieces in front of them. When they did not respond right away, I loosened the drawstring and tipped over the bag to reveal its contents. Dr. Gould slid his glasses from his forehead down onto his nose to study me, while Jonathan reached out for one of the gold coins and proceeded to drop it accidentally on the floor, where it tipped onto its side and rolled noisily to the wall behind him.

"What's this now?" Dr. Gould asked, trying to summon a smile. "Did you find buried treasure out there among the Indian cabins, Mr. Noyes?"

"There are many treasures to be found out there, I am sure," I said, "but, no, this bag came with me from Vermont. Its contents represent the vast majority of the Putney family's wealth."

"I see," Dr. Gould answered.

"Why did you bring the money to breakfast?" Jonathan asked.

"He doesn't want you to gift him the land. He wants to buy it from you. As he should," Lorinda said from the doorway, where she had been listening to our exchange. "How much, Mr. Noyes?"

"Lorinda!" Jonathan rose from the table, took his wife's stiff elbow, and escorted her into the kitchen.

When Dr. Gould started to speak in response, I held my hand up and told him I needed to have my say before he pressed with any more inquiries. I told him we would wait for Jonathan. When Jonathan re-appeared, I told him we would wait for Lorinda. When Lorinda re-appeared, with a pan of eggs and a loaf of brown bread, I commenced.

"The ownership of land, perhaps especially here in America, is a mysterious phenomenon, isn't it? Of course, I appreciate Jonathan's and

Lorinda's gesture in offering this land for the relocation of my family, but how it came to be theirs to give is a perplexing question."

"We bought it is how," Lorinda said.

Jonathan turned to her as if he were preparing again to chastise her, but when she met his eyes he kept silent.

"But from whom did you buy it?" I said "And from whom did that party buy it? And the Indians? How did they lay claim to it?"

"You're saying it is God's land," Dr. Gould said with a note of impatience in his voice.

"That's right. Wasn't it always God's? Isn't it still? I understand most people would consider your offer gracious, Jonathan, and I am glad to hear of your willingness to have my Putney family and me join you here as stewards of this land, but you are not gifting us the land. It's not yours to gift. If it's going to be gifted, God will be doing the gifting."

My words were met with silence. Jonathan and Lorinda looked at each other, and Dr. Gould focused on his plate of eggs.

"The money I have here is God's," I continued. "A collection of God's gifts to all the families that make up my family. If you are part of our fellowship, it is your money, too. Just as this land would be shared by all. There is no ownership in Christ."

"If I may, Mr. Noyes, how is it that you have your family's money, God's money, with you?" Dr. Gould said. "You didn't have foreknowledge of Jonathan's and my proposal. I find it curious that you're traveling with it. It would appear to be quite a bit. Does your family know you have it?"

"My family's trust in me is full-bodied and well-placed."

"That's not exactly what I asked," Dr. Gould said.

"It strikes me that you want to accept our proposition while making sure to point out my gesture of hospitality isn't all that generous after all," Jonathan said. "Rather than acting magnanimously, I am simply doing my duty."

"Please don't misunderstand me, Jonathan!" I answered him. "In the context of communal fellowship, there is nothing more magnanimous than doing one's duty. And it is certainly not my intention to de-emphasize the spirit of generosity behind your proposal. It is important to note, however, that one's place in the family, especially in terms of leadership, is not tied to how much earthly wealth one is able to contribute."

"So you are willing to move your members here and claim this land as home, but you aren't willing to recognize Jonathan's or my contributions?" Dr. Gould said.

"Each community member's daily happiness in this place will be recognition of Jonathan's and Lorinda's contributions," I said. "Specifically to what contributions of yours, Dr. Gould, are you referring?"

He straightened in his chair. "I am prepared to donate financially, of course," he said. "That said, I think my greatest contribution will be my leadership. I am wise, well-learned, widely read, experienced, and I am an effective communicator and organizer. I say all this under risk of sounding arrogant. I make these claims because you asked."

"That's not exactly what I asked," I said.

I realized at this point that Dr. Gould, Jonathan, and Lorinda were disappointed and frustrated. Of course, I knew this would be the case, but I could not afford to step lightly in guarding the sanctity of the vision God had afforded me for the nurturing of His kingdom. However, while certain precepts were non-negotiable, it was also true that I knew Oneida was the place where my family was meant to be, and I needed the Burts to ensure that outcome. Winning Dr. Gould's favor was perhaps less necessary, but I knew Jonathan respected the man, so, going forward, I would need to choose my words carefully.

I outlined for my audience the details of community life. Some of the things I discussed were descriptive—we were already doing them in Putney—while others were prescriptive, things I planned to implement upon establishment in our new home. I laid out for them the principles of mutual criticism sessions, clarifying that all members were expected to take occasional turns being criticized, and that I would be the chief facilitator and scheduler. I laid out the rules for complex marriage, emphasizing that I alone had final say on who coupled with whom. In addition, I also explained the basics of ascending fellowship, the notion that, in most cases, especially when it came to the young men, they would be trained as lovers by older women so as to minimize the chances of unintentional pregnancies. At this moment in the conversation, Lorinda rose from the table and walked out of the house with her apron still on. She took care to close the door behind her softly, but she might as well have slammed it.

Jonathan stared at the closed door as he spoke. "Lorinda would like to have children. One at least. It's been hard."

"The poor woman has lost two pregnancies," Dr. Gould said.

"It's not your place to give out that news, Dr. Gould," Jonathan said. He said this so quietly I barely heard.

"Children are definitely part of our project," I told Jonathan. "Of course, all plans need to be sanctioned, but I can tell you right now that you and Lorinda would have my blessing. Permission granted."

"How kind of you, Mr. Noyes," Dr. Gould said. Jonathan nodded in agreement, not hearing the edge in the doctor's voice.

"In terms of how we rear our children, though, it will be a community-wide effort. Just as jealousy and exclusivity have no place in marriage, these evils have no place in child-rearing. I'm still thinking through the particulars, but I imagine a children's house staffed with nurses. A place where the adults can visit to love the children equally, without favoritism. My own beloved son Theodore. He would live there with all the community's children. I imagine building this house after we built a great mansion—one building—where all the adults would live together under one roof."

It was less than a month later that Harriet, Mary, Fanny, and the rest of the Putney-ites arrived in Oneida. Harriet and I, along with the Cragins, stayed with the Burts, while everyone else spread out among the old cabins that Jonathan and I had been sprucing up in anticipation of their arrival.

Dr. Gould was present among us for a while, but his voice grew quieter as the weeks wore on, and he had trouble connecting with the other community members. Jonathan told me that Dr. Gould suggested to him that I had poisoned the Putney-ites' minds against him, but I had done no such thing. I had merely advised them that he was prideful and that we must, out of love, do our best to humble him. He was on the docket for the community's first mutual criticism session, but he did not show up. After that point, I would see him in town occasionally, and he would always take that moment to check his watch.

Within three years, our numbers had swelled from thirty to more than two hundred. I did not have opportunity to enjoy all this growth firsthand as I ended up spending a good deal of time directing our new branch in Brooklyn, out of necessity at first and then by choice. Harriet was good enough to stay behind and help manage affairs along with George Cragin and John Skinner, while Mary accompanied me. We stayed in a house that Abram Smith had inherited. Of course, he was not necessarily pleased that we were making use of it in this way—I think he imagined the community would sell the house and use the profits to help bolster our beginnings in Oneida—but he knew, given his history, that he had little room to complain, so he kept quiet, at least in terms of complaining to me directly.

At first I fled to Brooklyn because it appeared I had again ended up on the wrong side of the law. A woman, Tryphena Hubbard, and her miserable husband had joined our community in Oneida, and they had a row one night that ended with him beating her badly. Her father got involved before we could intervene, and in his dealings with the constable, he put more blame on the community and me for what had happened than he did on his own son-in-law. When it appeared I might be headed for another arrest, I contacted Larkin, who again counseled me to flee. At this point I was at my wit's end, deeply discouraged, and this is why Mary agreed to accompany me. She told me she worried that if I were to go off alone, she might never see me again.

Once the Hubbard incident resolved itself—when the Hubbards reconciled and disentangled themselves from our community, her father's wrath cooled—I asked Mary if she wouldn't mind staying in Brooklyn a while longer. City life agreed with me, and without the distractions of the constant physical labor that Oneida demanded, I had been able to write more than I had ever before. Despite Dr. Gould's arrogance and misplaced priorities, I had taken to heart his comments about my writing, especially my literary similarities to Emerson, and it occurred to me that my writing might be the best tool we had at our disposal to grow our community. Eventually, Stephen and Fanny Leonard joined us in the city to supervise the beginnings of a printing operation so my writings could be circulated, and the four of us became a true extension of the Oneida family. A few new converts joined us in our home, and folks from Oneida would often be granted permission to visit us in Brooklyn for a change of scenery and company, so the place was perpetually informed by positivity and new energy. For a good while, it seemed our lives were destined to be defined only by perfect happiness.

# Clark Emory Finds Love

I WAS IN LOVE for a short time with a woman named Caroline Coates. This was in Ann Arbor, Michigan, just prior to the war. In fact, I was in love with Caroline for more than a short time. It might be I am still in love with her.

My time with Caroline corresponded exactly with Charles Guiteau's presence in my life. Over the course of these months, I saw him everywhere. The opposite end of my pew at church. Two tables away at the tavern. Behind me in line at the post office. Up in a tree, on a roof, under a horse. On one otherwise splendid September afternoon, while picnicking with Caroline ten miles outside of town on the banks of Whitmore Lake, I was startled to watch Guiteau float by us on his back like an overgrown otter.

On these occasions, Guiteau never simply nodded or offered a typical sort of hello. Instead, he'd either look through me and pass by as if I were an apparition, or he'd rush me, plant the tip of his nose within an inch of mine, and pepper me with commentary about Homer, "that doughface Buchanan," the new water closet at the coffee house, or Latin conjugations. His breath was always stale, and as often as not there was food in his beard.

Caroline told me at the time that considering these encounters with Guiteau as anything but coincidental would be irrational. "Like the cube root of two?" I asked, and we had a hearty laugh. We were both mathematicians, so the witticism was well-targeted, and since I have never been a man to whom comedy comes naturally, there was an element of surprise that enhanced the joke. I think Caroline was charmed by my effort.

Caroline's reasoning regarding Guiteau's omnipresence in my life was based on the fact that he would periodically call on me in my office at the university. Since he evidently felt free to drop in on me there, why would he go to the trouble to follow me around surreptitiously? I figured she probably had a point. I admired many things about Caroline, not the least of which was her sound, steady mind. It might not be considered romantic to say so, but when I was courting her, I often thought of how comforting it would be to have such a partner by my side as I navigated my life. I wanted passion, but I also wanted peace. With Caroline, I thought I'd found both. We were often quiet together, but it wasn't a worrisome quiet. It was a thoughtful quiet. I liked thinking alongside her. I liked thinking about her thinking. I never felt inclined to interrupt our quietness just for the sake of interrupting it. This to say, it didn't take me long to realize I loved Caroline.

It is in this context, the context of love, that Guiteau became for me a tragic problem rather than a minor nuisance. The scoundrel inserted himself between Caroline and me, obfuscating what I should have known was the truth. I allowed a madman to sow seeds of doubt in my heart, and for this I will forever be ashamed and regretful.

Guiteau always referred to me as his mathematics professor despite the fact that I was not. I corrected him on this point numerous times, but he persisted. Rather than being his mathematics professor, I was a mathematics professor who had evaluated the mathematics portion of his university entrance examination, assigned him a failing grade, and thereby denied him admission to the university where I taught capable students. Although he tried diligently to persuade me otherwise, I knew from our first conversation that Guiteau would never be admitted to the university. I based this opinion on my observation that Guiteau was the worst type of student in two ways. First, he was woefully unprepared. Second, he believed himself a genius.

Many young men came to Ann Arbor every August with the intention of enrolling in the university. Those who were unsuccessful failed for one of two reasons: either they were unable to pay the tuition, or they were unable to pass the entrance exams. Guiteau possessed money but not rudimentary knowledge of mathematics or French. After receiving his examination results, he came to visit me in my office. He evidently passed the composition portion of his exam, so that's why he never darkened the doorway of Brooks's office, and although he tried to badger Pasqualle about his language exam, he surrendered efforts on that front after being foiled by the old codger's strict and strategic policy of conversing with students only in French.

Unsurprisingly, my meetings with young men who had failed the entrance exams were often unpleasant. Sometimes there were tears, sometimes threats. Other times, though, I would pick up on an odd sense of relief from the poor lad, or I'd sense he was genuinely looking for counsel about how to move forward with his life in the aftermath of this setback. In these cases, I often suggested military service or application to the university's new law school. At the time, all a young man needed to gain admission to the law school was tuition and a recommendation letter attesting to his "high moral character." I had written several such letters on the spot.

Guiteau was neither sorrowful, angry, nor relieved in our initial meeting, nor was he looking for advice. He told me in no uncertain terms that he had no interest in soldiering or lawyering because he was "destined for more." What he wanted was to retake the exam. He told me he had been ill on the morning of the test and seemed to believe I could administer a second exam to him then and there. I told him he could not retake the exam until the new year as per official policy, and I suggested that, given his abominable score, the result would likely be the same unless he was willing to prepare himself by undertaking remedial work. As I had in the past suggested to a handful of other young men in Guiteau's circumstances, I mentioned that he might inquire about enrolling in the local secondary school. The Union School had a good reputation and well-qualified teachers. He thanked me at that point and made an abrupt exit, promising on his way out he would keep me posted on his progress. I told him that was wholly unnecessary, but he had already turned the corner and was a few steps into the hallway by the time the words left my mouth.

So, ironically, it was I who sent Guiteau to Caroline, and it was Guiteau, in a sense, who brought Caroline and me together. He enrolled in her class that day, and it was the next afternoon that she called on me in my office to inquire about him. Guiteau had told her I'd suggested he sit in on her courses in order to familiarize himself with classroom protocol and pedagogical methods because I saw great potential in him as a future professor. Rather than work through problems with the rest of the students, Caroline told me he simply watched her all afternoon, nodding and smiling, and during lunch, when she was trying to mark the student's homework, he stood at her desk and sketched out for her his biography, a story extraordinarily rich in romance and heroism.

Of course, I was astounded by the brazenness of Guiteau's dishonesty and his disrespectful behavior, but when I explained the truth to Caroline, she seemed more amused than angry. She told me she suspected as much, that she thought Guiteau was probably embarrassed about his situation and that his lies had grown out of this embarrassment, and she assured me she would do her best with him. I told her she had no obligation to teach Guiteau. In fact, I recommended she dismiss him from her class, but she told me she took her responsibilities as an educator seriously. "Unlike university professors, we secondary school teachers don't always get to choose our students," she said and smiled at me in such a way that made me feel my life would be immensely diminished in the moment she would stop smiling.

Later, Caroline told me this hadn't been our first meeting. She insisted we'd been introduced a year prior when I arrived in Ann Arbor, but I do not recall it. If she was right, I do not understand what could have been on my mind, what could have possessed me to miss her exquisiteness. I told her this multiple times, and on each occasion she seemed both embarrassed and pleased, as I was both embarrassed and pleased to tell her. She asked me once why I supposed I had not seen her then as I saw her now. I wished I knew the answer. It was difficult not to think about the days wasted, especially considering the plans I had recently made to spend the next year in Munich as a visiting instructor. Within two weeks of her visit to my office to discuss Guiteau, I had already suggested to her that we get married upon my return from Europe, but she was hesitant to commit. She was worried we hadn't known each other long enough, and the prospect of a year apart worried her. She confessed she had never been much of a letter writer.

In his visits to my office, Guiteau would sometimes refer to Caroline by her first name rather than as Miss Coates. I always corrected him on this score, more sternly than when correcting him about my not being his mathematics professor. The final time I did so, however, his response gave me pause. He reported to me that Caroline had told him to call her Caroline. He said he felt oddly about it at first, but she had insisted. He told me he had no choice. "As you and I both know," Guiteau said, "Caroline is a hard woman to deny."

Why did I not at that point simply banish the reprobate from my office and be done with him? I have asked myself this question on many occasions. The answer, I am afraid, is that I wanted to hear what he had to say. Even though I told myself that much of what he reported to me was likely fabrication, my curiosity got the best of me. I knew from his ramblings that he had caught wind of my proposal to Caroline, my upcoming trip to Munich. How could he have known these things unless Caroline had confided in him?

Although Guiteau had previously dismissed out of hand a career in law, he possessed a conniving quality I have had occasion to observe in more than a few successful lawyers, and he would often pace in front of my desk as he spoke as if I were occupying a jury box. This would unnerve me, so I'd ask him to sit, and he'd try to accommodate me, but he never could contain himself for long. In our final meeting, though, Guiteau didn't pace at all. When he entered my office, I noted immediately he'd gotten a haircut and shaved his neck, and as he settled into the chair across from me, I was struck by his lack of fidgeting. He simply crossed his legs, folded his hands on his lap, placed his hat neatly on his knee, and smiled. Instead of launching into a monologue as was typical, he said he had a few insights he'd like to share with me if I could spare the time. Unfortunately, I nodded.

Guiteau proceeded to tell me that he had been thinking about the situation in which he, Caroline, and I would find ourselves come the new year. If he were to pass his exams and enroll in classes at the university, he doubted he would have any time at all for a social life. Specifically, he would not have opportunity to call on Caroline while I was in Munich, even though, he claimed, she had already made him promise that he would. "Of course, all this is moot if I am unable to enroll at the university," he said. "If there is again a problem with my entrance exams, I would have plenty of time to indulge Caroline. To take care of her for you. To stand in for you. It would be as if you never went away. In one sense it would be like this. But, of course, in another sense, in the truest sense, you would be very far away from Caroline and me. Maybe even after you returned you would be very far away from the two of us. Far away in the sense that things like this, like love, can change over time. Aren't women fickle?"

Before I knew what I was doing, I was already doing it. I came around the desk, grabbed a handful of Guiteau's jacket, and escorted the skinny troll out of my office before he had opportunity to protest. In the doorway,

I told him I did not want to see him again, and I wished him good luck in his future endeavors. When a few seconds later there was a knock at the door, I realized the nincompoop had left his hat. "Your chapeau is outside," I yelled before smashing the hat with my foot and then storming across the room to open the window and fling it into the breeze.

I did not call on Caroline for more than a week after this episode with Guiteau. On one occasion she came to campus to try to find me, knocking on the door of my office—the footsteps were a woman's; I imagined it was her—but I did not answer. I was angry and confused. If Guiteau was right that the two had become friends and confidants, if he were telling the truth about her asking him to attend to her in my absence, then surely all was lost. Even if he were being untruthful, though, didn't his lies point to a kind of truth? Why wouldn't Caroline commit to marrying me upon my return from Bavaria if she wasn't worried she might change her mind and come to love another in the space of a year? If a man like Guiteau could pose a threat to our bond, then what of the other more appealing men in town? There were at least four young professors I could think of who could be considered good prospects. There was Tuttle at the bank. And I'd seen Worstheimer the barber smile and tip his hat to her on more than one occasion. If Caroline was destined to be usurped by another man, then what kind of sense did it make to spend a year in a foreign land enduring torturous thoughts of jealousy and bitterness? "Guiteau might be a fool," I thought, "but perhaps no more a fool than I."

When my condition worsened to the point that I was having trouble meeting my classes during the day and was often unable to choke down my supper in the evening, I went to Caroline's house early one morning intending to find clarity and closure. The sun was just coming up. As I neared her door, I spotted Guiteau skulking towards me, carrying two satchels. Of course I would see Guiteau on my way to visit Caroline. I was surprised and not surprised. My mind ran wild with possibilities. When I took a step towards the knave, he turned tail and ran as if he were being chased by bandits. That was the last I ever saw or heard of the man until more than two decades later when, like everyone else, I read about him in the papers. When I would once again be both surprised and not surprised.

By the time I reached Caroline's porch, I had decided that one of the satchels Guiteau was carrying must have been hers. It was obvious they were running away together, catching the early coach. The door opened before I could knock. Caroline was in her shawl and hat, and when she saw me, she broke into tears and hugged my neck. She said she was on her way to see me, that she couldn't go another day without talking to me. Of course, I didn't believe her. I laughed scornfully and told her I'd just seen Guiteau carrying their bags on his way to the depot where I was sure he was waiting for her.

As I spoke, she let go of me and took a step back. When I finished, she wiped her tears and asked me to repeat myself, so I obliged. She opened her mouth to answer, closed it, and then opened it again. "Charles stopped in to say goodbye. He told me he's returning home to Wisconsin for the winter, and then in spring he plans to start a new life in New York. Something about God calling him to help lead a religious group there. As is typical with him, I didn't follow everything he said, but that was the gist of it. He wanted me to tell you that he appreciates all you've done for him, that he hopes you're not too disappointed by his departure, and that he wishes you the best in Munich next year." Caroline's voice grew steadier and louder as she continued. "Allow me at this point to join Charles in wishing you a good trip."

"So it's 'Charles,' is it?" I said. "Well, I suppose I see how it is. So, I will have a good trip. Thanks to you and your 'Charles,' I'll have a wonderful trip."

After Caroline slammed the door, I knew immediately I had made a grave mistake. I knocked a few times and called to her, pleaded for her to come out or let me in, but by that time the sun had risen, and people were appearing on the street, and I had begun to understand the irrevocability of what I had said and done. Resignation was already beginning to settle in.

Hoping against hope, I returned to Caroline's door each of the next few evenings, but she would never answer. The next week, when I tried to see her at the Union School, I was told by the stern headmaster that she'd spotted me through the window and had asked him to inform me she did not wish to converse.

When I departed for Europe after Christmas, I slid a letter under Caroline's door. I told her how sorry and embarrassed I was, and although I knew I had no right to ask it of her, I inquired whether she might consider allowing me, upon my return, to call on her so we might perhaps explore the possibility of starting over again. I told her I wanted to show her the real man I was.

I thought of Caroline every day during my time in Munich. I intentionally learned no German because I wanted to punish myself by feeling as alone as possible. I succeeded in my failure. When I arrived back in Ann Arbor the next year, I felt even more alone than I had in Bavaria due to the fact that I found Caroline married to Worstheimer the barber. A few months later, when Caroline gave birth to a daughter, I abruptly resigned my position at the university and found work with the government as a surveyor and cartographer in the Western territories, which is where I ended up waiting out the war.

In my new life, there were stretches of weeks traversing the mountains and canyons with my small crew during which I'd see no women, save for the occasional squaw, and when back at camp at the end of the day, I'd sometimes lay my head down and plead with myself to dream about those two months I had with Caroline in Ann Arbor even though I knew such a dream might ruin me. I never succeeded these nights in summoning Caroline, though. I could dream only of Guiteau.

# The Children's House Nurse Attends
## to Her Charges

JUST AFTER BREAKFAST, we received word that Mr. Noyes and Mrs. Cragin had arrived and that they wished to meet with all the girls, so the other nurses and I gathered up the lot of them, ran combs through their hair, and arranged them in a semicircle on the damp lawn near where Mr. Noyes and Mrs. Cragin already stood waiting.

When Mrs. Cragin walked over and sat down among the girls, Mr. Noyes stayed where he was. I thought he might drift over to exchange pleasantries with the other nurses and me, but he didn't. He appeared cross. Most probably with Mrs. Cragin, I figured—despite their affection for one another, they were known to squabble now and then—but then I worried that his apparent anger might involve me and the other nurses somehow. Perhaps even the children. I can't say why I thought this.

Mrs. Cragin asked the girls to raise their hands if they loved their dolls. All the girls raised their hands. Of course they did. One girl raised both her hands to show just how much love, and she offered to go wake her doll from her nap and bring her outside so Mrs. Cragin could see how precious, but Mrs. Cragin smiled and told the girl she should let her doll rest. The girls proceeded to tell Mrs. Cragin their dolls' names, ages, and favorite games. They described for her the clothes they had made for their dolls, and what each of their dolls liked to eat and didn't like to eat, and what songs each liked having sung to them, and what songs each did not care for. They told Mrs. Cragin that the younger boys were often enlisted into their doll play, but the older boys never played along even though they seemed sometimes like they wanted to. One girl assured Mrs. Cragin that even though the dolls sometimes grew fussy and were difficult to manage, they all loved living in the nursery. Mrs. Cragin laughed at this, and her laughing made the girls laugh, and the girls' laughter drew a smile from Mr. Noyes.

One of the older girls told me later how she thought at that moment Mrs. Cragin was going to announce that the children's house was going to receive a collection of new dolls. She thought this was why Mrs. Cragin was encouraging the girls to talk about their dolls. To set the mood for the surprise.

The girls' happy chatter seemed to relax Mr. Noyes. As they continued talking with Mrs. Cragin, he began walking slow circles around the group with his thumbs under his arms. The community had been blessed with a wonderful group of girls. I thought perhaps Mr. Noyes was thinking something along these lines as he listened. I was proud of the girls as they conversed with Mrs. Cragin. Proud of their bright spirits. Proud of how, even in their excitement, they tried to take turns and not speak over one another. Proud of how straightly they sat and how well they listened and how they didn't allow themselves to be distracted by the desire to capture ladybugs or braid dandelions or drill holes in the dirt with their fingers. I couldn't imagine what a better group of girls might have looked like.

I think the pride I felt for the girls distracted me. It kept me from anticipating Mrs. Cragin's mission. It allowed me to be taken by surprise.

Even though the dolls are fun, they are harmful, I heard Mrs. Cragin say. Is one to love objects? One is not to love objects. To do so is to commit idolatry. To pretend too deeply is to lie. To pretend to the point that one forgets one is pretending. It is to lie to oneself. Can one lie to oneself? Oh, yes. Surely one can. To lie to oneself is perhaps the most harmful type of lie. And while most kinds of love are good, some kinds of love are not good. That does sound strange, doesn't it? It's true, though. Some kinds of love take up too much room. If a mother's love for her child takes up so much room in her that she doesn't have room enough to love all children, that kind of love is not good. The right thing to do is to guard against that kind of love. That kind of love that tempts us to stick to one person instead of participating in the bigger, broader love that God intends for us. That sticky kind of love is not good.

Here's a big word: philoprogenitiveness. That's not an easy word to say, is it? The right thing to do is to guard against this sticky kind of love called philoprogenitiveness. You all love living in the children's house with

each other, don't you? That's right. Of course you do. You live with all your good friends and good nurses in the children's house because it's best. It's best you all get to love each other and the whole community gets to love you. Your mother and father love you. Of course they do. But not only your mother and father love you. Your nurses love you. And Mr. Noyes and I love you like your mother and father and nurses do. We are your mother and father like your mother and father. That's right. All the men in the community are your fathers and all the women your mothers. Love is best when it's not limited. When it's not sticky. When it has enough room. When it's not—remember the word?—philoprogenitive.

Listen. Here's something I want to tell you. The girls in the Brooklyn family formed a committee. Girls just like you. A committee is a group with a unified purpose. That's right. Listen to what this committee did. This committee decided they wanted to give up their dolls because they didn't want to learn philoprogenitiveness. Rather they wanted to learn community love. Isn't that brave? As a symbol of their commitment to learn to love in the right way, they decided to give up their dolls. They decided to give up their dolls by burning them. Aren't they brave girls to do that? As a symbol. To show how serious they were. In the stove. A symbol in this case is like a demonstration. It shows on the outside what's inside. Through giving up their dolls, they showed the love in their hearts. I wonder if you girls might like to form a committee like your sisters in Brooklyn. I wonder if you might show yourselves to be as brave as them. Yes, normally that's a good rule. Children should stay away from the stove. For this purpose, though, we can make an exception. For the symbol, yes. Yes, the girls in Brooklyn are your sisters even though you've never met them.

Mrs. Cragin raised herself to her knees, and some of the girls mirrored her. Then she went around the semicircle, pointing to them one at a time. To join the committee, each girl had to state that she was willing to give up her doll. No, she wouldn't get a new doll. This would be for good. For good as in forever and for good as in for the best. Each of the girls agreed when pointed to, and then they were no longer only individual girls, nor were they merely a group of sisters. They were a committee.

Mr. Noyes had strolled away from the yard just prior to the girls' transformation into a committee. I'd watched him wander off. Apparently, Mrs. Cragin hadn't noticed his leaving because when she dismissed the girls, she asked me if I'd seen where he'd headed. Even though he'd headed towards the South Garden, I pointed in the opposite direction towards the sawmill. I can't say why I did this.

On the whole, the girls seemed to enjoy the doll burning later that afternoon. Leading up to it, they were so excited they didn't want to eat lunch. News of the event had traveled around the community, so by the time the fire was built and the dolls had been gathered, the living room was nearly full. Mr. Noyes moved from group to group to explain the goings-on. The growing problem of the doll spirit among the girls and how they themselves had decided to vanquish it. Some folks smiled and nodded as he spoke, and others frowned. The more folks Mr. Noyes spoke to, the quieter the room became.

Somehow the girls had gotten the idea to say "Amen" as each doll was relinquished to the stove. Some of the girls' voices were quiet and solemn, while others emanated joy. Some of the girls seemed unnerved by the un-expected audience, while other girls bloomed. Some of the girls gripped their dolls by a hand or a foot and tossed them into the flames as they would a stick, while other girls cradled their dolls and nestled them into the mouth of the stove as if into a crib. Some of the younger girls, nervous about getting too close to the stove, sought help from the older girls, while others were insistently independent. It struck me that how a girl went about burning her doll revealed a lot about whom she was becoming and whom she might become.

As the emptyhanded girls filed one-by-one past Mrs. Cragin after making their sacrifices, she met each with a cursory hug. Up until the final girl, though, her eyes stayed focused on the stove. It struck me that she was waiting for a girl to backtrack on her pledge, but none did.

The only tears shed were by a couple of the younger boys who badly wanted to burn something. One boy fetched a giraffe and a camel from the Noah's Ark in the playroom and tried to worm his way into line with the girls, and when I caught him by the elbow and guided him back to the rear of the room, he protested loudly and proceeded to sulk for the rest of the afternoon. On any other day he would have been disciplined for his outburst and stubborn sullenness, but on this day, I did not feel inclined to follow through. None of us nurses did.

It wasn't until late that night that sadness descended on the rest of the children. It spread through their bedrooms like an illness. They weren't wailing or howling, just softly whimpering. Girls and boys alike. And not only the younger ones, the older ones, too. One here, one there.

Like crickets on a dark lawn. Each lonely, but in concert. None of them would tell us what the matter was—of course they wouldn't—but they wouldn't be comforted either. When we went to their beds, they didn't want us there. They pulled their pillows over their heads so we couldn't stroke their cheeks, and they balled their fists so we couldn't hold their hands. In the end we relented to their sorrow. It was something they wanted that we could allow them to have, so we let them have it.

Conversely, my sleep that night, once it came, was deep and restorative. I often found sleeping in the children's house difficult. When the children were silent, I'd find myself waiting for them to become un-silent, and the waiting is what would hold off sleep. On this night, though, the children had become un-silent, and the other nurses and I had decided to acquiesce to their un-silence, so there was nothing to wait for. Nothing to hold off sleep. When I rose in the morning, my energy and alertness were tinged with guilt. It felt like I had stolen my sleep from the children, and I couldn't think of anything I could offer them to make restitution.

At breakfast, the children were exhausted and gloomy. None of them was willing to say the blessing, and few wanted to eat. Their eyes were dark and heavy, and their quiet, grumpy exchanges with one another were punctuated by the clattering of dropped spoons. The exquisite weather seemed to make the children's dreadful mood all the more pronounced. I wondered aloud to one of the other nurses whether it might not be a bad idea to ask Mrs. Cragin to come for another visit to encourage the children, but the other nurse told me she'd heard that Mrs. Cragin and Mr. Noyes had already left to visit the new community in Wallingford. Probably to form another committee, she said.

So the decision was made to have the children make kites out of sticks and string and stray squares of material from the women's sewing circle that we had intended to help the girls turn into doll clothes. The nurse who decided this was me, and I decided it with the help of one of the boys. The morning prior, when the dolls were still with us, this boy had told me he'd had a dream about kites. When the dream began, the boy was himself a kite, and that had been exciting, but the dream quickly grew frightening because the wind was too loud, and large birds kept squawking at him, and he began to worry about falling and being ensnared in tree branches. So the boy changed the dream to make himself the boy on the ground who was flying the kite rather than the kite itself. It was much better to be the boy flying the kite because flying a kite wasn't frightening at all, and it was still fairly exciting. The boy told me that when he and his family had come to Oneida, he hadn't wanted to stay at the children's house. He'd had horrible nightmares his first few nights away from his parents, and his mother had taught him this trick to help him. The trick of how to change a dream from frightening to pleasant. It wasn't a trick, really. You simply needed to stay calm, and you needed to explain clearly and precisely to the dream how it needed to change, and then the dream would change.

We assigned two children to each kite. We allowed them to pair off on their own without direction or consideration regarding what pairings might become too rambunctious or loud or distracted or quarrelsome. With restitution in mind, we allowed the children this freedom to be close to whomever they wanted. Once they found their partners, we taught them how to make the kite frame by crossing two sticks, and how to attach the material to the frame, and how to tie one end of the string to the material and the other end of the string to a third stick, and how to lick their fingers to determine the direction of the breeze, and how to run in that direction alongside the breeze, and how to bring their kites along with them as they ran—not yanking their kites alongside them but rather gently and smoothly introducing their kites to the breeze—and how to slow their running as their kites climbed higher, and how to steer clear of trees and other kites.

All of the kites were red, save for one yellow one and one blue one. I thought I recognized the yellow material from the new tablecloths in the dining room. I don't know where the blue material came from. It would have made nice curtains.

None of the kites got very far off the ground. The wind seemed sufficient, but the kites would only be caught up for a moment before crashing. One nurse suggested it was possible that some of the children were running too quickly and others too slowly, and then she wondered if the string we had the children use was too heavy. Another nurse wondered if the instructions we had given the children had been flawed, seeing as how none of us had ever made kites or flown kites ourselves. That nurse was me.

The children weren't at all concerned about the lack of flight. Even the boy who'd had the dream seemed overjoyed to run back and forth across the lawn with his partner as they watched over their shoulders the bouncing kite that chased them. Most of the kites were damaged after only a few minutes of play, so a few of the older girls set up a kite infirmary in one corner of the yard, where they laid the patients in a neat row and worked on them with extra sticks and string.

While their battered kites were being administered to, some of the children persevered by flying imaginary kites, which over the course of the morning became stuck in the highest branches of the tallest trees, fell prey to hungry eagles, and burst into flames upon reaching the sun.

# John Humphrey Noyes Mourns His Beloved

IN THE WAKE OF THIS apocalypse, the family in Oneida needs to hear from me. I need them to need to hear from me. The words I need to share with them need to do important work. The words need to make clear the way forward, to redeem and pay tribute to the distances already traveled. As of yet, these words have not found me. I need them to find me.

THAT THE MEN SURVIVED while Mary and Eliza perished. All the men. Abram Smith, the self-appointed captain of the sloop, who at one point in his life had claimed to love Mary to the point of madness, was the first to make shore. And the Henrys, Burnham and Seymour, neither of whom could swim, clung to a large plank that eventually deposited them a quarter mile downriver from Abram. "If not for God's hand," they took turns telling one another until I told them that in saying this they were speaking mindlessly, heartlessly. And young Francis, the troubled wanderer whom Mary had found and brought into our fellowship. He had been at the helm when the sloop capsized. So Francis's hand, not God's. Francis's fragile nerve. Francis's weakness. Abram said after the young man waded to shore, he had turned and re-entered the water for a brief moment. Abram suspected his intention was to drown himself. "God help my soul, I don't think I would've have stopped him," Abram said. I told Abram that in saying this he was speaking mindlessly, heartlessly.

Mary and Eliza dead and these four cowards still breathing in and out. These four little boys, who let their sisters sink with a limestone-loaded boat to the bottom of the Hudson.

WE ALERTED THE ONEIDA family right away. Harriet wrote the letter, and I signed it. As of now, though, the loss is not yet real for our brothers and sisters in Oneida in the same way it is for us in Brooklyn. The Oneida family will not feel the full weight of the loss until they hear from me in person. It is in my presence that they will feel fully Mary's and Eliza's absence. It is through the words I will speak that they will hear fully Mary's and Eliza's silence. So I need to work out the words. For the family's sake and for my own sake I do.

IN THE IMMEDIATE AFTERMATH of the tragedy, I could not look Abram or the Henrys or Francis in their respective faces. Harriet could not do so either. Her stomach still turns in their presence such that she can't take meals with them. So Harriet and I are heading to Oneida because the family needs to hear from me in person, needs Harriet and me there in body to join with them in mourning, but we are also heading to Oneida because we seek respite from cowards whose presence is like poison to us.

George Cragin has gone on to Oneida ahead of us. He was in a hurry to go. Although Harriet tries to convince me otherwise, I know in George's eyes I am one of the cowards, and just as I seek to separate myself from them, he sought to separate himself from me. He knows better, but at present it is not about what he knows; rather, it is about what he feels. Harriet advises me to be patient, assures me he will come around, but I fear he is lost to me, and if he is lost to me, then how can he not be lost to all of us? This fear stems not from the way in which he looked at me in the days following Mary's death, but in the way he did not look at me. In the way he communicated with me only indirectly, through Harriet.

WHAT GEORGE AND THE Oneida family need is for me to shape the tragedy for them so it is something they can understood. My challenge in doing this is that I do not understand it.

MARY AND ELIZA DROWNED on a Saturday. When we received Henry Burnham's telegram in Brooklyn, I departed for Hyde Park immediately. *Serious news. The women went down with the vessel. The men were saved.* I read it aloud to George, who bowed and unbowed his head several times before turning up the stairs. I figured he was fetching his hat, but when he did not come down after a few minutes, Harriet went to check on him. When she came down alone, she said he would not be accompanying me. I figured he was simply too broken to make the trek. Even in the thralls of my own fresh sorrow, my heart went out to him. I did not know then that the true reason he was not going with me was because he was worried he might strike me down in the street once out of Harriet's sight. This is what he had told Harriet upstairs.

Upon my arrival at the site, the air barely stirred in the red evening sky, and the river ran so smoothly and silently it appeared solid. A miraculous summer freeze. As if a careful, faithful person could walk shore to shore.

Upon seeing me, the first thing Abram wanted to do was litigate his case. Assign blame elsewhere. A cowardly act in response to a cowardly act. According to Abram, Francis bore full responsibility for the wreck. As he paced and ranted about Francis's guilt, his clothes and hair still damp, one of the Henrys dropped to all fours and lurched like a gagging dog, and the other Henry patted his namesake's back as if he were burping an infant. "His negligence! His insipidness!" Abram roared, raising his voice to be heard over Henry's retching. When I asked Abram why Francis, the most inexperienced of an altogether inexperienced crew, was left alone at the helm, Abram answered it was because the sky had been clear, the river calm, and Francis had insisted on his own capability. "He lulled us into trust!" Abram said. "So the scoundrel bore false witness, too, in characterizing himself as competent! In overestimating himself!"

The Henrys did not argue with Abram's assessment. Even Francis himself did not protest. He sat apart from us but within earshot, facing the river with his legs folded like an Indian, poking at the mud with a stick. When I asked him if he had a rebuttal, he did not answer. From the moment I first met Francis, he had struck me as someone given to sullenness and cantankerousness, but Mary had tried to convince me that what I was actually noting in him was serious-mindedness and reflectiveness. In this way, she had said, the young man reminded her of me.

As the evening wore on, my cheeks became chapped from my tears, and my heart grew hot and rose higher until I could taste it in my throat. Abram and the Henrys, too, wallowed in grief, but Francis appeared to be at peace in his sorrow. As if his perpetual sullenness finally had purpose, and in this purpose he found a measure of relief. Mary had been wrong. The young man was in no way reminiscent of me.

For the first few nights after the wreck, I secured a skiff and charged Francis with keeping a lantern lit on the mast of the sunken sloop to mark it for passing vessels until we could find a crew to recover it along with Mary's and Eliza's remains, but the young man eventually abandoned this responsibility. On the third night, Abram and I caught him reclining on the shore, drowsily poking the mud with his stick even though the lantern had been extinguished. When I asked why he was not fulfilling his duties, he did not offer an answer. It were as if Abram and I were not there, as if no question had been asked. I rowed out in the skiff myself to re-light the lantern, and when I returned to shore, Francis was gone. Abram said he had simply risen to his feet and slunk off without a word, and Abram had not felt inclined to stop him. We never again saw nor heard from Francis. He is as dead to us as Mary and Eliza. No he is not. He is not as dead. He is more dead.

THE ONEIDA FAMILY DOES NOT need all these details from me. The stillness of the water, the tear-chapped cheeks, who shirked what responsibilities. What the Oneida family needs is for me to transform the tragedy into something they can bear and cling to like a promise. In order for me to author this transformation, I first need to find a way myself to bear and to cling.

FROM THE BEGINNING, I had never been wholly convinced by Abram's sloop scheme. Our coffers in Brooklyn were running low, though, and by the time he formally made his proposal to me, he had already arranged for most of the necessary preparations. At that point, it would have been more difficult and costly to say no than yes, and I understood better then how Mary, and to some degree George, had been manipulated by the man a decade earlier. Abram had a knack for making his assumptions your assumptions and was skillful at disguising his instructions as humble requests. Before I entirely understood the logistics of his project, it was fully underway. When I took leave for a few weeks to minister to the Wallingford branch of our community, Abram and his crew made two voyages to Kingston for limestone without my knowledge. When I returned to Brooklyn, it seemed everyone, even Harriet and Mary, assumed that I had sanctioned the expeditions, so I would have felt sheepish putting a stop to the operation at that point. I would have appeared petty. Besides, Abram's claim that there was a good market for the limestone seemed accurate, and I gathered that the community men who accompanied him on these errands found the work adventurous and interesting. So I allowed it to continue.

When Mary alerted me at the end of June that Abram had invited her and Eliza to accompany him and his crew on their next excursion, though, I was wary. Abram said the women could do the cooking along the way, and, if they fancied it, a bit of berry-picking in Kingston while the men loaded the limestone. Mary told me she was injured by my wariness, which she interpreted as mistrust. "Cooking and berry-picking," she said. "I hardly think there is reason to be suspicious." When I told her it was not her I mistrusted but rather Abram, she answered that she was injured by my lack of confidence in her ability to resist him. Mary did not put any stock in my suspicion that Abram was still seeking to possess her, but even if he were, she claimed there would be no room for him to work towards this end with Eliza there. Eliza would serve as a buffer, Mary assured me, and the two women would not leave each other's sides. So I acquiesced and gave her my blessing.

I did not know until after the tragedy that Harriet and Eliza had also quarreled about the voyage. Harriet told me she had asked Eliza not to sail to Kingston with Abram because she was worried it would be dangerous. The argument turned bitter, and the two women had still not made up with one another prior to Eliza's departure. This is something that haunts Harriet. The possibility that Eliza died while still angry with her.

From the moment they met in Wallingford, Harriet and Eliza had shared a soul. Harriet and I were in Connecticut to meet Eliza's father, who sought to donate land to the family and aid us in starting a branch of the community there on the banks of Quinnipiac. From the first day of our visit, Harriet and Eliza were inseparable, and as soon as we returned to Brooklyn, Harriet campaigned for Eliza to come live with us. I have never seen two closer sisters. Mary, too, was struck by the strength of their bond. She told me when it was just the three of them, she would often feel invisible, but she did not begrudge them their fellowship. "I choose to recognize the beauty in it instead, in the same way I hope folks choose not to begrudge you and me what we share, but instead recognize its beauty," she said.

"But of course they begrudge us our fellowship," I said and laughed. "It's different with two women, though, than it is with a man and a woman. It does not inspire the same sort of jealous spirit."

"Not necessarily different," Mary said, and before I could inquire further, she ended our conversation by beginning another with a kiss.

IT IS NOT ONLY ONE thing the Oneida family needs to hear from me. They need to hear many things. That is, each family member needs to hear something different. So the words I offer need to work in many different directions at once. The words need to have breadth as well as depth, and they need to be flexible and generous in terms of their connotations. What is at stake is everything. It is my conviction that in the aftermath of this tribulation, the family will either find that its bonds have grown stronger, or it will feel itself unraveling.

THE SQUALL THAT SUNK the sloop lasted five minutes. Abram and the Henrys agreed on this as readily as they agreed to lay blame on Francis. They repeated this fact to me and to one another repeatedly in shared disbelief. That the squall arose out of nowhere, without warning, and dissipated in the same manner, as an apparition would, seemed important to them. I sensed they believed the sinister immediacy of the storm somehow helped to establish their innocence, to excuse their ineffectiveness and inaction.

IN ORDER FOR ME to serve as an effective comforter for the Oneida family, my personal sorrow needs to make room for collective sorrow, but it does not want to make room. My confusion needs to yield to clarity, but it does not want to yield. My loneliness needs to acquiesce to fellowship, but it does not want to acquiesce.

IT WAS MORE THAN a month, well into August, before we found a crew in Poughkeepsie with the equipment needed to recover the boat and Mary's and Eliza's bodies. They were buried in the cemetery at the Episcopal church in Esopos. A man from the congregation there donated a small marble marker to memorialize the women he never knew. When Harriet and I met him to thank him, he seemed embarrassed by his own kindness. He looked pained. His voice barely more than a whisper. It were as if our brokenness and desperate appreciation of his kindness was his shame. He had done something graceful and perfect, but in his own eyes he had failed to do enough. His righteous act a filthy rag. If only one man like this, one possessed with his spirit of selflessness, would have been on the sloop. If only a man like this could have taken Abram's or Henry's or Henry's or Francis's place, I am convinced we would still have Mary and Eliza among us.

PERHAPS THROUGH CONSIDERATION of the respective griefs of Harriet and the Esopos Episcopalian, I can discover the nature of what the Oneida family needs to hear from me and discern how I might best express it. In bearing witness to Harriet's grief for Eliza, I might be able to study my grief for Mary as through a microscope, and in bearing witness to the Esopos Episcopalian's grief for my grief, I might be able to study my grief for Mary as through a telescope, and perhaps through these studies I might be able to move closer to imagining and helping the family imagine a communal grief. One sanctioned grief shared and, therefore, more manageable and survivable.

It is not only the Oneida family who needs to hear from me. There are many outside our community who seek to hold me responsible for the tragedy, who are eager to assign to my hands the blood of these women. Mary's blood, especially. Folks in Putney, Brattleboro, Ithaca, and New Haven. "Perhaps God slew John Noyes's adulterous lover to expose him as the heretic and fornicator that he is." Slander and false witness along these lines.

There is also the problem of what to make of the tragedy in light of my previous proclamation that no faithful member of our family would have to taste death. Our perfection, I have argued on many occasions, leaves no room for it.

In answer to this dilemma, I have worked out four possibilities:

First, God's promises are empty. He is not to be trusted.

Second, God's promises are only for the faithful. Mary and Eliza were not faithful.

Third, God's promises have been misunderstood and mischaracterized by me. I am not to be trusted.

These first three possibilities, of course, are not possibilities at all. Rather, they are blasphemies.

The fourth possibility, the only possible possibility, is that God's promises evolve. God's truth is dynamic rather than static. It bends with time. It is on a continuum. It passes through stages. It develops itself, forms its own forming, reveals itself to itself as it is revealed. Is the truth of our family's good and perfect work diminished by the fact that it originated in Putney, revealed itself more fully in Oneida, and continues to reveal itself in beautifully surprising ways in Brooklyn and Wallingford? The truth of our family's good and perfect work is not diminished. Is the truth of the freed slave's freedom proved false by the fact that he was once a slave? The truth of the freed slave's freedom is not proved false. Rather, the truth of his freedom, his understanding and appreciation of it, is to a great degree dependent upon his former enslavement. Paul writes in Romans 8 that the faithful are set free from sin and death. Is this truth undermined if some of the faithful may first have to die to gain their freedom from dying? This truth is not undermined.

I will not recant. How can I recant? To recant is not a possibility.

"I HAVE TAKEN AUTUMNAL walks along our beloved stream here in Oneida and in Putney along Sacketts Creek and in Wallingford along the Quinnipiac and in New York along the Hudson, and I have on occasion studied the plight of leaves that have fallen into the current. Surely I am not alone in this. Many among you have done this, too. Especially in the fall you have done this. You have spied in the water a red maple leaf or a golden spray of butternut leaves. Some leaves float along happily on the surface until out of sight. Other leaves, though, are drawn under. You have seen them swallowed up in the rapids. You have watched them whirlpool down into the flux, reminiscent of how the wind pulls them down from trees. A first falling and then a second falling. Our sisters Mary and Eliza are, in a sense, like these leaves . . . ."

After I am finished speaking and the family has been dismissed, they do not congregate to engage me at the front of the hall like they often do. Rather, they disperse quickly and quietly. George Cragin does not disperse with them because he has not shown up to the meeting at all. I have not seen him since my arrival in Oneida. He and Harriet, though, have already taken two walks together. Harriet continues to tell me I need to be patient with George.

Only Harriet lingers in the hall. She remains seated in the front row. When I drop my body into the seat next to hers, I know I will stay there forever.

"You will have other opportunities to address them, of course," she says.

"I need them to understand," I say.

"They do understand. They understand how difficult this is for you," Harriet says. "Perhaps especially for you. And they understand your love for them."

"I need them to understand more than that," I say.

Harriet shifts in her seat. I think she is going to reach out to me, to touch me, but she does not. She keeps her hands folded on her lap.

"Is it possible you need too much?" she says.

## Luther Guiteau Makes a Donation

DEAR MR. NOYES,

Greetings to you in Christ.

This is the second letter I have written you, but I take no offense if you do not remember the first, which was well-nigh ten years ago. Prior to that I followed with great interest news of your courageous initiatives in Vermont, and I have read all your writings, which have served to clarify for me much about the direction and content of life in Christ. I try to pray regularly for you and your community, although I admit this sometimes proves difficult because of the envy and regret that cloud my heart.

When I wrote that first letter, you were just settling in at Oneida. I included a donation with my correspondence then as I do now. In my previous letter I confessed to you that I was making my donation somewhat bitterly. I did not want to send you money; rather, I wanted to send you myself. A decade later, I recognize it as one of the great regrets of my life that I did not throw down my nets and follow as Christ instructed the faithful fishermen, but instead argued myself into believing the prudent thing was to stay put. At the time I had a houseful of children and a sickly wife, and I listened to voices who told me uprooting them would be irresponsible and selfish.

Now that I have a healthy wife and my children are for the most part grown, the only thing holding me back from joining you is my age. I am disappointed in myself for growing old—in my youth I could never have imagined such a tragedy—but I am writing to you today more out of hope than disappointment or bitterness. Although my regret over my missed opportunity to live in communion with you and your family lingers, I am trying to find for myself a sort of hope once-removed in my son Charles. With your blessing, I would like to see him claim the opportunity I missed.

I understand I could have simply sent you my son without introduction. I know many people come to you and your family in this way, simply showing up on your doorstep as it were, and I have heard you accommodate them and, after a trial period, admit them into full fellowship if they prove themselves fit. Charles, though, requires a letter. If not required by you, then required by me. I feel the need to explain my son to you before you experience him. Do all fathers feel this need? I believe I am right that you have at least one son of your own, so perhaps this concern of mine resonates with you.

I want all people with whom Charles comes into contact to help him, and I want him not to be in need of their help. I want to accompany him everywhere so I can make his way easier and undo his mistakes, and I want to be disentangled from him so I can be at peace. I want him to come to me for counsel so I may guide his footsteps, and I want him to seek out others instead so as to spare me the pain of his rejecting my advice. So I am concerned for my son, and I detest him a little, and I am unnerved by him, and I am disappointed in and proud of him, and I love him, and I am perplexed by him, and I want him not to embarrass me, and I want to do right by him, but I do not know how to do that. I have never known.

Given all this, it is difficult to put into words the relief I felt when the Lord laid on my heart the notion that you and your family might help me. Help Charles. Furthermore, I felt even more encouraged when Charles responded enthusiastically to my proposal. If we lived any closer to you—I am writing from Wisconsin—I think he would have already opted to forgo the train and strike out on foot. Since our conversation he has been studying your writings, which I provided him, and this has made him even more impatient for winter to yield to spring so he can make his journey to you.

(Is there any greater pleasure than to give your son a book and have him love that book? It's a singular, surprising joy.)

Charles is not whole now, but he is trying to become whole. It appears to me he is trying. His mother, who passed when he was a boy, was not whole either. He takes after her in this way. Charles's sister, whom he has often treated quite shabbily, loves him and is protective of him, sometimes to a fault. She tells me the key to making Charles whole is patience. While she is undoubtedly right that I should be more patient with not only Charles but with everyone, I cannot see how my patience or impatience helps or harms my son in terms of his pursuit of wholeness. My patience or impatience comes in response to words he has already uttered and actions he has already undertaken, and these words and actions are what make him unwhole. They are what reveal him to be unwhole.

When he was a boy, I would try to whip him towards wholeness. The whipping proved ineffective, but even then, I am convinced, the whipping was not the problem. The words and actions that necessitated the whipping were the problem. Even if I had the patience of Job, how would that help Charles become whole? Moreover, is it reasonable to expect the rest of the world to respond to him with this kind of patience? Of course not, and yet I cannot help but want to change the world to accommodate my son. I would whip the world to make this happen. Even as I write this, the notion of my son becoming whole seems impossible. (It is so easy to transition from a spirit of hope to a spirit of despondency, is it not? It can happen in the blink of an eye.) In Christ, though, I have to remind myself, all things are possible. What better example of this could I cite than what you have built in Oneida?

Perhaps this is not the first letter of this kind you have received. Surely I am not the only man tortured by concern for his son. Perhaps you hear my words and sentiments as familiar, whereas I consider them extraordinary simply because they are mine. In telling you that Charles is at once intelligent and dim, articulate and incomprehensible, prideful and filled with self-doubt, perhaps you are hearing descriptions typical of individuals, perhaps especially young unmarried men, who regularly make their way to you. Perhaps when I write that Charles is often in conversation with himself as if he is two different people, or that I worry he spends too much time alone in part because I do not think he feels alone when he is alone but rather feels alone when he is in the presence of other people, you are not alarmed because you welcome individuals like this on a regular basis. That some, my present wife included, have recommended to my daughter and me that Charles might respond well to spending time in an asylum perhaps does not worry you as you have heard this said before about people who ultimately turn out to be productive, steady, happy, and whole contributors to your community.

As for my conviction that Charles's best hope to become a new creation is not to lock him away but rather to foster his immersion in the freedom of love and fellowship offered at Oneida, I imagine you might think it so obvious that it does not even necessitate discussion. I imagine you might think it goes without saying. Perhaps this entire letter I am drafting is filled with things you believe go without saying. Perhaps I am wasting my time and yours going to such lengths to make a case for your reception of my son because of course you will take him in. I pray this is the case. I pray I am wasting my time and yours.

So I send you my Charles. When he arrives in the spring, he will, of course, freely give to the community all he has. (Since he does not have much that he can truly call his own, he will also be delivering to you another donation from me.) He tells me this is the aspect of life in Oneida he looks forward to the most, sharing all he has with his Oneida brothers and sisters and having them in turn share all with him. (It is perhaps presumptive on his part to be calling them his brothers and sisters already, but I choose to interpret this as a hopeful sign, so I have not discouraged him from doing so.) In the meantime, I hope you will accept the enclosed bank note as a stake in my son's future with you. I am confident you and your family can be everything to him, and I thank you in advance for training and edifying him with your guiding hand.

As long as Charles is in your stead, I hope it acceptable that I continue to write and, of course, supplement your work with financial donations. That you did not reply to the letter I wrote to you a decade ago is not something that overly concerns me—I realize it reached you in a tumultuous time—but if you would from this point forward prioritize reply to my letters, I would be appreciative. Even a few sentences to let me know you received my donations and to offer a sense of how Charles is doing would go far towards easing my mind.

Charles has already told me that he himself will not be writing any letters to me. He says this is not meant to hurt me, but he believes it will be best if, at least for a while, he looks only forward and not backward. When I told him he could write me about looking forward, about what that entails and what he sees, he told me that no matter what he wrote to me about, he would have to send the letter backward. These kinds of conversations do not lead anywhere with Charles, so I did not pursue the issue further. I tell you this because I would ask that you keep secret this letter and any further correspondence between us. Charles would not like knowing we are in communication about him. I do not wish to deceive him, but I see no other option. It is difficult to admit that my son sees my concern for him as undermining, but I must see it for what it is, acknowledge it, and do my best to protect him, even if from myself.

As I finish this letter, Charles is outside my window splitting logs in the snow. He knows manual labor will be expected from him at Oneida, so in recent days he has been pushing himself to perspire to prepare for his new life. It has been frigid, so sweat can be hard to come by, but he has taken to the axe with a dedication that surprises me. Charles always balked at menial chores when he was a child, and his mother allowed him to shirk them, so he does not have much experience with such things. He is trying to make up for that now. If he keeps up at this pace, the woodpiles he is stacking around the yard will outlast me. As it always has been and will be with fathers and sons, I suppose.

As he swings the axe, Charles's mouth does not stop moving. His inclination to talk with himself has always worried me, but maybe it should not. In writing this letter to you, I am probably communicating with myself as much as I am communicating with you. In going back over what I have written, I realize many of the sentences were probably more important for me to write than they were for you to read. Perhaps this is how prayer works, too?

So perhaps Charles is out there praying. Is out there writing letters to himself. In any case, I see steam rising from the back of his
damp shirt—he has stripped off his coat—and I see him wiping
his brow with the back of his glove, so I know he is satisfied and
hopeful, and this tempts me to feel the same.

Regards,
Luther Guiteau

# PART II
## 1860–81

# Charles Guiteau Loses His Shoes

FATHER NOYES WAITS OUTSIDE the shop for me again. He wants to know why I am late again. Since joining the community, whenever I encounter Father Noyes I shake his hand, and I shake it again upon parting. Father Noyes has told me this amount of hand-shaking is peculiar. Even bothersome and off-putting. Even potentially unsanitary.

We are drawing close to an unveiling.

I point to my stockinged feet to present Father Noyes evidence of my continuing persecution and harassment. Once again, Legion has pilfered my shoes.

*This nonsense is becoming tiresome, Charles. Surely we all have better things to do. To whom do I need to speak in order to put an end to this foolishness? Give me a name.*

It is all of them in spirit. In spirit they are legion. They who do not pilfer the shoes encourage the pilferers with their smirks and laughter. There is but one reason the pilfering is funny to them. Their shoes are not the shoes being pilfered.

The first pilfering occurred on my second night in Oneida. When I told Father Noyes, he nodded and assured me he would get to the bottom of the matter. He regarded my feet, and then he regarded his own feet, and then he told me he had an extra pair of shoes that would hold me over in the meantime. When I expressed to him my ideas regarding fit punishment for the pilferer once apprehended, Father Noyes lifted his gaze to regard my face.

*Here in Oneida, it is my responsibility to determine and administer discipline, Charles. Not yours. Is that understood?*

Father Noyes did not follow through with his promise to get to the bottom of the first pilfering. Due to this negligence, there was a second pilfering. When I informed Father Noyes of the second pilfering, he regarded my feet again and informed me my shoes were on my feet. I told him they were not my shoes. He regarded my feet again and noted the shoes I was wearing looked like his shoes. I told him they were his shoes. Then he asked how it had come to pass that I was wearing his shoes. When I reminded him that he had loaned them to me the first time my shoes had been pilfered, to hold me over in the meantime, he said he did not remember doing so. When I reminded him that he had promised to get to the bottom of the matter of my pilfered shoes the first time my shoes had been pilfered, but had neglected to get to the bottom of the matter, he cupped my shoulders with his large hands and regarded my face. As if he were holding me in place for a kiss.

*Have you talked to the young men, Charles? You need to find a way to talk to them. They need to hear from you directly. You need to work towards greater self-reliance.*

The third time I tell Father Noyes my shoes have been pilfered he is angry.

*I am not angry, Charles. I am, however, weary. Are you not weary?*

I am. I was weary of this the first time it happened, and I was weary the second time, and I am weary now. Again and in the meantime and presently.

*Where was it you found your shoes last time?*

Hanging in the shop above where the tools hang is where I found my shoes the last time. Which was the second time. And hanging in the shop above where the tools hang is where I found my shoes the time before that. Which was the first time. Legion likes to watch me get them down. I have to stand on top of two stacked crates to reach them, and Legion pretends to kick out the crates from underneath me. To cause me to exhibit fear. Because my exhibition of fear increases Legion's enjoyment. There is but one reason my fear is funny to Legion. It is not Legion's fear.

*So hanging in the shop above the tools is where your shoes are apt to be found this time, wouldn't you agree? Stay here, Charles.*

Father Noyes's voice is stern but quiet. Not quiet like he wants to avoid being overheard, but quiet like the words he is saying are not important because they are merely a preface to action. He strides quickly towards the door of the shop but then stops short to turn to face me.

*Where are my shoes, Charles? The ones I loaned you the last time this happened?*

Father Noyes did not loan me shoes the last time this happened. Rather, he loaned me shoes the first time this happened, which was two pilferings ago. Father Noyes's shoes are in Sunset Lake, which he and others call the turtle pond and I call the carp pond, but I do not tell him his shoes are in Sunset Lake, which he and others call the turtle pond and I call the carp pond. Rather, I tell him that I returned his shoes to him. He tells me I am mistaken about returning them. I tell him I did not pilfer them.

It was necessary to deposit his shoes in Sunset Lake, which he and others call the turtle pond and I call the carp pond. And it is necessary that he accuse me of having the shoes so that in his accusation he himself might be accused. And it is necessary that I make my denial so that he might bear witness to his own perfect and impossible guilt.

We are coming close to an unveiling.

When he turns back to the shop and opens the door, the dissonant rhythm of steel on steel and the lurid chorus of sweat-soaked voices drift into the thick morning air. Bile rises in my throat. Underneath these noises, not just today but every day, I forehear the yelps and whimpers of mangled animals. And underneath these noises I foresee the cracking of forelegs, paws, and hooves. And underneath these noises I forefeel the yelps and whimpers in my own throat. And underneath these noises I foretaste with my own tongue the blood-matted fur. Not just today underneath these noises, but every day underneath these noises.

Elijah directed the she-bear to devour the youths who had made mockery of him, and the she-bear devoured them.

Father Noyes lets the shop door close without entering and turns again to face me.

*Elisha, Charles. Not Elijah. And there were two bears, not one. And I don't recall the bears being identified as female.*

He combs his beard with his long fingers. He wrinkles his high forehead. He could be leading a meeting, delivering a homily.

*You would do well, Charles, to ponder on the notion that God was likely displeased with Elisha for this rash act. For using the power inherent in His name, for using His creation, to destroy young, redeemable lives. You might do well to ponder on whether being eaten by bears was or was not just punishment for those children.*

I never considered the story in that way. Nor will I direct myself to consider it in that way going forward. The story has been revealed to me in the way it has been revealed to me. Revelation cannot be undone. God shall not be mocked.

*Make no mistake, Charles. You are no prophet, and I am no bear. If your study of the Old Testament is to be sound and fruitful and revelatory, the likely possibility of God's displeasure with His people, perhaps most notably with kings and prophets, needs to be in your mind at all times. Page after page throughout the Pentateuch and the Books of the Prophets, God is more apt to be displeased than pleased.*

These are the final words Father Noyes says before disappearing into the building. So they carry more weight. Final words are weightier than words followed by, and therefore replaced by, other words. Due to the manner in which no other words come after and therefore replace final words, final words carry more weight. In the meantime they carry more weight.

When Father Noyes re-emerges from the trap shop, no noises follow him. He is carrying one of my shoes by the heel with two hooked fingers. A carp by the gills.

*I am told this was found hanging on the wall amongst the tools. Sewell tells me it was there when he opened the shop this morning.*

I take the shoe from him and fit it halfway upon my right foot, where it does not belong, and then I remove it and fit it the whole way upon my left foot, where it does belong. I sit on the ground to do this.

My right shoe was not hanging on the wall above where the tools hang alongside the left shoe? My right shoe must have been hanging on the wall above where the tools hang alongside the left shoe.

*I have been informed that your right shoe is in the orchard, in the pear tree nearest the east fence, and that a ladder would come in handy for fetching it.*

That my right shoe is hanging in the orchard rather than in the trap shop on the wall above where the tools hang alongside my left shoe is unlikely. Legion wants me to walk one-shoed all the way to the orchard for nothing. And then walk back one-shoed from the orchard for nothing. As part of the persecution. I stand up and start towards the trap shop door. Father Noyes puts a hand up to stop me.

*Your shoe is not in the shop, Charles. You can take my word for it. I looked and inquired so you do not have to look and inquire. In any case, I deem it best for you to stay away from the shop for a while.*

I do not want Legion to think I am frightened of them. I do not want Father Noyes to think I am frightened of Legion.

*Come. I will walk with you to the orchard. I know you are not frightened of those boys. What is to be frightened of? A bunch of rambunctious pups. Still. Just now it is not about being frightened or not frightened. Just now it is about the business of fetching your shoe. Walking to the orchard to fetch your shoe does not signify your being frightened. Walking to the orchard at this point in time is simply necessary because your shoe is there. And I will walk with you. I will accompany you on this errand because it will afford us opportunity to talk.*

It begins to rain. So lightly that the hovering droplets could be rising from the earth. As well as descending from the leaden sky. As well as rising from the earth. The same fallen droplets that had just descended. Rising again. Or different droplets. Descending droplets that only descend and rising droplets that only rise. Meeting in mid-air to hover.

*Since it is raining you'd do well to remove your sock from your un-shoed foot and put it in your pocket. That way, when we rescue your shoe from the pear tree, you will have a relatively clean, dry sock to wear.*

But then I will be putting a relatively clean, dry sock on my relatively wet, dirty foot.

*You might find some grass or leaves to wipe and dry your foot before putting on the sock.*

It is raining, so all the grass is wet. All the leaves are wet. One cannot dry one's foot with wet grass or wet leaves.

*You can certainly use damp grass and leaves to clean your foot. To wipe off mud. Your foot might not be bone dry when you put it into your sock, but you will be better off than you would have been had you walked the whole way to the orchard in your sock.*

I remove my sock, ball it, and place it in my pocket. Father Noyes nods.

We are coming close to an unveiling.

I walk through the drizzle in the damp grass beside Father Noyes, attempting to emulate his two-shoed gait. So that I do not stride lopsidedly like a man wearing only one shoe. As I am a man wearing only one shoe.

When I step on a sluggish bee with my un-shoed, un-socked foot, I stumble and curse.

Father Noyes kneels beside me as I attempt to remove the stinger from my heel. He chooses to pretend he has not heard me curse.

*About the other boys, Charles. I do not believe there to be true malice towards you in their hearts. You refer to them as demons, but I think that is a mischaracterization. They are not demons. They are no more demons than you and I are demons. Their hearts are not evil; rather, they are easily distracted by mischief, and they act foolishly because they are desperate to amuse and please each other. They are desperate to amuse and please each other because in doing so, they are able to feel good about themselves. If they feel they are liked by their companions, then they can allow themselves to like themselves. That's the crux of it. That's the crux of being a boy. I do not believe their primary motivation is to inflict pain upon you. I sincerely do not. I think it is primarily an excess of energy that drives their interactions with you. Energy can well up in boys, and they need to learn how to channel it appropriately. In learning how to do this, how to channel energy appropriately, boys become men.*

*So I think there is that aspect of what has been happening between you and your peers. The aspect of boys growing up. Also, I think they want to test you simply because you are new. They want to initiate you, to discover something about you by observing how you react. They want to know if you are a threat to them, if you are someone around whom they need to be careful, or if you might be someone with whom they might find friendship. You know Nathaniel, right, Charles? The tall tow-headed fellow who can do all the birdcalls? When Nathaniel and his family arrived in Oneida last year, the other boys would drop worms in his water cup and on his dinner plate when he was not looking. On at least one occasion, if I remember correctly, he swallowed one. Even so, he laughed along with them. This impressed the other boys, Nathaniel's easygoingness, and now he gets on well with all of them. He is like a brother to them, and they are like brothers to him.*

The stinger comes out of my foot cleanly, in one piece. I hold it on the edge of my finger and bring it closer to my eyes. A remnant of the bee's abdomen clings to one end. When I lower my thumb onto it and squeeze, a bit of venom oozes out.

Who are they to test me? Who are they that I should seek to impress them? To swallow worms for them?

*I suppose I do not understand your question, Charles. Who are they to test you? They are young men like you are a young man. Did you hear what I said about Nathaniel? About brothers? When I speak, it is my hope that you are listening. You will eventually need to come to recognize the other young men of Oneida as your brothers. Brothers are not always kind to each other, but they always have love for each other. They always need each other, and they know they can always rely on each other.*

I get to my feet, and Father Noyes and I recommence walking. I put the stinger on my tongue, press it against the roof of my mouth, and swallow it.

*When I was a boy, my brother and I went barefoot everywhere, all the time. The bottoms of our feet would grow tough and calloused. Hard as hooves. We walked on pine needles, rocks, sticks. I remember stepping on an arrowhead or two. I've surely stepped on more than my fair share of honeybees.*

Father Noyes grins, pleased to remember this about himself.

What about snow and ice? Frostbite? What about school and church?

*I am referring only to the summer months, Charles. I grew up in Vermont. In the winter our feet were fully dressed, of course. And in school and church we certainly wore shoes.*

When I was a boy, my mother told me about George Washington's men at Valley Forge trekking through the snow in their bare feet. I attempted to emulate them one morning. First just to the outhouse and back. And then a longer hike to our neighbor's. When I returned, my father gave me the switch for my efforts. But I could not feel the switch. All I could feel was that I could not feel my feet. I felt not feeling my feet so intensely that I could not feel myself feeling the switch. And then later, in bed, my feet burned. Given that snow had made my feet burn, I reasoned that fire might cool them. So I went to the stove. But this is not how it works. And the doctor did not know if the blisters had come from the cold or the heat. And the switch burns. Even if not right away. The switch has the final word.

We are coming close to an unveiling.

By the time we reach the orchard, the rain has steadied itself into the kind of soft, soaking rain that is good for an orchard. Over the east fence, the sky burns white, triggering the slow, cold crackling of fresh thunder.

When Father Noyes and I find the right tree and spot my shoe perched in the branches among the pears, we remember together the step-ladder, and we scan together the rest of the trees in the orchard for ladders, and we see together no ladders.

Father Noyes moves to the base of the trunk. Drops to one knee. Locks his hands. I put my hands on his shoulders. I put my shoed foot into the stirrup of his grip. My next step is onto his shoulder with my stung foot. My third step is into the tree.

When I have the shoe, I step out of the tree and back onto Father Noyes's shoulder. Then I step into and then out of the stirrup of his grip. When I land on the ground, my stung foot finds a rotten pear and, within the pear, another bee.

Scattered all across the ground are similar rotten pears. A good number of which contain similar bees. The way Father Noyes is standing suggests to me an invitation to place my hand on his shoulder to brace myself when I remove the second stinger from my twice-stung foot. But when I brace myself on his shoulder, he seems surprised. Like he did not intend to suggest to me an invitation to brace myself on his shoulder. Since I am already bracing myself on his shoulder, though, I continue to brace myself on his shoulder as I put my relatively clean, dry sock and damp right shoe on my wet, muddy, twice-stung foot.

When I let go of Father Noyes, I note the muddy footprint on his shoulder.

*The thing for you to do now, Charles, is to go back to your room for a while. Get some rest. Close your eyes, or perhaps find something to read. Soak your foot in a bucket. I will see you again at supper. Unless, of course, we still have something to discuss. Do we still have something to discuss? One more thing? I hope we still have one more thing to discuss.*

Father Noyes is squinting because of the rain. Otherwise he does not appear affected. I become aware of how I am tucking my chin into my chest due to the rain in the moment I notice that Father Noyes is not tucking his chin into his chest. And I become aware of how I have swept my wet hair back off my forehead in the moment I notice how his hair hangs in dripping strands across his temples and onto the bridge of his nose instead of being swept back off his forehead.

*Before we part, Charles, I want you to understand that I know what happened with your shoes this morning. Perhaps more importantly, the young men with whom you work in the trap shop know. Sewell knows. Soon everyone, the whole family, will know. You should act very soon to own up to your actions and ask forgiveness. Perhaps you might approach them one at a time, or, if you prefer, you might call them together to address them as a group.*

*Either way, you need to speak to them, and you need to do so soon. You do not want to let this fester.*

I tell Father Noyes I do not know what he is saying even though I know what he is saying. I tell him I do not know what he is saying as a test. To find out if he knows what he is saying.

Father Noyes pokes the air between us with his forefinger.

*Do not make things worse through denial, Charles. I am severely disappointed you did not have the courage to admit your deception to me on your own. I walked with you here to the orchard because I wanted to afford you the opportunity to repent without having to be told to repent.*

I again tell Father Noyes that I don't know what he is saying even though I know what he is saying. I tell him this again to test him again.

*This morning, one of the boys saw you at the trap shop before sunrise, and he witnessed you returning to your room shoeless. He told Sewell, and Sewell told me. They know it was you who hung your own shoes in the shop. To attempt to get the other young men in trouble? To get out of working this morning? Both they and I are unsure of your motivations. I hope by this evening you are ready to explain yourself.*

How did my shoe get in the pear tree? I did not put it there. To say I put my shoe in the pear tree is to say something untrue. To say I need to repent of putting my shoe in the pear tree is to say something unjust.

*No, you did not put your shoe in the tree, Charles. In response to your deceitful actions, the boys took one of your shoes from where you had planted it in the shop, and they ran it over here to the orchard.*

Legion should not have done so.

*Given the circumstances, I do not believe you are in any position to offer your opinion on what the other young men should or should not have done.*

The first time my shoes were pilfered it was Legion who took them. To say it was me who took my shoes the first time they were taken would be to say something untrue.

*They told me they took your shoes the first time, Charles. You are not being accused of that.*

The second time my shoes were taken it was Legion who took them. To say it was me who took my shoes the second time they were taken would be to say something untrue.

*You are defending yourself against accusations no one has leveled against you, Charles. You are doing so to avoid taking responsibility for those actions of which you are guilty.*

I do not think Legion has paid sufficiently for their pilfering. Neither for the first time my shoes were pilfered nor for the second time my shoes were pilfered. So this morning I did what I did. I am guilty of seeking to create an opportunity for justice to prevail. Since to this point in time all opportunities for justice to prevail have been missed.

*You are not the justice keeper in Oneida, Charles. This is not your role. To be direct, you are not off to a good start here. You need to alter your course.*

Father Noyes pulls an unripe pear off a branch and takes a small, careful bite with his front teeth. He winces as he chews. When he holds out to me the uneaten portion of the pear, I do not take it because it is unripe and because I have already eaten.

I am not like a piece of unripe fruit.

*You are like a piece of unripe fruit, Charles. Too crisp, too bitter. You are not ready for the harvest, but you will be. You made promises to your father when you came to Oneida, and your father made promises to me in seeking my approval of your joining us. Suffice it to say, Charles, that your father cares for you and wants the best for you. One does not worry for and fear for and make promises for those one does not care for. And your heavenly father cares for you. And your sisters and brothers and fathers and mothers here in Oneida care for you. And I care for you. We care for you because it is our duty to care for you. I am saying this to you now, but I could be saying it to any of the boys. The boys whom I would have you regard as your brothers. I could be saying it to my own son Theodore. Or my own son Victor. You have not met Victor yet. He is away. He is also like a piece of unripe fruit.*

Father Noyes takes four more quick bites of the pear and then tosses the core underhand over the fence. He wipes his fruit-wet hand on his rain-wet shirt and clears his gums with his tongue.

I am not a piece of unripe fruit. The promises of my father have no place here.

*In the figurative way in which I am speaking, Charles, you are. You are a piece of unripe fruit. Not just you. My son Victor, too. Your father and I have exchanged letters. Does it bother you to know that? It should not bother you. I tell you this so you understand how the promises of your father do have a place here. They have a place with not only you but with me.*

I am not a piece of unripe fruit.

*You are. What's more, I know you still have the shoes that I loaned you. I know that's another untruth you have told.*

I do not have the shoes you loaned me in the meantime. I do not have your shoes. That is not an untruth.

*It is an untruth. And you are. You are a piece of unripe fruit. My own son Victor is, and you are, too.*

These are the final words Father Noyes says before raising a hand to himself. Before the bee rises from the pear-littered grass into his beard, and Father Noyes slaps himself on the neck, and the bee stings his palm. As these words are final words, they carry more weight. Final words are weightier than words followed by, and therefore replaced by, other words. Due to the manner in which no other words come after and therefore replace final words, final words carry more weight. In the meantime they carry more weight.

We are drawing ever closer to an unveiling.

## Sewell Newhouse Grows His Operation

I DON'T KNOW. Mr. Noyes gets a notion in his head, and just because it's in his head he somehow knows it's right, and because he knows it's right he doesn't see the need for discussion or explanation. His notion that I would supervise Guiteau's settling in worked like this. He said it and that was that.

My question wasn't only why me, it was why anyone. When I first arrived in Oneida, I wasn't assigned a mentor. Mentor is Mr. Noyes's word. I was left to figure out things on my own. Mentored myself. It's when you start treating people differently from one another that things don't work. Some people get mentors and some don't?

"Maybe some people need mentors and some don't," William Inslee said to me. "You were a grown man with a wife and livelihood when you arrived here. This Guiteau chap comes to us alone, and he seems a bit aimless, doesn't he?" William's not wrong. But still.

When Eveliza and I joined the family, I told Mr. Noyes I wanted to keep being a blacksmith, building my traps, and I told him I worked best alone. He concurred. I reminded him of this a while back when I thought he needed reminding, and he said, "I concur that I concurred, Sewell, but that was a decade ago." So that's how that conversation went. I guess time passing is all it takes to void an agreement. William says he sees my point, but he also says I'm oversimplifying. He says it's a tendency of mine to do so.

When Eveliza and I arrived in Oneida all those years ago, she started in right away on readying our cabin—she didn't get a mentor either—and I headed down creekside with my tools to set up my tent and start in on my work. This was the first day. It was just Wolf and me then. He was just a pup. In a matter of thinking, he's been with me since even before he was a pup, since even before he was born, because before he was my dog, his mother Wolf was my dog, and before that, when I was but a boy, his grandfather Wolf was my dog, and his great-grandfather Wolf was my father's dog. Wolf wasn't a good name for any of them because none of them looked anything like a wolf. All of them skinny mutts with more than a little hound in them. Once a name sticks and gets passed down, though, there's not much to be done about it.

It was just Wolf and me and my tools in the tent by the creek for the first few months. Mr. Noyes had most folks working the fields and orchards back then, and, of course, there was a lot of construction to do. I rotated on and off construction projects like every other man, but I knew I wasn't a vegetable picker or a fruit tree man, and Mr. Noyes didn't push that on me, nor did he make me work on satchels and garter belts when he started up those operations. And when he started sending men on the road to sell wares, I stayed put. Due to what he'd originally concurred to. He didn't push this work on me even though I'm sure some people complained about me getting special treatment. "Why doesn't Mr. Newhouse have to pick beans?" or some such. That I never heard such complaints directly I take to mean Mr. Noyes didn't abide them and put a stop to them before they could spread. Otherwise I would've heard. For better or worse, things don't go unsaid here. For better or worse, even the secrets aren't secrets.

In the beginning when it was just Wolf and me in the tent, I sometimes forged up to five hundred traps a month. Mostly beaver and mink, but we started getting orders for cougar and bear, too. Eveliza got so she was cross with me because I had no time to sleep let alone be a husband. Her words. Wasn't I being a husband working in the tent, though? Working myself sick making traps to fill orders so she and the rest of the family could thrive? How was that not being a husband? Wasn't I her husband there working in the tent as much as I would have been her husband with my boots off twiddling my thumbs in the house? Maybe I was even more so her husband in the tent because of what I was providing through my labor. Would I have been more her husband out in the fields next to her hoeing potatoes? All that aside, the work, I admit, got to be too much to keep up with. Mr. Noyes always called the orders blessings when he shared them with me. So I guess we were being over-blessed was what was happening.

When Mr. Noyes saw I was struggling, he came up with all sorts of ideas how to help. Again, the way he thinks, since the ideas were his, each one was right and ready for immediate implementation. First idea was that he himself would become my assistant. This was the beginning of him starting to renege on his concurring. "I'm your apprentice! Teach me!" he said. The look on his face when he said it suggested that it was funny somehow, the idea of me teaching him. His stint with Wolf and me in the tent didn't last long. He'd put on an apron and swing the sledge a few times before taking a break to see how things were going with the barn raising or the peach harvest or lunch preparation. Rather than speeding me up, he slowed me down. All his stopping and starting. All the explaining and re-explaining I had to do.

He might be the smartest man I ever met—William tells me that reading one of Mr. Noyes's books is like reading three; I'll take his word for it—but he seems to have a hard time learning what someone else is trying to teach him, maybe because his mind is already so full of what he already knows. Another difficulty was that Wolf didn't like him there. Wolf was used to me, how I did things. How when I got to the tent in the morning I was there to stay. Mr. Noyes's gallivanting unnerved him, and he didn't like all the visitors. Folks wanting to see Mr. Noyes the blacksmith in his apron. Children stopping off on their way back from fishing. Women stopping off on their way to the creek with laundry. Wolf growling under his breath at all of them, making me nervous. Not that Wolf's a mean dog. He just gets used to things being a certain way, and it discombobulates him when things change.

Mr. Noyes decided after a few weeks that a better idea than him being my apprentice all the time would be for me to have a different apprentice every few weeks. This way, he explained, a lot of the men could get familiar with my how-to, and soon I'd have a whole team. Funny that he'd have an idea he described to me as being better than his first idea seeing as how he believes that all his ideas are flawless. Even William couldn't give me a satisfactory answer on that score.

As relieved as I was that Mr. Noyes was moving on, I wasn't pleased to have a new man to break in every few weeks, a new man for Wolf to get used to, but we got through it. These other men weren't as smart as Mr. Noyes, so it was easier to teach them, and Wolf tolerated most of them well enough because they stayed put and didn't talk so much.

Looking at it the way Mr. Noyes does, the way I suppose most do, it was a wise and shrewd move on his part to have me train all these men, just as it was wise and shrewd for him to put William to work on building water-powered machines to help me. Now the creek does a lot of the work, and I've got a team of workers who, for the most part, know enough to be helpful—some know more about maintaining William's machines than I do—and now I'm out of the tent and into a full-fledged shop with walls and roof. Whereas at the beginning my operation was on the periphery of things, now it's kind of a centerpiece. Even the children get involved when the orders are coming in fast. William couldn't figure out a machine for linking chains, so Mr. Noyes assigned that chore to the children, requiring that each child do a hundred links a day. They make a game of it. Race each other. Mr. Noyes says they complain when they have to stop linking to go back to their lessons. So while just a short time ago I was filling orders for five thousand traps a year and about killing myself to do it, now we sell more than one hundred thousand traps a year. William says he doesn't see why we couldn't do two hundred thousand next year or the year after. Easy for him to say.

Probably none of us would still be here but for the traps. All we have is thanks to them. They help our reputation, too. People have mixed opinions about Mr. Noyes's writings and the ways of our family, but everyone in the know admires Newhouse-Oneida traps. Mr. Noyes himself has acknowledged this on more than one occasion. Not only in informal conversations but up in front of everyone at meetings. He doesn't mention me specifically in making these declarations, though, and he doesn't mention William, either. In fact, instead of thanking us, he is always after the both of us to guard against pride. He declared once in a criticism session that I'd do well to remember that I am but one tool in God's workshop. One link in a long chain. People nodded. Eveliza nodded.

I tried to talk with William about this afterwards, how I felt Mr. Noyes was being unfair, and I could tell he wanted to agree with me, but he wouldn't let himself. He said if I were hurt by Mr. Noyes's failure to recognize my worth, then wasn't I acknowledging the very pride Mr. Noyes was warning me against? I said it wasn't so much the not being recognized that bothered me; rather, it was the admonishment not to be proud on top of the not being recognized. It was like I would be in trouble for feeling any kind of way about myself or the work I do.

So when Mr. Noyes asked me to serve as mentor to Guiteau, he wasn't thinking only of trapmaking. He wanted me to help Guiteau prepare for his first criticism session. Usually Mr. Noyes had new members go through their first session after a couple months. It was a sort of initiation. He told me that in mentoring Guiteau, I would also be reminding myself of my responsibilities to the community. My duty wasn't only to trapmaking, it was to whatever work Mr. Noyes gave me to do. When I again reminded him about his concurring all those years before, he told me I was out of line. He said my reminding him of his concurring was an example of how I needed to be reminded of my responsibilities. Mr. Noyes had never spoken to me this sternly before. Truth be told, I think he was always careful around me because he knew what my traps meant to the community. If Eveliza and I were to leave, what would happen to the operation? A thorny question I'm sure he didn't want to have to think about. With what had transpired that spring with Eveliza and Ransom, though, I think Mr. Noyes knew more confidently than ever before that I wasn't going anywhere. If what had happened with Eveliza and Ransom hadn't chased me away, he figured I'd never go. Can't say his reasoning wasn't sound.

I won't argue that I didn't make a mistake reacting the way I did to finding out about Eveliza and Ransom. When I saw the two of them walking in the garden, her arm entwined in his and her hair all disheveled and the both of them with straw clinging to their clothes, I should not have walked up stealthily behind them and choked Ransom's neck, and when I got him down—it was very easy to get him down—I should not have put my knees on his thin, boyish arms and filled his maw with dirt. Wolf shouldn't have bit his foot. Mr. Noyes acknowledged that Eveliza and Ransom were also in the wrong—they acknowledged this, too, admitted it was duplicitous not to have their interviews sanctioned, to keep from Mr. Noyes and me what was between them—but I received the brunt of Mr. Noyes's and the rest of the family's consternation because of the spectacle of my tantrum. And because it took a while before Ransom was able to walk without limping on account of how Wolf had nipped him pretty good. Now he walks fine until he sees me and Wolf, and then he suddenly gets a hitch in his stride. I've noted to William how sometimes it's Ransom's left leg that drags and sometimes it's his right leg, and I know William found this amusing even though I could tell he didn't think he should find it amusing.

I was still feeling pretty raw about all of this when Guiteau arrived. I was feeling raw about Eveliza, wondering how well I really knew her, and I was feeling raw about the community as a whole, the way most everybody chose sides over the incident and none of them, not even William, had chosen mine. I was also feeling raw about Mr. Noyes, specifically his suggestion that Ransom and I might heal our rift by doing a stint as bedmates. He said that back in the early days of the community, Abram Smith and George Cragin had done so after their row over Mary Cragin, and the men had come out the other side the better for it. When I told Mr. Noyes that my response to such an unreasonable assignment would be to swear off sleep and spend my nights working in the shop until I fell dead, he let the matter drop, but he did so in a way that made clear his disappointment. Finally, I was also feeling raw about myself on account of how I'd gone ahead and become secretly familiar with a woman named Iris because I thought it would make me feel less raw, but it didn't make me feel less raw. Instead, it compounded the rawness. In the aftermath, I almost hated to see Iris come walking by more than I did Ransom because I was more sure I'd done wrong with her than with him. If I had it to do over again with her, I wouldn't have. If I had it to do over again with Ransom, I don't know.

So I wasn't in the best spirits when Guiteau descended upon me. The way Wolf responded to him, though, surprised me, and on account of that surprise I started feeling less raw. Guiteau was queer. He had something in common with Mr. Noyes in the sense that he was hard to teach at first because his head was already so full, but I couldn't tell what it was full of because he didn't say much. He'd smile when there was nothing to smile at and look forlorn when the sun was out and we were ahead of schedule on orders and I had a few minutes to throw a stick for Wolf out on the lawn. So he was hard to figure, but Wolf took to him like I'd never seen Wolf do before. He let Guiteau pet him on the first day, and on the second day he greeted Guiteau in the morning with his tail wagging. I couldn't understand it. Whereas with most folks he'd growl under his breath like he wanted them to leave or, at best, kind of curl up at the other end of the work room and give them the cold shoulder, with Guiteau he'd whine and whimper and be at the man's ankles all day. It's like Wolf was always worried Guiteau was going to leave and break his heart by going. I still don't understand it.

As much as Wolf seemed to favor Guiteau, the rest of the community was having a hard time with him. The other young men wouldn't let Guiteau be queer in peace, of course. They had to agitate and torment him so they could feel better about themselves. To assure themselves that they weren't queer, too, I suppose. Because don't all folks suspect themselves of being queer? The girls also gave Guiteau a hard time, but in a quieter way. Almost a meaner way, I think. Like if Guiteau were eating a meal at a full table, a girl would walk by and give a personal hello to every chap sitting there but him. Singling out someone like that whom nature has already singled out. With this kind of cruelty, one episode at a time doesn't seem so bad. Seems like a person should be able to shrug it off. In aggregate, though, it takes a toll.

As Guiteau's criticism session drew closer, I became more nervous for him. I wasn't sure what to tell him. William advised me to think back to my own session following the incident with Eveliza and Ransom. He said I had done pretty well because I'd kept calm and quiet and looked like I was taking to heart what was being said. He said he could tell I was remorseful. What William said surprised me because, truth be told, I didn't listen at all to what was being said that night. I heard voices saying words, sometimes my name, but I wasn't really in the room. I was thinking about Eveliza's and Ransom's bodies together, and Iris's and my bodies together, and thinking about these bodies together was making me feel ill. My ill face must have looked to William like remorse.

After what felt like a long time I remember growing impatient and wondering how long the session would last because I needed to get back to work, so my impatient face must have looked like remorse, too. At the end of the session, just before it broke up, I was thinking about what Eveliza had said after we'd gone to bed together for the first time since everything had happened. After we were done coupling, she said that it felt the same as it always had, that nothing had changed. Lying next to her that night, it was a relief to hear her say this. Sitting at the front of the room as folks went on and on in their instruction and edification of me, though, I worried maybe I'd been wrong to be relieved by what she'd said. So I suppose my worried face, too, must have looked like remorse.

Based on what William said, though, I told Guiteau he needed to listen and show that he was listening. I told him he shouldn't respond to anyone's commentary, neither aloud nor through gesture. Maybe nodding would be all right, but he shouldn't shake his head in disagreement to anything. "It's something to get through," I said. "As your mentor, that's what I would say. They'll chastise you a bit about the incident with your shoes—you should expect that—and they'll complain about this and that, but it won't last too long I wouldn't imagine. Mr. Noyes says mutual criticism improves character, and I guess he's right, although maybe mostly in a different way than he means. It improves character because it's something you get yourself through. You ever get yourself through something before, Guiteau? It's a good feeling. You come out the other side knowing you can rely on yourself."

On the evening of the session, when Guiteau's turn came up, I was surprised when Mr. Noyes asked me to begin. I hemmed and hawed a bit before reminding Guiteau that he needed to be more responsible in taking care of the tools at the shop. I told him I'd found a pair of tongs on the floor earlier in the week, and when I'd asked around about who'd left them there, I'd been told it was him, and I told him that I was at present missing two hammers, and although I couldn't say for sure, I suspected him of misplacing them, too, on account of how precedent had been established in terms of his carelessness with the tongs. I made to sit down then, but Mr. Noyes wouldn't allow it. He said it was my responsibility as Guiteau's mentor to offer serious, meaningful criticism. He reminded everyone that to do so was to show love. So I stayed standing for another minute to tell Guiteau he'd do well to try to talk to himself less. Especially with other people around. Especially when it sounds like he is to talking to himself about the people around him. I told him gossip could be a destructive force, even when one gossips with oneself. Mr. Noyes was pleased enough with this comment to let me sit.

When I was finished speaking, the floodgates opened. In the past I've seen Mr. Noyes take steps to regulate a criticism session if a person, especially someone new, was being treated too roughly. He'd call on folks whom he knew would be gentler in their commentary, or he'd simply draw things to a close. I'd even seen him enumerate an individual's good qualities at the end of a particularly brutal session. With Guiteau, though, he kept quiet and let folks rip and tear. We were there for more than an hour. At one point folks in the room were laughing. At another point a few of the women were in tears. As for Guiteau, his face was as blank as water. He put me in mind of an owl on account of how wide open his eyes were and how his head swiveled to stare at whomever was talking. I could tell his demeanor unnerved folks. Afterwards I heard a few people praise him for how he held up, but other folks opined he came off as disrespectful.

Eveliza told me she found Guiteau frightening. She told me afterwards that she was worried she'd have nightmares about him, and even though I had plans to go back to the shop that night, she asked that I come to bed with her because of how uneasy and spooked she felt. We were out of our cabin and living in the mansion house with everyone else by that time. As we walked, she hooked my arm with hers and told me she was proud of me on account of how Mr. Noyes had asked me to start the proceedings that evening.

I watched Ransom watch Eveliza and me leave together. He looked forlorn watching us, and I took some satisfaction in that. I figured the satisfaction I was feeling was probably not something that Eveliza would approve of, so I tried to hide it. For just an instant I felt badly for Ransom. I thought maybe he and Iris might be happy together, but then I thought he better not go anywhere near Iris. Not if he knew what was good for him he better not.

It was still dark the next morning when I returned to the shop to find Wolf with his leg stuck in a beaver trap. When I released him and got a close look, I knew he was going to lose his leg. It looked like after the trap closed on him he got after his leg trying to chew himself free. Animals will do that.

I helped along the inevitable and took Wolf's leg with snips, and then I wrapped him up and took a buckboard into town to the horse doctor. By the time we got there, Wolf had stopped struggling, stopped snapping and whining, and I wondered for a while whether he was gone. The doctor was out, but his wife was there. She put some ointment on Wolf's stump and re-wrapped him with some clean bandages. She told me that what would happen would happen. She'd make no prediction on the matter. So I took Wolf back to the shop where he crawled under one of the tables and slept. I shoved his water bowl under there with him—he didn't want to eat anything—and three days later he limped out ready to get on with life.

I don't know what happened. Beaver traps don't climb down from where they hang on the wall and set themselves. Somebody. Probably Ransom. William said that was me being hasty in my thinking, but I could tell he figured the same as me. He was trying to slow me down. He didn't want me to do something I couldn't take back. As we talked,

William crouched down and reached out to Wolf under the table to give him a pet, but, of course, Wolf showed him his teeth. Still, I appreciated the gesture. I know that in trying to comfort Wolf, William was making to comfort me. "Maybe not Ransom," William said after he stood. He shrugged. "Maybe Guiteau. On account of what you said at his criticism session."

When Mr. Noyes stopped by later that day, he reported straightforwardly that he had talked to William and then had talked to Ransom, whose denials he characterized as believable and sincere. As for Guiteau, he dismissed the possibility out of hand. "Since Charles has come to us, no one's treated him better than your dog. Think about how sad that is, Sewell." In any case, he told me I was forbidden to interrogate either man, Ransom or Guiteau. "Not your place," he said.

"My dog," I said.

"That's why it's not your place," he said.

The next time I came upon Ransom, he put on his usual performance with the limp, but I could tell his heart wasn't in it. I'll never know for certain, but it struck me at that moment on the lawn that the kind of man who'd fake an injury to inspire guilt and curry sympathy probably wasn't the kind of man to take the initiative to tangle with a mean dog in a dark room. So maybe my thinking had been hasty.

Eveliza wouldn't say anything more than it was sad. Not so much sad for Wolf or sad for me, but sad for the family as a whole. That something cruel like that could happen here in Oneida where we all were supposed to be living in concert with Christ and in harmony with one another. Then she sighed. Not so much for the three-legged dog, but rather out of disappointment and discouragement over what the three-legged dog represented.

As for Guiteau, he didn't change one iota. I suppose that's one advantage of acting queerly all the time. If you always act queerly, folks can't one day up and accuse you of acting queerly. Maybe if he'd started acting like a normal person that would have been queer for him. But he didn't.

I waited for Guiteau to say something to me about the mutual criticism session, about Wolf's leg, but he never did. The only thing I noticed that was maybe a little out of the ordinary was that he started to slip Wolf a bread crust or a morsel of meat out of his pocket after returning to the shop from lunch some days. But I did that, too, sometimes, so maybe he'd seen me do it and was just following suit. Could be that's all that was. Could be just something he'd learned from me.

# Charles Guiteau Has Trouble
# Finding Fellowship with Women

IN THE EYES OF YAHWEH, there is no male or female. But I am not Yahweh. And I do not possess the eyes of Yahweh. Rather, I possess my own eyes. And my own eyes are differentiators and discerners.

There are three women here at Oneida whom I discern particularly. I particularly discern Dorcas Findley above the neck. Particularly her lips. And I particularly discern Claudia Hatfield below the neck. Particularly her bosoms. And I particularly discern Florence Snyder. I particularly discern Florence Snyder when, unbeknownst to her, I am high in the branches of a tree, and her bloomers are around her ankles, and she is relieving herself in a patch of foxglove.

When I asked Dorcas Findley for a meeting, I had been in Oneida for only a week. And I had not opened my mouth other than to eat. And to discuss with Mr. Noyes the pilfering of my shoes. And to ask Wolf if he was a good boy. And to yawn. This might explain why Dorcas appeared startled when I spoke to her in the garden. Where she was reading a book. Also that I approached her from behind might explain. Also that I was bleeding from my forehead might explain. I had hurt myself with a hammer while working in the trap shop earlier that day. By design I had hurt myself with the hammer. So I could be excused from working at the trap shop for the rest of the day. And the wound had scabbed over. But I was incapable of leaving the scab alone. I would tell myself to leave it alone, make a covenant with myself to leave it alone, but then moments later find myself breaking the covenant. Despite having just made the covenant. Which put me in mind of how I had been incapable of leaving alone my burnt, blistered-over feet when I was a child and had burnt, blistered-over feet. My mother would ask that I make a covenant with her to leave alone my burnt and blistered-over feet. And I would make the covenant. Sincerely and with resolve. But then I would break the covenant. Often as soon as my mother left the room.

When Dorcas was finished being startled, she offered me her handkerchief. Which I sniffed before folding it and pressing it against my forehead wound. Which I was incapable of leaving alone despite the covenant I had made with myself to leave it alone.

When I asked Dorcas if she would be willing to interview with me in the near future, perhaps even in the present moment, there in the garden, her lips smiled dimly. Not so much at me as at the leaden sky above and beyond the top of my wounded head. Against which I continued to press her handkerchief. Except for when I would remove the handkerchief from my wounded head to look at the blood on her handkerchief. Dorcas's dim smile was not a precursor to words, though. Her dim smile was a precursor to her regarding her book. As she had been regarding her book before I had startled her and she had given me her handkerchief to press against my head wound. Which I could not leave alone despite the covenant I had made with myself to leave it alone. Her regarding again her book suggested to me she had not heard me. Or perhaps had misheard me. So I asked again. Thinking I had gone either unheard or misheard.

In the time that passed between the first time I posed to Dorcas the question and the second time I posed to Dorcas the question, I determined it was difficult to discern whether Dorcas appeared more beautiful when viewed face on or when viewed in profile. I shuffled back and forth between the two vantage points for this purpose. For the purpose of trying to make a discerning determination of beauty based on two perspectives. When her lips asked what I was doing, I shushed them. I told them what was required from them at the moment was not a question, but an answer.

*Just now I am reading, Mr. Guiteau. When I read, I prefer to think about nothing but the book. Does this sound rude of me? I know you are new here, and I do not want to sound unwelcoming, but if we must converse, I wonder if it might occur at a later time. Also, if we must converse, my preference would be for you to stand still rather than dart back and forth. Your strange movements disconcert me. Another preference of mine would be that we not converse alone but rather in the presence of others, preferably a large group. Finally, I would ask that you not speak to me of an interview. I do not know you, and you do not know me. Your forwardness is both improper and puzzling.*

I challenged the claim her lips had made that she would rather read a book than speak with a man. I told her she was wrong to hold such a preference. I told her a man might pick her a bouquet of flowers, or protect her from danger, or sire her children, or build her a house, or save her from drowning, or tell her a joke, or pray for her, or instruct and edify her, or kiss her tenderly. I told her a book could only be read.

*Perhaps you are right, Mr. Guiteau, and yet, at the moment, in this context, I want no part of any of those things. Please do not pick a flower for me. We are in a garden. I like the flowers where they are. Please do not pray for me or tell me a joke. If I were drowning right now, I would implore you not to interfere as I would prefer sinking. Do you understand what I am saying? In this moment, I want nothing that cannot be given me by this book. My desire is to be inside the book. I am decidedly uninterested in anything outside the book. All the things you mention are outside the book as you are outside the book. When I am reading, I resent anything outside the book that tries to draw me away from being inside the book. Perhaps this seems silly to you, or frivolous, or simple, but I do not care a great deal about what you think at present because, again, you and what you think are outside the book.*

*So if you would be kind enough to take your leave from me now, I would be appreciative. It is likely that tomorrow or some other day soon I will seek you out to apologize for not being more gracious and patient on that afternoon in the garden when I told you how unappealing you were compared to a book, and my hope is that you will then be kind enough to forgive me. That will be another thing then that you could add to your list of things a man can do that a book cannot do. Extend forgiveness to an inhospitable woman.*

I told her lips they were clever but not as clever as they thought they were. I told them there is a difference between sounding clever and being clever. There is no difference, though, between looking beautiful and being beautiful. They are the same thing. When I said this, she regarded me in wonderment, as if I were being transfigured. As if she were re-startled by my presence.

When I attempted then to return her handkerchief, her lips told me to keep it. When I re-attempted, they insisted. And then they pursed tightly.

Prior to that afternoon in the garden, I told them, I had believed Dorcas to have the most beautiful face of all the women at Oneida. But now that I saw her up close, and in the full light of the afternoon sun, I think perhaps I was mistaken about Dorcas having the most beautiful face of all the women in Oneida. It is an interesting face in the sense that it is unique and distinctive from the typical face, I told them, but it is not necessarily an attractive face. Rather, it is an interesting face as opposed to an attractive face.

This was not true in the sense that it was honest. The more I regarded Dorcas, the more assured I became of her face's unrivaled beauty. What I said was true, though, in the sense that it was purposeful. In the sense that Dorcas needed to be humbled and tested. From both perspectives. Face-on as well as in profile. Dorcas was distinguishing herself as a haughty, prideful woman. That is to say as an ugly woman despite being a beautiful woman. And this ugliness needed to be addressed. Even in the face of beauty.

*If I am so plain, I am perplexed as to why it is so difficult for you to honor my wishes by leaving me to my book, Mr. Guiteau.*

Her lips said "plain," but I did not say "plain." Dorcas was neither a good listener nor a good conversant. Being a good listener is tantamount to being a good conversant. And she was not a good listener. Which disqualified her from being a good conversant. Insofar as she was not, in any sense, a capable listener.

When you take leave of a woman, she lingers with you longer than a man lingers with you after you take leave of him. A woman might linger for days or even weeks or even months or even years. Even women who are not beautiful linger. But especially beautiful women linger.

I walked out the other side of the garden and headed towards the orchard. And Dorcas's voice was still in my ears. And I hung her bloody handkerchief among the blossoms. In the low-hanging branch of a cherry tree. And her lips whispered protest. They told me I was not being chivalrous. When I asked them what a chivalrous man would do, they answered by moaning softly. And they called me into the tall grass on the outskirts of the orchard. Where the orchard is no longer the orchard but is not yet the field. And they pressed themselves on mine. Dorcas might have thought she was reading her book all afternoon. But she was not. The parts of her that lingered were not. The parts of her that lingered ministered to me for the better part of an hour. In the tall grass that is no longer the orchard and is not yet the field. And those parts that lingered and that ministered included her lips and her other parts that were called by her lips to linger and minister.

My interactions with Claudia Hatfield and Florence Snyder, although notably different from my interaction with Dorcas Findley, were largely the same as my interaction with Dorcas Findley. When I asked to interview with them, they asked if we could converse at a later time. Claudia and Florence were together when I spoke with them. We were not in the garden. Rather, we were in the summer house. Both Claudia and Florence offered the opinion that it was not proper for me to address them together. That is, they addressed me together in telling me how it was improper for me to address them together. They were of one mind on the issue of the impropriety of my addressing them together. When I later tried to address each of them separately, though, each expressed the opinion that I was better suited and more compatible with the other. When I approached Claudia after the evening meeting, she recommended I turn my attention to Florence's perfectly shaped eyes and her gentle, friendly wit. When I approached Florence the next day after breakfast, she delivered a homily on the subtle beauty of Claudia's singing voice and the divine wonder of her rose petal skin.

A few days later I made a new covenant with myself and approached Nan Polk on the path to the children's house after regarding the relatively satisfactory nature of her lips and her bosoms. Wolf accompanied me despite my pleas with him not to accompany me. Nan spoke to me but did not regard me with her eyes as she spoke. Rather she regarded Wolf with her eyes as she spoke. She said she was not supposed to talk to me alone. I told her we were not alone because Wolf was with us. When Wolf heard his name, his ears perked, and he barked. Nan said Wolf did not count. She said she was not supposed to talk to me alone as per the advice of Dorcas and Claudia and Florence and Mr. Noyes.

That night I went to the trap shop, and the trap shop was empty save for Wolf, who greeted me joyfully and whom I assertively ignored so that eventually he made to lie down in the corner to sleep. I then acquired two hammers, one for each hand, and went into the woods and hammered dead tree limbs until my arms were dead tree limbs.

Before hammering and as I hammered the dead tree limbs, I thought that after hammering the dead tree limbs I would throw the hammers into Sunset Lake, which Mr. Noyes and others called the turtle pond and I called the carp pond. But before hammering and as I hammered the dead tree limbs, I did not anticipate that after hammering the dead tree limbs my arms would be dead tree limbs. So instead of throwing the hammers into Sunset Lake, which Mr. Noyes and others called the turtle pond and I called the carp pond, I simply dropped the hammers. And they remained where I dropped them. Like dead tree limbs remain where they are dropped.

And on my way out of the woods, I made a new covenant with myself.

# Victor Cragin Noyes Recalls and Reconsiders Prior

THREE DAYS AFTER we were born, Victoria passed. Mother told me Victoria and I shared a face for the three days. From the waist up Mother couldn't tell Victoria and me apart for the three days, so she had to look below the waist. When she told me this I was too young to understand why below the waist. She said Father Noyes claimed he did not need to look below the waist to tell because he could tell by our chins. *He could not tell by your chins, though. Father Noyes talked of a dimple on your sister's chin, but there was no dimple. Your chins were as identical as your eyes, noses, ears, and hair. Your chins were perhaps the most identical parts of you.* When Mother told me this I was too young to know what a dimple was. *So for the three days Father Noyes called you Victoria as often as he called you Victor.* My sister, too? Did Father Noyes call my sister Victor just as he called me Victoria? *Yes. And Father Noyes continued to call you Victoria and your sister Victor even beyond the three days.*

IN FATHER NOYES'S MANSION there are many rooms, and in Dr. Brigham's mansion there are many rooms. In both Oneida and in Utica, rooms have been prepared for me. Father Noyes has told me it is ultimately my decision where I shall live, and he has told me it is ultimately Dr. Brigham's decision. Father Noyes has not told me it is ultimately his decision where I shall live, but that it is ultimately his decision where I shall live is understood insofar as it need not be said.

CHARLES ASKS IF I am jealous of my mother, which I take to mean do I still miss her. Yes I still miss her. *No, Vic.* He does not mean still miss. He means jealous. Jealous as in do I ever wish I could be drowned instead of or along with her. Charles tells me I should not be hesitant to answer truthfully. *We are friends, right, Vic?* Charles pulls my hand out of my pocket and shakes it like a doll's hand or a puppet's hand instead of offering his hand to me to shake of my own volition. *Friends should not be hesitant to answer one another truthfully, Vic.*

THEODORE IS MY BROTHER by Father Noyes but not by Mother. I am reminded of this when I try to see him behind his beard because behind his beard he looks like Mrs. Noyes. Theodore seeks to help me negotiate what Father Noyes demands of me so I may be allowed to live with him in Oneida rather than in Utica with Dr. Brigham insofar as it is ultimately Father Noyes's decision where I shall live. Theodore says I am fortunate because Father Noyes's demands of me are clear and actionable. Conversely, Theodore says, Father Noyes's demands of him are contradictory and impossible. Theodore says this causes him sometimes to be jealous of me, which I take to mean that sometimes Theodore misses me. Most probably when I am in Utica with Dr. Brigham. *Consorting with the likes of Guiteau is not helping your case with Father, Vic.* But Father Noyes himself consorts with Charles. And so does Mr. Newhouse consort with Charles. *Different circumstances, Vic. Father and Sewell are not consorting with Guiteau, they are mentoring him.*

FATHER CRAGIN CONFESSES HE is sometimes jealous of me. He confesses this when we walk together in the woods where we walk so as not to be seen by Father Noyes. *Not that John would mind seeing us together. In fact, John encourages me to mentor you, but I do not need his encouragement to do so. I resent his encouragement on this matter because even outside of his will and instruction I would do it. Even if he were to prohibit it I would do it. If John sees us walking and talking, he will think we are doing so because he advised it, and I do not want him to think we are spending time with one another in response to his advice. This is why I would have us walk together*

*in the woods. In order to avoid this misunderstanding.* Father Cragin says Mother's drowning is what sometimes makes him jealous of me. He was not jealous of me prior to her drowning, but he is now jealous because she is gone from him completely insofar as in her death he has no part of her, but I still have part of her, even in death, insofar as she is part of me by blood. Father Cragin says Father Noyes took too much of Mother from him in life just as he takes too much of her from him in death, but Father Noyes cannot take from me what I have by blood. Not even when I am in Utica with Dr. Brigham can Father Noyes take from me what I have by blood. *This is why I am sometimes jealous of you, Vic, and this is also why sometimes John is jealous of you. The difference is I admit to my jealousy whereas John does not.* Why does Father Noyes not admit to his jealousy? *Because John was not to spill his seed in fellowshipping with your mother, but he did spill his seed. So he, like your mother, is part of you by blood. This is why he does not admit to his jealousy that your mother is part of you by blood. Because of the nagging shame that he spilled his seed when he was not to spill his seed. Which is also my shame. You are not my shame. It is important for you to understand this. You are not my shame. My shame is the fact of John's spilled seed. But you are not my shame. Please understand this. Understand that you are not my shame. Do you understand this?*

MOTHER AND FATHER CRAGIN and I bobbed in the cold water. They passed me back and forth carefully. *Don't drop the baby.* Whenever they passed me they said this because it made me laugh. And we bobbed in the cold water because that made me laugh. So cold it took my breath away. Made colder somehow by the warmth of the bright sun. And Mother and Father Cragin stretched out my hands with their hands to cup the water spilling white off the rocks because that made me laugh. And whoever did not have me would submerge and then break the surface to peek-a-boo me because that made me laugh. Father Cragin says he does not know where this could have been or even if it could have been. He cannot think of such a place in Brooklyn, and he cannot think of such a place in Oneida. He remembers such a place in Putney, but does not remember taking me to the place. Father Cragin says I would have been too young to take swimming in Sacketts Brook. Too young then to remember Sacketts

Brook now. But I remember even prior. I remember even Victoria with whom I shared a face for the three days.

WHEN FATHER NOYES SENT me to Dr. Brigham in Utica, he told me it would be only for three days, but this was a miscalculation insofar as I stayed in Utica with Dr. Brigham for ninety days. *Not a sylum. An asylum.* In his office Dr. Brigham asked me how many times a day did I self-pollute. I told him no times a day insofar as the self-pollution occurred at night. *Do you know, Victor, that self-pollution is a doubly abominable transgression? Do you suffer from headaches, melancholy, weakness in the back, variable appetite, the inability to look others in the face, sudden flushes of heat in the cheeks, or clamminess? How about dull, sheepish eyes; dry, brittle hair; palpitations or pain in the region of the heart? How about shortness of breath, constipation, cough, bouts of weak eyesight, irritation of the throat? Any loss of memory?* No loss of memory. *Any twitching muscles in the arms and legs? Any attention lapses?* No loss of memory. Quite the opposite in fact. I remember things no one else remembers. Both things others no longer remember and things others have never remembered.

CHARLES ASKS IF I have ever conversed with Mother after her drowning. How? I ask. *If you have to ask how, then the answer is no.* He tells me to follow him to Sunset Lake, which folks call the turtle pond and Charles calls the carp pond. In the rain? I say, and then as if on cue the clouds part and the sun shines through. *What rain, Vic?* We follow the shoreline trail halfway around. Mosquitoes and sweat bees swarm our beards, and cottonwood seed drifts down around us like snow. The geese glide on the still, smooth water, so smooth and still it appears solid. Like ice. Like the geese are sliding rather than floating. Like someone could walk safely bank to bank if they stepped softly enough. If they had enough faith. We walk softly on the shoreline trail so as to be able to get close to the geese so that when we get close Charles can stomp and jump and fling his arms and loudly honk like a goose so as to scatter the geese, who do not scatter but rather relocate as one body to the other end of the pond. Charles grabs a dead branch and rakes under the black water along the edge of the spongy bank. He rakes out of the rotten muck one of Sewell's otter traps that has trapped an otter that isn't an otter but a goose. The otter that is a goose bobs on its bloated side, bounces against the shore, its long neck impossibly twisted, its beak opened wide as if to swallow the lake, one wing half unfurled above the surface as if trying to lift the rest of itself, and the other wing submerged, dragging it down.

*I don't like how he calls you Vic, Vic. Did you tell him to call you Vic, or did he just start calling you Vic on his own? Before Guiteau came along, only I called you Vic.* I did not tell Charles to call me Vic. He just started to call me Vic of his own volition. Theodore is just returning from Yale. When he is at Yale he wishes he were at Oneida, and when he is in Oneida he longs for Yale. It is the same with Ann Hobart insofar as when Theodore is away from her he longs for her, and when he is with her he longs to be away from her. It was the same with Theodore and Sam Hutchins. Prior to Sam enlisting, Theodore and Sam would grow cross and argue with one another to the extent that they would avoid one another for weeks at a time, but after Sam was gone, first to the war and then from typhoid, Theodore would long for Sam. *Sam was no less my brother than you are my brother. I don't want to lose you like I lost Sam. Tell me, Vic, what was the worst part of it? What was the worst part of the asylum? The just being away or something else?* The crib with the lid was the worst part. Seeing men kept in the crib with the lid. Instead of saying this, though, I say, The worst part of it was the just being away. *You must do all you can not to have him send you back then.* I am trying to do all I can. *But you're not, Vic. Consorting with Guiteau is not doing all you can.* Consorting with Guiteau was not on Father Noyes's list of things to refrain from in order not to be sent back to Utica. *Consorting with Guiteau is in the spirit of the list of things to refrain from in order not to be sent back to Utica, though.*

*If you strive and refrain thusly, as per the enclosed pledge, you can return to Oneida to be with your family.* The letters I received in Utica from Father Noyes smelled like rain. *Think of yourself as a piece of unripe fruit. Think of your adherence to the enclosed pledge as a means of ripening. Think of*

*your return to Oneida as the harvest. It is up to you to choose.* I will refrain from self-pollution. I will strive to keep my hands out of my pockets. *Dr. Brigham opines that you are capable of striving and refraining. He opines that you do not belong with him in Utica. That being said, you need to decide if you belong here in Oneida. If you want to be harvested, you must ripen.* I will strive to look folks in the face when I speak to them instead of looking over their shoulder or at their feet. I will refrain from walking away from folks in mid-conversation. *If you choose to reply to this missive with a statement affirming your commitment to adherence, which I hope you will do, that will not be the end of it. In fact, that will be only the beginning. Each day is a new opportunity for you to demonstrate your commitment.* I will refrain from taking too seriously my croquet matches with Theodore. I will strive to take more seriously my reading. I will refrain from moving my lips when I read. *While my demands may on their surface seem strident, I hold that I am not asking more of you than I ask of anyone else here. I surely am not asking more of you than I ask of myself.* I will refrain from eating too quickly or too slowly. I will refrain from chewing with my mouth agape. I will refrain from carrying on conversations with myself. I will especially refrain from carrying on conversations with myself that cause me to laugh or weep. *That we share blood is neither here nor there.* I will strive to be less squeamish about perspiration, dirt, insects, rodents, precipitation, and meat that no longer smells fresh but is still perfectly suitable for consumption. I will strive to study and emulate the characteristics of my more mature brethren, but I will refrain from clinging to my mature brethren too needfully. *That we share blood is neither here nor there except in the sense that folks expect more of you due to our blood connection and in the sense that how you comport yourself reflects not only on yourself but on me, whom the family looks to for leadership and guidance.* I will strive to be more courageous in and comfortable with conversing with women. I will refrain from blushing whenever a woman speaks to me. *For what it is worth, your mother would agree with me in regards to what I am asking of you. She would concur with me in terms of your ripening. She would sign her name to this letter alongside mine.*

WHEN I LEAVE ONEIDA, *Vic, you are welcome to leave with me.* Why are you leaving Oneida, Charles? *As per the covenant I made with myself. Come*

*with me to the turtle pond, carp pond, otter pond, goose pond.* In the rain? *What rain?* The rain pouring out of the sky. The rain in which we are standing and conversing. What are you hiding underneath your shirt? *Come with me to the turtle pond, carp pond, otter pond, goose pond, and I'll show you.* We follow the shoreline trail halfway around. The lightning and thunder follow us. Where are all the geese? *They have left Oneida as per the covenant they made with themselves.* You said you would show me what you are hiding underneath your shirt if I came with you, and I came with you, so show me what you are hiding underneath your shirt. *A goose,* Charles says, but he produces a violin. Why do you have Frank's violin? *What violin? You are not listening. This is an otter. I have brought this carp to the pond so that it may leave Oneida as one body with the other turtles as per the covenant.* He flings the violin into the rain over the pond in a long arc. It splashes and floats. *If it had more heft it could have flown further.* Why? *Physics is why.* I mean why did you do that? Why did you throw Frank's violin into the pond? *What violin?* The one you just threw. *Comeuppance. Insofar as comeuppance furthers fulfillment of the covenant.* A moment ago I would have thought it could not rain any harder, but it is now raining harder. *When I leave Oneida, Vic, you are welcome to leave with me.*

# Frank Wayland-Smith Witnesses a Defenestration

I HEARD MR. MILLS'S inquiry as innocent and sensible. I certainly did not hear the malice and disrespect Tirzah tells me Mr. Noyes heard. Mr. Mills had been with us for only a few months and had already seen himself and his wife sit for criticism twice, and he had seen Charles Guiteau and Victor Noyes each sit three times. In asking Mr. Noyes how often he submitted himself to criticism, it appeared to me Mr. Mills was simply trying to gain a better understanding of how things worked. He spoke his question clearly, straightforwardly. I should not have told Tirzah I found Mr. Mills's question refreshing, but I did tell her. I should not have told her because telling Tirzah was as good as telling Mr. Noyes himself.

Tirzah argued Mr. Mills would have done better to ask his question of Mr. Noyes in private rather than in the presence of the whole family. She asserted this was what had vexed Mr. Noyes and made him suspicious of Mr. Mills's intentions. She might have had a point. The fact that Mr. Mills asked his question freely and openly, though, is in large part why I found it refreshing. Not to mention the fact that Mr. Mills's question was a question in which I was interested, one I had often fantasized about posing to Mr. Noyes myself.

Tirzah and I were conversing in the rehearsal room where she was helping me search for my violin. My spruce. No one played it but me. No one but me was to touch it. I would never make this claim aloud, of course, but folks knew it to be true. In spirit, all the instruments belonged to the family as a whole, but in practice, folks knew the spruce was mine. The other musicians called it Frank's violin. The basswood instruments were everyone's. Anyone who wanted could sign out one of them like a library book. Not the spruce, though.

Mr. Noyes had gifted the spruce to the family three Christmases ago. He called me to the front of the hall to receive it on behalf of the orchestra. He did not call up our conductor, Mr. Joslyn; rather, he called me up. People knew from that day forward. Just like folks knew the trap shop was Sewell's and Tirzah was Mr. Noyes's.

"Is it back at the mansion house in your room?" Tirzah asked. "Tucked into your bed waiting for your return? Its neck reclining on your pillow?" She smiled at me not smiling. "Your sweetheart. Your pet."

"It might be back at the mansion house in someone's room but not my room."

"Whose then?"

"You tell me, Tirzah. Speaking of sweethearts. Speaking of pets."

Tirzah shook her head. "Mr. Noyes is long done with the violin. You know this, Frank. He's pecking out tunes on the piano now. Mr. Joslyn is tutoring him. It's comical to watch. John is an awful student. He doesn't take instruction well."

"I don't imagine Mr. Noyes would take my violin to play it."

"Why then?"

"To teach me a lesson," I said. "You heard him at my last criticism session."

"You can't be serious, Frank," Tirzah said, tilting her head. "He told you to take care not to let your beautiful playing and uncommon talent undermine your faith and distract you from your spiritual commitments. This was reminiscent of his criticism of Henrietta Combs back in April that she not allow her transcendent physical beauty to get in the way of maintaining her exemplary character. She walked on air for a week as a result of that horrific dressing down. Please. Someone criticize me like that."

"Again, as was the case with Mr. Mills's question, you hear things differently than I, Tirzah," I said. "When it comes to Mr. Noyes, you do."

"I am objectively right in this instance, Frank. It is a fact Mr. Noyes relishes your playing."

"He did at one time."

"He does still. He told me so just this past week."

"What did he say?"

"It wouldn't be right for me to tell you. What he told me was for my ears only."

"What he had to say about my playing the violin was for your ears only?" I said. "You're fibbing."

"He was making a comparison," Tirzah said. By the expression she wore, I got the sense she was trying to make herself blush. Is that something a woman can do?

"Come now," I said. "A comparison to what? Don't be cruel."

Tirzah tapped a finger on her cheek. "If I tell you, you have to answer a question for me," she said.

"What question?"

"You'll find out when I ask it. After I tell you what Mr. Noyes compared to your exquisite fiddle playing."

"Do not call it a fiddle," I said. "It is not a fiddle. I do not fiddle."

"My my," Tirzah said, raising her eyebrows. "Do we have an agreement, my haughty friend?"

"Fine," I said.

Tirzah crossed the floor, stuck her head into the hallway, stepped back into the rehearsal room and pulled the door shut. "Mr. Noyes and I were in bed at the time," she said.

"I am in shock."

She waved me quiet. "This was afterwards. Mr. Noyes was being sweet. He was describing what it was like to be with me. He said, 'There is as much difference between other women and you as there is between a tenpenny whistle and Frank's violin.'"

"I don't want to hear anymore," I said. "Forget I asked."

"But I haven't gotten to the important part," Tirzah said. "Mr. Noyes said to me, 'You are like Frank's violin. When I go to hear him play, I always expect something sublime.'"

Tirzah bowed and curtsied as I shook my head. "I cannot believe you told me that," I said.

"Yes you can," Tirzah answered. She took a step closer to me and rested her forehead on my shoulder. "You begged me to tell, Frank. You know I cannot deny you. Besides, what do I not tell you?"

"Sweet Tirzah," I said, patting her cheek. "Mr. Noyes is right. You are indeed an exquisite woman." When she straightened and smiled at me, I kissed the top of her head and folded my arm around her neck. "But you are by no means as exquisite as my playing."

She play-pouted at this and tried to push me away, but I braced myself and would not budge. "Have you changed at all since you were a child?" she said. "I don't think you have. When I am with you, we are ten years old again. This is equal parts frustrating and wonderful."

I smiled. "We bring out the frustrating and wonderful in each other, Tirzah."

"I suppose that's true," she said, disentangling herself from me and backing away. "Enough of this nostalgic nonsense, though. We had a deal. I have earned the right to ask my question."

"All right," I said. "But hurry, please. I really do have to find my violin."

"Quickly then. Do you love Cornelia?"

"Who?" I said.

"You heard me," Tirzah said as the smile left her face. With Tirzah, though, a serious countenance was often a precursor to frivolity. Conversely, she often grinned broadly and used a voice charged with laughter when discussing serious matters. This was how she disarmed you.

"Cornelia Worden?"

"Right," Tirzah said. "There is but one Cornelia here in Oneida."

"Cornelia and I have grown to be excellent friends," I said. "We are very fond of one another. At least I am very fond of her. I hope she is very fond of me. There. You have your gossip."

"Oh, she is," Tirzah said, still looking serious. "Fond of you, I mean."

"You know this how?"

"As you just said. Gossip. I am an awful gossip. So you probably should take anything I say with a grain of salt. I hope I learn my lesson someday soon. We should probably cut short this conversation right now before I let slip any scandalous news. I am incorrigible. I apologize."

"Very good," I said. "Very convincing. Now tell me how you know that Cornelia is fond of me."

Tirzah smiled tightly. "I'll just say that Cornelia knows when it comes to Frank Wayland-Smith, I am the resident expert. So she has come to me with lots of questions. She thinks you fascinating if a bit inscrutable. I think one word she used was 'enchanting.'"

"That's surprising to me," I said. I covered my mouth with my hand. "I thought Cornelia fancied Charles Guiteau. I always see them together."

"That's not funny, Frank," Tirzah said. "Seriously."

"It's a bit funny."

"It's not," Tirzah said. "All of us women have our Charles Git-Out stories, but the scoundrel has recently been pestering Cornelia above and beyond what can be laughed off. In fact, she has tried to dissuade him by evoking your name. She told Guiteau that, at present, she found herself favoring Frank Wayland-Smith to such a degree that being with another would be unfair, both to herself and to the man."

"I didn't realize he was pestering her like that," I said. "She hasn't said anything to me. Perhaps I need to have a word with my good friend Charles."

Tirzah smiled. "No need to mount your steed and rescue your damsel, good knight. I have alerted Mr. Noyes to the situation."

"Of course you have," I said. "Well, all shall be set right then. Mr. Noyes, knight of knights, will see to it I am sure."

"John has fielded so many complaints about Guiteau that he has become somewhat of an expert on the reprobate. Just as I am an expert on you."

"If he were truly an expert at managing Guiteau, wouldn't Guiteau have reformed his behavior by now?" I said.

"You seem lately to have soured on John, Frank," Tirzah said. "Aligning yourself with his critic Mr. Mills. Accusing him of theft. Insinuating that he isn't an effective leader. Is there something troubling you? Perhaps something I can help smooth over? Is this just a case of petty jealousy, or is there another matter I can help assuage?"

"You could have a word with your John about returning my violin to me," I said.

"You are putting me in a foul mood, Frank. I don't expect this from you. Usually when I am in your company my mood improves." She frowned. "I depend on you for that."

"Are you teasing me now, Tirzah?" I said, taking her hand. "If you are truly upset, I apologize."

"It's all right, Frank," she said. "True friends need not apologize."

"I don't believe that," I said. "I don't believe that to be true at all."

"As most of the community knows, Mr. Mills, I made the decision a while back that I would not subject myself to mutual criticism. I consider this choice one of the most significant sacrifices I have made for this body." As Mr. Noyes spoke, he walked across the hall to where Mr. Mills was seated and stood over him in making his answer. "I did not make this decision because I doubt the practice would benefit me. On the contrary, I hold that mutual criticism is one of the most important, healthiest habits we cultivate here among our family, and, as I hope you know, I count my-self a member of the family even though I also bear the burden of being its leader. Indeed, is not the head part of the body? Christ himself was King of his disciples, but wasn't He also a disciple himself?"

Mr. Mills did not respond to Mr. Noyes's question, but others in the hall nodded and murmured in agreement.

"This being said, Mr. Mills, Christ did not receive instruction from his apostles. Similarly, Paul did not receive letters from the churches in Corinth or Ephesus or Thessalonica directing him in regard to his life in Christ. This would have been backwards. Wouldn't it have been back-wards, Mr. Mills, for these folks to offer counsel and instruction to the Apostle Paul, who had received visions directly from heaven, who had suf-fered greatly at the hands of the Pharisees and Sadducees, who had been thrown in jail and had abandoned all comforts and earthly considerations for the gospel of Christ?"

The hall grew silent as Mr. Noyes's question hung in the air. As the silence wore on, it became apparent that Mr. Noyes intended to insist on an answer from Mr. Mills. No one would be dismissed until Mr. Mills acquiesced. It was during this silence that I felt bitterness swell in me. Not because of the words Mr. Noyes had delivered but because of his intent to humiliate Mr. Mills. It struck me as cowardly.

I was surprised when Mr. Mills stood. "I am sorry to have offended you, Mr. Noyes."

"No offense taken," Mr. Noyes said as he smiled. He clapped Mr. Mills's shoulder and turned back towards the front of the hall.

Mr. Mills, however, was not done speaking. "I must disagree with you on that score, Mr. Noyes. I believe it is obvious you have taken of-fense. Furthermore," Mr. Mills continued as he swept his eyes over the room, "I am sorry to all of you, the whole family, if my question was inap-propriate. I obviously still have much to learn about this community, and ever since I was a boy, I have had a knack for talking out of turn. Perhaps I did that here." At this point it appeared Mr. Mills was making to settle back into his chair, but then he straightened again. I sensed the man was in the middle of an argument with himself, and the side that beckoned him to keep talking won out.

"It's just that, well, I heard Mr. Guiteau being roundly criticized this evening for committing what is apparently a very serious infraction.

Eating fruit in the library. As a body, we spent quite a few minutes on this issue, and. . . ."

"All it takes is a couple drops of juice from a peach or a plum to render a book unreadable," Mrs. Hicks offered from the back of the hall. "Its pages will stick together."

"Understood," Mr. Mills continued, nodding to Mrs. Hicks. "I also understand that someone biting into a crisp apple might create a distracting noise that could cause a nearby reader to lose his train of thought."

"Especially, as was said, because Mr. Guiteau chews so loudly," Mrs. Hicks added.

"Right," Mr. Mills said. "I only asked my question of Mr. Noyes because I have witnessed him committing the same infraction as Mr. Guiteau. A pear if I'm not mistaken. And as for the complaint about the day that Mr. Guiteau became agitated and loud over the political literature he was reading, I would suggest that Mr. Noyes's dressing down of Mr. Guiteau that day was louder and somewhat more distracting than Guiteau's rather minor outburst."

"I simply told Mr. Guiteau, 'Let the dead vote for the dead. Christ is my candidate, and I will vote for no other if I wait a thousand years,'" Mr. Noyes said. He was seated now, having made the decision to give Mr. Mills the floor. I sensed he was invigorated by Mr. Mills's engagement.

"Certainly an interesting bit of advice to ponder," Mr. Mills said. "I am simply pointing out the fact that if Mr. Guiteau is going to be so severely chastened for what is considered his inconsiderate behavior in the library, then shouldn't Mr. Noyes be criticized for the same? As he himself says, he is part of the same body."

OVER THE YEARS, I had noticed how Mr. Noyes's countenance had changed during my playing. When I was a boy, he would smile and close his eyes at my recitals, and he would keep them closed after I had finished as if he were still relishing the notes. After one of my early recitals, he joined me at the front of the hall as the audience exploded in cheers— I remember the heat in my cheeks and ears and the conflicted feelings of wanting the applause to stop immediately and never to end—and he spoke to the room about how much he was already looking forward to my future recitals in the years ahead. This was a Sunday afternoon, so it was not only the family present but also a crowd of visitors who had come to enjoy picnic suppers on our grounds, indulge in strawberry shortcake, and listen to music. Mr. Noyes then turned philosophical and spoke for more than a few minutes about music as sacrament. He called it one of God's three sacred gifts to humankind, in addition to love and work, and he ranked it as the second most wonderful, just ahead of work and just after love. When he was finished, as the audience bustled happily out of the hall, Mr. Noyes put his arm around my shoulders and kissed the top of my head.

As I grew older and my skill evolved, though, Mr. Noyes became less enthralled with my playing even as others in the community, especially the women, fawned over it. He told me he was concerned that I loved my violin more than I loved my brothers and sisters, and he warned me against becoming addicted to applause and flattery. "Life is not a concert," he told me. "Your family's chief purpose is not to serve as your personal worshipful audience." On the other hand, Mr. Joslyn, who had served as conductor of the community orchestra since he had founded it, confided in me that I was the sole reason he kept serving in the role, and that on occasion when he had been tempted to leave Oneida to explore opportunities to play and conduct in Europe, the thought of my playing is what anchored him. I was a teenager at the time and was astounded by the compliment he was paying me, but more than the praise, what lingered with me was the notion of someone desiring to leave Oneida. At the time, the idea seemed bizarre. Mostly frightening, but also a bit exhilarating and, in another sense, relieving.

I thought of all this that evening in the hall as Mr. Mills challenged Mr. Noyes. Tirzah later used the word "defiant" in describing Mr. Mills's comments. That may be accurate, I suppose. He was defying Mr. Noyes in the sense that he was being honest with him, and as was the case when I was younger and Mr. Joslyn frightened, exhilarated, and relieved me by suggesting the possibility of abiding in a world outside Oneida, so did Mr. Mills's words frighten, exhilarate, and relieve me by the possibilities they suggested.

THE RUCKUS IN THE hallway woke me. I thought I was dreaming and told myself to go back to sleep, but then there was a bang against my door that made me sit up straight. Ransom, my bedmate at the time, whispered a curse, and the both of us rose, dressed, and hurried into the hallway.

In the room across the way, which at the time housed Mr. Mills and Mr. Guiteau, a small crowd had congregated. A couple of the men held candles, and in the wavering light I saw what appeared to be snowflakes dancing in the air. When I was able to make my way into the room, I saw that the window was wide open and that Mr. Noyes was standing over Mr. Mills and Mr. Guiteau, who were both seated on the bed. Mr. Noyes held a jug in one hand and its cork in the other. As he brought the jug to his nose to sniff, Mr. Mills stared solemnly at the floor, and Mr. Guiteau aimed his sleepy grin at me.

"Guiteau let slip about it earlier, so I sneaked in after they was asleep to see for myself, and there it was. Like he said. Outside on the sill." It was Jerome speaking. "Then I told Marcus to go summon you, Mr. Noyes. While I was waiting, Mills tried to get it from me, and I told him no, but he kept a-grabbing at it, so I had to. Once in the nose."

"That's a lie," Mr. Mills said. "Good God." When he looked up from the floor, I saw his nose was bloodied.

"The evidence would seem to support Jerome's contention that he did indeed punch you in the face," Mr. Noyes said.

"His lie is that I was grabbing for the jug. My head was still on my pillow when he punched me. I had just in that moment been awakened by the cold air coming in, and I told Charles to shut the window. I didn't even open my eyes to say it. Didn't even sit up. Next thing I know, I'm punched."

"I saw his arm twitch to grab for the jug," Jerome said. "Ask Guiteau. Aren't I telling the truth, Charles?"

Guiteau did not offer an answer other than to continue grinning at me, and Mr. Noyes did not seem interested in hearing from him.

"What is it?" Mr. Noyes said. He sniffed the jug again and wrinkled his nose.

"Cider," Mr. Mills said. "Good God."

"It's turned to alcohol," Jerome said. "Guiteau let slip that Mills drinks it every night. He leaves it out on the sill."

"Did Guiteau let slip he drinks it with me?" Mr. Mills said. "Good God. It helps me sleep. I have arthritis in my back."

"It tastes terrible," Guiteau said. His eyes remained on me as he spoke. "Why would I drink something that tastes as terrible as that tastes?"

"You made it?" Mr. Noyes said to Mr. Mills. "You stole from our God-given bounty of apples to make it?"

"A little mash from the cider making is all," Mr. Mills said. "Good God. Take it."

"I'm going to have to ask you to abandon the premises immediately, Mr. Mills," Mr. Noyes said. "We'll alert your wife in the morning to what has transpired, and she can make her decision then about how she wants to proceed, but tonight we need you out of the family's house."

"Where would you have me go?" Mr. Mills said. "It's snowing."

"You can spend the night in the trap shop."

"That dog is down there," Mr. Mills said. "It doesn't like me."

"Doesn't like anyone, save for Sewell and me," Guiteau said, continuing to grin at me. "The dog favors me well enough, though. Just Sewell and me it favors well enough."

"The barn then," Mr. Noyes said. "In the morning, you'll be allowed in to gather your belongings and your poor wife if she so chooses, and then you'll leave the community altogether and for good." Mr. Noyes sniffed the jug again before corking it.

"I will gladly take my leave in the morning," Mr. Mills said. He stood and took a step to confront Mr. Noyes face to face. "But I will not be staying in the barn tonight like an animal. The funds I submitted to you upon my arrival here and the work I have since done entitle me to this bed. I will not be put out into the snow. Good God." Mr. Mills wiped at his nose and saw when he looked at his hand that he was still bleeding. "Furthermore, I will keep that jar with me tonight, and I will take it with me when my wife and I depart in the morning."

"This is not a negotiation," Mr. Noyes said. "You will retire to the barn tonight. As for this concoction, you will not be getting it back. For your own good you won't."

"Return it to me, you arrogant charlatan!" Mr. Mills hissed, and when he lunged at Mr. Noyes, Jerome and Ransom intercepted him, lifted him off his feet, and slammed him against the wall by the window. Mr. Mills did not acquiesce. Arthritis or not, he persevered ferociously, and it looked like he might free himself until Guiteau joined the fray by dropping to the floor, grabbing one of Mr. Mills's legs, and sinking his teeth into Mr. Mills's thigh. Mr. Mills yelped in pain. At that point in the fracas, although I did not hear Jerome, Ransom, or Guiteau say anything to one another, they appeared to move as one with pre-ordained purpose and direction. Mr. Mills was carried to the open window and tipped out headfirst.

"What have you done?" I said.

"Go play your fiddle, Frank," Jerome said. "You don't like it, go play your fiddle."

"Yes!" Guiteau said, his grin breaking into full-fledged laughter. "Go play your fiddle, Frank!"

"You bit him like a dog," I said to Guiteau. "You're quite a specimen. Biting men and tormenting women."

My words changed Guiteau's face. His mouth tightened, and tears began to well in his eyes. "Go play your fiddle, Frank," Guiteau said again, but quietly this time.

"Let's not lose our bearings, boys," Mr. Noyes said. "That's enough, Frank."

"We need to check on Mr. Mills," I said. "We need to summon the doctor."

"I imagine he'll be fine," Mr. Noyes said without joining those at the window who peered down into the darkness. "It's only sixteen feet, and with the snow it would have been like landing in feathers."

"He's moving around," Jerome said from the window. "I can hear him."

"Why don't you go play your fiddle, Frank?" Guiteau said again.

When I made to rush him, Ransom stepped in front of me and put his hands on my shoulders. "All right, Frank," he said.

"Mr. Mills will be fine," Mr. Noyes said again, and as if on cue we heard cursing rise from the ground below. "Throw him his shoes and his coat, and then everyone back to bed. Enough excitement for one evening. So unfortunate. So very disappointing." Mr. Noyes leveled his gaze at me and exhaled sadly. "Tomorrow, though, is a new day."

As Mr. Noyes exited the room with the jug still in hand, Guiteau hastily gathered Mr. Mills's coat and shoes and hoisted them out the window. The joy had returned to his face.

"I'll take his blanket down to him and make sure no bones are broken," I said.

"No you won't, Frank. Mr. Noyes said everyone back to bed," Guiteau said, and then he stripped Mr. Mills's blanket from the bed, balled it in his arms, and pushed it over the sill.

"Mills treated you well, Charles," I said. "He shouldn't have."

"Charles?" Ransom broke in. "A word, please?" He made a spectacle of throwing his arm around Guiteau's narrow shoulders and drawing him close. "Weren't those your shoes you just chucked out the window for Mills?" Ransom grinned at his audience, and quiet laughter began to ripple through the room. "I'm afeard you also threw him your coat."

Even though I was the only man in the room besides himself not laughing, Guiteau aimed his scowl at me. "Go play your fiddle, Frank," he said.

# Charles Guiteau Makes His Escape

MOST DAYS THE SMOKE from Barnes Davis's smoke house curls into the air like tight pigtails. But today loose plumes.

Wolf whiffs the air and sneezes. Sewell yells into the shop. All the men come running out.

Two hills slope between the community's property and Barnes Davis's property. Slope enough for children's sleds when there's snow. The first hill slopes shallower for smaller children, and the second hill slopes steeper for older children. Wolf and I trail Sewell and the running men from the shop. As Sewell and the running men from the shop crest the second hill, Wolf and I crest the first. Wolf trails Sewell and the running men from the shop on account of his missing leg. I trail Sewell and the running men from the shop to keep them all in front of me. So I can bear witness.

Sewell turns his head to locate Wolf and me after descending the first hill, and he turns his head to locate us again after descending the second hill. "Go on back, Wolf!" he yells the first time he turns. But Wolf does not heed him. "Well, get on up here then!" he yells the second time he turns, and he stops at Barnes Davis's property line, and Wolf heeds him. Trots to Sewell's outstretched hand. Meets it with his panting muzzle.

Ahead of us, the running men from the shop join Barnes Davis and Barnes Davis's son in regarding the burning smoke house. Their heads swivel anxiously from the smoke house to the adjacent pig pens to the smoke house, but they take no action. They wait. For a sudden cloudburst to quench the fire. For a wind to rise up and extinguish the flames like breath does a candle. For Barnes or Sewell to tell them what to do.

Wolf waits on the men who wait. His ears perked, his tail rigid. His legs triangulated under him like an easel. Like a milking stool. Wolf whiffs the air and sneezes.

Jerome is the first to do something other than wait. Jerome who is always first up in the morning. First finished eating. First in the water when they swim and first out of the water when they are done swimming at Sunset Lake, which Mr. Noyes and others call the turtle pond and I call the carp pond. First to fill his basket with beans. First to snatch the hat off my head and toss it in the snow on the day last winter I wore the hat they kept snatching off my head to toss in the snow.

Jerome rushes the pig pen and unlatches the gate. This leads Barnes Davis's bald head to redden, and he gesticulates and yells curses at Jerome and the escaping swine. Barnes Davis's gesticulating and yelled curses lead Barnes Davis's son to grab Jerome's collar and knock him to his knees in the mud. Now all the men are led to moving, and there is much to bear witness to. I bear witness to those who are led to chase the pigs, and I bear witness to those who are led to pull apart Barnes Davis's son and Jerome, and I bear witness to Wolf, who is led to start in pursuit of a pig before deciding it folly and circling back to the mud, where he is led to clamp onto Jerome's leg like a beaver trap would clamp on. When Jerome shakes free, I bear witness to Wolf clamping onto Barnes Davis's son's leg like a beaver trap would clamp on. I bear witness to Sewell yelling after Wolf and stationing himself between the men in the mud and a charging Barnes Davis. I bear witness to Sewell placing his hands on Barnes Davis's chest to steer him back.

As I bear witness to the men in the mud, I concurrently bear witness to Ransom breaking away from the men in the mud to approach the burning smoke house. Ransom pauses when he gets to the door, turns himself, and enters the burning smoke house backwards. Enters like exiting. I think I am the only one to bear witness to this until I hear Sewell spit Ransom's name like a curse. Like what curses used to sound like before my coming to the community where there are to be no curses but where there are curses just the same. On account of how there are to be no curses in the community, the curses in the community are whispered rather than spat. But Sewell doesn't say Ransom's name like a whispered curse. Sewell says Ransom's name like a spat curse. Like a curse outside the jurisdiction of the community. Barnes Davis's property is outside the jurisdiction. But Mr. Noyes says the community moves with you. *Whither thou goest,* he says. To mean there is no outside the jurisdiction of the community. Sewell's saying Ransom's name like a spat curse says different, though. Says there is an outside.

Sewell removes one hand from Barnes Davis's chest to point to the burning smoke house's loft, where Ransom stands cradling a ham. Flames dance in relief behind Ransom and on either side of him like blown curtains. Like we are bearing witness to him in a window.

Barnes Davis's son rises from the mud, limps to the smoke house, and stations himself under Ransom. Ransom drops the ham, and it bounces off Barnes Davis's son's shoulder onto the ground. Barnes Davis's son grunts when the ham bounces off his shoulder. Grunts like a pig grunts.

The other men are led to fall in line behind Barnes Davis's son to take turns catching or failing to catch hams. Sewell yells instructions for the men to do this, but the men have already been led to do it, are already doing it when Sewell begins to yell instructions for the men to do it. "Get a hammer and help me with this," Sewell will sometimes say to me in the shop as I am already approaching him with a hammer already in my hand and helping him already on my mind.

One by one the men pile their caught or uncaught hams on the grass where the mud stops. Sewell tells me to get in line. Tells me I am not exempt. The ham Ransom drops on me hits me in the eye-bone and in the jaw-bone, shutting my eye and loosening my tooth and filling my mouth with blood. The ham hits me in the eye-bone and in the jaw-bone and shuts my eye and loosens my tooth and fills my mouth with blood because I do not bear witness to the ham's descent until it is too late because Ransom drops the ham before I tell him I am ready.

I leave the ham where it lies in the mud to walk to the grass where the mud stops to sit down. I bear witness to Wolf attacking the ham like it's a raccoon and starting to drag it away, and then I close my eyes because bearing witness hurts and makes my head hot, and then I hear Sewell yell Wolf's name, and I hear Wolf yelp.

The ham that hit me in the eye-bone and in the jaw-bone, shutting my eye and loosening my tooth and filling my mouth with blood, is the final ham. Barnes Davis and Sewell run to fetch a ladder from Barnes Davis's barn for Ransom to use for his descent from the loft, but Ransom makes his descent without the ladder. I bear witness to his descent even though bearing witness hurts and makes my head hot. Ransom jumps from the loft and lands in a crouch in the mud like a cat would land.

My eye-bone aches and my jaw-bone aches and my eye is shut and my tooth is loose and my mouth is full of blood on account of the ham that hit me in the eye-bone and in the jaw-bone, shutting my eye and loosening my tooth and filling my mouth with blood, and Barnes Davis's son's clavicle is broke, either on account of the ham breaking his clavicle or on account of Jerome breaking his clavicle, and Jerome's knee is twisted either on account of Barnes Davis's son twisting his knee or on account of how Jerome had to twist his leg to wrest it free from Wolf, but Ransom, who leapt from the loft of the burning smoke house and landed in a crouch in the mud like how a cat would land, is whole.

After Ransom makes his descent from the loft, landing in a crouch in the mud like a cat would land, Barnes Davis and Sewell leave the ladder they fetched leaning against the loft of the burning smoke house even though Ransom has already made his descent. They leave the ladder they fetched leaning against the loft of the burning smoke house like kindling.

"Handsome Ransom," one woman said to another woman after supper one night. I bore witness to her saying this. I bore witness to her whispering it, but not like a curse is whispered in the jurisdiction of the community. And I bore witness to these two women whispering "Handsome Ransom" to a third woman. And I bore witness to the third woman whispering back to the two women who had whispered to her, "Handsome Ransom, indeed." And I bore witness when Ransom and I were bedmates. I bore witness to how he would come to bed late. To how he would come to bed late smelling of women and their whispers.

Handsome Ransom Indeed. Like three names.

When Ransom lands in a crouch in the mud like a cat would land, Wolf darts towards him to circle and bark. Sewell calls to Wolf, but Wolf does not heed him, and Ransom does not heed Wolf. Does not even make to shoo him away. As far as Ransom is concerned, Wolf is not barking at and circling him. On account of Sewell, as far as Ransom is concerned, Wolf is not barking at and circling him. On account of how Ransom does not want to be condemned by Sewell, as far as Ransom is concerned, Wolf is not barking at and circling him. I bear witness to this. To how Ransom does not want to do anything that might condemn him in Sewell's eyes more than he is already condemned in Sewell's eyes. Sewell calls to Wolf again, but Wolf does not heed him.

"Hey, Wolf!" I say from where I sit in the grass where the mud stops, and Wolf's ears perk, and he comes to me to where I sit in the grass where the mud stops. Trots to my outstretched hand. Meets it with his panting muzzle.

"Your dog's down a leg," Barnes Davis says to Sewell. "Unless I'm miscounting."

"Don't call my dog," Sewell says to me. "Don't call my dog when I'm calling my dog. You don't call my dog. Not when I'm calling him you don't. From here on out, you leave Wolf alone." He whispers this to me like a curse in the jurisdiction of the community. With his eyes in the mud he whispers this to me.

"How?" Barnes Davis says to Sewell. "What took it?"

I start back to the shop before the other men, who linger to bear witness to the smoke house's burning. I do not feel led to bear witness to the smoke house's burning as I have already borne witness to its burning. Through fore-knowledge I was fore-led to fore-witness its burning. So I do not feel re-led to re-bear witness to its re-burning.

When I pass the pile of hams, I bear witness to a piglet rustling there. Rooting through the warm meat. I shoo it, but it does not shoo until I kick it in its flank, and then it shoos.

On my way back to the shop, I encounter a legion of pigs dragging their snouts through the grass. I aspire to kick them all in their flanks, but the pigs do not allow me to get close enough to kick them in their flanks. Some of the pigs I aspire to kick in the flank make for the woods. Some of the pigs I aspire to kick in the flank double back towards the burning smoke house. One of the pigs I aspire to kick in the flank is scooped up by and then wrests its way out of Mr. Noyes's arms.

Mr. Noyes and the piglet he is carrying and then not carrying crest the steep sloping hill as I crest the shallow sloping hill. Mr. Noyes and I meet in the space between the steep sloping hill and the shallow sloping hill, which is itself a hint of a hill in that it inclines and declines but does not incline or decline enough to be regarded as a full-fledged hill. If there were snow, no children could sled on it. Not even the youngest and smallest of children could sled on it.

*Is Victor there with the other men, Charles? Have you seen Victor?* When the piglet wrested itself from Mr. Noyes's arms, it landed on its back unlike how a cat would land, rolled over onto its feet, and made for the woods. It ran straight but with its haunches drifting sideways like a crooked wagon. Like how a dog runs straight but with its haunches drifting sideways like a crooked wagon.

Barnes Davis's smoke house is burning.

*Yes, Charles. I see. Is everyone safe? Have you seen Victor? Is he there?* More or less.

*Everyone is more or less safe? You have more or less seen Victor? Victor is more or less there?*

The ladder Barnes Davis and Sewell fetched for Ransom to make his descent from the loft even though he did not need it to make his descent from the loft is now leaning against the burning smoke house like kindling.

*Why is your face swelled, Charles? Why is your eye closed? Why is your mouth bubbling blood?*

I don't answer Mr. Noyes except to spit blood into the grass like a curse outside the jurisdiction of the community.

*Did someone strike you, Charles? Who struck you? Did Jerome strike you? Did Sewell strike you?*

Ransom dropped the ham before I said I was ready for him to drop the ham, and the ham hit me in the eye-bone and in the jaw-bone, shutting my eye and loosening my tooth and filling my mouth with blood. I do not know where Vic is.

*Well, go clean yourself up and then get two rags and dip them in cold water from the creek and put one of the cool rags on your eye and the other cool rag in your mouth and bite down on it and lie down and rest. If you see Victor, tell him I seek him. Send him this way.*

Mr. Noyes continues towards the fire, and I continue towards the shop. I turn to watch Mr. Noyes crest the second hill as I crest the first hill just as Mr. Noyes turns to watch me crest the first hill as he crests the second hill.

I do not feel led to go clean myself up and get two rags and dip them in cold water from the creek and put one of the cool rags on my eye and the other cool rag in my mouth and bite down on it and lie down and rest. Rather, I feel led to retire to my room and pack my bag and a second bag and wait until dark, until everyone else is lying down in their beds, to make my departure from the community with my bag and the second bag.

When I pass Victor exiting the mansion house as I am entering the mansion house, he is his father's echo. *Who struck you, Charles? Did Jerome strike you? Did Sewell strike you?*

Your father seeks you.

*I know he seeks me, but you're not telling me he seeks me because you're not seeing me. If he asks later, you didn't see me, so you didn't tell me he seeks me. How could you have told me he seeks me if you didn't see me?*

When I make my departure late that night, the moon is full, but clouds occlude it. I leave the jurisdiction of the community by cresting and descending the two hills between the community and Barnes Davis's property, and then I leave the jurisdiction of Barnes Davis's property by reaching the road beyond Barnes Davis's property. The stink of Barnes Davis's smoldering smoke house follows me on the road. Follows me into and out of jurisdiction after jurisdiction. Follows me for hours. For miles. For years. Follows me whither I goest.

# John Humphrey Noyes Picks Strawberries

MY BROTHER GEORGE and I picked strawberries into one basket on a warm June afternoon in Oneida.

"It was not that your questions made me scared of ghosts, exactly," George told me. "It was not only that. More specifically, they made me worry I was a ghost. Your asking, 'Which George are you, George? The living George or the dead George?' made me fear that the living I thought I had been doing had not been living at all, but haunting. Haunting not only you and the rest of our family but somehow also haunting myself. A specter I would never be able to vanquish."

"You've carried this with you forty years without sharing it with me," I said.

"Your question has stalked me through boyhood and into manhood and, to be truthful, is never far from my mind. Even now, I imagine it will be the final thought I have in this life," he said. "I have had many dreams in which I am asked this question by different individuals in different scenarios, and, as of yet, I have not known how to answer. In some dreams, I direct the question back at the questioners, but they never know the answer, either."

I stood from my crouch and pulled my brother up with me. I did not let go of him as I spoke. "I am grieved by this revelation, Brother," I said. "I understand why the words I spoke would upset you and linger with you. I am very sorry. It pains me that the most important experience of my life, the event of my salvation and calling, proved to be, for you, a source of life-long fear and unease."

We both wore wide-brimmed straw hats even though the sky was overcast, and when I took mine off to wipe the sweat from my forehead,

George did the same. When he reached into the basket for a strawberry and tossed it into his mouth, I bent to pick and eat a half-green berry from the bush.

"Do not be sorry, John," he said. "I have not told you this after all these years to solicit an apology. Rather, I am hoping you can offer me some answers."

As we spoke, Helen, George's wife, came into view, and the two of us watched her lead a pony around the circumference of the field. Atop the animal was a young girl, Emma, who was new to the community. She and her parents had been with us for only a few months, but I could tell already they probably would not last. Emma's parents were quiet and tended to cling too exclusively to each other and to their daughter. It was a shame. Emma, especially, would have been a wonderful addition to the family. She was tall for her age, long-limbed and strong, bright and quick, and she had a wide mouth and full lips the color of the ripest strawberries in our basket. Everyone in the community had adored her at first sight. Helen, especially, had taken a liking to the girl. She and my brother had lost a child the year before. Under normal circumstances I might have stepped in to advise Helen to be on guard against besiegement by the mother spirit, but in this case, I let it go. In part because Helen and George would be returning soon to Wallingford, in part because I know she had been injured, as I had, in learning that Tirzah would soon be giving birth to George's child, and in part because I empathized with Helen's adoration of Emma. Being around lively, healthy young boys always made me thankful and proud, but being in the presence of young girls of Emma's quality made me feel as if I were being afforded more than just a glimpse of the divine.

"Truthfully, I do not know why I told you all this now, John," George said. "Nor, conversely, do I know why I kept it from you all these years. In any case, I feel foolish on both accounts. I wish I could put the words back in my mouth, but if I were able to do so, I suspect I would immediately want to say them again."

Over my brother's shoulder, I caught a glimpse of two acrobatic finches, jealous of our berry harvest, chasing each other towards the creek. "I would be negligent if I didn't once again remind you, George, that you are to keep no more secrets from me. What you and Tirzah allowed to happen without seeking my approval is gravely distressing. If it weren't you and Tirzah, if it were any other members of the community, I might have been forced to expel you from fellowship. I know the matter of which we are now speaking is of a different nature, but it is still something you have kept from me that you should not have kept from me."

"I know," George said. "I am sorry."

"I know you are sorry, George," I said. "As I am sorry that I evidently scarred you with my words, albeit unintentionally, all those years ago. I'm glad you have finally told me so that I can be sorry. I hope now that you have spoken of the matter with me you will cease from worrying over it anymore." I plucked and ate another berry. "Let's talk of more pleasant matters now, shall we?"

"Just one more thing if you would indulge me," George said. "I want to know about the fox. When you asked me which George I was, you referred to a fox. Killing a fox. Tell me this one thing, John, and then we can let the matter drop. What were you referring to? And the first George, my brother George, what was he like?"

"That is two things!" I said, and I waited until my brother reluctantly returned my smile to continue. "George, this is the George you are," I said, and I took a step back and gestured towards him with both hands, like I were showing him off to someone, as if he were a painting or a new piece of furniture. "You are the kind, decent, dependable, selfless, sensitive George. You are the George who has won my confidence to head the community at Wallingford."

"And in installing me at Wallingford, you can rest assured I will not come into contact with Tirzah or the baby," George said. He folded his hands and rested them under his nose. "I apologize for saying that," he said.

"Apologies are in the air today, aren't they?" I said. "You must trust me, George. You must trust my judgment. If you will not trust me, who will trust me? I need you to trust me. I need you to trust me more than I need anyone to trust me."

"I trust you," he said.

"I trust that you trust me," I said, and I put my hand on his cheek.

"I still want you to tell me about the first George, though," he said. "Please, John? Who was he? It always seemed to me that Father, Mother, you, and our siblings were careful not to remember him around me. I am not a child now."

"Did we do that?" I said. "If so, it was out of love. No one in our family, not even Mother, was loved more deeply than you. Still, we should not have made you feel like we were keeping secrets from you. Again, I am sorry."

"I know I was loved," George said. "But being loved is not all there is."

"Here is what I can tell you," I said. "Our brother George was ten when he passed. I was twelve. He was a wonderful companion despite the fact he always hated being my younger brother, and this resentment made him daring and mischievous. He was cleverer than I by half and could run like a deer, and in the summer his skin turned brown as a nut as if he were part Indian. He was mesmerized by frogs and turtles and preferred swamp and pond over field and wood.

"I remember whole stretches of days during which we would fish from dawn until dusk. I also remember we shared a bed for a while, which I complained about because George would often urinate in his sleep. Mother thought perhaps there was some medical reason for this—the local quack advised she give him Milk Thistle tea, add a pinch of salt to his mug of milk at supper, and allow him to fall asleep only on his side—but to this day, I think he was simply too lazy to get up to use the outhouse.

"When he got so ill at the end, I remember being jealous because Mother would whisper to him words I could not hear, and she would stroke his hair and hold him all night even though she was pregnant with you at the time. In this way, I was jealous of you, too, because even before you took your first breath, you also were in a sense held by her all night, and because you were able, in how you were a part of Mother, to hold George all night. I just now remembered this as I was saying it. What a thing. To be simultaneously jealous of a dying boy and a boy who had not yet been born. What a foolish, selfish youth I was.

"Let's see, what else? I do have a memory of you and George being in the same room. The whole family was circled around George's bed, joined in prayer. Mother was holding you. One of our sisters wanted to hold you—they always wanted to carry you around, even after you had grown to be as big as them—but on this occasion Mother told her no. I have not thought about that scene in years. Thank you, George, for affording me the opportunity to revisit this memory. Despite the sad occasion, I am persuaded our family was never more together than we were in that moment. I am going to study the memory later tonight and pray I might dream about it."

"I would like to have that dream, too," George said. "Pray that I will dream it, too, will you?"

"I will," I said.

"When I pray myself, I am not always sure I am doing it correctly," George said. "The folks at Wallingford look to me as their leader, like I am an extension of you and, in turn, an extension of God and his will, but I cannot even pray with confidence. I know your thoughts on praying aloud, how it is often melodramatic and extraneous, but you do it so well, so effortlessly. It affords others insight into your spirit."

"Your concern is not uncommon," I said. "Many godly people find themselves uncomfortable communicating with God through language. But, George, what we all need to understand and remember is that we pray constantly, without ceasing. We are perpetually addressing God. We are perpetually in his presence. Your whole life is a prayer. When you move your body, you are praying. When you have a thought, when you tell a joke, when you weep, when you speak crossly, when you make love. When we engage in mutual criticism, we are praying. I need to remind everyone of this, and I will at our next meeting. Do you follow what I am saying, Brother? Now, here together amongst the strawberries as we remember and share and confess and forgive, we are sending up prayers. God is present here. He is an active conversant in our dialogue."

"You are delivering a homily, Mr. Noyes!" George said and chuckled. "Here in the strawberry patch! We have not even had lunch yet, and you are already bent on edification and instruction!"

"Always!" I said, and I laughed at his laughter.

"Father was never much for prayer, was he?" George said.

"You are right. Not traditional prayer, anyway. Shortly after George took ill, though, Mother told me that Father asked God to make him sick in place of his son. When she told me this, she seemed both immensely proud and profoundly disturbed. She wept. As you might imagine, she wept a lot in that period around George's death. When you fussed and she rocked and nursed you, I think you were comforting her just as much as she was comforting you. Even then and there, George, as a babe with your mother, you were praying. Each coo, each suck a supplication."

"I think Father was like me—I should say, I am like Father—in how I do not understand the ways of God," my brother said. "If it were not for you, John, I do not know where I would be in terms of the state of my soul." George brought his hand to his mouth and smoothed his beard. "As for what you just said about Mother, it saddens me that I was born into so much sadness."

"You and Father are not alone in believing you do not understand God," I said. "Even I am still rarely satisfied that I hear and understand everything I should in the way I should. Augustine writes, 'When you believe you are understanding God, it is not God you are understanding.' That is a rough paraphrase, anyway. And as for having been born into sadness, Brother, I have to ask you, who among us has avoided that curse?"

"Perhaps little Emma," he said, and I again followed his eyes back to the girl, who, with Helen's help, dismounted from the pony and ran towards the nursery. "Perhaps Tirzah's child. I hope Tirzah's child. I will pray that for him or her."

"As will I," I said.

A few months after our conversation in the strawberry patch, I received word from Wallingford that George had passed. Only a week earlier the doctor had told Helen the malaria was relenting, so I had put off my trip to see him. When I got the news, I was distraught not only by George's death, but by the fact that I wasn't there to comfort him at the end. It is never a perfect endeavor to put your trust in men, even in learned men like ministers, professors, presidents, generals, and doctors. I have been reminded of this truth in one way or another most every day of my life.

After George passed, Helen left Wallingford, but not to return to Oneida. Neither I nor anyone else in the community ever heard from her again. It was around this time that my prediction came true about Emma and her parents, who also left the community. They told us they were taking leave to tend to a sick relative in Massachusetts, but they did not mention a return date, and they never came back. This collection of losses deeply grieved me and the rest of the community for a time. It was one of the darkest seasons we had to endure.

Adding to my sorrow was a rumor Tirzah shared with me. She told me she had heard that on Helen's way out of Wallingford, the woman had leveled some vile accusations against me. She accused me of wanting to bring her back to Oneida so I could have her for myself. As a stroke of revenge for what had transpired between George and Tirzah. This was not true. Helen and I had only the one interview, and I did not find it to be an especially worthwhile experience. We were not compatible. This happens. Sometimes the requisite magnetism is not present for the coupling to be anything more than polite fellowship. Her misdirected thinking about my desire for her was especially bothersome, though, because it suggested to

186

me I might have made an error in judgment in encouraging her and my brother to produce a child. I thought they complemented one another in compelling ways and that their offspring would prove to be exceptional. Had I known Helen's true nature, I would have not made this request, and we all might have been spared the pain of the resulting stillbirth.

Of course, if Helen truly said the things about me that Tirzah heard and reported, it is possible the new widow was speaking under the influence of grief, which, if left unchecked, can turn easily to bitterness. Knowing this, I was persuaded to afford her grace and forgiveness even though she never asked it from me. For the sake of my dear brother George, and my second dear brother George, and Tirzah's dear son George I was.

# Chet Randolph Takes in a Ball Game

I KNOW THE FIELD is called a diamond because of its shape, but it's beautiful like a diamond, too, especially at the beginning of the game when the bright, freshly raked grass is brought alive by the players running on in their smart-looking uniforms. People talk about the spectacle of horse races, and they're right to do so—I once took the train to Saratoga and had a grand time—but baseball is better, I think. A horse race requires your undivided attention—it won't let you see anything else—and then it's over. Too quick if you ask me. With baseball and all its pauses, starts, and stops, you can watch the game with one eye and keep your other eye on the world. You almost have to keep your other eye on the world, considering some of the characters in the grandstand with you.

The minister of the church I've been attending here in Hoboken says folks are better off staying away from baseball. Given my experience at the last game I attended, one might think I'd be apt to agree with him, but the trouble I found there doesn't seem to me like it was the game's fault. The fellow I tangled with, I could have met him at the train station or at the market and he would have been just as objectionable and ornery. I got that feeling from him, like wherever he went he was looking for trouble.

My minister says it's not only the unsavory characters baseball attracts, though. He's suspicious of the ballpark itself. Elysian Fields. He says the name is un-Christian in that it refers to a place pagans believed in, a heaven for heroes. I thought it was a pretty name for a place before I learned where the name came from, and, to be honest, despite my minister's misgivings, I think I like the name even more now. I can see why the pagans wanted to believe in such a place. Dead heroes or not, I like thinking of heaven as a big field rather than a place filled with mansions and golden streets. Maybe just because where I'm from and what I knew growing up. I don't know what Greece looks like, but in Pennsylvania, I was always surrounded by farms and meadows and sloping hills and quiet woods. I've been here in the city for close to a year now, and thinking of these kinds of places I used to know upsets me sometimes. When I took the train up to Saratoga and we were rolling through the countryside, I had to stop looking out the window because my stomach began to ache.

We never played baseball in Pennsylvania. Not in my town, anyhow. Not in a full-fledged way. We'd sometimes throw rocks to each other and try to hit them as far as we could with sticks, but there weren't any bases to run around, and no one went to any trouble to chase after the rock after it was hit. Plenty where that one came from. The idea that you would get a whole crew of folks together, split them into teams, and find matching clothes and caps to wear never crossed our minds. In the city people are better imaginers than they are where I'm from. Is it maybe that folks where I'm from are too easily satisfied? It was pleasurable enough hitting rocks with sticks, so we didn't think to go any further?

I have to say, it makes me feel a little stupid now looking back at it. Simple-minded me swinging a dumb stick at a dumb rock when dapper men with sharp uniforms and impressive mustaches were playing real baseball in a place named after a heaven for ancient heroes. Makes me feel a little embarrassed to be from where I'm from, and then it gets complicated and confusing because that embarrassment makes me embarrassed. Baseball isn't the only thing that's made me feel this way since coming to Hoboken. I like living in the city, but on occasion it makes me feel bad about myself in a way I never felt in Pennsylvania. It makes me feel like I should try to hide parts of myself that I previously thought were good parts.

Sometimes I go to the baseball games with Lloyd, a friend of mine I guess you could say, whom I met at the boarding house, but this last Saturday Lloyd wasn't feeling well on account of having just found out that his best girl from back home was getting married to his cousin. He'd just received the letter from her and needed some time to be alone to wallow in his sorrow, so I ventured to the ballpark on my own. Lloyd's from Illinois. I suppose I'd do well to watch out for girls from there.

At the beginning of the game, the chap seated next to me seemed easygoing enough. He was plenty hungry and thirsty for sure. Before the first inning was over, he'd already eaten three sausage sandwiches, and he was taking regular pulls from the flask in his pocket. So I thought I'd strike up a conversation. He was sitting in the seat Lloyd would've been sitting in, and I was feeling neighborly. I didn't have anything important to say. I just wanted some friendly give and take. When I left Pennsylvania, Pop told me I needed to learn to keep to myself and not bother everyone with the first thing that enters my head. He told me folks I'd come across in Hoboken wouldn't be as patient with me as folks back home and that I needed to learn that people have their own lives to live and don't wish to be bothered with the details of me living mine. Pop is wise about a lot of things, but I disagree with him about this. Pop and me, we see some things differently for sure, which is one reason I decided to leave home and see how life might be lived elsewhere. It's my opinion Pop might cheer up some if he talked with a few more folks on a regular basis. The older he gets, the more sour he gets. Saddens me to think about him growing old like this, whether I'm there in person to watch it happen or not.

So I said to the man next to me, "Are you a supporter of the Mutuals or the Metropolitans?" I asked him twice because the first time he didn't answer me. He just stared at me blankly, which gave me the impression he hadn't heard and needed me to repeat myself. The second time he answered by asking me which side I was aligned with.

"The Mutuals, I suppose," I said. I liked the way their pitcher kicked his leg when he threw, and I thought the Metropolitans' uniforms were a bit drab in comparison. I didn't offer him this explanation, though. I didn't know how most folks chose which teams to support. Considering how passionate some of them were, though, I thought the reasons must be more significant than the ones I had come up with.

"Well, I support the Metropolitans!" he said, jutting out his chin. His face put me in mind of an axe-head. "It would seem we're rivals!"

Despite the sausages and whatever was in his flask, his breath smelled sweet, like new hay. "Well, all right then, friend!" I said. "Good luck to you and your side, but not too much luck!"

"Care to put a wager down?" he asked. He lowered his voice in saying this and looked behind him and to either side as if to identify eavesdroppers.

"Oh, no," I said. "That's not me. My minister wouldn't like that." I said this smiling. I know I did.

"Art thou holy?" he asked. "Holier than I?" Whereas before he had seemed to want to keep our conversation private, he now projected his voice and gestured at me in such a way as if to invite the attention of those around us.

"Not me," I said. "I'm far from holy."

"I should say so!" he said. "About two hundred miles away, give or take!"

"I don't know how you mean," I said.

"No, you don't," he said. "And you won't, either. You are not meant to. You have not been chosen."

"I suppose I've been Methodist most of my life," I said, "and since I came to Hoboken, I've been going to a Congregationalist service. Just to see."

The fellow threw back his head and forced a laugh. He meant it hurtful. To mock me. "You might as well stay in bed Sunday mornings," he said. "You might as well stay in bed and roll over on top of your fat, ugly wife."

"I'm not married, mister," I said. "If I were, though, I sure wouldn't appreciate you describing my wife using that vocabulary." I could feel the heat rush into my cheeks, and I felt that familiar surge. Back home in Pennsylvania, I liked to fight when I was a boy, and I was always pretty good at it.

"You have nothing over me on that score!" the fellow said. "I'm not married, either!" He grabbed a handful of his own scraggly, billy goat beard and gave it a yank as if trying to get his own attention.

"You don't say," I said. "Well, friend, I can't say I'm surprised." I heard a few titters over my shoulder, and when I turned, the two couples seated there smiled at me.

"You two are a couple of fortunate chaps," the older of the two men said to my neighbor and me. "Don't get caught up in the marriage game. It's a deal with the devil." The woman sitting next to him laughed and poked the man playfully in his round stomach, and he doubled over in feigned pain.

"That's what I've been trying to tell my friend here," the queer fellow sitting next to me said. "Mr. Holier-Than-Thou here."

"That's not at all what you were telling me," I said. "You were telling me not to go to church, and you were insulting the wife you didn't know I didn't have." I don't know why what the rascal said got me so worked up, but I was having trouble shaking it off. "I suppose if you would apologize, mister, we could put this conversation behind us and take in the game."

I had barely finished speaking before he swooped in with his long, wiry arm and swiped my hat off my head. When I reached to get it back, he stood, dodged me, dropped my hat on his seat, and sat on it.

Next thing I know I had one hand wrapped around the man's chicken neck, and I was rearing back with the other to give him a couple proper ones in the nose when I felt something whistle past my ear. I hadn't swung my arm, but my intended target had already crumpled in pain, and when I let go of him, he had blood streaming out of a gash over his left eyebrow. The portly man behind us scurried out of his seat into the aisle and picked up the baseball that had evidently collided with my neighbor's eye-bone.

I felt some guilt watching the wounded man exit Elysian Fields. Holding both hands over his bloody eye, he looked unsteady as he shuffled out of the bleachers. I'm not sure what was affecting him the most, the contents of his flask or the baseball in the noggin, but watching him stumble off, it didn't seem likely he was going to make it to wherever he was headed without some difficulty. The folks behind me, though, didn't share my concern. The portly man and his pal both reached down to shake my hand as if I'd achieved something, and even the two women smiled at me. Appreciative for the excitement, I suppose. In any case, I lasted only a couple more innings before I slunk off myself. The empty seat next to me and the happy chatter between the couples behind me were making me lonely, and I figured I'd head back to the boarding house and swing by Lloyd's room to see if he might be ready for company.

I still have the baseball. The portly man presented it to me, and when the usher came looking for it, the portly man fibbed, claimed he'd seen my bloodied neighbor tuck it in his jacket as he left. No one sitting around us, myself included, spoke up for the sake of the truth, and when the usher left, the portly man nudged me and winked like we'd schemed the whole thing, like it had turned out just as we'd planned.

I don't know. Does anything turn out like that?

I keep the ball in my suitcase. I figure next time I go home to Pennsylvania for a visit I'll give it to one of my little cousins. He and his chums can knock it around in lieu of rocks. Maybe start to get a better idea than I had at his age of what the real world is like.

# Charles Guiteau Does Time

THE OFFICERS WERE OUT of their jurisdiction.

The Shunamite woman prepared a room for Elisha and his servant Gehazi. And Elisha and his servant Gehazi did not pay rent to the Shunamite woman. For Elisha and his servant Gehazi to pay rent to the Shunamite woman would have been an abomination in the sense that for them to pay rent to the Shunamite woman would have been to undermine her graciousness and thereby cancel her blessing.

I said this to Mrs. O'Bryan through the door. I had opened it a crack to allow for just enough room for my one eye to see and to be seen and for my words to be spoken and to be heard. "Chicago is Shunem. You are the Shunamite woman. Annie is Gehazi. I am Elisha. To forgive the rent would be your graciousness. For me to pay the rent would be an abomination."

Mrs. O'Bryan walked away from the door rather than make an answer, which I interpreted to mean she had acquiesced or was considering acquiescing. But I misinterpreted. Rather than acquiesce or consider acquiescing, she summoned two wiry police officers to remove me bodily.

"You shall not be blessed with a child in your old age," I said to Mrs. O'Bryan as I was being removed bodily down the hall toward the stairs by the two wiry officers. When the two wiry officers had knocked, I had opened the door a crack to allow just enough room for my one eye to see and to be seen and for my words to be spoken and to be heard, but the two wiry officers' fingers pried the crack wider to make just enough room for their arms to reach in and then wider for me to be removed bodily.

"Unlike the Shunamite woman, your womb will remain barren," I said.

"You the one who bashed him in the side of the head?" the wirier of the two wiry officers, who led me by my sleeve and the back of my collar, respectively, asked Mrs. O'Bryan. "There's a mess of dried blood in his hair."

"I've had seven children already, you imbecile," she said, and the two wiry officers snorted like pigs snort. "Please, Mr. Guiteau," she said, "bless me, please, with the curse of barrenness, you hornswoggler. Please, where were you ten years ago, you nincompoop?"

"Ten years ago I was preparing my flock, who did not understand they were my flock and did not understand they were being prepared," I said.

"You're a loon," Mrs. O'Bryan said. "You're a muttonhead."

"Should one of your children expire, I shall not stretch my body over him and breathe into him new life," I said.

The two wiry officers, who led me by my sleeve and the back of my collar, respectively, took the stairs in such a way that simultaneously pulled me and pushed me. "Do not threaten the lady's children," the wirier of the two wiry officers said. "It's one thing to be a deadbeat drunk. It's wholly another thing to bring harm to a child."

"I'd rather my child stay dead than have the likes of you touch him, you derelict," Mrs. O'Bryan said. She leaned over the banister to say this so that I was able to catch a glimpse of Annie behind her.

"So it shall be, Mrs. O'Bryan," I said. "Everyone in your family who dies from this point forward will stay dead. You had your opportunity to turn your heart to the right, and you have mismanaged it."

"I hear men in jail often get their throats slit when they sleep," Mrs. O'Bryan said. "Have you heard that, Mr. Guiteau?"

I missed the last step so that my foot landed heavily on the foot of the less wiry of the two wiry officers, who led me by my sleeve and the back of my collar, respectively, and in response the less wiry of the two wiry officers sunk an elbow into my ribcage. "Here's one for your trouble, you oaf," he said. "Watch your step now unless you're looking for one in the nose."

"How do you suppose throwing me in jail will get you your rent, Mrs. O'Bryan?" I called up the stairs after regathering my wind. "Additionally, don't you think these good officers have better things to do than busy themselves with a simple misunderstanding involving a few dollars?"

"Not at all," answered the less wiry of the two wiry officers.

"The job is the job," added the wirier of the two wiry officers.

"I know I'll probably never get another nickel from you, you ne'er-do-well," Mrs. O'Bryan said. "At least this way, though, I get some satisfaction." She turned her head then and noticed Annie. When Mrs. O'Bryan addressed me again, I noted how Annie's presence had softened her voice like how darkness or snow or an empty room or a passing train or a ship ribboning out from shore or a flock of geese descending on a pond will soften a voice.

"I don't suppose anyone will be the worse off if you disappear for a while, Mr. Guiteau. Your wife included. If I were her, God help me, I'd fill my apron with rocks and walk into Lake Michigan. Alternatively, I would take this window of opportunity to make a run for it, return to my people if I had any, initiate divorce proceedings, and reflect on the missteps, mis-decisions, and misjudgments that have led me to such a sorry circumstance as to have you as a husband."

"Annie is the woman you are not," I answered Mrs. O'Bryan. "She knows her place is with me as I know mine is with her. What God has rightfully joined, let no iniquitous demoness put asunder."

"You some kind of a preacher?" asked the wirier of the two wiry officers, who led me by my sleeve and the back of my collar, respectively.

"I think I know what kind," answered the less wiry of the two wiry officers, and the two wiry officers snorted like pigs snort.

"If it wouldn't be too much to ask, I'd greatly appreciate a couple hours to gather my things and get my bearings," Annie said to Mrs. O'Bryan. At the top of the banister where it started, Annie's voice was a whisper, but in its descent it gained volume so that when it reached me at the bottom of the stairs where I lingered in the hands of the two wiry officers, who led me by my sleeve and the back of my collar, respectively, it rang in my ears like a gunshot. "I'll be gone before supper," Annie said.

"Take until tomorrow morning if necessary, dear. I can't imagine what such a man as this must've put you through." Mrs. O'Bryan patted Annie's hand. "Well, I can imagine a little. I'm no busybody, but these walls are thin."

As the two wiry officers, who led me by my sleeve and the back of my collar, respectively, continued to remove me bodily, I kept my head turned over my shoulder for as long as I could, determined not to miss the opportunity should it present itself to meet Annie's eyes, but the opportunity did not present itself insofar as Annie decided to turn and disappear down the dark hall towards our room rather than present me the opportunity to meet her eyes.

In the wagon on the way to the jail, I questioned the quality of the two wiry officers' horse, and in response the two wiry officers sunk their respective elbows into my ribcage.

"I am thirsty," I said after regathering my wind.

"You don't smell thirsty," the wirier of the two wiry officers said. "You smell like you've had quite enough to drink. You smell like you shouldn't be thirsty again for a good while."

"You can have some water when we get you to the jail," the less wiry of the two wiry officers said. "Then you can settle in and sober up."

"There were two thieves," I said. "One mocked Him and one treated Him with kindness and reverence. Care to guess which of the two He remembered in glory?"

"What is he babbling about?" the wirier officer asked the less wiry officer.

"Christ on the cross," the less wiry of the two wiry officers answered. "Sorry to tell you that you're off to hell, while I'm bound for heaven."

"Hell, huh?" the wirier of the two wiry officers answered, and then he sunk his elbow into my ribcage. "If it's already decided, I guess I might as well get my licks in."

"You make a good point," the less wiry of the two wiry officers said, and then he sunk his elbow into my ribcage. "If the die has already been cast."

In the cell where I was deposited there resided three other men: one large man, one middle-sized man, and one man who appeared not much more than a boy. The large man strode over to me and sat down on the bench beside me. "Why are you wincing and writhing, sir?" he said.

"My ribcage," I said. "My escorts took turns assaulting me with their elbows."

"They'll do that," the large man said, nodding in commiseration. "Like this, right?" he said, and then he sunk his elbow into my ribcage. Whereas the elbows delivered by the two wiry officers took my wind and produced a warm pain that gradually relented, the large man's elbow produced a cold, sharp pain that gradually increased in intensity.

"You hear that crack?" The large man snickered at the middle-sized man and the man who appeared not much more than a boy. "This bloke's rib broke."

"What'd you go and do that for?" the middle-sized man said. When he stood, the cap he had tucked in his waistband fell out so that he had to re-tuck the cap in his waistband. "Geezum, Neil."

"Geezum, Neil." The man who appeared not much more than a boy parroted the middle-sized man.

"I didn't aim to break it," the large man said. "I was just being rambunctious. I didn't even hit him hard. I sure could've hit him harder. Someone bashed him in the head. His hair's a mess of dried blood on this side. That wasn't me."

"Geezum, Neil," the man who appeared not much more than a boy said again.

"Clam up, Jerry," the large man said, and then he addressed the middle-sized man. "I didn't do it purposefully, Reuben," he said. "What would I ever want to break this bloke's rib purposefully for?"

"Geezum, Neil," the middle-sized man said again.

"Oh, geezum," the large man said. "I was just being rambunctious. I apologize, friend," the large man said to me. "I was just being rambunctious. I didn't even hit you hard. I sure could've hit you harder."

The middle-sized man walked over to the bench, tapped the large man, waved him up, and sat down. "A busted rib is a painful encumbrance," the middle-sized man said to me. "And dangerous. Our ribs are there for a reason. They're meant to protect all the soft, essential parts we carry in our middles."

"Our kidneys and pancreases and livers," the man who appeared not much more than a boy said.

"What do you know, Jerry?" the large man said. "You don't know."

"It hurts to breathe," I said.

"You have to breathe, though," the middle-sized man said. He leaned into the space between us. "Concentrate on taking short, shallow breaths as opposed to long, deep breaths. And whatever you do, don't cough or sneeze."

"I feel like I have to do both," I said.

"That's your mind telling you that," the middle-sized man said. "I just told you not to, so your mind is telling you that you have to. That's how minds work. Tell your mind to mind its own business."

"Sneezing is involuntary," I said. "I think coughing might be, too."

"We'll have to agree to disagree on that score," the middle-sized man said.

"I didn't even get him hard," the large man said. "I sure could've hit him harder." His back was to us as he leaned into the far corner of the cell where he made use of the chamber pot as he rested his forehead against the clammy wall. "Probably the cops beating on him brittled up his rib so all it took to bust it was a tap. I didn't even hit him hard."

"My body was made to be broken," I said.

"How's that, friend?" the middle-sized man asked.

"I have been overcome by bees and have tumbled from the mow of a burning barn and had my leg snapped in a bear trap and been brained by a ham and dented by a baseball and unjustly defenestrated in the middle of the night by thugs."

"Hell," the man who appeared not much more than a boy said, "our father shot off his own finger once, and when we were kids, Neil hit me in the back of the head with a shovel and I didn't wake up for almost a whole day."

"You three are brothers," I said.

"It probably wasn't so much how hard I hit him because I didn't hit him hard at all as much as it was I hit him in just the right spot," the large man said.

"Your brother with the shovel or me with your elbow?" I said.

"Yes, we are brothers," the middle-sized man said. "To this point we have been, anyhow. Although lately I've been considering ending the relationship."

"That's a joke he makes," the man who appeared not much more than a boy said. "Making like one can get rid of a brother like a sweetheart or a wife."

"What God has rightfully joined, let no man put asunder," I said.

"You have one?" the middle-sized man asked.

"A brother or wife?" I asked.

"Either. How about wife."

"Annie," I said. "I do."

"None of us has a wife," the man who appeared not much more than a boy said. "None of us even has a sweetheart."

"We've dodged that bullet," the large man said, turning away from the wall to face us. "Reuben came closest, but he wised up just in the nick of time."

When I stood, the pain in my ribcage flared so that I could speak only in a whisper. "I need to use the chamber pot if you wouldn't mind making way, please," I said.

"Sure thing," the large man said. He took two steps to the side and watched me undo my drawers and relieve myself.

"Give him some breathing room," the man who appeared not much more than a boy said. "Geezum, Neil."

"He's pissing blood," the large man said as he watched me. "I didn't even hit him that hard. I sure could've hit him harder."

"Our ribs are there for a reason," the middle-sized man said.

I tried to stop myself from pissing blood, but stopping burned more than pissing, which also burned but not as much as stopping. When I returned to the bench and sat, I coughed, and the cough turned into a sneeze, which turned into another sneeze, which turned into another cough, which made me have to return to the chamber pot not to piss blood again but to spit blood, after which I returned to the bench where I again coughed and sneezed.

"You have come full circle," the middle-sized man said and clapped me on the shoulder. "I'm sorry you're feeling so poorly, but your suffering might prove fruitful. Sometimes the powers-that-be will turn you loose if you're sickly. They'd rather a body die on his own recognizance rather than on their recognizance."

"They won't believe whining and crying, but if you can show them you're pissing and spitting blood, that might work," the man who appeared not much more than a boy said. "Depending on the nature of your infraction, of course."

"Temporary financial difficulties and an unreasonable landlady," I said. "My wife will be by shortly. She'll bail me out and tend to me."

"With what will she bail you out?" the middle-sized man said. "Given your temporary financial difficulties, I mean."

"Maybe she won't need money," the large man said. "Is your wife comely? If she's comely, maybe she won't need money. Maybe she and the jailer will work something out."

The man who appeared not much more than a boy smirked. "Maybe she'd be able to work something out for all four of us."

"Forgive my brothers, friend," the middle-sized man said.

"I will not forgive them," I said. "For they know what they do."

"I wonder what's keeping your wife," the man who appeared not much more than a boy said. "Perhaps she has other priorities today."

"I will not forgive them," I said. "For they are not destined to be forgiven."

"How's that?" the middle-sized man said. "How is it you won't forgive my brothers when I'm asking you kindly to do so?"

"She sure is taking her time," the man who appeared not much more than a boy said.

"She worth waiting for?" the large man asked, and he snickered. "Maybe I'll wait for her once or twice."

"How's that?" the middle-sized man said. "How is it you won't forgive?"

"They took turns mocking Him and struck Him again and again," I said.

The middle-sized man slid closer to me on the bench. "How's that?" he said, and he sunk his elbow into my ribcage, and the cell was filled with blinding light and deafening thunder, and its walls cracked like ribs, and the mouths of the large man and the middle-sized man and the man who appeared not much more than a boy filled with blood, and the large man and the middle-sized man and the man who appeared not much more than a boy prostrated themselves, and the earth swallowed them up, and the cell door was thrown open by a rushing gale, and I was restored, and I was delivered.

# Annie Bunn Guiteau Recalls
## and Reconsiders Her Marriage

I AWOKE TO THE SOUND of them. To the sound of him. She was silent. So to the sound of him and to the silence of her and to my own silence. To the sound of him breathing through his mouth too fast like a dog. To the bed moving under the three of us in the pitch black room.

We were the same, she and I, lined up next to each other in the bed like twins, like matching dolls. Our backs straight on the rigid mattress, our heads haloed on our pillows by our nighttime hair. When I awoke, he was on her, but I felt the weight of him, too.

I tried not to stir because I knew stirring would bring about what would come next. My nighttime logic told me that if I lay there without stirring, I could keep at bay what would come next, but after lying there a while and listening to him breathing through his mouth too fast like a dog, I awoke more fully, and my daytime logic reminded me that what comes next can never be kept at bay, and whatever would come next could not be more awful than what was currently unfolding. So I felt for the candle holder on the bed stand and swung it blindly in the dark and, by grace, landed it solidly upside his head so that what came next was that he tumbled off the whore and over the edge of the bed with a thump you wouldn't think could come from a man so skinny.

My stepmother wept for me when I married him, and when I divorced him, she wept again, so I could not discern the logic of her weeping. There were only two choices. I could be married to him or not married to him. If my cleaving to him was worth weeping over, then how was my disentangling myself from him worth weeping over? If I cut off my arm with an axe and she were to weep, would she also weep if by some miracle my arm were restored?

"You can leave now," I said into the darkness.

I was addressing both of them, but only the whore answered. "Of course," she said. Her voice was familiar. I tried to make out her face, but I could not other than to see she had long hair, a nose, a mouth, two dark eyeholes.

"Your husband said you wouldn't wake up and that if you did wake up you wouldn't mind, but you did wake up, and you do mind, don't you?" the whore said.

"He told you I wouldn't mind if he committed adultery in the bed in which I, his wife, was currently sleeping?" I said.

"Yes," the whore said. She sat up and commenced pulling on her bloomers. "He claimed the two of you had a complicated marriage that made it all right." She sounded like someone.

"Complex marriage."

"That's what he said. Yes, ma'am."

"Don't men lie to you all the time?" I asked.

"What they most often do is lie to themselves out loud in my presence," the whore said.

"Then why would you believe him?" I asked. "Or any man for that matter?"

"You understand, don't you, ma'am, that this is my work? That I get paid for this?" the whore said.

"So for money you believed him," I said.

"Wives," the whore said. "Does not your husband lie to you all the time? Why do you believe him?"

"Do you and I know each other?" I asked. "You sound like someone."

"I don't know who I know," the whore said. "I don't know who I sound like."

When she slid to the bottom of the bed and swung her legs out over my feet, I caught a whiff of her that was the same as catching a whiff of him. Behind her, I saw the shadowy blur of him raise his head to peer over the edge of the bed. When he saw me see him, he ducked again.

"Did you also believe him when he told you he had money?" I said. "I'm sorry to have to tell you that was a lie, too."

"That's not how this works, ma'am," the whore said.

I could make her out standing by the door, dressing. I think she pulled a brush through her hair a few times. In the light you don't think about the sound a brush makes moving through hair, but a whore rising from your bed, brushing her hair in the dark, you think about the sound. Sounds like someone's shushing you.

"It's the truth," I said. "He has no money."

"Me getting paid up front is how these transactions work, ma'am," the whore said, and then I heard the door close.

Our only money had been recently sent me by my stepmother. I had asked her for enough to make rent. I did not think he knew of it. I thought I had hidden it well enough in my satchel, but he must have sniffed it out.

The room was silent after the whore's exit. I wished there were a way it could stay so. I wished I were the whore having left and she were me having to linger behind. I shut my eyes and tried to pray that he would disappear. That when morning light filled the room and I got out of bed, he would not be here anymore or anywhere anymore. In trying to pray I promised that I would gladly accept life-long lonesomeness as my fate in exchange for him not being anywhere anymore come morning.

When I finished trying to pray, I heard his voice in my ear. The opposite of an answered prayer. Soft and slurred and teary. I imagined him slithering around the perimeter of the bed to get to me. "Annie," he said, like he had too much breath in his mouth. "I'm bleeding from where you dented my head with the candlestick. Will you light the lamp and see to it?"

"I will not light the lamp," I said. "I will not see to it."

"What happened was I was walking on the street, and she called out to me, and I heard her as you. She called to me in your voice. The alley was dark. I thought she was you."

"I was lingering in an alley?" I said. "I sound like a whore?"

"No, Annie," he said. "The whore sounded like you."

"And then when you saw she wasn't me, what occurred and why?" I asked.

For a short while he just panted into my ear for an answer. "I'm just explaining how I came upon her in the first place," he said. "If you would please light the lamp and see to where you dented my head with the candlestick, I'd be appreciative."

"I will not light the lamp," I said. "I will not see to it."

"Annie," he said.

"Did the whore in New York sound like me, too?"

"I told you the whore in New York was not a whore," he said. "She and I recognized each other from when I led the faithful at Oneida. She had been one of my wives there during the first dispensation. I attempted to explain to her that I had passed into the second dispensation, but, as you know, this is a complicated thing to comprehend, and she could not comprehend it. Besides," he said, "you told me you would not be returning to our room before supper, but then you returned to our room before supper."

"You need to prepare yourself for the third dispensation," I said. "This is a simple thing to comprehend."

"You are fading," he said, "on account of the blood seeping out of my head where you dented it. If you would only light the lamp and see to it."

"I am not fading," I said. "You are fading."

"You make the choice to remember only our trials and not our periods of bliss."

"You went through my satchel like a common thief," I said.

"What is yours is mine, and what is mine is yours," he said. "When I receive the funds the Oneidans owe me, do you not think that money will also be yours?"

"You will not receive funds from the Oneidans," I said. "I read the letter sent you by their lawyer."

"You did not have permission to do so," he said.

"What is yours is mine," I said.

"That letter means nothing," he said. "Lawyers don't know. My partner Mr. Noyes and I need to work it out between the two of us directly."

"Lawyers know about money," I said.

"Mr. Noyes is who matters," he said. "He is the one who knows what I am owed for the time I spent in ministry at Oneida." He raised himself to his knees and leaned his elbows on the edge of the bed as if he were a child saying prayers. "If I could just rest in the bed, I would be appreciative," he said.

"The letter said you were not welcome in Oneida and advised you that any correspondence you initiated with any party there would go unanswered," I said. "It was signed not only by the lawyer Mead but also by Mr. Noyes. You would lie to me knowing I read the letter. You may not get in this bed," I said.

"It's not that I would lie," he said. "It's that I know the truth, and the truth does not match the letter." He dropped his forehead on the mattress and then raised it and then dropped it again.

"You may not get in this bed," I said.

He then screamed into the mattress so that it sounded like a scream from far away, and he pounded on the bed with his forearms in a motion reminiscent of chopping wood.

"The poems I wrote to you!" he screamed, raising his head off the bed, and there was a pounding on the other side of the wall behind the headboard. "I am the author of those poems! I am that man!" he said, and again there was a pounding on the other side of the wall behind the headboard. "Whatever else you think I am, remember I am the author of those poems!"

"You are not the author of those poems," I said.

"'But when a soul, by choice and conscience, doth throw out her full force on another soul, the conscience and the concentration both make mere life, love,'" he said, his voice shrinking again to a pained whisper. "If I am the man who has transgressed with whores, I am also the man who composed those words for you."

"Elizabeth Barrett Browning wrote those lines," I said. "I knew from the moment you gave them to me. For some reason I thought the lie charming at the time."

"It was charming," he said and began to weep. "You were right to think it charming. If you would only light the lamp and see to my head where you dented it and allow me to rest in the bed."

"I will not light the lamp," I said. "I will not see to it."

"Hosea and Gomer," he said. "Gomer was a whore sanctioned by God to be His prophet's wife. Through faith and matrimony they were both restored."

"You are confusing yourself now," I said.

He stood then and struck me across the face, but his heart was not in it. He returned to the floor at the foot of the bed, and I did not hear from him again until morning when the landlady came to the door and then the police.

After they had taken him away, my bare foot stepped in the blood on the floor where he had lain his head all night. The dark spot had disguised itself as a shadow and had grown tacky like tree sap.

Throughout the relatively short duration of our marriage, the short duration that seemed a long duration, he twisted everything, tried to get me to see things twisted. Was the twisting intentional, or did his mind do the twisting without his knowing? For a while after our parting, I would frequently ponder on this. Not just regarding the whores, but regarding everything. When he tried to get me to see things twisted, was he trying to get me to see things as he honestly saw them, or was he being deceitful? And why was I willing to hear him out? If he were a lunatic, and I was suspicious of his lunacy, then what was I for my willingness to hear him out?

I would ask myself these questions all the time until I understood the answers did not matter. The fact of the whores was what mattered, not the explanation nor the nature of the whores. The fact of the twisting was what mattered, not the explanation nor the nature of the twisting. The fact that I heard out a lunatic was what mattered, not the explanation of why I did so or what hearing out a lunatic made me.

One evening, years after the fact of him in my life, after he had done what he had done and had paid for it and was not anywhere anymore, I made the mistake of presenting these impressions to my stepmother. I did so due to my lonesomeness, due to the lack of any other available conversant. She did not offer any spoken reply to my words, but she was nonetheless adamant in her response. Again through her tears she was.

# Tirzah Miller Recalls
# and Reconsiders Her Girlhood

HE SAT UP AFTERWARDS, his back to her, and raised his arms like heavy wings. He grunted softly as he stretched his neck in wide, slow circles. When she heard it crack, she thought of a fox's foreleg being snapped. She had been working at the trap shop for the past month and had not been able to get wounded forest animals out of her mind. Raccoons and beavers and bears and wolves and mink. Cubs and pups separated from their mothers. Blood-matted fur.

"You're getting old," she said to him. "I forget this just before we make love, and I don't think about it as we're making love, but as soon as we're finished, I remember."

When he turned to face her, she wished she had not said it. She thought she had wanted to hurt him a little, but now she knew that is not what she had wanted at all. The look on his face reminded her of the previous summer when he had confided in her that he had overheard two nurses at the children's house laugh with each other about his swollen belly.

His pained expression lasted only a moment, though, before one corner of his mouth lifted into a smile. "The logical solution, then," he said, "would be for us never to stop making love."

She sat up next to him and brushed his whiskered cheek with the backs of her fingers. "Would that not make it difficult to take our meals?" she said.

He was too many things to her, and that made it hard to know him. That is, she knew him in too many ways to know him truly. This is how she had explained it to Cornelia. She did not have a relationship with him, singular. She had relationships with him, plural. You would think that knowing him as a lover would trump the other ways of knowing him—as her mentor, her friend, her confidant, her uncle—but this was not the case. She often found herself thinking of him as one thing when she should be thinking of him as something else. She had not told him this, not straight out, but a few days ago she had asked him how he thought of her. A lover? A niece? A friend? A disciple?

"How I think of you is that I love you," he had said. "Agape, eros, philia, storge. I love you sacredly, like God loves you. I love you passionately with my body. I love you loyally like a friend. And I love you like family. That is, I tolerate you. I love you with a tolerating love." He had smiled. "I don't love you in these ways one at a time or according to occasion. I love you in all these ways all the time."

They had been walking in the woods, and his answer had stopped her in her tracks. She had to lean against a tree to steady herself and catch her wind. She felt like this sometimes when she listened to Frank's violin. Dizzy. Outside herself.

Later, though, when she shared Mr. Noyes's words with Cornelia, her friend's mouth had tightened, and she had snorted. "Sounds about right," Cornelia had said. "You ask him to tell you how he feels about you, and he answers in Greek."

Tirzah moved to climb past him in order to get up to dress, but he stopped her, placing his hand on the back of her neck. "You seem especially pensive these days, my dear," he said. "I know you've always had a busy mind—you did even as a child—but it seems even busier than usual lately. Tell my why."

She ducked his hand and settled back into the space beside him. "Do I seem abnormally preoccupied?" she said. "I'm sorry. I don't believe it's anything to be alarmed about. I suppose I have been feeling anxious lately. I don't know. Feeling anxious about what I don't know, I suppose."

"Your future?" he said

"That's partly it," she said. "Not only my future. The future writ large, I suppose. And not just the future. The past, too. Not to mention the present."

"So nothing significant then," he said, taking her hand and bringing it to his chest. "You're just anxious about yourself, everyone else, and all that was, is, and ever shall be."

"Right," she said. "And since it's everything, it's probably nothing, right?"

"Is it possible that Towner and his maneuverings are putting you in this unsettled state?" he asked, looking at the ceiling. "I sense you are not the only one given to worrying right now. Towner has everyone worked up. Has he attempted to enlist you in his cause?"

"He's smarter than that," Tirzah said.

"I know he's been talking to Frank."

"Yes."

"What does Frank say?"

She pulled away from him and pressed the heels of her hands into her eyes. "You know I don't like being the go-between when it comes to you and Frank," she said. "You two need to talk to each other."

"You used to tell me the same thing about George," he said. He lay back down and turned his head on his pillow so he was facing away from her. "You told me this first to deceive me and then to put the responsibility on him to tell me about your relationship and your pregnancy."

"Why was it my responsibility and not his to tell you?" she asked.

"It was both yours and his," he said. His voice had grown stern before softening again. "We've been through this, Tirzah."

"Too many times," she said. "I believe I've done my penance."

"All right. You are right."

"It's been more than five years. G.W. is five years old."

"I miss George," he said, his voice breaking. "Maybe arguing about him with you is a way for me to keep him alive. Also, Mary Cragin. My arguments with you about George and Frank are reminiscent of my arguments with her in years past about Abram Smith and her husband." He reached around himself to scratch his back, and she moved to help him, running her nails from his shoulders to his waist. "This just now occurred to me," he said.

She moved her hands up his neck into his thinning hair. "I love being with you, John—you know I do—but I often wish we were more alone when we were alone." When he did not answer, she retrieved her hands. "I believe a healthier way to remember your brother would be to visit with G.W. at the children's house more often. He asks about you, wonders when Father Noyes is coming to see him. He still talks about the size of the orange you gave him at Christmas. And to remember Mrs. Cragin, perhaps you might seek out Victor more often. Take a meal with him. He seems to be doing quite well lately. It would encourage him to know that you are noticing. That you approve of the progress he's made."

He sat up again. "Your advice is good advice," he said. "The things you recommend are things I often recommend to myself."

"Is Towner putting you on edge?" she asked.

"He is."

"I sense you getting tired. I teased you about getting old, but it's not old really, is it? It's tired. This is part of what is making me anxious, I think. Seeing how tired you are."

"Yes," he said. "I am tired."

"Don't men like Towner come and go?" she said. "Haven't they always come and gone? That Mr. Mills from a few years back. The one Charles Guiteau threw out the window. Even Guiteau himself. Haven't rascals like these always come and gone?"

"You're right," he said. "They have."

"Perhaps there is no cause for worry then," she said.

"There is a difference this time." He moved to the edge of the bed, slowly unfolded his body to stand, and then crossed the room and pulled on his trousers. "Towner is being listened to. He's found an attentive, sympathetic audience. I sense his audience is growing."

She thought about rising to dress along with him but instead moved to the middle of the bed and pulled the blanket up to her chin. "Despite his arrogance and presumptiveness, do you think. . . ." She stopped herself. "Please don't misunderstand my question, John, but I wonder if there might be something legitimate in what Towner is saying? Underneath his self-important braying, is there anything he is speaking to that the family might do well to take into consideration?"

"You tell me. Do you think so? Does Frank think so?"

"Yes. Frank thinks so." She tried to read his face for a response, but he was expressionless. She watched him pull on his shirt and walk to the window to look out at the rain. "Frank doesn't like the gossipy, underhanded way Towner is seeking to drum up support for his ideas, but he does think some of the ideas in and of themselves have merit."

"Frank thinks Towner is right that I have too much authority." He took a step back from the window and began buttoning his shirt. He always started with the bottom button. He was the only man she had seen do this.

"Not exactly. Frank thinks you have too much to do. He thinks your authority might be suffering because it is spread too thin. If you were to share some of your duties, he thinks it would be good not only for the family but for you, too. He sees what I see. That you are getting tired."

"Towner wants complete autonomy when it comes to cavorting with women," he said. "He wants to answer to no one. He wants no one to answer to anyone."

"That would appear to be his position," she said. "He holds that in order to be truly perfect, freedom is necessary. One's perfection is made manifest by one's own choices as led by Christ, not by following a set of dos and don'ts administered by a man, no matter how righteous the man." She closed her eyes and wished to be elsewhere. Wished to be struck deaf and dumb.

"Curious line of thought coming from a military man, don't you think?"

"Now that you mention it," she said.

"The one-eyed war hero offers his views on human authority. The Cyclops holds forth on freedom." He returned to the window and leaned on the sill with his fists. "I thought you said Towner hadn't spoken with you?" he said. "You seem to know quite a bit about his convictions for not having spoken to the man."

"He didn't speak to me," she said, and she felt her stomach drop. She knew she had made a mistake. "He didn't approach me directly. He sent his wife. Cinderella didn't say so, but it was obvious she was on assignment."

"You should have told me. When I asked if Towner had spoken to you, you should have told me he had through Cinderella. You said no, but your answer should have been yes. If you aimed to be honest, it should have been."

"I'm sorry," she said.

"Between the spread of Towner-ism and the local clergy again hell-bent on having me arrested, maybe it's time I think about abandoning Oneida to its own devices," he said. "Even you, Tirzah, might be better off. In my absence, my family wouldn't have to worry about how to go about keeping things from me. How to go about sparing my feelings as they undermine me." He laughed quietly, bitterly. "You tell me I seem tired, but it must be exhausting for you and Frank and everyone else to have to worry constantly about how to negotiate the old man."

She was weeping when he finally looked at her. She did not try to hide it. She wanted him to see.

"Do you remember taking scissors to your mother's curtains in Putney?"

"What?" she said, wiping her face with the edge of the blanket. "What?"

"You would have been three or four. My sister brought you to me and told me she needed help. She said she was at her wit's end with you. No matter how much she punished you, you wouldn't behave. The last straw was that you had taken scissors to the new curtains she had just made for the sitting room. Do you remember the sitting room at the family house in Putney?"

"I suppose I do remember vaguely," she said. "I remember the sitting room. I don't remember Mother taking me to see you, but I remember her being cross with me for doing something naughty with her good sewing scissors. She took me to you?"

"You were terrified," he said. "At least you appeared to be. I believe in her anger and frustration Charlotte had filled your head with the horror of the punishment I would administer."

"What did you do to me?"

"I brought you over to sit on my lap, and I gave you a bite of the apple I was eating, and I told you to look me in the eye and tell me the truth. And you did. You looked me in the eye, and you chewed the apple, and you told me between chews how you had taken the scissors and cut up the pretty new curtains. When I asked you why you had done so, you said you did not know."

"And then what?" she said. "What was my punishment?"

He sat down in the chair by the door to put on his shoes. When he bent over, he groaned, and when he straightened, he groaned again.

"You received no punishment," he said. "I praised you for being honest. I made funny faces to make you laugh so you would forget your fear. I went into the kitchen to fetch you an apple of your own."

# John Humphrey Noyes Makes His Escape

I CARRY MY SATCHEL in one hand and my shoes in the other. According to Myron, footsteps echo through the hallways of the mansion house like drumbeats, especially in the middle of the night. I have never noticed this myself, but I follow his directions nonetheless. I appointed Myron to be the architect of my escape, so not heeding him would be tantamount to not heeding myself.

On the ground floor I pause to peer into the meeting hall. At two o'clock in the morning the room is as dark and silent as a cave, but I cannot shake the sense that the space is filled to capacity with souls, all of whom are waiting for me. Before departing I lean into the abyss and whisper, "I am sorry," and as soon as I do I feel foolish, both for addressing an empty room and for apologizing. If an apology is owed, it is not by me.

Outside the mansion house, the rain falls as softly and quietly as snow. I do not even realize it's raining until I find myself standing in a puddle as I try to wrestle on my shoes. Bending over is no longer a specialty of mine, and by the time I am shoed, I am winded.

"You are sixty-eight years old," I tell myself.

As I traverse the grounds with my wet feet, I am surprised and annoyed to be reminded of Charles Guiteau, specifically an incident in which the lunatic had lost his shoes. We were in the orchard in a downpour where I was attempting to talk sense to him. I might as well have been talking to one of the trees.

When Guiteau finally left Oneida, it took the family, me included, half-a-week to notice he was gone, and then folks responded sheepishly. I remember being surprised by this. I would have expected the more pious and serious individuals among us to bemoan the fact that we had not been able to help the lad, and I would have predicted some of the younger, more frivolous folks to make jokes about him as they had since he had joined the community. The quiet embarrassment exhibited by the family was unexpected. Later, this discomfiture was replaced with a rash of stories about Guiteau, some containing a whiff of truth, some outlandishly unfounded. Guiteau's habit of urinating in the flower garden was why Henry Thacker was having so much trouble with the peonies. Guiteau had set the fire that consumed Barnes Davis's smoke house. Guiteau had somehow consorted with Mr. Mills in his cider making operation. Guiteau had defiled several women as they slept. Guiteau had hidden a pipe in the woods where he habitually smoked jimson weed. Guiteau was a spy planted in our community by the Quakers. The Confederacy. The Methodists.

In fleeing Oneida, I wonder if Guiteau left in the middle of the day or made his exit in darkness. Before tonight I would have believed myself to be more than capable of negotiating the community's property blindfolded, but as it turns out, finding my way without even the hint of moonlight is quite challenging. I know I have arrived at the pond not because I can see the shapes of the shoreline trees or the shimmer of the water but because can I hear it. My footsteps on the path are met by a series of splashes. Maybe frogs. Maybe turtles. Maybe carp.

"You are sixty-eight years old."

AT A QUARTER-TO-THREE I am to meet Myron, who will be waiting a mile beyond the pond with a buckboard. He will have a lantern to signal me. When I asked if the lantern were to assist me in distinguishing between his buckboard and all the other buckboards waiting on the side of the road at three o'clock in the morning, he corrected me. Our meeting was set for a quarter-to-three. If I were to arrive at three o'clock, I would be late.

Myron and I had finalized the details of my departure the previous afternoon in my bedroom, where we were careful to speak in hushed tones. We would arrive at the depot in plenty of time, where Myron would purchase my ticket. I would wait in the buckboard hidden under a blanket until it was time to board. If the trains were running on schedule, I would be in Niagara Falls by nightfall. There I would rendezvous with a Mr. Brett, who would be tasked with accompanying me across the border to his family's farm. Myron assured me that Brett, a devout Perfectionist and enthusiastic admirer of my writings, was trustworthy.

"Thank you, Myron," I said. "Is it possible I haven't thanked you before just now? I apologize. I have been preoccupied with sorrow on the one hand and anticipation on the other."

"I do not require thanks for doing my duty," Myron said. "I am sorry it has come to this, but I am glad you turned to me for help." He then reminded me yet again that I was not to tell anyone about our plans, advising me that deniability was the best going away gift I could give my allies. "Even Tirzah, John," he had said to me sternly. "Perhaps especially Tirzah."

"You seem to have little confidence in my ability to keep quiet, Myron," I said.

"This is crucial, John," he said. "You can't say any goodbyes. Not until after the fact. Then you can write all the farewell letters you please."

"I understand," I said. "The cruelty of the deception we are undertaking, though, disturbs me. It is cruel not only to my loved ones but to myself."

Myron nodded at first but then shook his head as if having a silent argument with himself. "If after you are gone it were discovered that some individuals knew of your plans, they could be in legal jeopardy," he said. "Perhaps more importantly, the rest of the family would be furious with them."

"I understand," I said. "I also understand I will be called a coward."

Myron hunched forward in his chair and looked at the floor. "Some might call you that," he said. "Others will blame themselves, thinking they must have failed you somehow."

"Those who should feel guilty, of course, will not," I said. "It will be the innocent who torture themselves."

Myron rubbed his beard. "I imagine one half will aim their anger at our hypocritical, fervently self-righteous neighbors who have been harassing you with legal threats, and the other half will lay blame at the feet of Towner." Myron levelled his eyes at me. "Which of these parties will be more correct?"

"They will be equally right," I said, "which will make for some lively arguments."

Myron did not return my smile. "There will be anger, guilt, and cross talk a-plenty, but—please don't misunderstand me, John—I believe there also will be relief."

"How do you mean?" I asked. I knew exactly how he meant, but I wanted to hear him articulate it.

"Things have been tense," he said. "Your retreat will ease this tension." As soon as the words left his mouth, Myron seemed to realize he was in a conversation he did not want to be in, and he rose to leave.

"Retreat?" I asked.

"Is that the wrong word?"

"I don't know," I said. "Words matter."

"When you approached me, that's the word you used," Myron said. "You said 'retreat.'"

"I did?" I asked.

Myron hid his hands in his pockets, hovering in limbo. He wanted to leave but did not know if he should.

"I've been self-centered, Myron," I said. I stood to face him and clapped his shoulder. "I haven't until this moment considered what is at stake for you. Some folks will be very angry with you."

"It will take them a few days to catch on," he said. "I imagine most will assume you've gone to Brooklyn to visit Harriet."

"After they figure it out," I said. "When it dawns on them that you enabled and kept secret my departure, some will turn on you."

"My popularity will likely not increase," he said. "That is why as soon as I see you off on the train I am heading to Wallingford."

"There will be questions for you to answer there, too," I said. "I'm sure folks will want to know about Towner's insurrection and my legal problems."

"I can handle such queries well enough," Myron said. "Folks don't tend to expect many meaningful revelations conversing with me."

I sat back down. "Of course, as you rightfully mentioned, some will be relieved by my exit, so maybe among these folks your reputation will improve. Perhaps this will work out well for you in the long run. You'll enjoy the distinction of being the man who finally, literally, drove off the old codger."

"A comforting thought," Myron said. He allowed himself a subtle smile as he reached for the door.

"I haven't asked you, Myron. What do you make of my decision? Do you think it wise?"

"I believe in your judgment, John," Myron said, turning back to me. "I have not made my life here in Oneida under your leadership in order to second-guess you. To be frank, I do not understand those who make a habit of doing so."

When the door closed, I could not help but think that if I had been blessed by more Oneidans like Myron, there would be no question of whether my leaving were a retreat or something else because I would not be leaving at all.

I rose and crossed the room to look out the window onto the sunny lawn, where a group of young people were engaged in a spirited croquet match. One of the boys missed an easy shot and responded by howling at the sky and raising his mallet over his head as if to strike his opponents. All the participants and onlookers scattered gleefully, hooting in delight and happy fear.

I PAUSE TO CATCH my breath in the heavy mist that seemingly rises from the earth as much as it falls from the sky. I switch my satchel to the other hand and check my watch. Out of habit I do this. Of course, the action is purposeless as I cannot see my own fingers six inches away from my face let alone the hands and numbers of the watch face. I wonder how many more times I will check the time over the next few days. I remember how as a boy I had detested this habit of my father's. On more than one occasion I had fantasized about swiping his watch and depositing it at the bottom of Sacketts Brook Falls.

Were my father alive, I wonder what he would make of my current situation. I have often wondered what he would think of what I have built in Oneida, if he would regard it as an achievement or an embarrassment. I asked my mother on several occasions over the years, and she assured me he would be proud. She told me he might be fretful over the ferocity and frequency of the criticisms leveled against me, but he would be impressed by how I had brought people together to live and work in harmony. Gone for more than a decade now, my mother was spared having to watch the spirit of the community deteriorate over the last few years. And I have been spared having to watch her watch.

Tirzah often encourages me to share with her memories of my mother and father, her grandparents. I know how disappointed and forlorn she will be when she realizes I am gone. She informed me at supper yesterday of her intention to come up to my room to visit later in the evening, but I told her I was tired. When she pressed I grew impatient, and we ate the rest of our meal in silence. That this is how I left things with her is something I cannot allow myself to dwell on or I will lose all resolve.

I retired to my room alone immediately after supper, before the sun had even set, to commence packing and pacing. I desperately wanted Tirzah there, and the fact that my desire for her comfort stemmed from my sorrow about having to keep from her my impending departure was an unbearable irony. To occupy my mind, I attempted a letter to Harriet but abandoned it after only a few sentences. Had Harriet been in Oneida, I suspect I would have been unable to keep my plans from her, and she would not have approved of them. She might have even argued strenuously enough to change my mind. It has happened before, God knows. Perhaps it is fortuitous, then, that she is in Brooklyn. Perhaps even more than Tirzah, I hate arguing with Harriet. If leaving Oneida without consulting these soulmates were unfortunate, leaving Oneida after they had argued with me to stay would have been all the more woeful.

OCCASIONALLY, OFF TO THE side of the road, I hear rustlings in the brush. They unnerve me. Skunks have been prevalent this summer—even tonight, there is a strain of musk in the damp air—and I do not wish to make my long journey to Canada after having encountered one. I would cross the road to walk on the opposite side, but there are rustlings there as well, so I try to stick to the center as best I can.

"You are sixty-eight years old."

Not long after his arrival at Oneida, I shared a meal with James Towner during which he enthralled a table of young men with stories of his adventures as a soldier. At one point he revealed that, while serving in Arkansas, he and his men had developed a taste for skunk, but after returning to Ohio after the war and going to the trouble of bagging and eating a couple of the animals, he had been disappointed. His post-war skunks did not taste the same. He seemed to want to suggest some deeper meaning by this story, but judging by his audience's crude, immature reactions, I do not believe they heard it the way he intended.

Towner had lost his left eye at the Battle of Pea Ridge. He had been gifted a glass replacement by a widow he had come across in his adventures at the free-love commune in Berlin Heights. It had been her husband's. In Oneida, though, Towner almost always wore a patch. He said the glass eye was too snug and felt cold in his face, and although it was brown like his other eye, it was a different shade of brown, a darker brown, like an Indian's or a Negro's eye. I gathered all of this from Tirzah and some of the other younger woman whom Towner fancied. He seemed just as enthusiastic to converse with young women about his glass eye as he did with young men about eating Arkansan skunks.

I twice forbade Towner and his family from joining our fellowship. He had sent a letter from Ohio asking permission to join, and even though I promptly answered in the negative, he showed up undeterred a few weeks later, at which point I again refused permission. It was not the case then that I considered Towner a threat to my authority; rather, I worried he and his wife would pollute our family with their free-love spirit. The world might have seen Oneida and Berlin Heights as one in the same, but whereas our system of complex marriage was organized, supervised, and regulated, the fornicators in Berlin Heights answered only to their lustful instincts. Despite Towner's repeated assurances that he and his wife had forsaken and repented from this iniquity and, in fact, had fled Berlin Heights to escape it, I doubted his sincerity. I knew the population of the Berlin Heights community had been severely diminished due to the aggressive actions of the local authorities, so I suspected the true reason the Towners had come east was because our healthy numbers provided good opportunity for them to continue their defiled carousing.

It was Myron Kinsey and a few of the other senior men in the family who finally compelled me to allow the Towners opportunity to prove themselves. I believe this fact probably has something to do with why Myron has been so helpful to me recently. At least in part, he might be fueled by guilt and regret. Of course, Myron's dedication also might have to do with Towner's recent efforts to curry favor with Jessie Hatch, whom Myron cares for greatly. Usually I would note this kind of inclination as problematic, but in this case, I think it has had a good effect. Through Towner's attempted seduction of Jessie, the scales have fallen from Myron's eyes.

It was startling how quickly the gratitude expressed to me by Towner and his wife was replaced by challenges and complaints. Towner, for instance, claimed to understand the need for governance of sexual relationships in the community, but he argued the governance should be more widely shared. He felt similarly about my role as first husband to the young women who came of age in our family. Towner spread rumors that the community's young women were repelled by me and thereby sexually uninspired and disenchanted from the beginning of their development. Not only these women but their future partners, then, were victims of my incompetence. Towner, of course, thought himself to be up to the task of helping the community correct this shortcoming. He disguised his desire to plow through our young women as a desire to protect them. He used the word "liberation." The young women of Oneida needed to be liberated from Mr. Noyes's hand.

Frank Wayland-Smith tearfully revealed this to me one afternoon in his practice room. Tirzah had advised me that I should speak to him. She was worried because he was distraught about Towner and, as a result, was talking about leaving Oneida. So I paid Frank an unannounced visit and instructed him to unburden himself. I told Frank I had heard he wanted to leave Oneida and that I would not attempt to stop him so long as he told me why. He did not want to tell me the details of Towner's insubordination, but I advised him I would not stop quizzing him about the matter until he acquiesced. What Frank told me affected me like a sudden fever. I shivered and burned.

Not only was Towner talking of liberating the young women from me, but some of the young women themselves were parroting him. When I asked Frank to name the women, he hugged his violin to his chest and refused. This angered me at the time, but I realized later he was right to protect them. If I would have acted punitively against these misguided souls, it would have further empowered Towner. Frank went on to tell me that Towner often held forth about consanguineous relationships like Tirzah's and mine. Whether or not such unions were blessed, Towner said, was beside the point. They were bringing unwanted attention and judgment from the outside world, so those who participated in them were acting selfishly. Towner suggested that since I would never be persuaded to make the necessary changes on my own, what was needed was an elected board of advisers to check my authority.

"He's calling for a more democratic organization," Frank said, staring at the sheet music on the stand in front of him. "Some folks are sympathetic to this notion. Your recent suggestion that Theodore could one day take over for you as head of the family does not resonate well with folks.

They worry about how the outside world regards us and about our fate after you are gone."

"After I am gone?" I said. "Where am I going?"

"Towner has some complaining that Oneida is a monarchy."

"Oneida is not a monarchy," I answered. "That said, what Oneida is or is not does not rely on what anyone wants. God has decreed what Oneida is. Towner might think he is stirring resentment against me, but he is actually doing so against God."

"If he heard you say that, he would point to it as an example of the authoritarianism he is encouraging folks to resist," Frank said. His eyes had dried, but he looked pale and tired. "It pains me to tell you these things," he said. "I want you to know I think Towner is a duplicitous, selfish man."

"Do you think his criticisms have merit, though, Frank? Is that why you are considering leaving?"

"I think there are ways our community could improve. I don't think Towner is going about it in the right way." Frank closed his eyes and wearily lowered his arms to his sides. His violin and bow seemed extensions of his hands. "I sometimes think of leaving Oneida in the same way I sometimes think of dying," he said. "I imagine the quiet."

I am not angry with Frank, nor am I angry with the young women who evidently no longer prefer me, nor am I angry with Myron and the other men for initially being fooled by Towner. I am not even all that angry with Towner himself. Yes I am. I am very angry with him. Primarily, though, I am angry with myself. For acquiescing when I should not have and for not acquiescing when I should have. I am also angry at myself for leaving, just as I would be angry with myself for staying, and I am already angry at my future self for both regretting and not regretting having left.

There is a rustling in the woods to my left, and then a scurrying around my feet, and then a rustling in the woods to my right.

"You are sixty-eight years old."

THERE IS STILL NO sign of Myron's lantern. If there were more than one road to take, I might assume I was on the wrong one. Perhaps I have taken the wrong one regardless.

My journey has barely begun, and I am already tired. I knew I would be. Prior to my departure I pleaded with myself to sleep for a few hours, but I could not even stay in bed. As the evening wore on, I moved back and forth between my desk and the dark window, assuring myself that I would sleep on the train. I told myself this with full knowledge that I am unable to sleep on trains, that I have never slept a wink on a train. I was talking like a stranger to myself or like someone who should not be trusted. A liar.

Previous to last night, the only other completely sleepless night I remember occurred a few summers ago when I met Jessie Hatch in the orchard. She confessed to me later that she thought I had made our midnight appointment for amorous reasons, so she was nervous. Of course, she admitted, she would have been even more nervous had she known the actual reason I wished to meet.

Jessie was the nineteen-year-old daughter of Catherine Baker. Eventually, Eleazer Hatch admitted to being Jessie's father and subsequently endured a particularly stern criticism session due to this fact. Miss Baker had not expressed willingness to become pregnant, and even if she had, neither she nor Eleazer had conferred with me about the matter. Eleazer had denied responsibility for the pregnancy until he saw baby Jessie and held her in his arms. At that point, he said, he knew the sin was his.

When Jessie arrived in the orchard, the sky was clear, illuminated by a full moon. After greeting her, I immediately led her by her elbow to a stump and asked her to remove her shoe and stocking. She was bewildered by this request. Of course she was.

"I need to see your foot, child," I said. "A strange ask, I know. Please don't be afraid."

"I am not afraid, Mr. Noyes," she said, attempting to convince herself she was speaking truly, and she lifted her dainty foot onto the stump and undressed it. I regarded it and wept. Her toes were webbed.

"What is the matter, Mr. Noyes?" Jessie asked, her voice breaking. "What have I done?"

In answer I took off my own shoe and stocking and placed my foot next to hers on the stump.

"You have webbed toes like mine," Jessie said. "Duck feet. That's what Nurse Abner at the children's house used to call them." She paused. "If I may, Mr. Noyes, I don't think our feet are anything to weep about."

"I remember Nurse Abner," I said. "You children were blessed to have her."

"I remember her breath had no smell," Jessie said. "All the other nurses' mouths had distinctive smells. Hers had none."

I laughed quietly. "What a thing to remember."

Jessie laughed nervously at my laughter. "It's true! More importantly, though, I remember that when I was ill with malaria, she prayed with me differently than others prayed with me. Others prayed that I might be well. She prayed that I might be strong to accept the will of God. Her praying frightened me, but it seemed more powerful, too. Do you remember when I was sick with malaria, Mr. Noyes?"

"I do," I said.

"Why are we here in the orchard in the middle of the night with our webbed feet on a stump, Mr. Noyes?"

"Do you remember what made you well, Jessie?" I asked.

"God's mercy," she said. "My faith and the faith of the community."

"And quinine," I said. "I hadn't allowed it in Oneida until you fell ill. Then I allowed it. I allowed it because I was frightened you would die, that faith wasn't going to be enough."

"I didn't know that, Mr. Noyes," she said quietly.

"It would appear that I am your father, Jessie," I said, pointing at our feet.

"I thought Mr. Hatch," she said. "Mr. Hatch himself says so."

I stepped off the stump and pulled Jessie into my arms. "Eleazar seemed so certain of it at the time," I said. "I wondered if it were me, but Eleazer claimed you with such assuredness."

"I see," Jessie said, stepping away. "I am sorry, Mr. Noyes."

"There is no need to be sorry," I said.

"Thank you," she said.

"There is nothing to thank me for," I said.

After we walked back to the mansion house, I kissed her cheek and told her to sleep well. I did not retire to my room, though. I walked all night and thought of and prayed for not only Jessie but for Theodore and Victor and all of my children. I prayed they might possess the discernment to embrace what should be embraced and reject what should be rejected, and I foolishly prayed that they might always remember me kindly.

"You are sixty-eight years old."

The first letter I will write to Oneida when I reach Canada will be an edict ending complex marriage. The hearts of the community are being torn in half. Some are lusting after monogamy, and others are lusting after uncontrolled, unbridled freedom. Both kinds of lust are imperfect, but allowing the marriage spirit to enter Oneida, while perhaps destroying the community, will at least save it from Towner. And this way Myron and Jessie can have each other. As husband and wife. A gift, albeit an imperfect one, that I owe both of them.

DESPITE THERE BEING NO sign of a lantern—Myron will tell me later he was not able to keep it lit in the rain—I finally hear my name being called. Just as I am trying to decide if I have not yet walked far enough or have somehow walked too far. A voice coming out of the darkness that, at first hearing, sounds like my own.

# Charles Guiteau Fulfills His Purpose

SAY TWO SHIPS COLLIDED. Say the SS *Narragansett* and the SS *Stonington*. Say in Long Island Sound. Say in spring. Say in heavy fog. Say the *Narragansett* burned to the waterline. Say the *Stonington* made it to port, all her passengers spared. Say you were a passenger on the *Stonington*. Say what you had been gifted. Say what good and perfect purpose had been unveiled.

Say a man won a victory he was not seeking. Say the Republican Party's presidential nomination. Say in Chicago. Say in spring. Say in heavy fog. Say victory was foisted upon the man like a burden. Say the man attempted to protest his victory but was silenced by those who had foisted victory upon him like a burden. Say the burden of foisted victory was then increased via the American electorate. Say you were the foisted upon president. Say you were the American electorate. Say you were a voice crying out in the wilderness. Say you were a passenger on the *Stonington*. Say what you had been gifted. Say what good and perfect purpose had been unveiled.

I did my due diligence. Upon disembarking from the *Stonington*, I embarked on a train to our nation's capital and served as a faithful instrument during the campaign, lifting my voice pen-wise to help foist the victory. And I lifted my voice pen-wise after the victory had been foisted to reveal myself to the chosen who was the victor as one chosen must reveal himself to another chosen in order to be established in my rightful place at the chosen who was the victor's right hand. But rather than being heeded and established in my rightful place at the chosen who was the victor's right hand, I was held at arm's length. I was condescended to and rebuffed as one chosen should not be condescended to and rebuffed by another chosen. Not directly condescended to and rebuffed by the chosen who was the victor, but condescended to and rebuffed indirectly via the chosen who was the victor's lieutenants.

So again I lifted my voice pen-wise to reveal myself to the chosen who was the victor as one chosen must reveal himself to another chosen in order to be established in my rightful place at the chosen who was the victor's right hand. "To rebuff me indirectly via your lieutenants is still for you to rebuff me, and to rebuff me is to rebuff not only me, but it is also to rebuff none other than the Chosen of the Chosen." And my voice, which I had again lifted pen-wise went unanswered, and the un-answering left me no choice but to make a final answer to the un-answering. A final answer to make straight not what God had made crooked but rather to restraighten what God had originally made perfectly straight but then had been made crooked by the chosen who was the victor's shirking of his chosenness via rebuffing another chosen indirectly via his lieutenants. A re-straightening to be made not by lifting my voice pen-wise but by lifting my voice pistol-wise with a pistol that felt foreign in my hand insofar as I had never held a pistol in my hand before the day I held the pistol in my hand and lifted my voice pistol-wise into the dark Potomac in preparation for the day I would hold the pistol in my hand and lift my voice pistol-wise not into the dark Potomac but into the body of the chosen who was the victor, who had shirked his chosenness via rebuffing another chosen indirectly via his lieutenants.

Prior to my lifting my voice pistol-wise into the body of the chosen who was the victor, who had shirked his chosen-ness via rebuffing another chosen indirectly via his lieutenants, there were ten days of lifting my voice pistol-wise into the dark Potomac, and there were two days of unfulfilled promise. All these days were nights.

On the first day of unfulfilled promise, the promise went unfulfilled because either the chosen who was the president was not present or the chosen who was the assassin was not present. The chosen who was the president's hands locked themselves behind his back as he strolled, his head bent to the street. When the chosen who was the assassin passed by the chosen who was the president with his hands in his pockets, one of his hands gripping the pistol in one of his pockets, and cleared his throat in order to cause the chosen who was the president to raise his head from the street to meet his gaze, the chosen who was the president did not raise his head from the street to meet the chosen who was the assassin's gaze, and when the chosen who was the assassin sneezed, the chosen who was the president did not acknowledge the chosen who was the assassin's sneeze. The chosen who was the president's head stayed bent to the street as if the chosen who was the assassin's throat clearing and sneezing had not occurred, as if the chosen who was the assassin were not there or as if the chosen who was the president were not there. The chosen who was the assassin could not lift his voice pistol-wise into the body of the chosen who was the president without both chosens being present, and the chosen who was the president's lack of acknowledgment of the chosen who was the assassin's throat clearing and sneezing had called into question these requisite presences. Having not been acknowledged by the chosen who was the president, the chosen who was the assassin's throat would not clear and the chosen who was the assassin's sneezing would not be quelled. The chosen who was the assassin's throat grew fuller, and the chosen who was the assassin's sneezing became legion by begetting itself and begetting itself and begetting itself, chasing the chosen who was the assassin back to his room. And the chosen who was the assassin's throat would not be cleared until it had been cleared by whiskey. And the chosen who was the assassin's sneezing would not be quelled until it had been quelled by a whore.

On the second day of unfulfilled promise, the promise went unfulfilled not due to the absence of requisite presences but rather due to the superfluous presence of the chosen who was the president's wife, Lucretia. Lucretia carried the chosen who was the president's arm in her arms as they strolled, creating a proximity problem insofar as the chosen who was the assassin was concerned that in lifting his voice pistol-wise into the body of the chosen who was the president, he might by miscalculation lift his voice pistol-wise into the body of Lucretia in addition to or instead of the body of the chosen who was the president. And once again the chosen who was the assassin was plagued with sneezing, although on this second day of unfulfilled promise, the sneezing was quelled by the first lady's gracious "Bless you," which quelled the assassin's sneezing before it could become legion by begetting itself and begetting itself and begetting itself.

Later that night in his room when the chosen who was the assassin wanted whiskey and a whore, he denied himself. The chosen who was the assassin drank water, and he lifted his voice pen-wise via a series of long letters to some individuals whom the chosen who was the assassin had never met and to some individuals whose whereabouts were unknown to the chosen who was the assassin and to some individuals who were deceased.

The two days of unfulfilled promise and the ten days during which the chosen who was the assassin lifted his voice pistol-wise into the dark Potomac rather than into the body of the chosen who was the president were agonizing insofar as the chosen who was the assassin would inquire heavenward as to whether the cup could be removed from him, but each time he inquired heavenward whether the cup could be removed from him, he would immediately reconsider his inquiry, wish he had not lodged the inquiry heavenward, and then inquire heavenward as to whether his previous inquiry could be un-lodged. That is, as soon as the chosen who was the assassin fretted that he could not bear following through with the re-straightening, the chosen who was the assassin fretted that he could not bear not following through with the re-straightening.

To be a husband had also involved conflicting inquiries heavenward and fretful self-negotiations for the chosen who was the assassin when the chosen who was the assassin had been a husband. And when the chosen who was the assassin had been a minister to those who would not repent in the den of iniquity, the chosen who was the assassin's ministry had likewise involved conflicting inquiries heavenward and fretful self-negotiations. A husband must marry. If he does not marry, he is not a husband. A minister must minister. If he does not minister, he is not a minister. An assassin must assassinate. If he does not assassinate, he is not an assassin. A chosen must choose. If he does not choose, he is not a chosen. Insofar as what is conflictingly inquired or fretfully self-negotiated is not pertinent only to what will be done or what will not be done, but is also pertinent to whom one is or to whom one is not. To whom one will be or to whom one will not be.

Say you are the chosen who was the assassin. Say you finally lifted your voice pistol-wise via a pistol that still felt foreign in your hand into the body of the chosen who was the president. Say at the Baltimore and Potomac train station. Say in summer. Say in heavy fog. Say the chosen who was the president did not die despite his body finally absorbing your voice pistol-wise and then did not die despite his body finally absorbing your voice pistol-wise and then did not die despite his body finally absorbing your voice pistol-wise. Say the chosen who was the president's not dying became legion by begetting itself and begetting itself and begetting itself insofar as your pistol-wise voice had lodged itself in the chosen who was the president's body in such a manner as to incapacitate the chosen who was the president but not kill the chosen who was the president.

Say for weeks and then months the unclean hands of the unchosen tried in vain with their unclean instruments to dislodge and thus silence your pistol-wise voice that had lodged itself in the chosen who was the president's body in such a manner as to incapacitate the chosen who was the president but not to kill the chosen who was the president. Say the chosen who was the president's not dying became legion by begetting itself and begetting itself and begetting itself until the day the chosen who was the president finally died.

Say in the moment the chosen who was the president finally died, you were finally transfigured. Say you were finally transfigured in such a manner that the unchosen could not recognize that you had been finally transfigured but that only you yourself could recognize that you had been finally transfigured. Say by the time the unchosen lawyer finally visited you in your cell to alert you to the chosen who was the president's death, you were not in need of the unchosen lawyer's alert because you had already been alerted by the fact of your transfigurement, which the unchosen lawyer could not recognize but only you yourself could recognize. Say by the time the unchosen lawyer finally visited you in your cell to alert you to the chosen who was the president's death, you had already all but assumed your rightful place at the right hand of the Chosen of the Chosen. Say in fall. Say in heavy fog.

# Lucretia Garfield Mourns Her Husband

DURING MY BOUT WITH malaria this past spring, Dr. Edson told me on more than one occasion that while Washington's swampy air was not ideal, she nevertheless felt strongly that I should continue breathing as the alternative would be even less conducive to my making a full recovery. James didn't always appreciate Dr. Edson's bedside humor, but I rather liked it. This distinction was curious because, of the two of us, James was usually the one more appreciative of and in tune with wit. If Dr. Edson had been a man, I wonder if her jokes would have struck him differently. When I once asked Dr. Edson how she was typically received by her patients and their families—"Dr. Edson with the med'cin" is what my children took to calling her—she said most everyone seemed more comfortable in referring to her as a nurse rather than a doctor, including even her male colleagues who knew her credentials and had comparatively less training and experience. She told me she had given up on correcting the mistake.

One evening shortly after my fever broke, I told James I wanted to venture out and take the air. I was finally beginning to feel myself again and desired a short respite from the damp and stuffy White House. James's agreement to accompany me was cheerful, but I knew if he had his druthers he would have stayed in and worked. It was the way he did not meet my eyes and how he was almost too cheerful in his concurrence. Over the course of our time together, James often did things for me and for others that he did not care to do. This made him kind, I realize. This selfless graciousness. Still, I wish he had wanted to do more of the things he kindly, selflessly, graciously did, especially those things he kindly, self-lessly, graciously did for me. On behalf of James as well as myself I wish this.

He and I eventually found our way to happiness as husband and wife, and I am glad we did so before death parted us, but I think we might have been happier, and we might have arrived at happiness more quickly, if he would have allowed himself more often to want to do what he did, to want to be with whom he was with. If by some miracle I could have James back, I would be overcome with joy. Of course I would be. I would even be willing to share him with the country again. The shape she is in, she would benefit from his miraculous resurrection as much as I would. I think even President Arthur would acquiesce and make way. That I would want James back a bit different than he was the first time does not change the fact of my love for him. I would have him back a bit different than he was for his own sake as much as for my own. I should mention that given such an opportunity, I would try to be a bit different myself, too. And the country. I hope she would also try to be a bit different.

James and I did not talk as we strolled that evening, and our pace was slower than I would have chosen. I think James wanted to make sure I did not overexert myself, but I could tell, too, that he was tired and preoc-cupied. At any rate, walking so slowly caused me to imagine James and me as an elderly couple, and that made me melancholy, so I told James I was ready to return home after strolling only a few blocks.

"Christ," he whispered under his breath, and I thought at first he was cursing my fickleness, but that was not the source of his displeasure. "The miserable man approaching is a tireless stalker of mine," he said. "It's as if he's a stray dog and I carry kibble in my pockets. Do not look at him."

"For what purpose does he pursue you?" I asked.

"Ostensibly because he wants a job. Guilford. That's not it. Gilbert. Something like that. I don't know him from Adam. He told Blaine he aspires to be named minister to France. Blaine thinks he'd be a better fit for minister to St. Elizabeth's Insane Hospital." James bent his head to regard the dark street as the man drew closer. "Don't acknowledge him, Crete," he whispered.

So what did I do? It was not in intentional defiance of my husband. The man sneezed, and before I knew the words were forming on my lips, I had blessed him. It was instinctive. Blame my good breeding. After Mr. Guiteau had walked by, James was incredulous. He did not relent in his upbraiding of me until I began to weep. I was not weeping in response to James's crossness, though, as much as I was in response to how the whole evening had unfolded. All I had wanted was a walk with my husband to celebrate in a small, quiet way my renewed health, and that desire had somehow resulted in his anger and frustration. Such is sometimes the nature of marriage, I suppose.

The next morning I awakened to a fever, and although my head had cooled and I was feeling better by evening, Dr. Edson suggested that we might make arrangements to have me complete my convalescence in a more hospitable locale. She suggested ocean air might be ideal, and before I even had opportunity to weigh the idea, James had made arrangements for Mollie and me to vacation in New Jersey. The plan would be for he and the boys to join us in a few weeks. Although his logic was flimsy, I knew James connected my returning fever with his sharp words the previous evening, and in the following days as I prepared for Mollie's and my departure, he was overtly attentive to and tender with me. As attentive and tender as he had ever been. Out of guilt and shame he was determined to show me love. Such is sometimes the nature of marriage, I suppose.

His benevolent looks, words, and caresses did not lead me to comfort, though. At least, they did not lead me only or directly there. The way in which he was treating me reminded me of how compassionate and kind he had been seventeen years prior in the weeks after confessing to me that he had betrayed our vows in New York with that widow. I had been pregnant with our first child Harry at the time. The widow's name was Lucia. The similarity of her name to mine, of mine to hers, had made the betrayal even more bitter somehow.

I was again visited by this memory two weeks later upon receiving the telegram in New Jersey. All I knew for certain in that moment was what the telegram told me—James had been seriously hurt and he hoped I could soon make my way back to Washington to see him—but I knew for certain more than what the telegram told me. That is, I knew for certain more than what I knew for certain. I thought of our evening stroll, our encounter with the sneezing Guiteau, James's long ago betrayal, and his habit of guilty tenderness, and I knew for certain that it was Guiteau who had harmed James, and I knew for certain James would die, and I knew for certain James had not loved me when he had his dalliance with Lucia the widow all those years ago, but I also knew for certain that he had not loved her. Moreover, I knew for certain that he had grown to love me since then, so he would die loving me. I knew for certain he was thinking of and loving me now, in the moments I held and read and reread the telegram, even as I knew for certain that I loved him and loved that he was in those moments thinking of and loving me.

I knew for sure more things later that afternoon as Mollie and I headed back to Washington on the one-car train that had been arranged for us. I held Mollie much of the way, stroking her hair. She usually did not stand this for long, but on this afternoon she indulged me. A selfless, gracious kindness. When an hour outside of the city mayhem struck and our car was nearly derailed after decoupling from the engine, I knew we had not come close to serious harm, not that close, not as close as the blanched faces and quiet murmurs of the men around us suggested. I knew we had not come close because serious harm had already struck, because once something is broken it cannot be broken, because once something is gone it cannot be taken away, because God is not so cruel. I was wrong about this, of course. We escaped harm that afternoon on the train, but over the next seventy-nine days I was proved wrong over and over again. What is broken can be broken. What is gone can be taken away. God is that cruel. His capacity for mercy and grace does not surpass His capacity for cruelty. It had been wrongheaded and irreverent for me to think otherwise.

Months later, after James had been taken away from me again and again—he still is being taken away from me—and after the most tragic parts of the tragedy were over and done, I told Dr. Edson that if she had been in charge of James's care rather than Dr. Bliss, the country would still have its rightful president. I did not ask her what she thought of this impression. Rather, I stated it to her as a fact. Trains run on tracks. Children are echoes of their parents. Men who hear God's voice are dangerous. Men who don't hear God's voice, too. If she had been charged with James's care, he would still be alive.

In response, Dr. Edson blew softly on her teacup. "Still too hot," she said, but she was wrong to say this. The tea had cooled enough to drink. Maybe it was even a bit too cool.

"You know I'm right whether your humility allows you to agree with me or not, Dr. Edson," I said.

"Does no good," she said, raising her cup again and resting its brim against her chin. "What good does knowing do?"

# PART III
## 1882–86

# James William Towner Mourns His Eye

HAVING BEEN TO WAR, it is difficult not to see the world and its mechanisms thusly framed. Noyes discouraged this in me, telling me a military man's viewpoint was not of God and was not conducive to the realization of His heavenly kingdom in Oneida. I challenged Noyes on that front, one of my first challenges to him, a man who was not accustomed to being challenged and did not know how to negotiate challenges honorably or fruitfully. How can one be an effective leader without this skill? Someone tell me. So I pushed him. What of the Israelites' initiatives to claim the Promised Land? What of King David's battlefield prowess? What of John's final vision in the Book of Revelation?

Instead of answering me substantively, he told me he hoped I would do more thinking on the matter and get back to him. He said this as if he had to wait for me to catch up to him intellectually and spiritually before further discussion would be possible. I suppose he is still waiting, the expatriate coward, growing old in his stone cottage, feeling death's hot breath on his neck, trying to convince himself he lived his life as he should have.

My battlefield service came to an end at Pea Ridge. No harm was done me there by any enlisted rebel soldier; rather my eye was taken by the uncoordinated but combined efforts of a Chickasaw savage and a sonofabitching Missouri bushwhacker. The Indian did his part before the proper battle had even gotten underway, and the bushwhacker did his days later in the aftermath of our decisive victory.

In the case of the Indian, I was one of the first to emerge from timber as we closed in on Foster Farm. I felt the impact of the ball in my face even before hearing the crack of the shot or the war whoops. Blood filled my socket, but wiping it away I could see well enough to stumble back into the trees for cover and get off a few shots of my own before we readied the cannons and scattered the filthy heathens. Indians tend to get spooked by cannon fire more so than white men. Someone tell me why. Hand-to-hand close in, I would rather square off with white men any day of the week, but when the big artillery come out, savages will disperse with alacrity.

My wound was not so bad that I could not tend to it myself. I got the bleeding stopped, and I could still see some. Blurred shapes and colors. Well enough to aim and fire. I still had the other eye, of course. So I fought for two days like that, changing out the bandage during lulls, and after we had vanquished the enemy and claimed the victory, I for the most part felt none the worse for wear. But then the sonofabitching bushwhackers.

In our exhausted self-satisfaction on the way back to Missouri, we let down our guard and rode right into their meager ambush. I do not know what those treasonous dullards had in their minds, what outcome they expected. There were only about a half-dozen of them, and we killed them all in short order, but one of the few shots they got off went straight through the middle of my bandage. The medic dug out the ball with tweezers easily enough—he said easily enough—but when he was done he told me I had lost my eye for good. The next night in camp, one boy addressed me to tell me how lucky I was being dotted in the same eye twice, and no sooner did he get up and relinquish his seat by the fire then another oblivious sonofabitching rube replaced him to tell me how unlucky I was for the same series of occurrences. These two Iowans could not have rehearsed it better. Same could be said for the Chickasaw savage and the sonofabitching Missouri bushwhacker, I suppose. Like they were all in cahoots without knowing it. Which, if you consider things from the right angle for long enough, you wonder if this is exactly how the world works. In any case, reason would suggest that at least one of the Iowans must have been right on the matter, but I cursed out the both of them. I suppose I still owe an apology to one of them at least, but I still do not know which one. Someone tell me.

Suffice to say, then, that I know what it means to be tested, and I know what it is to deal with sonofabitching scoundrels, and I knew these things well before I met Noyes, who, two months before he fled Oneida, a deserter on tiptoes under the guise of darkness, found me one evening in the library among the newspapers and asked for a word. I sensed him coming up behind me despite his sneaking. Losing an eye enhances your other senses. A blessing to complement the curse.

When we stepped out into the warm evening air, Noyes motioned for me to follow him across the lawn to the summer house. Four boisterous young people were congregated there, two males and two females. As we approached, they quieted their laughter and happy chatter—by that time, Noyes's and my differences were well known enough that any resident of Oneida would have been struck dumb seeing us strolling together across the lawn—and when it came clear we aimed to stay, the youths politely but abruptly bid us farewell and scattered into the shadows like retreating Indians.

Without any preamble to establish context, Noyes cleared his throat and began to hold forth. As he spoke, he alternated between looking at me directly and gazing out over the surrounding stretch of darkening lawn as if there were an invisible third party out there listening in on our meeting. I got the sense during the relatively brief time I spent abiding with Noyes in Oneida that he was always performing for invisible audiences, souls to whom, for some reason or other, he was desperate to ingratiate himself.

Chief among Noyes's myriad of oddly unrelated topics that evening was his contention that he himself was chiefly responsible for William Lloyd Garrison's abolitionist work. He informed me he had known Garrison in Vermont and Ithaca in years prior to the war and that Garrison had absorbed his influence from their conversations and shared prayer.

"You're saying Garrison's thoughts about the evil injustice of slavery originated from his conversations with you?" I said.

"Correct," Noyes said. "You are hearing me accurately more or less. Mr. Garrison and I met on at least two occasions. Strike that. Three occasions. My commentary gave his vague notions discernible, actionable shape and fueled them with purpose." Noyes smiled and then frowned and then smiled again as if unable to decide on the appropriate visage. "I am telling you this, Lieutenant Towner, because of your brave service in the war. Your eye. A personal tragedy in the context of our national tragedy, both of which I feel partly responsible for. You might still have it if it weren't for me. Your eye, I mean. In a roundabout way. If I hadn't made such a strong and principled stand against slavery and agitated Mr. Garrison, who, in turn, agitated this nation against the God-forsaken institution, you might be whole rather than diminished as you are. I cannot apologize for it, though, I trust you understand. The loss of your eye, I mean. Whether you understand or not, I cannot apologize for your diminishment. While I recognize your tragic sacrifice and the instrumental part I played in its coming to pass, there will be no apology forthcoming from me. Not for the loss of your eye there won't. Not for your diminishment."

"Captain," I said.

"Pardon?"

"I was a captain. You said lieutenant."

"I said lieutenant. I did. I am sorry," Noyes answered. "For that I can and will apologize. Not being a military man myself, I'm not sure in which direction I made the error. Did I promote you or demote you? Nevertheless, either way, I beg your pardon."

"Mr. Garrison was a pacifist, of course," I said. "As such, it would be difficult to assign him or you, by extension, any blame for the war."

"He was a pacifist," Noyes said, "as many of us were. In the beginning. In the end, though, Mr. Garrison hated slavery more than he loved peace."

"In the end, after all the blood had already been shed, it was an easier choice to make," I said.

At this point in our exchange, without transition, Noyes informed me that at the community's next evening meeting, he was entertaining the idea of presenting on stage a couple in the act of lovemaking. He suggested specifically that Frank Wayland-Smith and Tirzah Miller might be good candidates to play the principals. He said the audience's response to the performance would serve to separate the sheep from the goats. "Those who revel in the beauty of the spectacle and are renewed and inspired by it, like one is moved by music, versus those who are unwholesomely titillated or ashamed to watch, therefore exposing themselves as spiritual neophytes."

When I asked what role I had in this, why he was approaching me with his proposal, he said he wondered if I thought the presentation was a good idea. When I answered that I most assuredly did not, he agreed with me immediately, telling me that as he spoke his idea aloud, he realized its impracticality and potential for fostering confusion and division, and he thanked me for serving as his sounding board. He then took a step towards me, tenderly placed his hand on the back of my head as if I were a child or a woman, and told me he hoped he could trust me to keep his confidence and not mention our conversation to anyone. He then abruptly stepped back, pulled out his watch, informed me he was due for a meeting, and trudged away towards the horse barn.

I left the summer house bemused by this exchange. It was not until later that evening when I shared the experience with Cinderella that the matter was clarified for me. "He is mocking you, husband," she said, "and also perhaps setting a trap. Mr. Noyes floated these absurdities and asked you not to repeat them in order to bait you, to tempt you to betray his confidence."

"What if I were to do so?"

"He's relying on the premise that people would not believe that he would say such things, thus painting you as a liar and an agent of disharmony."

"When he handled my head, the notion entered my mind to pummel him," I said. "Why did I not snap the charlatan's arm in two? Someone tell me."

"That's likely what he half-intended. Your pummeling him would've played to his purposes all the more," she said.

"Of course, you are right," I said, marveling at Cinderella's perception. "Such machinations in the Kingdom of God. Who would have thought?"

"Both God and man would have thought, Husband," she said. "And both from firsthand experience."

The next day I shared Noyes's vile proposal with Frank Wayland-Smith and John Skinner, whom I knew favored Tirzah Miller, and I instructed Cinderella to inform Tirzah. In doing so I stepped into Noyes's ambush purposely and purposefully to demonstrate to him his lack of authority over me. I do not know if this was the right course of action or not. Someone tell me.

It was not until after Noyes had removed himself from Oneida that I learned he regularly referred to me as The Cyclops. If he meant to cast aspersion on me by labeling me thusly—furthermore, if he intended to cast himself as Odysseus in making this comparison—he reads Homer differently than I do. Certainly both parties, Odysseus and Polyphemus, should have comported themselves more honorably, but of the two, I would suggest Polyphemus is the lesser scoundrel. In explaining my interpretation to Cinderella, she interrupted me to suggest I was overthinking Noyes's allusion, that he likely was referring only to the fact that I had one eye and did not intend anything more profound than that. If she is right, I think I must hold Noyes in even more contempt than I would otherwise.

I admit to being surprised when, hearing the cannon fire, Noyes turned tail and scurried away not unlike a heathen savage. Also not unlike

Odysseus, incidentally, who, despite foolishly and greedily leading a number of his faithful men to their deaths, somehow felt the right to be puffed
up with pride as he retreated from Polyphemus's island. Should I have
been surprised? Someone tell me.

Noyes-ites versus Towner-ites. I regret the struggle took that shape.
It was not my intention for factions to form. 'Tis human nature, though,
and, for better or worse, 'tis my nature to lead. When a leader such as
President Lincoln recognizes another man as a leader, as he did in commissioning me Captain of the Invalid Corps after my injury, is that not a
notable endorsement? Someone tell me. Noyes would say he is a leader,
too, and since he believes his commissioning comes directly from God,
he would likely argue that his leadership trumps mine, but where are his
commissioning papers? Where is his letter? I have both documents signed
by Lincoln himself. The Bible says to walk by faith and not by sight, but it
also says that the faithful will be known by the fruits of their labor. Look
me in my eye to see my fruit. Look me in my not-eye. As for Noyes, how
can you look a man in the eye if he is nowhere to be found? Someone tell
me.

When Noyes fled to Canada, he left behind three contingents: one
group of individuals stubbornly faithful to him who wailed over his abandonment of them like they had lost their own souls, another group who
exhaled with relief and wished him good riddance, and a third group defined primarily by their confusion. Leaving the first contingent to itself and
wishing it no harm, I stepped up to lead the other two, and they seemed
grateful for my willingness, Cyclops or no, and after much discussion in
which all voices were encouraged to participate, we are California-bound
to begin a new work, to bear new fruit. I am not anyone's king, and I am
not looking to do anyone's thinking for them. It is work enough doing the
thinking I am required to do for myself. It is true I have ambitious plans,
and those traveling with me to California have signed on to work with me
to help fulfill these purposes, but they do so by choice. What God wills for
them is between Him and them. If I am an intercessor or prophet, I am
not the same kind as Noyes fancied himself to be. The Lord is not telling
me to do this or not to do that. I seek His blessing, and I certainly do not
seek to be at cross purposes with Him, but what I want to build comes
from my own free will, which He in His eternal wisdom has bestowed to
each and every man.

Let us build the place first and see what it turns out to be before we label it paradise, before we call it perfect. This is my plea to my fellow laborers. Will we who build it possess the necessary perspective to accurately assess our handiwork? Someone tell me. We will build and then we will leave the labelling and the assessing to those who come after. Our children. The children of our children. And in turn they will add to or tear down what we leave them. As it should be. In America. Under God.

# Frankie Guiteau Scoville Endures a Trial

I WAS IN THE COURTROOM every day during Charles's trial. It was difficult to be there in my grief, like how being at a funeral of a loved one is difficult, but it would have been more difficult not to have been there, like how not being at a funeral of a loved one would be more difficult.

So I was often reminded of my mother's funeral over the course of the trial. I remembered holding Charles's hand during the service—he was still shorter than me then, too thin and always cold, and his hands, too, thin and cold—and I recalled being perturbed at his inattentiveness and restlessness. I think he loved Mother more than any of us children, even more than Father, and I think Mother loved Charles more than she did any of us children, even more than she did Father, so Charles's misbehavior angered me because I thought he owed her better.

I told Father after the service that I thought he should whip Charles for how he had comported himself during the service. Father wordlessly agreed and promptly followed through. That was the worst thing I have ever done. Never mind I was still a girl. A child can be wicked. Never mind I did not do the whipping myself. I conceived of it. More than once I wondered if Charles might have turned out to be a different man if he had not been whipped that evening upon returning home from his mother's funeral. If I had not conceived of his whipping. I spent the rest of my childhood and Charles's childhood trying to make up for this wickedness. Beyond even my childhood and Charles's childhood. I am still trying to make up for it.

My burden entailed more than grief and guilt during those days in the courtroom, though. Boredom tormented me, too. I learned over the course of the trial that grief, guilt, and boredom complement one another more readily than one might think. The inevitability of the trial's outcome made it tedious. In saying the outcome was inevitable, I am not saying I thought the trial unfair. Rather, I thought it unnecessary. Even though I knew my brother would be sentenced to death at the end of the exercise, I could not help but wish for it to move more quickly. Grief can be difficult to sustain—some grief can—and I did not want to spend all mine in that courtroom. I knew I would need to keep a sufficient measure in reserve for the hanging.

To help time pass during the trial, I would try to imagine things were different. I tried to imagine Charles was on trial not for assassinating the president but for swinging that axe at me five years prior. His wife had divorced him that spring, and he was running from his debts, and he was my brother, so I convinced my husband that it was our bounden duty to accommodate him.

One morning a few days after he had arrived, Charles was in his drawers in the mud in the yard chopping wood, and I was hanging laundry to dry in the cold morning sun. My back was to him. It was his shirt I was hanging when he raised the axe over my head. I saw him raise it in shadow on the muddy grass, and I did not know whether to believe it or not. My mind did not know whether to believe it, but my body knew to believe it, and I stepped aside just in time, so instead of cleaving my skull, the axe met Charles's own damp shirt that I had just hung from the line, doing it no harm other than billowing it like the wind would billow it, and then the axe met the earth, burying itself half-head deep in the soft April mud. I ran inside before Charles could swing the axe again, but he did not intend to swing it again. He left it sticking half-head deep in the mud. That's how my husband found it when he arrived home that evening. Charles had taken his leave by then. I tried to talk to him before he lit out, but he would not talk to me. I was not frightened of him for what he had done because I could tell he was frightened of himself for what he had done. That I was not frightened of him for what he had done made me foolish, my husband said.

I next saw Charles eighteen months later. First he denied swinging the axe at me, and then he denied remembering swinging the axe at me, and then he claimed he swung the axe at me because he remembered that once when he was a boy I had criticized the way he chopped wood. He claimed I had told him he had no strength in his swing not only because he was too thin but because he gripped the axe cross-handed. Watching me hang laundry that morning in the cold morning sun, he said he thought it was in that moment that I had said he was weak and thin and cross-handed, so that is why he had grown angry and swung the axe at me. Time was what had confused him, he claimed. He had not realized how much had passed. He then apologized and asked for money. I gave him some and forgave him because he did not mention how I had conceived of the whipping our father administered to him after our mother's funeral, which is what I had feared he would mention as his reason for having swung the axe at me. And I gave him some money and forgave him because he was my brother. I was not the one who had told him when he was a boy that his wood-chopping swing had no strength in it because he was too thin and because he gripped the axe cross-handed—it had been our father who told him this—but I did not correct him because even though his memory was inaccurate, there was a fairness in the inaccuracy because of the whipping I had conceived of and our father had administered after the funeral of our mother.

My husband said I should not have given Charles any money, brother or not. My husband said rather than give Charles money, I should have summoned him so that he could have boxed Charles's ears. When a loved one asks you for a fish, though, you are not to give him a scorpion. The Bible tells us this so we will know it, but even if the Bible did not tell us this, it is something we should know.

So during the trial, to stave off boredom and help time pass, I tried to imagine Charles was standing trial for swinging the axe at me instead of assassinating the president, but I was not able to do it because I could not imagine how to make the case against him. Perhaps I could not imagine how to make the case against him because the axe did not cleave my skull but only billowed his shirt as the wind would billow it and buried itself half-head deep in the soft April mud. Perhaps I could not imagine how to make the case against him because I had seen the axe above my head only in shadow. Perhaps I could not imagine how to make the case against him because of the whipping I had conceived of and my father had administered after the funeral of our mother.

So as the trial wore on, I tried to imagine other things to stave off boredom and help time pass. I tried to imagine I was not me. I tried to watch the trial as someone other than the defendant's sister. I tried to hear Charles's nonsensical testimony as someone who was not his sister might hear it. His claim that he was temporarily insane because his will was not his own but God's. His claim that if the courts condemned him they would be condemning God. His claim that it was neither he nor God who killed the president but rather the president's doctors. His claim that in failing to save the president, the doctors had also failed to save Charles, so Charles, like the president, was a victim rather than a perpetrator. I tried to hear these claims as someone who might hear them as tragic but not personally tragic. I was not able to imagine this either, though. I was not able to imagine myself as anyone other than Charles's sister. I was more Charles's sister and he was more my brother there in the courtroom than I had ever been his sister and he had ever been my brother.

When I insisted five years ago that we ask Charles to come live with us, my husband had accused me of imagining naively that all would be well, but his accusation was false. If I had possessed a capable imagination, I would not have insisted on asking Charles to live with us; rather, I would have chosen to imagine that he would be all right on his own, that he would be capable of taking care of himself. Contrary to my husband's accusation, it was only because I did not possess a capable imagination that I insisted we ask Charles to come live with us. I have never possessed a capable imagination. Even as a child I could never see through what was real. When Charles was able to imagine conversing with our mother after she was gone, I was jealous because I could not imagine doing so. In addition to being jealous, I was nervous because Charles's imagining made our father angry, but I think it made our father angry because he was also jealous. And then my father and I realized Charles was not imagining. We realized it was real to Charles. So my father and I grew even more jealous and nervous and angry.

I moved around the courtroom over the duration of the trial, a different seat each day to stave off boredom and help time pass. Sometimes even in the same day an afternoon seat different than my morning seat. Charles never once acknowledged me during the trial, but he knew I was there. He would frequently scan the room, and he would allow his gaze to rest on many faces, but he would never allow his gaze to rest on my face. The manner in which he would never allow his gaze to rest on my face told me he knew I was there. That is, the way he did not see me told me he saw me. I had been seen by him by being unseen by him many times previously, so I knew well what being seen by him by being unseen by him looked like.

I spent one morning in the witness chair, where my husband told me I neither helped nor hurt my brother's case saying what I said, which was that sometimes I thought Charles insane and sometimes I thought him sound-minded.

Not long before Charles shot President Garfield, he sent me a letter. It had no salutation, no closing. He did not mention my mother's funeral and how I had held his thin, cold hand, and he did not mention the whipping conceived by me and administered afterwards by our father, and he did not mention swinging the axe in shadow above my head in the cold morning sun and billowing his shirt as the wind would billow it and burying the axe half-head deep in the soft April mud. The meandering madness contained in the letter does not matter. What matters is all the letter did not contain.

Mrs. Garfield was not in the courtroom every day like I was every day, but she was there some days. When she was there, Charles comported himself differently. Everyone did. I did. Charles tried to sit straighter, and I did, too, and we both tried not to fidget. If I were capable of imagination, I would have imagined that there in the courtroom, Mrs. Garfield, like me, sometimes attempted to imagine she was someone else to stave off boredom and help the time pass. Perhaps she knew who I was and knew where I was sitting despite my choosing a different seat each day. Perhaps she made sure to keep tabs on me because my plight intrigued her. Perhaps she tried to imagine my plight. Perhaps she tried to imagine she was me.

## Charles Guiteau Recalls
## and Reconsiders His Future

"I DOUBT I WILL HANG."

"So say those who end up hanging. That's been my experience," says the guard who has not made to stick me dead with his knife, at least not yet. "And them who fret over it, weeping and wailing and carrying on calling themselves goners, they are the ones who tend not to hang. It's the damnedest thing."

The guard who has not made to stick me dead with his knife, at least not yet, is escorting me once again from the courtroom to my cell. As is always the case when he escorts me between the courtroom and my cell, the guard who has not made to stick me dead with his knife, at least not yet, is not shackled as I am shackled, so the two of us walk at cross purposes. The unshackled escort should adapt to the necessarily shuffling pace of the shackled escorted, but the unshackled escort does not adapt to the necessarily shuffling pace of the shackled escorted, so the shackled escorted is forced to attempt to adapt, but the shackled escorted is unable to adapt. Shackled as he is at the ankles as well as at the wrists. Bound to himself as he has always been bound.

"I will most assuredly hang."

"That's the spirit, Guiteau! In truth, though, I think you will likely hang," says the guard who has not made to stick me dead with his knife, at least not yet. "You oughtn't to have done what you did. Mad or not. Plenty of mad people around who avoid shooting the president dead. That's what I get stuck on. Just because you're mad doesn't mean you have to shoot someone. Let alone shoot someone dead. Let alone the president."

"I doubt I will hang."

"And those lawyers you have. I can tell the jury isn't taking a shine to them," says the guard who has not made to stick me dead with his knife, at least not yet. "Those who have the type of lawyers the jury doesn't take a shine to tend to hang. That's been my experience."

"I will most assuredly hang."

"The noose is as good as around your neck already, I'm afraid. Or maybe it's not. In my experience, it's difficult to say one way or the other. In any case, you should take this time to make things right with God. That's the best you can do now, Guiteau," says the guard who has not made to stick me dead with his knife, at least not yet. "In my experience, that's the best you can do now."

"I doubt I will hang."

"She loves me, she loves me not," says the guard who has not made to stick me dead with his knife, at least not yet. "Like a heartsick youngster."

"I will most assuredly hang."

"That's right. On and on. Back and forth. This type of thinking," says the guard who has not made to stick me dead with his knife, at least not yet. "In any case, one thing you can know for sure is that you'll get what you get, Guiteau. Either you'll get what you get, or you won't. Maybe you won't get what you get. I suppose that could happen. I said the same thing to Everett. He lost his job because of you, you know. It's not only the president you've hurt with your evil."

Everett is the guard who made to stick me dead with his knife at night in my cell while I slept so it would look like I made to stick myself dead with a knife. When I awoke to Everett making to stick me dead with his knife, he said God told him to make to stick me dead with his knife. He did not say God told him to make to stick me dead with his knife because God told him to make to stick me dead with his knife but rather to mock me on account of how God had told me to make to shoot the president dead with my pistol. Other guards came when I cried out, and they stopped Everett from making to stick me dead with his knife, and they removed him from my cell, and when I thanked them for removing him, they told me to recant my thanks or else they would re-fetch Everett and allow him to make to stick me dead with his knife so it would look like I made to stick myself dead with a knife, so I recanted my thanks.

"Like I told Everett, when it comes to justice, there are no shortcuts," says the guard who has not made to stick me dead with his knife, at least not yet. "Justice requires patience. Which leads me to a question I've been wanting to ask you, Guiteau. No matter what entity inspired your deed, whether it was God or madness or your own evil nature, why couldn't you have shown more patience? We elect a president in this country every four years. God or your madness or your own evil nature couldn't have waited four years to see if President Garfield might be unseated bloodlessly by the will of the people? Seems your crime was a crime of impatience as much as anything else."

God's calendar and man's calendar are not the same calendar because God is in time as opposed to up against time, but man is up against time as opposed to in time. When God instructs man to take action, the instruction is conceived according to God's calendar, which is not up against time, but God's instructions are enacted by man according to man's calendar, which is up against time. This makes for misunderstanding and second-guessing, but the misunderstanding and second-guessing are conceived of by those using man's calendar, which is up against time, rather than God's calendar, which is not up against time. So the misunderstanding and second-guessing are ill-conceived. That I must plead insanity for fulfilling God's will is a necessity given that the court in which I am being tried is based on man's calendar. Were this God's court, based on His calendar, I would not need to plead insanity. I would not need to enter a plea at all because I would not be tried.

"Well then who would be tried, Guiteau?" asks the guard who has not made to stick me dead with his knife, at least not yet. "Everyone else, save you? It sounds to me like that's where your reason leads. If you're the only one on the right calendar, on God's calendar, then everyone else, save you, is on the wrong calendar and thus in line for divine punishment. Am I getting warm?"

In Oneida the calendar has wound down. It wound down all the way to Canada, where he winds down. In my letter to him I explained the error of his ways and laid out for him how he might have better served as a more worthy vessel and how he might have better served to prepare my way. For a prophet to be welcomed, he must be accommodated. If not in his own country, then in another country where he can make up his home. If he is not accommodated, he cannot make up his home, and he will be forced to shake the dust off his feet upon leaving, and the country will wind down in his absence.

"Which is why your lawyers are talking about the Mormons and Oneidans, bringing up Joseph Smith and John Noyes, right? To offer examples of other mad folks, mad like you, who think God is talking to them directly. And these other mad folks aren't being hanged, so it's not fair that you should be hanged. That's the point your lawyers are seeking to make, right?" asks the guard who has not made to stick me dead with his knife, at least not yet.

"To tell you the truth, Guiteau, I have a hard time following that logic. As I've said, those lawyers of yours, I don't think you got the best team from the livery. Joseph Smith and John Noyes didn't shoot the president dead. That's what I'd tell my lawyers if I were you. Tell them to keep in mind that you shot the president dead. Remind them of this simple fact. The fact that you're on trial because you shot the president dead, not because you're mad for saying God talks to you directly. Furthermore, if I were you, I'd tell the lawyers to pursue the argument that although you shot the president, there's a way of looking at it that you didn't shoot him dead. Looking at it this way, it wasn't so much you killed the president as much as it was the doctors didn't prevent him from dying. When your lawyers raised this argument last week, my ears perked, and I could tell the jurors' ears perked, too. The notion that the doctors weren't good enough doctors. The notion that they could've undone your crime by being better practitioners of medicine. That's where I'd hang my hat if I were you. If I were your lawyer. Do your lawyers even ask you what you think, Guiteau? If they think you're mad, maybe they don't ask."

I do not want to shake the dust off my feet again. I do not want this country to wind down in my absence.

"Don't go calling yourself a prophet or blathering about different calendars," says the guard who has not made to stick me dead with his knife, at least not yet. "That would be my advice about what not to do. That nonsense isn't going to get you anywhere. Well, it will get you somewhere, but not the somewhere you want."

The next day in the courtroom, those who want to see me hang produce a fragment of the president's spine, which they say demonstrates the damage done by the firing of the pistol, and those who want to see me hang proceed to pass around the jury box the fragment of the president's spine, which they say demonstrates the damage done by the firing of the pistol.

One juror receives the fragment of the president's spine in his flat, open hand as if he is receiving a coin or a key in his flat, open hand, and he weeps. Another juror runs his finger carefully along the edge of the fragment of the president's spine as if he is running his finger carefully along the edge of an axe-blade, and he weeps. Another juror fumbles the fragment of the president's spine onto his lap, as if the fragment of the president's spine leapt up out of his hands and onto his lap as a fish might leap up out of his hands and onto his lap, and he weeps. Another juror closes his hand around the fragment of the president's spine as one might close one's hand around a loved one's hand, and he weeps. And many others in the courtroom, including she who calls herself a wife and including she who calls herself a sister, weep in turn in seeing the jury weep.

"I will most assuredly hang," I say at the end of the day to the guard who has not made to stick me dead with his knife, at least not yet. Today as he escorts me once again from the courtroom to my cell, he and I do not walk at cross purposes as we typically walk at cross purposes. Today the unshackled escort adapts to the necessarily shuffling pace of the shackled escorted. Shackled as he is at the ankles as well as at the wrists. Bound to himself as he has always been bound.

"The noose is as good as around your neck, Guiteau," says the guard who has not made to stick me dead with his knife, at least not yet. "As it should be. As the noose should be as good as around your neck. As I pray it is as good as around your neck."

As he speaks, the guard who has not made to stick me dead with his knife, at least not yet, weeps in turn as the jury wept in turn and as many others in the courtroom, including she who calls herself a wife and including she who calls herself a sister, wept in turn in seeing the jury weep and as I weep in turn in seeing the guard who has not made to stick me dead with his knife, at least not yet, weep.

## John Humphrey Noyes Takes Visitors

IN THE LAST DAYS they make visitations to the Stone Cottage. There is a string of them, but I would have the string be longer. I would have thought the string would have been longer. The string of them is not nearly as long as I would have thought it would have been.

Some in the string I summon, and others summon themselves. I turn my head on my pillow to face them and tell them they can hear the Falls from here if only they will listen. "Use my ears if you must," I say to them.

"No," Harriet says. "We are too far away from the Falls to hear. The Falls are too far away from us."

"Not if we are quiet," I say. "Quietness closes the distance."

"Whether we are quiet or not," Harriet says. "We are too far away from the water here in the cottage. The water is too far away from us. When you are feeling better, we will stroll outside and draw closer. We need to draw closer to listen. We will when you are feeling better. Not just to listen, but to see. When you are feeling better."

"We are plenty close to the water here to hear," I say. "The water is plenty close to us here to hear. Use my ears if you must."

"The truth is I do not care to hear the Falls," Harriet says. "Not just now I don't."

"No," I say.

"I long to hear other water."

"Yes," I say.

"Not Niagara Falls," Harriet says.

"No," I say. "Sacketts Brook."

"The Quinnipiac," Harriet says. "I long to hear her just now."

"Yes," I say. "Use my ears if you must."

"All I can hear is you," Harriet says. "If you would be quiet perhaps."

"Yes," I say. "Quietness closes the distance."

"Shh," Harriet says.

"BENEATH THE SURFACE THERE is more to hear," Mary says. "It is quieter beneath the surface, but there is more to hear."

"Yes," I say. "Beneath the surface in the cleft of the rock where He covers us with His hand."

"Not this water. Not Niagara. Other water," Mary says.

"Yes," I say. "Sacketts Brook."

"Water other than that other water," Mary says. "The Hudson."

"Yes," I say. "Use my ears if you must."

"Beneath the surface of the Hudson it is much quieter, but there is much more to hear," Mary says.

"Yes," I say.

"Beneath the surface where one must stay quiet and listen for the Resurrection," Mary says.

"Yes," I say.

"Beneath the surface where one's listening is the Resurrection. Where if one fails to listen to one's own listening, one misses it," Mary says.

"Yes," I say. "The Resurrection. We will know it when we hear it."

"It is not what one hears but the hearing itself," Mary says. "One must take care not to miss one's own hearing."

"Yes," I say. "A trumpet. An army. A thief in the night."

"Are you not listening?" Mary says. "I just now said it is not what one hears but the hearing itself."

"I'm listening," I say.

"I fear you're not listening," Mary says. "Even now I fear you're not."

"I HEAR IT," VICTOR SAYS. "Clear as a bell."

"Yes," I say. "Good. Are you sure? Use my ears if you must."

"The wind gathering the storm. The gathering wind of the storm. The storm-gathering wind," Victor says.

"No," I say. "You are mishearing. Listen for the Falls. Use my ears if you must."

"I don't believe I am mishearing," Victor says. "Clear as a bell."

"The water, not the wind. The Falls. Listen together with your brothers and sisters so their listening might guide your listening. Gather together Theodore, Jesse, John, Pierrepont, Gertrude, Constance, Irene, Godfrey, H.V., Dorothy, Miriam, and Guy. Listen together with them so their listening might guide your listening."

"It is only me here," Victor says. "I have only gathered myself."

"Fetch them all, so you might listen together, so their listening might guide your listening," I say.

"In this weather?" Victor says. "With the storm-wind gathering? Fetch whom? Listen to what?"

"Use my ears if you must," I say.

"I don't believe I am mishearing," Victor says. "Clear as a bell."

"I HEAR IT," TOWNER says. "It does. It does sound like that. It does sound like wind."

"No," I say.

"A strong gust sweeping across a scarred battlefield pocked with makeshift graves."

"No," I say. "The Falls. Not the wind. The water. Use my ears if you must."

"It whistles through my eye, through the hole where my eye would be, so that I hear it and feel it and see it in an all-encompassing way. It's more than hearing. It's more than you say. It's more than you could know."

"No," I say.

"It inhales and exhales like breath. I hear it and feel it and see it thusly. The inhaling a desperate, dry suck. The exhaling a gasp. A final gasp."

"No," I say.

"Yes," Towner says. "Use my eye if you must. The hole where my eye would be."

"Lovely," Tirzah says. "Like music. I hear it like music. I want to sing. It makes me want to."

"No," I say. "Do not sing. You do not know the words. There are no words to know."

"I did not say I would sing. I said I want to sing. The sound of the water makes me want to sing. That I am made to want to does not mean that I will."

"Shh," I say. "Listen with my ears if you must."

"It makes a lovely song is all I am saying," Tirzah says. "Its loveliness makes me want to sing it, but I do not need to sing it because it is already being sung."

"Shh," I say.

"It is the loveliest song I have ever heard," Tirzah says.

"There are many lovely songs," I say.

"And many ugly songs," Tirzah says.

"Ugly songs?" I say.

"Shh," she says. "You told me to shh."

"Name one," I say. "Name an ugly song."

"First verse, you're chewing an apple in my ear," Tirzah says. "Second verse, you're telling me in my ear to take a bite of the apple you just chewed in my ear."

"Shh," I say.

"Shh," Tirzah says. "Shh, yourself."

"If you hear it, John, then I hear it," George says. "George hears it, too, if you hear it. If one of us hears it, then we all hear it. We hear it together like brothers."

"The three of us," George says.

"Yes," I say. "Use my ears if you must."

"Our ears," George says. "Of course. What other ears would we use?"

"Yes," I say. "Our ears."

"It is loud," George says. "For water it is loud. I did not know water could be so loud."

"I have never heard wind so loud, either," George says. "For wind it is loud. I knew wind could be loud, but not this loud."

"As if they are aiming to drown out each other," George says. "The water and the wind."

"The fox was loud," I say. "Loud for a fox. In the way of its wheezing, yelping, panting, squawking, gnashing, and gagging it was loud. Loud for a fox."

"Not as loud as this water, though," George says.

"Not by half," George says. "Not half as loud as this wind."

"You are asking me to listen to nothing," he says. "There is nothing to hear."

"You have to be quiet to hear," I say. "Think of it like this: you have to bury your own voice so the voice of the water might live. Use my ears if you must."

"You are asking me to listen to nothing," he says. "Falling water cannot be heard as it is in mid-air and silenced there as all things are silenced there, save birds. Water landing on the rocks can be heard by virtue of the solidity of rocks. I can listen to the water landing on the rocks by virtue of their solidity if you would have me listen to that. But I cannot listen to water falling. No one can hear water falling as it is in mid-air and silenced there as all things are silenced there, save birds."

"Shh," I say. "You are not doing as I instructed. You are not burying your own voice so the voice of the water might live. Use my ears if you must."

"It does not matter whose ears I use to listen to nothing," he says. "I do not need anyone's ears to listen to nothing. I do not need ears at all. I would be better off without ears. Without ears I would be prepared to listen to nothing perfectly."

"Please," I say. "Shh. You must bury your own voice so the voice of the water might live. You must be still to hear the water."

"Still water can be heard," he says. "Still water can be heard by virtue of how it becomes unstill, by its occasional lapping against the muddy bank, by its rippling out from the ascension and descension of geese, and by its gulping down and then burping up of wind-blown leaves."

"Then listen to the still water becoming unstill," I say. "If you are incapable of listening to the falling water, listen to the still water. In any case, no matter which water, you must bury your own voice so the voice of the water might live."

"All right," he says. "Agreed. I will listen to the still water becoming unstill, and I will bury my own voice so the voice of the water might live."

"Good," I say. "Use my ears if you must. Listen to Sunset Lake. Listen to the turtle pond."

"No," he says. "I will use my own ears. Yes," he says. "The carp pond."

# Acknowledgments

Excerpts of *The Substance of Things Hoped For: A Novel* previously appeared in *Ascent, Kenyon Review, Literati Quarterly, Story,* and *West Branch*.

In writing this novel, I was inspired and informed by a long list of books, including: Robert David Thomas's *The Man Who Would Be Perfect: John Humphrey Noyes and the Utopian Impulse*; Robert Allerton Parker's *A Yankee Saint: John Humphrey Noyes and the Oneida Community*; Spencer Klaw's *Without Sin: The Life and Death of the Oneida Community*; Constance Noyes Robertson's *Oneida Community: An Autobiography, 1851–1876*; Robert S. Fogarty's *Desire and Duty at Oneida: Tirzah Miller's Intimate Memoir*; Candice Millard's *Destiny of the Republic: A Tale of Madness, Medicine and the Murder of a President*; Charles E. Rosenberg's *The Trial of the Assassin Guiteau: Psychiatry and the Law in the Gilded Age*; David G. McCullough's *Insanity on Trial*; George Wallingford Noyes's *Free Love in Utopia: John Humphrey Noyes and the Origin of the Oneida Community*; Pierrepont Noyes's *My Father's House: An Oneida Boyhood*; Walt Lang's *waltsmusings*, an Oneida Community blog; and the Oneida Community Mansion House's serial publication *The Oneida Community Journal*. I also gleaned a lot from several books by John Humphrey Noyes himself, including: *The Berean: A Manual for the Help of Those Who Seek the Faith of the Primitive Church*; *Bible Communism*; *Home-Talks*, Vol. I; *Slavery and Marriage: A Dialogue*; *Confessions of John Humphrey Noyes*; and *Hand-book of the Oneida Community, with a Sketch of Its Founder and an Outline of Its Constitution and Doctrines*.

Thanks to the helpful staffs at, respectively, Penn State Behrend's Lilley Library, especially Jane Ingold; Syracuse University's Special Collections Library; and the Oneida Community Mansion House and Museum.

Thanks to the Erie (PA) Arts Council for its support of my work through its Established Artist Fellowship Program and to Penn State Behrend's School of Humanities and Social Sciences Endowment for the research grant.

Thanks to my extraordinary colleagues Nathan Carter, George Looney, Kristy McCoy, Aimee Pogson, Evan Ringle, and Joshua Shaw, the Edinboro Six, who read early drafts and afforded me rigorous and encouraging commentary.

Thanks to Gregory Wolfe, Ian Creeger, and Shannon Carter at Slant for their expertise and dedication.

Finally, thanks to Josie and Wyatt for their inspiration and energy, and to AJ, always my first and most important reader, for her patience, positivity, and love.

This book was set in Adobe Jenson, named after the fifteenth century French engraver, printer, and type designer, Nicholas Jenson. His typefaces were strongly influenced by scripts employed by the Renaissance humanists, who were in turn inspired by what they had discovered on ancient Roman monuments.

This book was designed by Shannon Carter, Ian Creeger, and Gregory Wolfe. It was published in hardcover, paperback, and electronic formats by Wipf and Stock Publishers, Eugene, Oregon.